About Annie Groves

Annie Groves is the pen name of Jenny Shaw, an accomplished writer of fiction who has been published previously under a pseudonym. She lives with her family near the Western Approaches, where she enjoys exploring local history and walking by the sea.

Annie Groves was originally created by the much-loved writer Penny Halsall, who died in 2011. The stories drew on her own family's history, picked up from listening to her grandmother's stories when she was a child. Jenny Shaw has been a big fan of the wonderful novels by Annie Groves for many years and feels privileged to have been asked to continue her legacy.

Annie Groves

Winter *on* *the* Mersey

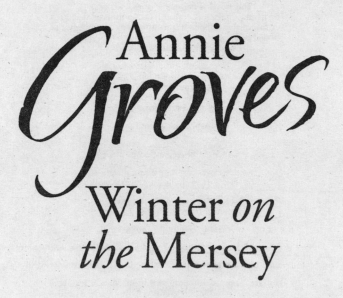

HarperCollins*Publishers*

HarperCollins
PUBLISHERS
Since 1817

This novel is entirely a work of fiction.
The names, characters and incidents portrayed in it are
the work of the author's imagination. Any resemblance to
actual persons, living or dead, events or localities is
entirely coincidental.

HarperCollins*Publishers* Ltd
The News Building
1 London Bridge Street
London SE1 9GF
www.harpercollins.co.uk

This paperback edition 2017
1

A catalogue record for this book is
available from the British Library

ISBN: 978-0-00-755086-9

Typeset in Sabon by Palimpsest Book Production Ltd, Falkirk, Stirlingshire

Printed and bound in Great Britain by CPI Group (UK) Ltd, Croydon CR0 4YY

MIX
Paper from
responsible sources
FSC
www.fsc.org   FSC™ C007454

FSC™ is a non-profit international organisation established to promote
the responsible management of the world's forests. Products carrying the
FSC label are independently certified to assure consumers that they come
from forests that are managed to meet the social, economic and
ecological needs of present and future generations,
and other controlled sources.

Find out more about HarperCollins and the environment at
www.harpercollins.co.uk/green

This book would not have been possible without
Kate Bradley, inspiring editor, and the support
of the wonderful Teresa Chris

CHAPTER ONE

Early Spring 1944

Dolly Feeny tried to shut out the sound of her oldest daughter screaming.

The sound echoed around the small terraced house, seeming to go on and on. Probably the whole road could hear the noise – Empire Street wasn't long, leading as it did down to the dock road in Bootle, with a corner shop at one end, a pub at the other and the Mersey beyond the dockyards. On a normal day Rita would be behind the counter in that shop, either before or after working her shift as a nursing sister at the nearby hospital. But today wasn't a normal day. Besides, everyone would know the reason for the screaming and would be with Rita all the way. Dolly put the kettle on again for what felt like the hundredth time that morning. No, it wasn't every day that she prepared to welcome a new grandchild into the world.

Pop, Dolly's husband, came into the kitchen, his white hair bright in the gloom of the cloudy day. He'd been up half the night, thanks to his duties as an ARP warden. Even though the raids that had plagued Merseyside for the earlier years of the war had died down, there was still the threat of danger from the crumbling buildings, or streets that hadn't yet been cleared, and last night there had been a fire in an abandoned warehouse. Try as he might, he couldn't get the smell of burning out of his hair or from his skin. If it had been a normal day he would have had a bath, filling it right up to the four-inch regulation line they all had to adhere to nowadays, and staying in it for as long as the water retained any comforting warmth. Today, however, there were more important things on his mind.

'Do you think she's all right?' he asked anxiously. He very rarely admitted to being worried about anything; he was the rock on whom the whole family depended. But the cries from upstairs were enough to shake anyone's confidence. He dearly loved Rita, as he did all his children, and couldn't bear the thought of anything happening to her.

'Course she is.' Dolly spoke warmly but firmly. 'You weren't in the house when I had any of our five. It sounds much worse than it is, and remember she's had two already. She'll be right as rain.' She smiled reassuringly, hoping that what she said was true. Nine years had passed since Rita had last given birth and she'd lost weight since then, thanks to the wartime diet and her non-stop hard work. But she was fit and healthy and, even more importantly, was no longer married to that cowardly deserter Charlie Kennedy.

Now she had finally married her childhood sweetheart Jack Callaghan, a pilot with the Fleet Air Arm, and as steady and loving a husband as any woman could ever hope for. Dolly knew that Rita wanted nothing more than to bear this baby safely so that Jack could come home on leave and meet the precious creature. This must be the most longed-for child in the whole of Merseyside. God knew both of its parents had been through hell and back before getting together.

Dolly's ears pricked up. 'Listen, Pop.' She wiped her strong, reddened hands on her faded print apron. 'That's a different noise, that is. Won't be long now.' She lifted the boiling kettle across to where the teapot stood ready. 'Best have a cup now, as who knows when we'll get the next one.'

'Are you sure? Sounds just the same to me.' Pop looked doubtfully at his wife. He wanted to believe her but didn't trust himself to do so. It seemed no time at all since Rita herself was a baby, a pale-skinned little beauty with deep red hair. Now here she was having her own third child. Where had all those years gone?

'Mam! Have you got any more hot water down there?' came a voice from the top of the stairs.

'I'll bring it right up, Sarah love.' Dolly emptied the rest of the water from the kettle into a large enamel jug, and then set another lot to boil just in case. 'Pop, why don't you fill the biggest pan from the tap and put that on to heat up as well.' She bustled to the door, all anxiety gone now that there was something useful to do.

Pop looked around uncertainly. They'd lived in this house for almost all of their married lives and yet he still wasn't sure where all the utensils in the kitchen were kept. That was Dolly's territory. Still, this was no time to complain. He opened every cupboard door until he found the pan he hoped she meant.

Meanwhile, Dolly raced up the stairs as quickly as she could, belying her fifty-something years, but careful not to spill a drop of water. 'Here you are, love.' She handed the battered jug to her youngest daughter, who swiftly turned back to the bedroom and the screams.

If anyone had told Dolly at the beginning of the war that just a few years later young Sarah would be supervising the birth of Rita's child, she would have laughed them to the other side of the Mersey. But now she could think of no better person. Sarah might be only nineteen, but she'd started her nurse's training with the Red Cross as soon as she could and had been thrown in at the deep end, tending injuries during the bombings, coping with all manner of indescribable horrors, as well as delivering babies in the most unlikely places – ruined buildings, air-raid shelters, and once in the middle of a deserted street. Overseeing a birth in the comfort of her own bedroom, with her patient an experienced mother who just happened to be a senior nurse, with the support of their own experienced mother, and endless supplies of hot water and all the necessities, was a comparative luxury.

Rita could have chosen to give birth in her own bedroom, above the shop just across the road from her childhood home. But Sarah had persuaded her to cross the narrow alleyway that separated the two buildings and have the baby here. That way the shop could stay open and their sister-in-law Violet could look after it, along with Ruby. Ruby was a strange young woman who scared easily and was, they all agreed, unlikely to cope with the grim reality of childbirth at such close range. She was better than she had been back when Rita had first brought her there to live, but her neglectful childhood had ill-prepared her for the world at large, let alone a world at war. She was wonderful with children, though, adoring Rita's first two – Michael and Megan – and also little George, the toddler son of Dolly and Pop's middle daughter, Nancy.

Dolly and Sarah looked at Rita now, as she lay whey-faced on the old off-white bed linen, her usually lustrous red hair dark with sweat, her face screwed up with effort. But her eyes were bright. 'It's coming,' she gasped. 'I remember this bit. Mam, hold my hand, will you? Help me through these last few pushes.' Dolly immediately knelt down beside her and took her damp hand, just as another wave of contraction and pain broke and Rita's face contorted as she let out a loud scream.

Sarah stood at the bottom of the bed, her eyes never leaving her patient. 'Come on, Rita, that's right, you're almost there. One more push could do it.'

Rita lay back exhausted, drawing in air in painful gulps. 'It's taking ages, though. Is everything all right? You'd tell me if it wasn't, wouldn't you, Sarah?'

'Everything is just right.' Sarah spoke with authority, for all her young age. 'It's been pretty quick actually, Rita. It just feels like a long time but it really isn't.' Her eyes narrowed a little as they assessed her big sister, registering that she was tired but not dangerously so, and that the next contraction seemed to be building. 'Right, here we go, give me a big, big push and . . .'

Rita let out a piercing cry and then fell back against the pillow, but it had done the trick. As her own cry faded away it was replaced by a higher, more penetrating one, the unmistakable sound of a new-born child. 'Rita! She's here, she's here! It's a girl!' Sarah struggled to remain professional as she picked up her niece and wrapped her carefully in a towel, automatically checking her as she did so, while Dolly stood to admire her latest granddaughter.

'Oh, Rita, she's beautiful.' She gazed at the little face, red and puckered and screaming, but a miracle all the same. 'Are you ready to hold her? Can you sit up?'

Rita raised herself against the pillow and Dolly stepped across to slip another one in behind it so that her daughter could prop herself semi-upright. 'Are you all right like that? Come on then, Sarah.'

Gently Sarah handed the little bundle to her sister. 'You did all right there. Anyone would think you'd done it before,' she smiled. 'Made it look easy.'

Rita reached for her new daughter and gasped with joy at the sight of her. 'Look at her hair. It's dark like Jack's.' She bent in to give the baby a kiss. 'If you turn out as good as your daddy you'll never have to worry. He's going to be so delighted to meet you. You're perfect, you are. Look at your little hands.' The baby's tiny fingers curled around her mother's thumb, gripping on tightly, as if her life depended on it.

'We'll send Pop to get a message to him,' Dolly announced, standing up straight, easing her aching back. 'He'll be made up, so he will. Now, Rita, did you have a name or is it too soon?'

Rita paused and then looked her mother in the eye. 'It's all right, we decided on Jack's last leave. If it was a girl she'd be Ellen, after his mother. So this is Ellen.' She turned her adoring gaze back to the baby.

Dolly found herself for once unable to speak for the lump in her throat. Ellen Callaghan had been her best friend in the whole world. They'd laughed together, done their housework together, raised their children together on Empire Street. But Ellen had died in childbirth when not so very much older than Rita was now. Dolly had looked out for the Callaghan children ever since – even though all but one were grown-up, and indeed the eldest was married to Rita. She could think of no more fitting tribute to her beloved friend.

'That's lovely,' she managed to say. 'We'll tell the priest as well. You just lie there and get your strength back. Here, it looks as if the little one is hungry already.'

Rita shifted herself so she could feed little Ellen, and it was all Dolly could do not to cry – with relief for the safe birth, with the unexpected emotion of hearing her friend's name spoken aloud after so many years and also with wonder at this miracle of new life. Somehow, despite the terrible hardships they had all endured since war broke out, and the atrocities that were going on still, she felt blessed to be in this world at such a marvellous moment.

'So you're sure you've got everything on your list, Mrs Mawdsley?' Violet Feeny pushed her horn-rimmed spectacles back up the bridge of her nose from where they kept slipping. 'Can you fit it all into your basket?'

The older woman pulled on her gloves, ready to face the bitter wind outside the small corner shop. 'Everything that is available, anyway. Such a treat to find some Oxo. Thank you, dear. I know you do your best. I expect it's even more difficult with your Rita so near her time, isn't it?'

'Oh, we manage all right, don't we, Ruby?' Violet turned to the shy figure behind her. 'I put out the stock and serve the customers and Ruby does the books – she's clever like that.'

Ruby raised her head, shaking her cloud of pale blonde hair which made her look so much younger than she was. 'That's right, Mrs Mawdsley.' That was enough polite conversation for Ruby – she found it excruciatingly hard, so she turned back to the long columns of accounts spread out before her.

Violet kept her cheerful smile in place as Mrs Mawdsley left, banging the squeaky shop door behind her, and then she slumped down on to the hard wooden stool by the counter. She knew her customer meant well – she was one of Dolly's best friends and had nothing but goodwill for the Feeny family. Violet herself had long since been accepted as one of them, as she'd married Eddy Feeny and come to live with her in-laws while Eddy was away serving with the Merchant Navy. She loved living with them and she enjoyed helping out in the shop, but her feelings about Rita's new baby were plaguing her.

Violet longed more than anything for children of her own. Yet she and Eddy had been married for over three years and there was no sign of anything happening in that department. It wasn't for lack of trying – Violet's long face broke into a smile at the thought of that – but they hardly ever saw each other. His spells of leave were so rare, and so short when they did come, and then by the time he'd seen everyone he wanted to see and who wanted to see him, they had precious few moments on their own. Eddy was a quiet fellow – certainly compared to his more extrovert big brother Frank and middle sister Nancy – but he was very popular, and now he'd been doing his duty in the dangerous Western Approaches he was hailed as a hero every time he came home. Violet couldn't argue with that – he was her hero, no doubt about it, and he'd already been a serving seaman when she'd met him, so it wasn't as if she hadn't known what their life together would be like. But it was so hard.

Violet knew her unofficial role was to keep everyone's spirits up, and usually that suited her down to the ground, but today, knowing that Rita had gone into labour, she felt absolutely rotten. It wasn't as if she didn't get on with Rita – the two of them were thick as thieves and had worked together for years in the shop, helping the customers and putting on a brave face so that nobody around Empire Street went without. Violet didn't like to admit it even to herself but she was filled with envy of her sister-in-law. Rita and Jack had had precious little time together either since their marriage just over two years ago, and yet here she was, about to give birth. It wasn't fair. On top of that she had two children already. Violet knew full well that Rita had had to make an agonising decision as to whether to have Michael and Megan evacuated, and she missed them still even though they were relatively close out on a farm in Freshfield in Lancashire. Once the blitz had stopped, there had been talk about bringing them home, which Rita was desperate to do, and yet she had to acknowledge that farm life suited them both and they were flourishing in the fresh air, eating plentiful good food that they could never hope to get in war-ravaged Bootle.

Reluctantly Rita had agreed – with Jack's backing – that the two children should stay away, at least for the time being, much to the delight of the farming couple, who had no children of their own and there-fore spoilt them terribly. Michael and Megan had been promised that they could come back for a visit as soon as their new sister or brother was born. So Violet was steeling herself for the big family reunion, and while she knew it would make Rita's joy complete, she dreaded the thought of it.

'Violet, can you come and look at this?' Ruby asked from behind her, and Violet jumped. How long had Ruby been speaking to her when she was lost in her agonising thoughts? She had to snap out of it, pull herself together, and not begrudge the generous Feenys their pleasure in the new arrival.

'What's wrong?' Violet asked, bending her tall, willowy frame over the account books. She didn't understand the figures; she knew Ruby was more than capable of sorting out any problem with them and was probably just asking her to make her feel wanted. That was a kind thing to do. But it didn't come close to easing the longing that was eating away at her. 'Oh, Eddy,' she whispered to herself. 'Come home soon, and let's hope we can have the family we so badly want at last.' But she didn't breathe a word of this to Ruby. Instead Violet pitched up the sleeves of her moth-eaten cardigan and got back to the grind of keeping the little shop in business.

CHAPTER TWO

Kitty Callaghan pushed a dark curl out of her eyes as she squinted at the keyhole in the fading evening light. There was just enough brightness left in the sky to find it. Of course there would be no street lamps coming on as they hadn't been permitted since the outbreak of war. In a big city Kitty would have felt happy to stay out longer, knowing that there would be other people about, even if it meant navigating the potholed pavements with a shielded torch. Yet here, in this small town on the south coast, she felt reluctant to come back after dark. She wasn't a country girl and there was something about her billet's isolation that made her uneasy. Not that she would admit that to anybody.

Pushing open the door with its flaking paint, she listened for any signs of the other occupants, but the place was quiet. She shared this small house with two other Wrens and their landlady, who had been only too happy to let out her spare rooms after her husband had been called up. The rooms were small but clean, with comfortable if slightly battered furnishings, and Kitty couldn't complain. She'd had much worse. When she'd first joined up, she had had to share a big dormitory with the other trainee Wrens, sleeping on a bottom bunk and with absolutely no privacy. Then there had been the filthy fleapit she'd been allocated when she'd been transferred to Portsmouth, which she'd managed to leave by claiming it was too far from her place of work. It wasn't as if she came from anywhere grand either. Her terraced home on Empire Street was no bigger than this and certainly hadn't been as comfortable, although she'd done her best. But having to run the household pretty much single-handed after her mother had died so young had been a struggle. Her big brothers had tried to help but their father drank away all the money that should have gone towards the housekeeping, and so it had been a matter of survival, with nothing left over for little extras. If it hadn't been for their kindly neighbour, Dolly Feeny, they'd never have got through.

From Portsmouth Kitty had been transferred again to this small town hugging the coast. It was an ideal place from which to pick up signals from the continent, and in her capacity as a telephone operator she was much in demand. She had proved herself to be calm in the face of crises – when messages were arriving at an impossible pace, she was efficient in recognising which to prioritise, and unflappable when the callers were panicking or aggressive. Fortunately that didn't happen often. But you never knew what or who you would be dealing with down the line and it was important to respond appropriately. Lives might be lost otherwise. Her exemplary work had led to her rising to the rank of Leading Wren, and everyone could see that this was well deserved.

The door to what had once been the sitting room opened and a young woman poked her face out into the corridor. 'Oh, it's you, Kitty. I thought I heard something. Fancy a game of cards?'

'Sorry, did I disturb you, Lizzie?' Kitty smiled at the young Wren who now used the ground-floor front room as her bedroom.

'No, I was just writing a letter home . . . You don't fancy playing cards for a bit, do you?' Lizzie looked wistful, and Kitty remembered how homesick the girl had been when she'd first arrived. Maybe she should make the effort and play cards with her to try to cheer her up. But the truth was she really didn't feel like it.

'Maybe just one round, and then I think I'll go up, if you don't mind,' Kitty said apologetically. 'It's been a long day.'

Lizzie nodded. 'That would be nice; I need to finish my letter afterwards anyway. Mum and Dad are always going on at me for not telling them enough of my news.' She opened the door to her room a touch wider and Kitty went in, sat at the little wooden table in the small bay window, and prepared to play. But her mind wasn't on it and Lizzie beat her easily.

'Sorry,' she said. 'I wasn't much competition there, was I?'

'It's all practice,' said Lizzie, not hiding her delight

at beating her housemate, who was usually a sharp player. 'Better luck next time.'

Kitty pulled a rueful face and stood, going through into the empty kitchen. Carefully she drew the blackout curtain before putting on the light and reaching for the tea leaves. She took a small scoop, mindful that there was only ever just enough to go round. She wondered whether to turn on the Bakelite wireless but decided against it.

The other Wrens in the house were lively and meant well, but Kitty found it hard to be anything other than superficially friendly with them. It wasn't just because of the age difference; although she was older, it wasn't by much. She just didn't have a lot in common with them. Technically she was their superior in rank, which set her a little apart, but it was more than that. They were keen to go out, have fun, make the most of what little entertainment this place could offer. She wasn't.

Once she had been, but that was before Elliott had died. It had been over two years now, but Kitty knew she would never again be that young Wren eager for adventure. Dr Elliott Fitzgerald had shown her a side of life that she had never thought would be open to her when she'd first met him. He'd been working in the hospital where two of her brothers were being treated, and she had found it hard to believe that he'd preferred her company to that of all the many pretty nurses he saw day and night. Yet he had, and their courtship had stood the test of separation, with him remaining in Liverpool while she began her training in north London. He'd given her confidence, stability, faith in herself and hope for a shared future – until he'd been killed in one of the final raids of the blitz over Bootle. After that she had hardened her heart and directed all her time and energy into her work. There seemed little point in going to nights out at the local hall or nearest air base. Elliott had been a wonderful dancer – even a champion when at medical school – and once she'd had him as a partner and tutor, there was little chance anyone else would come close. She didn't begrudge her co-billettees their evenings with the airmen, but had no wish to join them.

Slowly she made her way upstairs, carrying the tea, relishing its welcome warmth in her hands. Her bedroom faced the back garden and she stood at the sash window, looking at the vegetable beds in the last of the daylight. Her landlady had dug over her lawn and taken to supplementing the rations with home-grown produce. Soon it would be time to start spring planting, and Kitty had offered to help. Whenever she was home on leave she would be roped in to help in Dolly Feeny's victory garden, so she knew a little of what she was meant to do. She'd never begrudged helping Dolly on her precious few weekends back home, as it was largely thanks to the Feenys that the young Callaghans had survived their childhoods. It had made the two families particularly close. At one point Kitty had fancied herself falling for the oldest Feeny son, Frank; but now she knew better. He saw her as another little sister, and there had been no more

16

to it, no matter how fast her heart had pounded at the sight of him. These days he was walking out with one of the young women based at his place of work and that was much more suitable all round. She forced her mind away from the image of them together.

Turning back to her room, she sat on the narrow bed with its rather worn candlewick spread, setting down the tea on a little wooden table that the landlady's husband had made. Kitty sighed. The other reason she wasn't keen on spending the evening playing cards with Lizzie was that she couldn't help contrasting her with the two friends she'd made when they had all been trainee Wrens together. Both of them had known and liked Elliott and had helped her through the bleak time after he'd died. Then they'd all gone their separate ways, but had resolutely stayed in contact, mostly by letter, meeting up if their work allowed.

That was what Kitty had been doing today. Marjorie was someone she would never have met if it hadn't been for the war: a teacher, who had moved in very different circles to those of Empire Street. Kitty had been overawed by her cleverness to begin with, but then again Marjorie had been shy, ill at ease with the opposite sex, unsure of herself in social situations. Kitty had grown up with three brothers and had then managed their local NAAFI canteen, and so was completely at home with young men and their teasing banter. Gradually she had realised her humble beginnings didn't matter now they were all throwing themselves into the war effort, and Marjorie had relaxed enough to enjoy dancing with the young men from the Forces they'd met in the clubs Elliott introduced them to whenever he'd managed to visit London. She'd always been deadly serious about her work, though. She had been picked out for her brains and aptitude with languages, and was now stationed not far from her own home in Sussex, where she'd been working in signals. That was the official version, anyway.

When they'd met for lunch today, Marjorie hadn't exactly contradicted that idea. However, she'd insisted on taking the corner table in a quiet little café, far from where anyone could overhear them, staring at the chequered cloth as if trying to decide what to say. Finally she had looked at Kitty and given her a small smile. 'Look, you know how it is,' she said. 'I've been given a new posting and thought we should meet up before I left. I can't say when I'll be going, but it'll be sooner rather than later.'

Kitty had raised an eyebrow, desperate to know more but only too aware that you didn't ask questions.

Marjorie shifted in her seat. She was still birdlike, seemingly tiny enough to be blown over by the first hint of a strong wind. But Kitty knew inside she was made of sterner stuff. 'So, I realise I can't tell you what I'll be doing but – well, this one I really, really can't tell you.' She rolled her eyes. 'You'll just have to put two and two together, Kitty, like I know you're good at doing. Who knows, one day you'll be putting through a call that's a result of what I've been up to. That's as much as I can give away.'

Kitty had sat up straighter. Adding that to Marjorie's

crammer courses in French and German, this was a strong hint that her friend was going to be sent abroad – and that must mean it was very hush-hush. There were rumours of young women being sent on secret missions into enemy territory. Now maybe her friend was to be one of them.

'Really?' Kitty was impressed and filled with trepidation on Marjorie's behalf. 'And you are happy about it?'

Marjorie's chin went up and her eyes were alight. 'Yes, absolutely,' she'd said. 'I can't tell you what I'm doing, Kitty – but I can tell you I'm pretty darn good at it.'

Kitty nodded. Coming from someone else it could have sounded like boasting, but Marjorie had never been like that. For all her social awkwardness to begin with, she'd never had any doubts about her academic abilities. She'd had to fight her family for the chance to use those talents as a teacher and now she was turning them to good use in the service of her country.

Kitty had grinned. 'Well, good luck then.' She'd raised her tea cup. 'And let's hope wherever it is there'll be some dishy airmen to fill your leisure hours.'

Marjorie beamed. 'Suppose there might be. It's hard to say – they never brief you on all the really important things like that. If I'm really lucky there'll be some fair-haired ones. That'll take my mind off work very nicely indeed.'

'Marjorie!' Kitty pretended to be shocked, but she knew there was nothing Marjorie liked better than being whirled around the dance floor by a fair-haired pilot, particularly if he'd promised her a martini. It didn't hurt to dream. Though there might not be many cocktails for her friend in the near future.

They'd parted shortly after, with hugs and promises to keep in touch if possible, and neither had given in to the thought that Marjorie was going into danger and they might never see one another again. Kitty picked sadly at the bedspread now, wondering what was in store for her friend. She didn't doubt she had reserves of courage and resourcefulness, but she had seemed so small as she'd waved her goodbye on the train platform. 'I haven't been able to see Laura,' Marjorie had said. 'I'll write of course, but if you see her, will you tell her I was thinking of her?'

'Of course,' Kitty had promised. Laura was the third of the group who'd bonded so closely during the initial weeks of training. She was still in London, working as a driver, horrifying her very well-to-do family with her willingness to get her hands dirty fixing engines rather than sitting in their ancient pile in Yorkshire making polite conversation.

Clearly Marjorie was so close to being sent off to do whatever it was that she couldn't even make it up to London; if that was the case, perhaps Kitty could go in her stead. She brightened at the thought. She'd see when she next had leave and if it coincided with Laura being able to take some time off. That would be something to look forward to.

Danny Callaghan drew the rickety wooden chair closer to the fireplace. He had lit the kindling when he'd got in from work, and now he poked it and added a few pieces of coal, just enough to take the chill off the room which had been empty all day. He warmed his hands and then reached into his pocket for the letter he'd picked up off the worn doormat. The writing was familiar, scrappy and uneven, clearly done in a hurry.

Ripping open the envelope he was curious to see what his young brother Tommy had to say for himself. Tommy wrote often but never at great length. He had been evacuated to the same farm as their neighbour Rita's children, where he'd soon taken to the life. Seth the farmer had been delighted as, having no son of his own, he had begun to struggle with all the daily tasks once his young farmhands had been called up. Tommy had become a real help. The arrangement suited everyone. In the past Tommy had been a proper handful, and had nearly got himself killed in a burning warehouse down at the docks, where he had had no business being in the first place. His older siblings had been at their wits' end trying to work out how to keep him safe at home, and so sending him to the farm had been the best solution all round.

Danny drew out the single sheet of paper and scanned it quickly, then looked again more carefully. He'd been expecting more of the same sort of news that Tommy had been sending for the past couple of years: what fences he'd helped to mend, if the fox had managed to get into the hen house, what treats Joan, Seth's wife, had baked. There was some of that, but the main reason Tommy had written was he wanted to come back to Bootle.

Danny groaned. Of course his little brother was growing up. He was thirteen now and would soon turn fourteen. It hadn't escaped Tommy's notice that this meant he could leave school. So he thought the best thing would be for him to move back in with Danny and then see if he could help the war effort in any way – he had heard that boys of fourteen could join the Merchant Navy.

'Oh no,' Danny breathed, knowing full well the sort of life that would mean. Plenty of the men and boys he knew who'd grown up around the docks had joined the Merchant Navy, and of course Eddy Feeny would come home with tales of what it was like, so Tommy knew all about it – or at least the tales of adventure, dodging U-boats, mixing with seamen of all nations, all working for a common cause. It would appeal to any boy. But Danny didn't want his little brother to be in danger like that. He groaned aloud once more.

'Danny! Whatever's the matter?' Sarah Feeny pushed open the back door and set down a scratched enamel pot on the hob in the back kitchen. 'Mam made extra stew and thought you might like some. Don't get your hopes up; it's nearly all potato and beans, hardly any meat in it. Seriously, what's wrong? You haven't taken bad again, have you?' Her animated face was etched with sudden concern.

'No, no, nothing like that.' Danny shook his head and his thick black hair glinted in the firelight. 'You shouldn't have.' He nodded at the pot. 'Thank your mam for me, she spoils me.'

22

'She likes to,' Sarah said with a grin, pulling up another chair. 'So, tell me what's happened.' She shivered and drew her nurse's cloak more tightly around her.

Danny let out a long sigh. 'It's our Tommy. This arrived today. He's reminding me that he's going to be fourteen soon and won't have to go to school any more. He says he wants to join the Merchant Navy.'

Sarah gasped. Like Danny, she thought of Tommy as the young tearaway who'd settled down once he was given responsibility on the farm, and although if she'd added it up rationally she would have known how old he was, it was still a shock to realise he was well on the way to becoming a young man. 'It doesn't seem possible, Danny. Surely you don't want that.' She tried not to let her anxiety show, not only for Tommy but for Danny too. She knew better than anyone what he struggled so hard to keep hidden. Although technically now part of the Royal Navy, Danny had never gone – and could never go – to sea. All of the armed forces had turned him down, despite his obvious courage and willingness to sign up, as rheumatic fever had left him with an enlarged heart. Any extreme physical activity would put him at risk. They'd only found out when he'd stood in for a fallen fireman at a vast blaze down at the docks. Danny had taken the man's place without hesitation but had collapsed afterwards. Sarah had rescued him but the news had got out. When it came to fighting for his country, Danny Callaghan was damaged goods.

By a stroke of luck, Danny had shown an uncommon

aptitude for solving puzzles and crosswords while recuperating, and this had led to him being recruited to join Western Approaches Command, as they were in desperate need of that rare kind of skill to help decipher enemy signals. Frank Feeny worked there as a naval officer, and had recommended his old friend, against some opposition from the more traditional superior officers. Danny had only ever worked down on the docks up till then and had been a tearaway himself when in his teens.

This was exactly what was on Danny's mind as he reread his little brother's letter. He recognised that feeling of wanting to join up, do his bit, and also see the world and test himself against the odds, take a risk and worry about the consequences later. It was precisely why he wanted to protect Tommy from it. Now he was older, he wished he'd paid more attention at school, but at the time he couldn't be bothered, couldn't wait for it to end so he could get out and live his own life. It had meant that his work at Derby House had been extra hard to begin with as he'd had to learn so much from scratch. He could see with hindsight how he would have benefited from listening to his teachers when they'd insisted he could have gone further. All right, the family had needed him to go out and earn his keep – but he'd wasted the last year in the classroom. He wanted better for Tommy.

Now he looked across at Sarah, with her sleek brown hair pulled back away from her caring face, knowing that she'd be worried for him. He didn't want his anxieties to burden her. 'No, I'd much rather he stayed where he is. At least we know he's safe there, and well fed.'

'And Michael and Megan look up to him,' Sarah said. 'They'd miss him if he came back.'

'It's been good for him to be like a big brother to them,' Danny agreed. 'The trouble was, we all let him get away with murder because he was the youngest and he could wind us round his little finger. Now he's had to grow up a bit.'

'Sounds like he's started to grow up a lot,' Sarah said ruefully, getting to her feet and opening a cupboard. 'Here, Danny, I'll put this on a plate so you can have it now while it's still warm. News always feels better after a full meal.'

She knew her way around the Callaghan kitchen as well as her own, as – ever since Kitty had left – Dolly would often make a bit extra for Danny and have Sarah take it across the street. 'There you are.' The delicious smell filled the small room, and Danny tucked in gratefully.

'Thanks, Sar.' Finally he pushed the plate away. 'You're right. You can't make good decisions on an empty stomach.'

'I wonder what Kitty thinks?' Sarah replied. 'Do you think he'll have written to her as well? It's not up to just you, is it?'

'She'll have to know,' Danny said. 'Even if he hasn't asked her, I'm going to tell her. Sometimes he listens to her. She can persuade him to stay at the farm better than I can.'

'Not much she can do about it from wherever it is

25

she is down south,' Sarah pointed out. 'All the same, you'd better write to her. And she'll want to know all about the new baby. Mam sent everybody a letter to say Ellen had been born but didn't have time to give any details.'

Danny looked sceptical. 'That's more your sort of thing, isn't it? I don't know what Kitty will want to know. I'm glad for Rita, of course I am, but all babies look the same to me.'

'Danny!' Sarah gave him a straight look. 'That's your niece you're talking about. Honestly, you men, you're hopeless sometimes.' Her expression was affectionate though. She could never be truly cross with Danny. He was too good a man for that. She knew he was just teasing – in that special way he seemed to reserve just for her.

'You tell me what she'll want to know, then,' he grinned. He had realised long ago that Sarah knew him better then he knew himself. 'Better still, write a note and I'll put it in with my letter about Tommy. That'll sweeten the pill.' He grew serious again. 'Sar, just think of it, young Tommy wanting to put his life on the line like that. I can't have that. It's too much. Somehow, we have to stop him.'

CHAPTER THREE

Frank Feeny held the heavy door open for Wren Sylvia Hemsley as they made their way out of Derby House at the end of their shifts. It was unusual for them both to finish work at the same time and he thought they should make the most of it, so earlier when they'd met at tea break he'd suggested going to the cinema. She had said she'd think about it, but wasn't sure if she would have to stay late to cover for a sick colleague.

Now, though, luck was on their side. Sylvia had been able to get off on time, and they emerged into the early spring evening. Liverpool city centre had taken a pounding earlier in the war and the ruined buildings stood testament to the bombing raids, but also to the indomitable spirit of the people, who had refused to be cowed. At first everyone had been hesitant to walk through the damaged streets, and there had been real danger from falling debris and potholes opening up, especially as there could be no street lighting. They'd got used to it now, though, and the area was beginning to come to life again. The evenings were slowly lengthening and a feeling of optimism was in the air. There had been no major raids over the city for some time, and there was a tangible sense of the tide of war being on the turn. The Allies had won the battle at El Alamein in North Africa and were making inroads into Italy. The attacks by U-boats on vessels in the North Atlantic had dropped considerably, much to the relief of many in the city, whose fathers, sons and brothers sailed that route, as members of the Royal Navy, Merchant Navy or Fleet Air Arm. Frank knew that many of the gains in the North Atlantic were down to what went on in the two levels of basement rooms in Derby House and the nearby Tactical Unit, all plotting the enemy's positions, working out the best way to intercept and destroy them.

He looked at Sylvia and grinned. They deserved their evening off. 'What do you fancy seeing?' he asked.

Sylvia smiled back. 'How about *Casablanca* again?'

Frank shrugged. He'd have preferred to go to something new, but Sylvia was a big fan of Humphrey Bogart. 'I don't mind,' he said. 'It's on near your billet, isn't it?'

Sylvia beamed at him. 'Yes, and we'll just have time to get there. I'd love to see it again.' She began to sing as they walked along. 'Ta da ta da ta . . . as time goes by . . .'

Frank raised an eyebrow. Sylvia was a dedicated Wren and highly skilled at her job, very pretty and great company, but even her nearest and dearest couldn't claim she was musical. She couldn't hold a tune to save her life. He told himself not to be so judgemental – she had plenty of other fine qualities. But he'd been brought up with music in the house, as Pop was always playing his accordion as they grew up, and many a time he'd taken it down to the Sailor's Rest and joined in when someone else was on the piano. The children would gather outside and join in the words of any songs they knew. Frank couldn't remember how old he had been the first time he'd gone along, it was so much a part of his childhood. He had never questioned it – keeping in tunc was just what you did. He realised he should count himself lucky that he could hold a note without thinking about it.

Involuntarily his mind flashed back to one occasion when Kitty had been there, singing along in her school-girl voice, perfectly in rhythm and in key. She was another one who'd never had to work out how to sing, she just did it naturally. He wondered where she was now – somewhere down south, Danny Callaghan had said, living out in the sticks. Frank gave a small smile. She would hate that.

'What are you laughing about?' Sylvia demanded, catching sight of his expression. She turned to face him. 'Are you making fun of my singing? It's all right, I know you do that; you're not the first.' She sighed. 'We can't all be Vera Lynn, or what's her name, your friend from round here? Gloria Arden. Some of us have to make do with the talents we were born with.'

29

'Of course I'm not making fun of you,' Frank assured her hurriedly. He didn't want to have a row on this rare occasion of sharing an evening off. 'One Gloria in the world is quite enough. All right, she's got a great voice, but she can't bake a Woolton pie like you can. She never was keen on spending time in the kitchen.'

Gloria Arden was now one of the country's best-loved singers, riding high in the public's esteem, her golden voice offering entertainment and comfort in equal measure, and was often to be found touring with ENSA, the Entertainments National Service Association. She'd started her life in Empire Street, though, daughter of the landlord and landlady of the Sailor's Rest, and had been his sister Nancy's best friend – still was Nancy's best friend, in fact, and whenever a tour brought Gloria back to the north of England, she would make a point of seeing her. Even before she made it big, Gloria had never had any domestic inclinations. She'd worked in a factory before she got her lucky break, singing at the Adelphi in the city centre when they had a vacant slot.

'Bet she can't mend a uniform jacket like I can either,' Sylvia went on. 'Or type as fast.'

'Or type at all, as far as I know,' Frank added dutifully. He carefully put his arm around Sylvia's shoulder – not because he thought she might object, but because he had to be mindful of his balance. He'd lost a leg back in the early days of the war and had used a false one ever since. He could manage most day-to-day things, although his reign as a boxing

30

champion was over, but any sudden movement could be a problem. It meant he couldn't be as spontaneous as he'd like to be. He'd met Sylvia long after the accident and she'd always said she didn't mind, but sometimes he wondered. While they were very fond of each other, if pressed he would have to say they were 'in like' and not 'in love'. Then again, he reasoned that the war distorted all relationships. Some couples flung themselves at each other, in case one or both of them weren't here tomorrow. There had been plenty of over-hasty affairs and marriages, some of which were lasting and others that had already crumbled. Other couples chose to tread much more cautiously, wary of enforced separations or the heightened emotions that inevitably came with prolonged fighting conditions. He suspected that was what had happened to them. Before his accident he had been anything but cautious, but that and the war had matured him, and now he had the added responsibility of being a lieutenant, responsible for training many of the new recruits at Western Approaches Command. He couldn't be seen gadding about in the streets, even if it was with a highly respected young Wren.

'Glad to hear it,' said Sylvia sparkily. 'I like to know I'm appreciated.'

'Oh, you are,' said Frank warmly, and meant it. He brushed her dark curls where they were coming loose from the base of her uniform cap. 'I'm a lucky man and I know it. It's not every old crock who has a beautiful young woman on his arm.'

'Old crock – get away with you.' Sylvia punched

him on the arm. She'd known about his leg from the start and it had never bothered her, though she sensed it still troubled him far more than he let on. All she could do was carry on as normal and hope that one day he'd believe her that it really didn't matter. He was devastatingly good-looking, he was widely respected at work, and she knew she was the envy of most of the female members of staff at Derby House to be walking out with him. Fair enough, he might not be able to take her dancing at the Grafton, but in all other respects he was just what she'd always wanted. If only he could believe that. Sometimes she wondered if he ever would.

'Let's get the bus,' she suggested, rounding the corner and not even registering the damage to what had once been the large John Lewis department store, so familiar was it in its wrecked state. 'We don't want to miss the beginning. That's the moment I like best – when the lights begin to go down.' She looked up at him brightly, and winked.

Frank squeezed her shoulder. They halted by the bus stop, busy with workers returning to the outskirts of the city, many in uniforms of the various armed forces. There was a hum of chatter, and Frank thought for a moment how much he loved his home city, with everyone pulling together and getting on with what needed to be done, despite the horrendous bomb damage all around. The people of Merseyside were bigger than the attacks of the Luftwaffe. This is what they were fighting for – the spirit of the place and the people who lived there. He was proud of his uniform, and Sylvia's, and could see that other people were looking at them approvingly. His earlier qualms seemed unjustified and silly now.

'Come on, this is ours.' Sylvia stepped onto the bus and Frank let her choose where to sit. Miraculously there were two seats together, but this was near the start of the route, and later on it would be standing room only. He was secretly glad – he'd of course get up and offer his place to anyone who needed it, but standing for any length of time in a moving vehicle was something he'd rather avoid. As more passengers got on he was pressed closer to Sylvia and he noticed yet again how her cleverly altered uniform jacket curved around her shapely body. No wonder the men in the bus queue had looked at him with envy.

'What shifts are you on this weekend?' he asked, his mouth close to her ear as yet another group of passengers squeezed inside. 'I'm off on Sunday. Shall we make a day of it?'

Sylvia sighed and turned towards him. 'Oh, Frank, I'd love to, but I didn't know you'd have any free time. I've got both days off for once and I promised I'd go to see my parents. It's been ages, and they worry if I don't visit them now and again. They think I've wasted away or something.'

'Ah well, never mind.' Frank knew that was true. Sylvia came from the Lake District, and even though it was in theory in the same corner of England, the journey was often complicated and took ages. He couldn't blame her for grabbing the chance to spend some time at home. He was lucky – he only had to travel along the Mersey to Bootle to see Dolly and Pop. He couldn't begrudge her this opportunity to see the parents he knew she missed dearly, even if she rarely admitted it. He reached down and squeezed her hand. 'You'll enjoy that. Give them my best.'

'I will.' Sylvia had been nervous at first to introduce Frank and her parents, never fully sure how he felt about her, but after they'd officially been a couple for six months she'd taken the plunge. Of course, they had loved him, and now they never stopped asking her when he was going to pop the question, but Sylvia couldn't answer that one. If these had been normal times, things might have been different – and yet without the war, she and Frank would never have met at all. 'Mum will probably load me up with her home-made jam for you.'

'I'll use it to sweeten my landlady,' Frank laughed. 'It's about the only thing that works.' He'd chosen to live in a service billet rather than go back to the little house on Empire Street, as that was already full to bursting, but his landlady was taciturn at best and mostly plain sour. He didn't complain – he wasn't there for entertainment.

'Excuse me,' said a trembling voice from behind his shoulder, 'I hate to ask but . . .'

Frank swivelled round in his seat and saw an old woman, leaning on a walking stick, making her way unsteadily along the aisle. He stood up immediately. 'Please. My pleasure.' He took a firm grip of the well-worn metal pole so he wouldn't embarrass himself by falling as the bus jerked back into action along the

34

potholed road, and the lady sagged in relief as she sat down. Sylvia shuffled along the seat a little to make room.

Frank noticed that slight movement and reminded himself how caring she was and how little fuss she made about it. Some women might have made a song and dance about having to share a seat with someone other than their boyfriend, but not Sylvia. She was simply good-natured like that. She was kind, and very attractive, and she wanted to be with him – so why was he hanging back from committing himself more fully?

'Is she sleeping?' Violet leant over the little cot to see Ellen's tiny face. 'What beautiful eyelashes she has, Rita. She's going to be a model in a magazine when she's grown up.' She straightened again and tugged at the sleeves of her old cardigan. They must have shrunk again in a too-hot wash, but it was one of the very few she had left.

Rita sat up on the couch, gazing adoringly at her new daughter. 'She's been like that for half an hour. I managed to nod off myself, just for a quick nap. I ought to be getting ready for tea but somehow I needed the rest.'

'Don't you worry yourself about that,' Violet tutted. 'I'll see to it. You put your feet up while you can. You've a lot of rest to catch up on, running round like you did practically until that child was born. Is Ruby minding the shop?'

Rita glanced towards the internal door that led to

the shop. 'Yes, she's getting better all the time. I think it's because beforehand she always knew that if things went wrong you or I would be there to sort it out. Now I've got Ellen to see to, and you've been over at the victory garden, it's all been down to her. I stick my nose in now and again when you aren't around, but she's been forced to speak to people and she's found they don't bite after all.'

Violet shook her head in disbelief. 'It's been a long time coming, that has. I'll just put my nose round the door and see if she's happy with Spam fritters.' She carefully shut the door to what used to be Winnie Kennedy's breakfast room, which Rita had turned into a cosy sitting room now her ex-husband's mother was dead. The once stuffy, over-formal space was now warm and inviting, as Rita had collected scraps of fabric and made patchwork cushions and rag rugs, even if there was no new furniture to be had. She had stored away Winnie's favoured dark, heavy pieces and kept only the softer, lighter ones, and had begged some tins of paint off Danny Callaghan to brighten the walls and woodwork. Danny, in his former occupation down on the docks, had been able to get hold of the most surprising items, and he still had the odd few tucked away. Usually Rita disapproved; but for this – making a home fit for her new baby – she'd made an exception. Ruby had as much of a claim to the place as she did, but hadn't objected. Hardly anyone knew but Ruby was actually Winnie's unacknow-ledged daughter, but the mean old woman had gone to her grave keeping the secret of who the father was.

Charlie had never so much as indicated he'd known this was his sister, either. He'd gone to his own grave despising Ruby as much as Winnie, their mother, had.

Violet pushed open the door to the shop and saw Ruby was out in front of the counter, not hiding in the account books for a change. There was a man there, not young but not elderly either, in a faded brown overall and peaked cap. He looked familiar but Violet couldn't place him.

'Oh . . . oh, hello, Violet.' Ruby jumped back. She was a little red in the face. Violet supposed it had taken a considerable effort for the shy young woman to talk to the customer, and forgave her the nervousness.

'Ruby, I've just come to see what you'd like for your tea,' Violet said directly. She turned to the man. 'I'm sorry, I can't quite place . . .'

The man stepped forward and she could now see that he must be about forty. His hair, or what was visible of it, was beginning to grey and he had wrinkles around his eyes, but his expression was friendly. 'James. Reggie James. It's Mrs Feeny, isn't it? My dad told me about you.'

Violet nodded as the penny dropped. This must be the son of old Mr James who'd been so helpful when they'd first started work on the victory garden and hadn't really known what they were meant to be doing. There behind him were some boxes of vegetables. He must have brought them to be sold in the shop. 'Very pleased to meet you,' she said. 'Your father was very kind to us, you know. We would have been stumped without him. Has Ruby been sorting you out?'

'Oh . . . yes. Yes, she has.' The man seemed suddenly at a loss for words and Violet wondered if he was one of those men who didn't know what to say to women – some didn't like to see women running a business, even if it was a corner shop and all the men had been called up or kept in reserved occupations like down on the docks. She noticed he didn't stand quite straight and wondered why that was. He saw her looking and got in his explanation before she could ask.

'I was wounded at El Alamein,' he said, slightly self-consciously, rubbing the top of his leg like a reflex. 'Some folks think I took a Blighty, but it wasn't like that. I'd never have dodged my duty by deliberately injuring myself, but it means I can't go back into active service.' He smiled sheepishly. 'I wasn't as young as most of them and it takes that bit longer to heal at my age, you see. Anyway, now I'm up on my feet again I'm going to help Dad out on the allotment, and do a little sideline in vegetables when I can.'

'Oh, I'm sure that's a good idea,' said Violet hurriedly, a little embarrassed to have been caught staring. She couldn't imagine for one moment that any son of trustworthy old Mr James could have hurt himself on purpose to avoid further action in the war. 'We can always sell fresh vegetables, can't we, Ruby?'

Ruby nodded mutely, seeming to have regressed now that there was someone else to do the talking.

Violet remembered why she'd come in the first place. 'So, Ruby, Spam fritters for your tea tonight?'

Ruby looked at her feet and then appeared to snap out of it. 'Yes please. Thank you, Violet.'

'I'll leave you two to it then,' said Violet, turning back towards the living quarters, but not before registering the glance that Ruby exchanged with Reggie James. Then she told herself not to be silly. Ruby had hardly any friends, and sometimes could scarcely say hello to people she'd known for years, she was so withdrawn through sheer habit. She would be far too hesitant to make a new friend of an unfamiliar acquaintance. It must just be that she was pleased with the new business arrangement. Ruby liked the numbers to be in order. That could be the only explanation.

CHAPTER FOUR

'Are you sure you don't want to go to Lyons Corner House?' asked Laura as she met Kitty off the train at Victoria. 'Somewhere nice and warm?' She was in civvies, and even though clothing was rationed and generally hard to come by, she'd somehow managed to look devastatingly fashionable as ever, with her swing coat and little matching hat on her beautifully cut blonde curls. Heads were turning as she swept along the concourse but Laura blithely paid no notice.

Kitty had come in her Wren's uniform. Now she no longer shared a billet with Laura, her chance to borrow her friend's clothes had gone, and she hadn't felt like turning up in her slightly battered tweed coat, now several years old and looking it. Besides, she was proud of her uniform. She'd worked hard to be worthy of it, and she appreciated the approving glances it won from many of the other passengers whirling around them. She took her friend's arm.

'I'd really rather go for a walk, if you don't mind,' she said. 'I'm cooped up inside most of the time, you know.'

'Of course, I completely understand,' said Laura at once. 'But surely there are plenty of places to go walking where you are? What else is there to do, frankly? Count the cows?' She glanced down at her feet. 'Good job I didn't wear my high heels. I found some divine ones in Peter Jones, did I tell you in my last letter? Anyone would have thought they were just waiting for me.'

'Lucky you,' said Kitty, meaning it. 'Just don't try driving your lorries in them. Tell you what, if we wander across Green Park we could find a Lyons after that. I don't want to deprive you of your teacake.'

'Come on, then.' Laura led the way, weaving through the press of people, many in uniform, some carrying kit bags over their shoulders. Some were saying goodbye to families and loved ones. Others were waiting, maybe for a long-hoped-for reunion. Despite the ever-present threat of disruption to the trains, nobody appeared to be complaining. Kitty had been lucky; she'd come up from her small local station without a problem for once. It meant she had most of the day to spend with her old friend. Almost without realising it, she felt a weight lift from her shoulders. Confiding in Laura always made her feel better and she knew the feeling was mutual.

As they passed through the streets and headed towards the park, the crowds thinned out, but there was still a sense of bustle and activity. Kitty grinned, relishing being back in a big city. It was where she felt at home, jostling around people, being in the thick of it. Growing up on Merseyside had made her feel that this was normal, and it was where she was comfortable, despite knowing rationally that big cities were more dangerous, being targets for the enemy's attacks. Yet she couldn't shake off the sense that this was the sort of place where she belonged, not a quiet country town where everything went silent after dusk.

Green Park loomed ahead, with its avenues of old trees, and as they began to wander down one of its wide paths, Laura turned to face her. 'All right, Kitty. I know you – you would usually rush straight to Lyons or somewhere like it. What's up? What do you have to say that's so secret you can't tell me where anyone can overhear?'

Kitty laughed ruefully. She should have known there would be no fooling Laura, who might act the dizzy socialite when it suited her, but who underneath was as sharp as a tack. There was no point in beating about the bush.

'Have you heard from Marjorie recently?'

'Marjorie?' Laura stopped to think. 'I had a letter a few weeks ago; it had taken ages to get to me, and loads of it had been censored anyway. You wouldn't think signals in Sussex could be that exciting. I was impressed.'

Kitty shrugged. 'Well, let's just say if she wrote down what she hinted at to me the other day, then you wouldn't have had much of a letter at all. It would all have been blacked out.'

'Now you have got me intrigued,' Laura said. 'Tell all, Callaghan. Out with it.'

Hoping that she wasn't exaggerating, or hadn't got the wrong end of the stick, Kitty explained what had happened. 'So you see, she asked me to have a word with you rather than write, as she didn't think she'd be able to get leave to see you in person,' she finished, gripping her handkerchief in her jacket pocket in anxiety for her friend. 'This sounds serious, doesn't it? Can you imagine it, Marjorie going into enemy territory, probably undercover?'

Laura came to a halt. 'Well, I don't know what I expected you to say, but it wasn't that,' she admitted. 'I thought you were going to tell me that she'd finally fallen properly for one of her blond pilots, or she'd been chosen to learn Danish or one of those other language things she gets so worked up about. Golly, Kitty. That's ever so slightly terrifying, isn't it? I mean, when we first knew her, she was scared of Leicester Square on a Saturday night.'

'She's changed since then,' Kitty reminded her. 'She was so certain she was doing the right thing as well. Honestly, Laura, she showed no doubt at all. She knows what she's getting into and she's ready for it. I'm afraid for her and yet I'm proud too. That she should be chosen – well, she must be really good at what she does.'

'She is, I'm sure,' said Laura with certainty. She held on to Kitty's arm more forcefully. 'Look, we mustn't worry about her. That will do no good and we can't change what she's decided to do or what will happen. She will be needed.' She paused, casting her glance from left to right and back again. 'No one around, is there? Well, I bet she is going to northern France.'

43

'What?' Kitty leaned closer. 'What do you mean? What do you know, Laura?'

Laura closed her eyes briefly and then made up her mind to share what she'd heard. 'All totally hush-hush, of course,' she said, as if it was even necessary to stress such a thing, 'but it's sort of common knowledge in certain circles that something big is going to happen. I don't know when, and of course not exactly what, but something's brewing.'

Kitty raised her eyebrows. 'Has Peter said something?'

Captain Peter Cavendish was Laura's boyfriend, and very well connected, with an uncle who was an admiral and who had attended meetings of naval top brass ever since they'd known him. At first Laura had called him Captain Killjoy, as their working relationship had begun with hostility on her part and near-silence from his; he'd also shown an uncanny knack of knowing when Laura had planned a night out, always calling her to drive him just when she was getting ready. That had lasted until they'd both been involved in rescuing a baby from a burning building after a bomb had gone off in a north London street. Peter had nearly died, and after that it had become obvious that the two of them were meant for each other.

'Not as such,' Laura admitted. 'You know he's careful never to breathe a word of what goes on at those interminable conferences of his. But I can tell something's changed. I mean, it makes sense. Look at all the Allied success of the past year – North Africa, Italy. You'd have to say it would be no surprise if they were thinking of going into France now. Wouldn't you, if you were in charge?'

Kitty took a step back. 'I . . . I don't know. Seeing as I'm never going to be in charge of something like that, I don't think about it. I just get on with what I'm asked to do.'

'Oh, so do I,' Laura said hastily. 'I'm just guessing. But it would be the obvious thing to do.'

Kitty glanced at her friend. Of course she would hear conversations like this all the time, even if they weren't full of detail. But Laura was used to being around discussions at that sort of level. Kitty wasn't, and she didn't feel qualified to offer an opinion. Also, even after having been friends for so long, Laura sometimes still had that effect on her: making her feel inadequate, that she was on the outside looking in, while the likes of Laura forged ahead, effortlessly taking charge, knowing they were born to make the key decisions. Then she gave herself a mental shake. Laura didn't do it deliberately. It was just Kitty's own habit to feel under-confident in the face of such assurance. But Kitty herself had changed since the early days of training – she had to remember that.

'Besides,' Laura said, her tone sadder now, 'he's been hinting that he might not be shore-based for much longer. Nothing definite, naturally. But it's true; ever since I've known him he has been mostly behind a desk rather than on board a ship. I can tell he misses it, and he feels he should get back to sea and into the heart of the action. I admire him for it, of course I do, but I can't help wanting him to be safe as well.'

'Oh, Laura.' Kitty gave her friend's arm a squeeze. 'He'll have to go where he's sent, won't he? Like the rest of us. We know he's brave, there's no question of that.'

'He feels he hasn't taken his share of the risks,' Laura said flatly. 'We both know it was taking the risk of jumping through that window with all the shattered glass that injured him, so you can hardly accuse him of taking the easy way out with a desk job. They had to keep him from active service for ages while he built up his strength again – not that you'd get him to admit it. But he feels everyone thinks he's taken the cushy postings, when really the opposite is true. He lives with the consequences of that injury every day; he'll never be fully free from pain.' She pulled a face. 'Anyway, there we are. Nothing I can do about it. If he does take part in whatever's coming up, maybe he'll bump into Marjorie, to say *bonjour*.'

Kitty gazed up to where the tree branches almost met in an arch above their heads, the new leaves beginning to bud. 'It feels like it's all a long way off, doesn't it? Standing here in this quiet bit of the park.'

For a moment it was easy to forget that they were in the middle of the biggest city in the country, millions of people going about their business to fight for everything they held dear. The spring sunlight filtered through the swaying branches with just a hint of warmth to come.

Laura smiled. 'Yes, but it's not, is it? So, my girl, we have to grasp every moment. And in my book that means a nice cup of tea and maybe a cake if they've got any. Or a crumpet at least. Come on, I'll treat you.'

Kitty relented. Laura clearly wasn't going to be kept from a café for much longer. 'All right, you win,' she said. 'Now you know the news and I know yours. Peter's all right otherwise, isn't he?'

Laura gave an even bigger smile. 'Yes, still the dashing captain.'

Kitty knew that Laura had tried to keep her friendship with Captain Cavendish under wraps, as such relationships, while not exactly frowned on, and not uncommon, were not actively encouraged within the service. Once it had come to light, there had been a fair bit of jealousy of Laura and some very hurtful comments had been aimed her way. It being Laura, they had just bounced straight off her, but even so, Kitty was aware her friend never put herself forward for promotion or any kind of privilege, concerned that the immediate assumption would be that her boyfriend or his illustrious uncle had used their influence. Laura loved her job as it was, and she was very good at it, but Kitty wondered how long that would last, especially if Peter was called back to active service as seemed likely.

'As long as you're happy,' Kitty said loyally.

'I am,' Laura assured her. 'He's the best thing that ever happened to me, I don't mind telling you, and even better he says the same about me. I just adore him, however foolhardily brave he might be. Wouldn't have him any other way.'

Kitty nodded, pleased for her friend. 'And no news about—'

'No, none,' Laura said hurriedly. She didn't have to check what Kitty meant; there was one person they both knew was never far from Laura's mind. Her cheerful attitude masked a deep-seated sorrow for her lost brother, a pilot missing in action since before they had started their training. No confirmation had ever come about what his fate had been, and so there was no way of knowing if he was alive or, more likely, dead. So Laura kept going, trying to remain positive, but with a little bit of hope dying away every day.

'No, nothing. Of course I'd tell you if there were. And who knows what might happen if we invade France? I might at least find out, one way or the other. But for now it's limbo as usual. Come on,' she tugged on Kitty's arm, 'I'm perishing. I've put on my most glamorous new coat for you, I hope you recognise, and it turns out to let the breeze right through it, so if I don't have a hot drink soon I might well expire, and you wouldn't want that on your conscience, would you?'

'Definitely not, Peter would kill me,' said Kitty, allowing Laura to lead her towards Piccadilly and the promise of tea and crumpets.

'So will you look after Georgie on Saturday evening, Mam?' asked Nancy, quickly checking her reflection in the mirror over Dolly's fireplace. She carefully smoothed her victory roll, making sure every hair was in place. She had red hair like her sister Rita, but Nancy's was more Titian in tone, and she always styled it, whereas Rita usually made do with anything

48

that was tidy enough to fit under her nursing sister's cap. Nancy nodded quickly in satisfaction. She'd been told she had a look of Rita Hayworth about her, and thought there might be some truth in it.

Dolly looked up from the comfy armchair, where she was knitting something in mustard yellow with wool unravelled from Violet's old cardigan, which had finally given up the ghost. 'Saturday evening? Are you off out, young lady? Don't forget your poor husband, stuck in a Jerry prison.'

'Of course I never forget Sid,' snapped Nancy, annoyed, 'but it doesn't mean I have to spend every hour God sends with his miserable mother in her horrible house. Honestly, Mam, she keeps it so cold it's a wonder I haven't turned blue. It's making Georgie ill, I swear it. He's got a bad chest again, poor little soul.' Sid Kerrigan had been a prisoner of war since Dunkirk and had never even seen his little boy. Now and again Nancy felt guilty about that, but usually she was too preoccupied by the idea of her youth disappearing fast and having nobody to go dancing with. 'Anyway, it's not as if I'm off gadding about. My WVS group has joined forces with the WI to put on a dance for the visiting servicemen and they need volunteers. Of course I said I'd help out when they asked. They rely on me for that sort of thing.'

Dolly sighed. She'd tried for ages to get Nancy involved with the local branch of the Women's Voluntary Services, of which she was a mainstay. Then Nancy had outmanoeuvred her by announcing she was indeed joining the WVS, but the branch in the

49

city centre. Nancy assured her mother it was because they were most in need of help – and as it was just after the dreadful days of the Liverpool Blitz, this was true – but it also had the advantage of being away from her mother's eagle eye, and mixing with the influx of American servicemen, a trickle which grew to a flood after Pearl Harbor. Nancy was fooling nobody – and the fact that she was never without a new pair of nylons spoke volumes. Dolly had a pretty shrewd idea what Nancy got up to in order to get them, but she had no proof. She wasn't going to stand for her middle daughter letting the family down, and had warned her often enough. Now she had another reason to object.

'That's all very well, Nancy, but I said I'd have little Ellen that evening,' Dolly told her. 'Rita's worn out with her, and I promised to give her a few hours when she can grab some unbroken sleep. And no, before you ask, Sarah's working, Ruby's apparently going out with a friend and Violet is keeping the shop open late. I can't risk having Georgie if he's got a bad chest; he might pass it on to Ellen and she's far too tiny to cope with that.'

Nancy all but stamped her foot in frustration. 'But, Mam—'

'Don't you give me any of your soft soap, my girl,' said Dolly sternly. 'I love Georgie to pieces, and well you know it, but there's someone else smaller than him to consider now. You might as well get used to it. You've got his other grandmother who could help out, after all.'

Nancy huffed in indignation. 'I'd sooner let him play in the dock road. She's useless, Mam, all she goes on about is how she's suffering 'cos Sid's a POW, as if she's the only one who's got anything to complain about. I wouldn't trust her to notice when Georgie was hungry or if he needed anything. She's not like you and Violet, you know.' She turned on her dazzling smile, but it was wasted on Dolly.

'Well, has she got him now?' she demanded.

'You have got to be joking!' Nancy pouted. 'No, she hasn't.'

'Where is he, then?' Dolly wanted to know.

'With Maggie Parker, as was. You know, Betty Parker's big sister. Her house got bombed out and she's moved back in with her family here and she's got a kiddie just a bit younger than Georgie,' Nancy explained. 'I thought it would be nice for him to have a playmate the same age. Particularly if everything here is going to revolve around a new-born baby,' she added crossly.

'Nancy, you can't be jealous of your own little niece,' Dolly sighed in exasperation. 'Betty Parker, now there's a name from the past. She was Sarah's best friend all the way through school, then she went and joined the Land Girls, didn't she? They're a nice family, so they are. Why don't you ask them to mind Georgie on Saturday? It's not as if you'll be out late, is it?' She gave her daughter a straight look.

Nancy squirmed, but couldn't exactly say what she'd had in mind for Saturday. It certainly didn't involve coming home directly after the dance. Common sense told her to quit while the going was good, though. 'That's an idea, I'll ask,' she said. 'I'll go and do that right away – it's time I was picking Georgie up anyway.'

'That's right, love, you do that.' Dolly approved of the Parkers, and felt she could rest easy that Nancy couldn't get up to anything now. She picked up her knitting again, Pop coming though the back door just as Nancy went out.

Pop shrugged off the heavy donkey jacket that he wore for his salvage work, and turned to wash his hands at the kitchen sink. 'Did I miss anything?' he asked, coming through the narrow doorframe between the back kitchen and the kitchen proper. He bent to kiss Dolly on the cheek. 'What did Nancy want? The usual?'

Dolly laughed up at him. 'Of course. She can't have her own way this time, though.' She recounted their conversation.

Pop raised his eyebrows. 'She'll have to get used to the new way of doing things,' he declared, running his hand through his shock of white hair. 'We've helped her a lot and we'll do so again, but she has to realise little Ellen needs us too. I don't want our Rita took bad because she's tried to do much too soon. You know what she's like.'

'You're right, she'll be angling to get back to work any day now,' said Dolly, untangling a length of wool that had tied itself in a knot. 'She's not to rush it. We'll have to keep an eye on her, see that she takes her time.'

'She never thinks of herself, that one,' Pop said. 'What's that you're making there, Dolly? That looks familiar.'

'So it should.' Dolly held her work at arm's length and inspected it critically. 'It's the wool from the cardigan Violet's been wearing these past three years, which was more hole than cardie by the time I came to use it. I don't know, it's been washed so often it's gone all scratchy and uneven. I reckoned I could make it into a bolero for her so she could still get the warmth, but we'll have to see.'

'If anyone can do it, you can,' said Pop proudly. He never ceased to be amazed at his wife's skill, even though they had been married thirty-odd years. She could sew, knit and cook, she was the street's auxiliary fire-watcher, she ran make-do-and-mend classes as well as working for the WVS. She had raised five children, helped with three grandchildren so far and was hoping for more, though she never said anything in case Violet got upset. There was no doubt where most of their children got their work ethic from. He returned to the subject of the one child who hadn't.

'Our Nancy all right, was she?'

'She's got some do on, and says she's been asked to volunteer. I don't doubt she has, but it's what she gets up to while she's there that worries me.' Dolly clacked her needles together. Both she and Pop were very strict about the sanctity of marriage and had brought their family up to hold the same view. That was why it had been so hard to stand by when Rita was married to that manipulative bully Charlie

Kennedy, but Rita had never given them any cause to worry, even when he treated her so badly. The same could not be said for Nancy, who'd been caught out with Stan Hathaway, a local boy now in the RAF, in a bus shelter a couple of years back. Nancy had sworn nothing had really happened and she wouldn't go so far again, but Dolly knew only too well what she was like.

'Don't see trouble where there isn't any,' Pop warned. 'She's a good girl at heart, our Nancy. You can't blame her for hankering after a bit of excitement. Sid's been gone a long time and she's still young. It'll all be harmless fun, you see if I'm not right.'

'Yes, I'm sure that's all it is really,' said Dolly, not wanting to worry Pop. 'Anyway, she's found someone else to babysit occasionally, so all's well.'

'There you are then.' Pop rubbed his hands in front of the little fire. 'Now tell me something really important. What's for tea?'

Dolly brightened up. 'Funny you should ask. I found a recipe from the government that uses parsnips in a pudding, and we've just dug up the last ones from the victory garden. It's perfect. You mix them with cocoa and milk and it says it'll be just like a chocolate pudding.'

Pop's eyes widened. Even with Dolly's talent in the kitchen he couldn't see how this idea would work. 'Lovely,' he said loyally. 'Can't wait.'

CHAPTER FIVE

Violet hugged the envelope to her chest and hummed to herself, standing stock still in the middle of the empty shop. She knew she had to open up so the dock workers could come flooding in and buy their morning papers and tobacco, but she wanted to savour the moment. It was so rare to have any time to herself, any space to think, and she just had to relish the good news, let it sink in, before the hectic rush began.

Eddy had written to say his ship was on its way back to Liverpool and he would be home before embarking on the next trip. He'd be back for a whole week. Seven whole days. Violet hadn't seen him for that amount of time since they'd first met and married. She couldn't quite believe it. Of course she had to keep calm and not jinx his return voyage; there was still danger in the Atlantic, but there was nothing like the risks of earlier in the war when the U-boats had sunk so many vessels. Eddy had survived all of that. Now the worst thing he'd have to contend with was the weather. Even that was improving, though – they were out of the season of winter storms and spring was finally here. He'd be home for Easter if all went to plan. She could collect eggs and decorate them, maybe hide them for Georgie and make a big game of it. Eddy would love to join in with that. Then they could all have a proper Easter dinner . . .

'You opening up today, love, or have you won the pools and decided you're too grand for us?' called a voice from outside.

Violet snapped out of her dream and pushed up the sleeves of her moth-eaten cardigan. 'One moment, hold your horses,' she shouted, snapping up the blinds and unlocking the door. Several men had gathered, huddled in their jackets, scarves wound tight against the biting wind. Spring hadn't managed to warm up this particular corner of Merseyside this morning, and the familiar smell of the river combined with that of the docks drifted into the shop.

'You're looking cheerful this morning,' said one of the men, a regular customer who Violet had known since she began helping out behind the counter. 'Maybe you have gone and won the pools an' all.'

'Better than that,' grinned Violet, picking up the paper that she knew he liked, 'much better. You can keep your old pools. My Eddy's coming home on leave for Easter and he'll be here all week. How about that?'

'Blimey, love, that is good news,' the man said, fishing in his pocket for his change. 'Did you hear that?' He turned to his workmates. 'Eddy Feeny's coming home on leave. You make sure to tell him we'll buy him a pint down the Sailor's Rest. He's a good man, your Eddy.'

'He is,' said Violet, beaming widely. 'He's the best there is. Don't you go keeping him out late down the pub – his place is home with me.'

'Oh aye, you'll be giving him a warm welcome all right,' said another man at the back of the group, nudging his friend, but the others weren't inclined to make a smutty joke with him. Eddy was well known and admired, and if anyone deserved a spot of leave with his young wife then it was him.

'You leave her alone, Arthur,' said the first man, 'or you won't find your favourite baccy ready for you like you expect. You make sure you tell your Eddy we said hello, Mrs Feeny. If it wasn't for the likes of him, we wouldn't have our jobs. Him and his lot, they defended our docks when Jerry wanted to destroy them. They took on Hitler's submarines and won. We wouldn't be here today if it wasn't for the Eddy Feenys of this world, and that's a fact.'

The men nodded sagely, knowing he was right. The docks were vital to the war effort – supplies of food, raw materials, and service personnel all arrived in Britain via the ports, and nowhere more vital than those of Merseyside. Hitler had done his best to disrupt the shipping in the Atlantic and destroy the docks themselves, but despite feeling the full force of the enemy power, the ships had kept sailing and the docks kept receiving them and their cargoes. The men of the Merchant Navy had run huge risks, playing a deadly game of cat and mouse on the high seas, and many had lost their lives. No wonder Eddy and his comrades were so well regarded. Violet could feel herself getting tearful at the very thought of it, but forced herself not to give way to the emotion threatening to overpower her. Instead she smiled again and made sure everyone had what they'd come in for.

In a matter of minutes the morning rush was over, and she could settle into the calmer routine of sorting out the remaining newspapers, stocking the shelves and checking the change in the till before the house-wives started to arrive for their daily shopping. She made sure she knew where the stamp was for the ration books, gave the counter a quick wipe down and then settled back on the wobbly wooden stool that wasn't quite the right height, as she was too tall for it. With a little thrill of anticipation she opened the envelope again. She'd just read the letter one more time before anyone else came in. Sighing with delight, she gazed at the familiar handwriting, giving her the news she'd waited for so long.

Kitty stared straight ahead of her at the slightly faded olive green wall, with its dog-eared posters and lists of instructions. She couldn't believe what she'd just heard down the telephone line. It had been in every way a routine call. It was just that she could have sworn she'd recognised the voice.

The caller hadn't identified himself but merely said, 'May I speak to Captain Squires, please? It's rather urgent.'

All she'd had to say was, 'Certainly, sir. Putting you through now,' and no further interaction was needed.

There was a slight hesitation, almost as if the caller was about to say something other than the 'thank you,' that followed. The voice was troubling in its familiarity. Did the tone of it betray that he had known it was her, too?

She told herself to calm down. It was important that nobody saw her brief lapse of concentration. She was the most experienced operator in this unit and it was her duty to lead by example as well as coaching the newcomers. She couldn't allow them to notice she was flustered. Besides, all she'd actually said were the very same phrases that she used scores of times every day.

Forcing herself to focus on the job in hand, she took the next call, but she was on autopilot. Try as she might to avoid admitting it, all her nerves were fizzing. Logically the speaker could have been any young man with a Scouse accent, and heaven knew there were plenty of them in the service. He'd spoken only those few words. But they were enough. She knew deep in her bones that it had been Frank Feeny. Although her mind could come up with umpteen excuses why she shouldn't jump to that conclusion, her body betrayed her and reacted in the way it always did when she heard someone mention his name or read about him in a letter from home.

'Everything all right?' asked Lizzie, her co-billettee who also formed part of the same unit. 'You look as if someone just walked over your grave.'

Kitty snapped back into her role. 'Yes, quite all right, thanks,' she said shortly. She saw Lizzie's face fall – the junior Wren probably thought she'd made a faux pas – and quickly made an excuse. 'Something in my eye, that's all. It's gone now.'

Really, she told herself as she connected the next call, this wouldn't do. She couldn't allow herself to be thrown like that. She was meant to be showing the younger ones how to conduct themselves, and getting into a flap would only lead to mistakes. So what if it had been Frank Feeny? He was entitled to call any naval establishment. He most likely did so all the time, and so in some ways it was actually strange that their paths hadn't crossed before now. It was irrelevant to her work, and he was nothing to her other than as a former neighbour and big brother of her great friend Rita. Yet her heartbeat told her differently, as it took ages to settle down to its regular pace. She made herself breathe in and out slowly, fighting against the knowledge that somehow, deep down, that profound and familiar pull was very much still there.

'You were keen enough a moment ago. What's changed?' The young GI was slurring his words a little as he planted his arm against the rough alley wall right by Nancy's shoulder, blocking her way. The dance was over, night had fallen, and people were making their way home, or at least back to their billets. Nancy looked into the man's face, which had been pleasant enough early in the evening, and saw an unwelcome gleam in his eye. He was having trouble focusing and his breath smelt unpleasantly of sour beer.

'You've made a mistake,' she said as lightly as she could. 'I'm a married woman. It was just a dance, nothing else.'

'No, it's you who's made the mistake.' He brought his face closer to hers and the stench of alcohol grew even stronger. 'We got a word for girls like you and it ain't pretty. You come along, all dolled up and making eyes at us, and then you try to run off when we take you up on what you've been offering all evening. You're just a tease, aren't you?' He tried to touch her face but missed, and she twisted away.

'I promised you nothing,' she said, keeping her voice even, knowing she couldn't let him see any fear. She reminded herself she'd dealt with worse than this. Some of Sid's friends used to get out of control when they got drunk, and any time he turned his back for a moment she'd had to be on her guard for leering comments or wandering hands, even though they knew she and Sid were an item. She could usually talk her way out of anything. The trouble was that this young man seemed too far gone to take in what she was saying.

'Yes, you did. That's what you come to these places for,' he insisted, making a lunge for her hair with his other hand. 'Cm'ere. Let me show you what you've been missing. Show you what we Yanks can do that your Limey boys can't.'

'Get your hands off me,' Nancy snapped, angry now.

61

'Don't know what you mean,' the GI said, his smile menacing. 'You want my hands all over you, don't you, you know you do.'

'I most certainly do not,' she half shouted, glancing around to see if anyone was nearby. There must still be some people around. They were only a stone's throw from the hall where the dance had been held. All she had to do was make enough noise, or distract him, then she could run for it. She had hardly had anything to drink and had no doubt she could outpace the staggering GI, but first she had to make a break. Was that a figure out on the main road, lit by the bright moon? She raised her voice still further. 'You take your hands off me right now. Go home . . . What do you think you're doing?'

She almost screamed as he brought his hand clumsily down on her mouth, trying to shut her up. She wondered if she should bite his thumb. That might distract him enough so she could run off.

'Gonna show you what you been asking for,' he half crooned, eyes bright but glassy, stumbling a little as he said it. 'Show me some of that . . .' he hiccupped. '. . . British hospitality. That's what you all reckon you're famous for, isn't it? British hospitality . . .' He dragged his hand over her cheek and this time she screamed properly as his hand wandered down her neck, threatening to go lower still.

'What do you think you're doing, soldier?' The half-glimpsed figure from the road turned and ran towards them, and in the dim light Nancy could see he was also an American serviceman but quite a bit older than her unwelcome companion. 'You leave the lady alone. She said she wanted you to take your hands off, so just you get away from her.' He grabbed the younger man's outstretched arm from behind and the GI almost fell now that his prop had gone. He glared woozily at the older man and evidently saw at once that this was no contest – he didn't stand a chance.

'She said she wanted it,' he protested feebly.

'Get out of here and be thankful I'm not putting you on a charge,' hissed the older man. 'I'm going to remember your number and I'm going to get your unit to issue you a warning. You don't go round attacking young ladies in dark alleys. You go back to your base and sleep off the booze. If you can't take it, you shouldn't drink it.'

'She's no lady,' slurred the GI, but he did as he was told, walking unevenly back to the road, one hand against the wall so he didn't fall.

Nancy sighed out a breath she hadn't realised she'd been holding. She blinked hard. That had been a close one. One minute she had been making what she'd thought was polite conversation with the young GI with whom she'd danced earlier on in the proceedings, the next he'd taken her arm and thrust her into the mouth of the grim little alleyway. She'd obviously misread him. She had been stupid. It wasn't a risk she could afford to take. Now she was calmer, she took a better look at her rescuer. He must be in his early thirties, with laughter lines around his dark eyes, and high cheekbones. He had a friendly and very good-looking face. 'You all right?' he asked with concern. 'I do apologise for my fellow soldier. I'm sorry, some of these young guys have never been away from home before and don't know how to behave.'

Nancy gave her hair a shake. 'No, I'm all right, really,' she said. 'Thank you for taking the trouble to get rid of him. He was quite drunk; he didn't really know what he was doing.' She hoped that was true.

'No trouble, ma'am.' He looked at her steadily. 'You take care, now. Tell you what, I'll walk you back along the road. Have you got any friends waiting for you?'

Nancy wondered what had become of the man she had been intending to meet. It hadn't been a date exactly, but he'd promised to be there at the dance and had suggested they might go on somewhere afterwards. He'd been very persuasive and insistent a few days ago, and she'd been flattered and intrigued. Then again, she'd only seen him around a few times at the WVS canteen and didn't really know if he was the type to keep his promise. He hadn't shown up tonight. He might have said the same thing to a dozen young women across the city. Or he might have been shipped out at the last minute – you never knew. More fool her to be mooning around wondering if he'd turn up, and making herself seem vulnerable. She was getting careless.

'I'm going back to the friends who are looking after my son,' she said, as that made her seem respectable, and not the sort of woman who let herself be picked up by random strangers outside a dance hall. Besides, it was true. She needed to go to the Parkers' and they wouldn't wait up all night.

'May I walk you to the bus stop then, ma'am?'

Nancy decided that was a harmless enough request, and they would be back on the busy street so he was hardly likely to try anything. He didn't look the type anyway. He seemed a real gentleman. He had the look of a man who'd trained hard and carried himself easily, a very attractive combination.

'Well, thank you very much,' she breathed. 'Please don't feel obliged, if it's taking you out of your way . . .'

'Nothing of the kind,' he said. 'It will be my pleasure. Staff Sergeant Gary Trenton at your service, ma'am.' His eyes twinkled at her in the moonlight.

'Pleased to meet you, Mr Trenton, and I'm very grateful,' said Nancy, wondering at the change of luck in her evening as she counted the chevrons on his jacket. 'Nancy Kerrigan.' She held out her hand, they shook, and he gently took her arm as he shepherded her towards the bus stop.

CHAPTER SIX

The southerly wind bore the sharp smell of the nearby sea. Kitty lifted her head automatically to catch it, as she used to do so many times when back home the westerlies would carry the scent of the River Mersey to her front door. It took her back to her childhood, to when her mother was still alive and before she had had to take on the care of the household. She'd played in the street, looking up to Rita back in those days, chasing Nancy and borrowing her skipping rope, watching Sarah learn to walk and talk. Even though times had been tough, she hadn't known any better and had just accepted how things were. Sometimes they'd hear Pop Feeny play his accordion and they would all sing along to songs from the music hall, or ones that Pop and Dolly knew from their own childhoods over in Ireland. Kitty could just about remember her mother joining in. She'd had a fine voice. It might not have been up to Gloria Arden's standard, but they'd all gathered round on the rare occasions Ellen Callaghan stopped her never-ending housework and started a song.

Kitty smiled to herself. Now there was another little Ellen Callaghan on Empire Street and Rita had written to say she also had a voice – a loud one, which she'd given vent to every night of her short life so far. Rita hadn't sounded cross, simply delighted that her small daughter had such a healthy pair of lungs. She'd mentioned a date for the baby's christening but Kitty had hardly registered it, as it was so very unlikely that she'd be able to go. Father Harding was going to do it; he'd been slightly put out that Rita and Jack hadn't married in his church, although he'd understood that, given Jack's brief and often unpredictable shore leaves, they hadn't been able to arrange a ceremony in time. So they'd had a civil ceremony. But Father Harding had known both families for years and wasn't going to turn down the chance to welcome the youngest member into his fold, Rita had written with relief.

Kitty reached the square brick building that had been requisitioned for their office, quickly checking her watch to see if she was on time. She was very rarely late and only ever because of something out of her control, such as damage to the road forcing a detour. Even that was uncommon in this small town, whereas it had been an everyday occurrence when she'd lived in north London, and you just got used to it. She took off her light scarf and tucked it into her favourite handbag, now showing a depressing amount of wear and tear.

'Miss Callaghan, you're wanted in the boss's office,' said a young clerk, hurrying towards her.

'Oh.' Kitty refastened her bag to buy herself a moment. She couldn't imagine what it might be about, and racked her brains to see if she'd done anything wrong. Surely it couldn't be about that lapse of concentration a few mornings ago? Only Lizzie had noticed it, and she wouldn't have reported it – unless Kitty had read the girl wrong for all this time. It wasn't as if any calls had been missed or wrongly connected. 'Do you know what it is about?' she asked, keeping the uncertainty out of her voice, even as she realised it would be highly unlikely a junior member of staff like the clerk would be told anything serious.

'No, ma'am. I mean miss. I mean, Leading Wren Callaghan.' The clerk shuffled nervously, holding a manila folder to her chest for protection, overawed at being asked a question by one of the senior Wrens she looked up to so much. She wanted to please and impress her but didn't know how.

Kitty realised the young woman's dilemma and instantly sought to put her at her ease. 'Don't worry, there's no reason you should know,' she said hastily. 'Thank you for telling me. I'll go through right now.' She beamed at the clerk to allay any remaining nerves and the young woman's face brightened, before she scurried back to her desk.

Kitty squared her shoulders and knocked on the old oak door separating the most senior officer from the rest of the crowd and the ever-present noise of the telephone operators.

'Come.'

Kitty went in.

Superintendent Knowles looked up from her impressive desk, which had once graced the local bank. The deputy manager had signed up for duty with the navy even though he hadn't needed to go, and his wife had been so upset that she could not bear to have his desk returned to their home. She had offered it to the Wrens and Superintendent Knowles had eagerly accepted. It lent the little office some dignity – and a huge amount of paperwork could be stored in its capacious drawers.

'At ease,' she said at once, as Kitty stood smartly before her. 'Let's not stand on formality, Callaghan. Kitty. Sit down and do have a biscuit.' She pushed a beautiful rose-patterned china plate across the highly polished desktop, and Kitty was astonished to see it held a variety of biscuits such as she hadn't seen since the beginning of the war.

'A perk of the job,' said Knowles.

'Thank you very much,' said Kitty, sitting down as instructed, and helping herself to a bourbon. If she had been slightly worried before, she was completely confused now. She had always had a good working relationship with Knowles, but nothing had ever hinted at anything closer, still less anything informal. She wondered what was coming next.

'Oh, take two,' said Knowles. 'That's the spirit. Now, Kitty, are you happy here?'

Kitty couldn't stop her eyebrows from rising a little. 'Well, yes. Of course,' she said.

'Excellent,' said Knowles. 'I'd expect nothing else from you. You clearly have a firm grip of your job and everything it entails, and you have also shone in your role of coaching the younger members of our unit.'

'Thank you,' said Kitty, still none the wiser about what was going on.

'How do you feel about that final part of your work?' Knowles wanted to know. 'The training aspect, I mean?'

Kitty thought for a moment. 'I enjoy it,' she said. Then, 'No, more than that, I love it. It gives me enormous pleasure to see someone come in fresh from initial training but not really knowing what to do when the pressure starts to build, and watch her change into a fully competent operator who can cope with anything. It's more than a pleasure, it's a privilege, ma'am.'

Knowles nodded, as if she'd anticipated nothing less. 'That is good to know, Kitty. In fact it is exactly what I predicted you would say.'

'Oh,' said Kitty, at a loss for words. Predicted to whom, she wondered.

Knowles sat forward and clasped her hands on the beautiful old wooden desktop. 'You see, Kitty, I have been asked to recommend one of my Wrens for a highly sensitive training position,' she said. 'It requires someone who is accurate and discreet, obviously; someone, in fact, who has immense and meticulous attention to detail. It also needs someone who can bring on others to the highest level, and to do so quickly. It is a position of great responsibility. Lives will be at stake; there can be no slip-ups.' She paused to let her words sink in. 'The first person I thought of was you,' she concluded.

'Me?' said Kitty.

Knowles nodded gravely, all pleasant friendliness gone. 'Yes, you, Miss Callaghan. You are one of the finest telephone operators I have worked with. Your work is impeccable, and besides that you go above and beyond what is asked of you. You work long hours and extra shifts with no complaint, you are encouraging but firm with the less experienced Wrens, and you are never, but never, known to gossip. That would be essential in this new position.'

Kitty blinked, delighted with the compliments and flattered that all her hard work had been noticed. 'Thank you,' she said again.

Knowles looked at her seriously. 'So now, I need you to consider this carefully. It would require a move away from this unit.'

Kitty nodded, and a treacherous little thought formed in her head. Maybe it would be back to London. She could see more of Laura. They could go out together and she would be on hand for when Captain Cavendish went back to his ship. She could distract Laura and Laura could take her to all the places she'd known before the war . . .

'I know all you girls enjoy the fresh air and less frantic pace of life here beside the sea,' Knowles went on.

Kitty kept her face from showing her real feelings – that she would far rather be somewhere livelier with more going on.

'I am afraid this post is in a major city,' Knowles said, as if this was a point against it.

'I see,' said Kitty carefully, while trying not to build up her hopes. How good it would be to be back with Laura, if not exactly recreating the days of their training, then at least being close to someone who understood everything she'd gone through.

'I realise it would be a disappointment to leave this beautiful countryside,' Knowles went on, 'and of course to be in such a city would mean being back in danger of a potential attack from the enemy. While it can never be ruled out anywhere, urban or rural, it is my duty to warn you that this place has been the target of much bombing in the past.'

Kitty's chin went up. 'I understand,' she said, 'but I have had experience of this already and I know I could continue to work under such conditions. I would be ready to do my duty wherever I am needed.'

Knowles nodded. 'Again, exactly what I thought you'd say. That's precisely the attitude we require. So, you would have no problem returning to the north-west?'

'The northwest?' Kitty's jaw dropped.

'Why, yes. This position is in Liverpool. I understand that is where you come from?'

Kitty struggled to respond and swallowed hard to conceal her surprise. 'Well, yes. I mean, of course, yes, I grew up on Merseyside. In Bootle, right by the docks.' She glanced down at her hands, which were tightly gripping each other, the knuckles white. 'It has been very heavily bombed. But many of my

72

family and close friends are still there, or nearby.' She paused.

Knowles looked at her directly. 'Kitty, it is my job to know as much as possible about my senior staff and I have to ask you this now. I am aware that you were in a relationship – am I right in thinking it was a fairly serious relationship? – with a young doctor based there, and that he was killed in one of the bombings. Would that be an impediment to you returning to the area?'

Kitty gasped. So Knowles had been investigating her background. That came as a shock, and also a clue as to the level of sensitivity of the position. She wasn't sure whether to feel flattered or offended. Realistically, she knew it must be necessary – someone of Knowles's level wouldn't waste time on it if it weren't. So how would she feel, going back to where she had first met Elliott? She took a moment to consider.

'No, ma'am,' she said after a brief pause. 'To tell you the truth, although that is how I came to know him, we spent most of our time together in London. I don't believe it would affect my work. I have been back several times over the past few years, for my brother's wedding and things like that, and it gets a little easier every time. Thank you for asking.'

'No need for thanks,' said Knowles briskly, 'I can't recommend you if I think you will fall apart every time you walk down a certain street with memories. Not that I believe for a moment that you would. So I had to ask.' She picked up a pen and glanced at a piece of paper to one side of her desk. 'Right, well, you don't have to make up your mind straight away. It's more important we get the right person for this position than rushing it, but I need you to give me your answer by tomorrow. This is not exactly routine procedure, I'm sure you realise, but I didn't want to order you to take up the posting without giving you a chance to take on board what it means. Not a word to anyone else, obviously.'

'No, obviously not,' said Kitty. She rose. 'I'm . . . honoured you think me capable of this, ma'am. I'll have my answer for you tomorrow, if not sooner.'

'Excellent, Kitty.' Knowles rose too, and ushered her to the door.

Kitty stood in the cold little corridor, painted the same dull institutional green as the room where she usually worked, her head reeling. Back to Liverpool. How would that feel?

She could see Rita and the new baby. She might be back in time for the christening. That would be wonderful. She would see Danny, and they could work out what would be best for Tommy – his most recent letter had worried her, and she knew they would have to decide about that soon. If they were both in the same place it would be so much easier. She'd see all the other friends and neighbours, whom she'd missed with a dull ache that she rarely allowed herself to think about. She would be back in a big city, with all that had to offer, away from those aspects of country life that she knew she should relish, but which had in fact been testing her patience ever since she'd arrived.

She drew a breath. She had been chosen for this honour, and she knew she had to accept. It was what she'd sworn to do after Elliott died – to go where she was needed, where her patriotic duty lay. This alone would be enough to say yes. He would have done whatever was asked of him and it was now up to her to carry on in his wake.

Excitement and dread battled within her. She would see Frank Feeny; there would be no way of avoiding him. Frank Feeny with Sylvia. Every time she'd gone home she had wondered if she would meet his new girlfriend, but even though she'd seen him very occasionally, he'd always been on his own. She didn't know how she'd feel about seeing them as a couple, forced to face the reality that he loved someone else.

Well, that wasn't enough to put her off. Plenty of people were dealing with far worse things day in and day out. He would be nothing to her. If their paths crossed she would be friendly and strictly professional and that would be that. There was no reason at all to think any more of it.

Resolution made, she turned back and knocked on Knowles's door.

'Come.'

Kitty went in.

'Ma'am, I don't need until tomorrow. I'd be delighted to accept. I'll go back to Liverpool.'

Rita pushed open the door to her mother's kitchen with one hand as she held her baby closely to her with the other. 'Anyone in?' she called. She saw the teapot was on the table and she reached across to the spout. It was very warm, so that was a good sign.

Dolly came bustling through the door from the parlour, duster in hand. 'Who's this, then?' she said in delight, immediately checking to see if her newest grandchild was asleep or not. 'Will you look at the eyelashes on her, Rita. They are even darker than Michael's, and his were gorgeous at that age, weren't they?'

Rita smiled to herself. Even her own mother didn't know for sure that Jack was Michael's real father – if she had guessed, she'd never said as much. It was true; both his children had been born with eyelashes that would be the envy of many a film star. At this moment, though, Ellen was oblivious to everything, sleeping peacefully on her mother's shoulder, rosy cheek against Rita's rather bobbled woollen jumper in deep sea green. Rita used to think it brought out the colour in her eyes, but now she didn't have time to consider such things.

'Have you heard the news?' she asked her mother.

Dolly put down her duster. 'Depends what news you mean,' she said briskly. 'Sarah tells me that Danny's had a letter from young Tommy saying he wants to come back here to live now he's almost fourteen. Was that what you meant?'

Rita sat down at the table, carefully positioning herself so that Ellen couldn't reach out and grab the old chenille tablecloth if she woke up. 'No, it's not that – though Danny did say something about it when he came in for a newspaper earlier in the week. It might make a difference to his plans, though.' She looked up at her mother, a wide smile on her face. 'No, it's Kitty. She's being posted to Liverpool. She's coming home.'

'Is she now!' Dolly's face was full of pleasure. 'Well, sure, that's wonderful! When's she coming, does she say? Will she live in her own house again or will they expect her to stay in one of their billets?'

Dolly had never felt right about her son Frank's return to the city of his birth, only to have to live with a landlady, not back in his old home with her. The fact that there wasn't actually any room for him any more didn't make a difference to her mother's instinct to have him home to look after him. She'd felt hurt, even though she'd known logically he needed to be closer to the centre and Derby House. It wasn't about logic, it was about the deep urge to take care of him, no matter how old he was and how far he'd risen through the ranks. Now she felt the same about Kitty. She was almost like another daughter to her, and she wanted nothing more than to see she was safe and well.

'She's not really sure,' Rita replied, shifting a little to make Ellen more comfortable. 'She's told them she wants to live back at home. I suppose that would make it better for Tommy, come to think of it. Between Kitty and Danny, they should be able to keep an eye on him if he does come home. Isn't it the best news, though? I can't wait to have her back again; we've hardly seen her since she left. She says she should be back before Easter. Jack will be made up when he hears.'

Dolly poured two cups from the pot and pushed one across. 'Here, let me hold my little granddaughter while you enjoy your tea.' She reached out and Rita gratefully passed Ellen over, taking great care not to disturb her.

'The thing is, I need your advice,' Rita went on. 'Jack's too far away – I wouldn't get a letter to him and a reply back in time – so I want to see if you think this is a good idea or not.'

Dolly looked up expectantly, while cradling Ellen's head in its tiny crocheted bonnet against her shoulder. 'What's on your mind, Rita, love?'

Rita took a sip before explaining. 'It's who to have as godparents at the christening. Jack and I agreed we wanted to do this properly, seeing as our wedding wasn't in the church. Now we've got time to plan everything. We want to be fair. Jack's already said he wants to ask Danny, that's only right, and I thought I'd ask Sarah, being as how she was the one who brought little Ellen into the world. With your help, of course.' She grinned, glad that part of the process was over and done with.

'Now don't be selling yourself short,' Dolly admonished her. 'We just cheered you on – you did all the hard graft there.'

Rita nodded. 'Worth it, though.' She gazed in adoration at her little girl before carrying on. 'So now Kitty is coming back, I would really like to ask her. She's always been such a good friend to me, as well as being Jack's sister. I couldn't think of anyone better, and she'll be a good example to Ellen too.'

'She will that,' said Dolly. 'None better. She's done well for herself, and all through her own hard work and talent. I take my hat off to her. She'd be a grand choice, Rita, and I'm sure Jack would agree if he was here. Why would you even think twice?'

Rita nodded. She had no doubts about Kitty's suitability. That wasn't what was troubling her. 'I don't want to offend Violet,' she told her mother. 'She might have expected to be asked. We'd have asked Eddy too, if we could have been certain he'd be back, but even though he's due leave for Easter week, you know what it's like – they could be delayed, or the weather could turn, or anything like that. But Violet – she's here every day and she loves Ellen. I wouldn't want to put her nose out of joint for anything. It's just that it seems unfair to have two godmothers from my side and none from Jack's.'

'So that's why you wouldn't ask Nancy,' Dolly said, more as a statement than a question. She looked at Rita.

Rita nodded. 'Yes, we have to be fair.' She didn't say that she wouldn't have asked Nancy anyway, as she didn't think her middle sister was any kind of suitable role model. She knew full well that Dolly was thinking exactly the same, but neither of them needed to put it into words. Even though Sarah was four years younger, she was far more steady and reliable. God forbid, if anything were to happen to Rita, she knew she could safely entrust the care of Ellen to Sarah or Kitty. She wouldn't feel nearly as happy relying on Nancy.

'I'm sure Violet will understand,' Dolly said. 'She's not one to take offence. Look what a hard time some people gave her when she first arrived and they didn't know who she was. She ignored them and they soon stopped their carping. I wouldn't think you'd have to worry about her.'

Rita gave a little shrug of acknowledgement. Violet had arrived out of the blue, as Eddy hadn't told his family he'd got married, and everyone had had to get accustomed to her strong Mancunian accent and braying laugh, which could shake the walls. Her lanky frame and general resemblance to Olive Oyl from the *Popeye* cartoons made her an easy target for gossip to begin with, but it had soon died down, particularly when she had begun to help out in the shop. Now she was accepted by all but the most petty-minded, such as the occasional older dock worker, who pretended he couldn't understand what she was saying.

Dolly was sure what she was saying was true, but she kept to herself her other thoughts. She knew, though she never mentioned it, just how desperate Violet was for a family of her own. Violet had never talked about it but, with her sharply honed instinct, Dolly could tell. It was the way Violet looked after little Georgie, never complaining; always ready to play with him even when she was dog-tired. Or the way she was with Michael and Megan on their rare visits, never too busy to listen to them and their stories of life on the farm. Dolly recalled how, when she'd first arrived, Violet hadn't told them about her real background, letting it be known she was an only child, the orphan of a respectable vicar and his wife. In fact she was too ashamed of the real version, that she was one of eight. It was true her father was dead, but her mother had still been alive then, an alcoholic married to an abusive second husband. Violet had visited her mother for the final time just before a bomb had killed her. So now Violet was genuinely an orphan with nowhere else to go, but she had found her true home with the Feenys.

'I do hope not,' Rita said, pausing to drain the last of her tea. 'I couldn't do without her help, you know. I'm glad you think I've made the right decision.'

Dolly nodded vigorously. 'And besides, she can be godmother next time,' she suggested. 'You'll not be stopping at little Ellen here, now will you?' She raised her eyebrows and smiled.

'Honestly, Mam!' Rita didn't know whether to be embarrassed or cross or pleased. She ended up a mixture of all three. 'I've barely given birth to this one; it's far too soon to be thinking of any more.'

'Well, you never know,' said Dolly, who had never regretted having five children, her heart full of love for all of them, even though she couldn't remember when she'd last had a minute's peace. A large family was a blessing. She'd known far bigger families back in Ireland, and five seemed nothing in comparison. Her children were the centre of her world, and she wanted nothing more than for them to have the chance to feel the same.

'We'll see,' said Rita, calm again. 'First let's see if we can come through this war, and then I can have my Jack back with me all the time. He hasn't even seen Ellen yet. He's counting the days until Easter – he can't wait to meet her.'

'Of course he is!' said Dolly, with extra enthusiasm to hide her secret worry that Jack would have his leave cancelled at the last minute, as so often happened. If Rita was openly concerned that Eddy wouldn't make it back on time, then the same risk must apply to Jack. She would have to keep her fingers crossed that both young men would manage to get the leave they'd been promised. 'Anyway,' she said with a sly note, 'by the time you have the baby after that, Sid might be home and then he and Nancy can be god-parents to that little one.'

'Hmm. Maybe.' Rita knew she must not speak ill of a prisoner of war, but if he was still the same old Sid, then there was no way on earth she'd entrust a child of hers to him. Then again, he would be changed by his experiences when he came home – if he came home.

Dolly patted Ellen's back, through the layers of knitted blankets wrapped around her, at least one of which she'd made in her make-do-and-mend class. 'So you've got Kitty and Sarah as godmothers,' she said. 'You've got Danny as the godfather. That's not right, is it? Don't you want another godfather, even if you can't have Eddy?'

'Oh, didn't I say?' Rita shook her head. 'I must be getting forgetful with all the lack of sleep. It's already been settled ages ago. We've asked Frank, of course.'

CHAPTER SEVEN

Nancy Kerrigan was spitting with suppressed fury, with nobody to vent it on. 'Hurry up and boil,' she muttered at the tea urn, which Mrs Moyes had asked her to see to while she herself made sure everything was ready to open up in the WVS canteen in the city centre. The urn refused to do so, making what was already a bad morning even worse.

First, Georgie had started coughing again, leading her mother-in-law to be even more unpleasant than usual, implying Nancy was a bad mother, when anyone could see she was trying her best, and with precious little help from the miserable old woman. Nancy had debated leaving him at home in her care, he sounded so bad, but she decided that wrapping him up warmly and rushing him round to Dolly was the lesser of two evils. At least she'd know he was cosy and well fed with her. She wouldn't put it past her mother-in-law to forget to keep an eye on the little boy, she was so mired in her own sense of the world doing her wrong.

Nancy hadn't stayed long at her mother's, as she

was still full of rage at the slight of being overlooked in favour of Kitty as godmother to Ellen. Kitty Callaghan, for heaven's sake! What did she know about bringing up babies? All right, she'd helped raise Tommy when their mother had died, but she hadn't given birth to him, had she? She hadn't gone through all that, and she knew nothing about a mother's feelings for a baby. Despite all her frustrations, Nancy loved Georgie with a genuine and sometimes almost overwhelming love, and she simply could not believe that Kitty was capable of experiencing anything like it.

Also, Kitty had been away for over three years with hardly a visit home in between. That made her out of touch with everybody and what the family was like now. The war had changed everyone and all their relationships, and surely Kitty couldn't begin to realise this. Fine, so Rita wrote to her, and Danny probably did as well, but it wasn't the same as being here with them all. Kitty had hardly exchanged two words with Violet; she hadn't been here for the Liverpool Blitz when so many had been killed or injured from their own small patch of Bootle, and she certainly didn't know Ellen. You couldn't just assume all babies were the same – even Nancy, living a few streets away, had picked up from her sisters' and mother's chatter that the little girl had her own sleep patterns, her preferences for how she liked to be carried, what made her comfortable and what didn't. Kitty would be a useless godmother. She herself, Nancy, would be a far better one, and yet she'd been royally snubbed. She thought she would burst at the insult.

She glared at the urn and wondered if it was broken. She hoped not, as finding spare parts would be almost impossible. Maybe Mrs Moyes would know of someone. Nancy sighed and turned away from the hateful machine and decided to sort out the cutlery while she waited. She picked up the butter knife and all but stabbed it into the box where it belonged. It wasn't as if there was much butter in the first place.

'Are we ready, Mrs Kerrigan?' Delia Moyes was much older than Nancy and had a motherly way about her, a sensible but immaculately well-pressed apron stretched across her neat peppermint-coloured twinset, an amber necklace at her throat. Matching tiny earrings twinkled behind her greying curls. She was the epitome of respectability, the embodiment of the WVS.

Nancy liked to think she herself represented the other side of the Women's Voluntary Service, bringing a little much-needed glamour to the proceedings. However, she didn't feel very glamorous this morning, with all the cares of the world on her shoulders. Gamely she painted on a smile, as there was no point in annoying her supervisor. 'Almost there, Mrs Moyes,' she replied, and just at that moment the reluctant urn finally began to boil. Nancy thought it was a lucky sign and that maybe this shift wouldn't be so bad after all.

'Excellent, Mrs Kerrigan, you know we don't like to keep our brave boys waiting,' said the older woman, smiling encouragingly. 'They look to us for comfort now they are so far away from home, as you are well aware.'

'Yes, Mrs Moyes, they count on us, don't they?' said Nancy loyally. She swiftly sorted the teaspoons while her supervisor went to open the main door. She could see through the window that a few servicemen were already gathered waiting for their tea, sandwiches and company. She told herself to snap out of her bad temper – she had a job to do.

The shift was almost over and Nancy was on her last legs. For ages she had secretly mocked her sisters, both nurses, for their frequent complaints about sore feet and tiredness from running around all day at work, sure they were exaggerating to get some sympathy. Now she understood better. Her calves ached and her toes were pressed up against the blunt ends of her shoes, chosen for their stylish effect rather than their practicality. Now she knew why her sisters always wore flat heels. But she'd been so desperate to cheer herself up this morning that she'd gone against her better judgement and dug out her old two-tone stacked heels with their jaunty red bows.

'Do sit down, Mrs Kerrigan, you haven't stopped all day,' advised Mrs Moyes. She'd often had her doubts about her youngest recruit, but today she had to admit the girl had done her share and more, nipping between the tables to collect used crockery, dispensing tea with a wide smile that never wavered, staying just on the right side of friendliness before it tipped over into flirtation. 'Why don't you have some soup? We ought to get rid of it anyway before we have a fresh batch for tomorrow, so you'd be doing us all a favour.'

'Oh . . .' Nancy could barely get out a sentence as she sank heavily on to a wooden chair, the cushion for which had long since vanished. She knew full well that the soup could equally well be heated up again, but she wasn't going to turn down the offer. 'I'd love some, Mrs M. That will put me right back on my feet in no time.'

'Then I'll fetch you some,' said Mrs Moyes, thinking how wan the girl looked today once she let the cheerful mask slip. Perhaps she was worried about something – maybe her little boy was sick again. Children picked up everything at that age, she remembered from her own brood.

Nancy threw a quick glance over her shoulder towards the rest of the room, and then raised her legs to rest her feet on another chair, almost groaning as the pain in her stubbed toes eased a little. That would teach her. She'd be back in her low brogues tomorrow. In some ways she hated them, they were such a dull brown and screamed 'sensible', but her feet couldn't take another shift like this. She'd have to bathe them in warm water when she got back. She took her mind back to her pre-war, pre-Sid days, working at the big George Henry Lee department store, and the fabulous lotions for sale there – what she wouldn't give for a bottle of one of those to ease her throbbing feet.

'Miss Kerrigan? It is you, isn't it?' A voice came from behind her.

Swiftly she threw herself round, feet back on the ground, and looked up. For a moment, with the light streaming in the open door and window behind him, she didn't recognise the figure. He was tall and well set, in the uniform of the US Army, and had an easy, relaxed bearing. Then the penny dropped.

'Mr Trenton, or Staff Sergeant Trenton, I should say.' She took a swift glance at his chevrons and counted them to check she was right – she'd become an expert at reading the different insignia by now. She stood up, her weariness gone. 'Well, fancy seeing you here.'

'I might say the same, Miss Kerrigan – Nancy, wasn't it?' He took a chair and sat down, and so she sank back on to the old wooden one she'd collapsed on beforehand.

'That's right. Fancy you remembering,' she laughed, conscious of how different he appeared in the daylight. Although she'd tried to take a good look at him as he walked her to the bus stop after the recent ill-fated dance, she hadn't really been able to get a proper impression of him. Now the broad light of day confirmed he was every bit as good-looking as she recalled, and his face was even more friendly. 'What would you like – we've still got some soup, or there are Spam sandwiches, and there's always tea.'

'Of course. This is England. There's always tea,' he echoed, but not in a teasing way, and he smiled to show he meant nothing by it. 'There's no rush, Miss Kerrigan. Look, here comes your friend with something for you.'

Mrs Moyes placed a deep bowl of soup in front of Nancy, along with what these days passed for a bread roll. Nancy thanked her gratefully, even though she knew the roll would taste like sawdust. You just couldn't get proper flour any more, just the low-grade type that everyone had to put up with but which made the bread tasteless and grey. She didn't care. She was used to it – they all were – and it would fill her up until she could get back to her mother-in-law's house. 'It's my break,' she explained, wondering if she should postpone it; whether Gary Trenton would think the worse of her for not being on her feet, serving behind the counter.

'You don't have to apologise to me,' he said at once. 'I tell my men, make sure you take your breaks while you can. You're not much use to me if you're too darn tired to put one foot in front of the other. Reckon it can get pretty busy in here, with all my fellow countrymen arriving.'

Nancy swallowed a mouthful of the soup. It was mixed vegetable, as it often was, and it didn't always do to ask which vegetables were in it, but she was past bothering about that. Then she nodded. 'It can. It sure can.' She attempted an American accent.

'Not bad.' Trenton grinned in appreciation.

'More and more of them every day,' Nancy went on, then left the sentence hanging. She'd noticed the increase in numbers, they all had, and the rumours were spreading about something big in the offing. She wondered if her new friend could be persuaded to talk, but quickly realised he hadn't got to staff sergeant by gossiping.

'If you say so,' he replied amiably. 'Pretty crowded city, ain't it? Pity about the hollowed-out church up the road.'

Nancy nodded as she nibbled at the dry roll. 'You should have seen it before the blitz. St Luke's was lovely.' She paused ruefully. 'We lost so many buildings in just a few days. Most of the rubble has been cleared away now, but you could hardly walk around because of the bricks and stones and glass, and the smell, oh boy, you don't ever want to come across such a thing again. Burning and all that.' She sighed at the memory of that terrible, frightening time, and then grew quiet, figuring that if Trenton and his men were over here, then they would most likely be called to take part in equally grim scenes, or possibly worse. She had better shut up – the men came to the canteen to take their minds off such things, not to be reminded of what they were about to face.

'Everyone says it was a great city,' Trenton said.

'Still is,' Nancy replied robustly. 'There's nowhere better, and you'd better believe it. We might not have that church or our cathedral, we haven't even got a proper John Lewis any more – that's a store, a lovely big department store – but you won't find our spirit's been broken.'

Trenton smiled even more broadly and nodded in approval. Nancy couldn't help notice he had very fine hands, with tapering fingers and clean, square-cut nails. She wondered how strong his grip was, or how delicate his touch could be. Maybe if he were to touch her . . . She shook the thought from her mind. 'You said it, Miss Kerrigan,' he agreed. 'That's what everyone tells me. The people of Merseyside won't be beat.'

'No, sir.' Nancy swiftly wiped the last of her roll around the dregs of the soup and popped it into her mouth. She was too hungry to leave any food, good-looking staff sergeant or not, but then she shook the crumbs from her fingers and swiftly pushed back her hair. She flashed him her best Rita Hayworth smile.

'So how does a person get to see the real Liverpool?' Trenton asked now. 'I can't say how long I'm around for, but I kinda think I should get to know the city while I'm stationed here.'

Nancy pushed her bowl away and sat up straighter. 'Well, the WVS has been known to run tours. Just short ones, as a way of helping our visiting servicemen find their way about the place.'

'Ah.' Trenton nodded. 'See, that's sort of what I had in mind, but as I already know my way about, I was looking for something more . . . customised. Something special. The Liverpool most visitors don't get to see, that kind of thing.'

Nancy nodded, enjoying the way this was going. 'I think I get your drift, soldier.' She looked him right in the eye. 'A personal guided tour, you mean? Was that what you were after?'

'Depends on the personal guide,' he said, raising an eyebrow.

'One might be available in about an hour when she finishes her shift,' Nancy informed him. 'She knows the place like the back of her hand, she was born and bred here, and could probably tell you a thing or two you couldn't begin to imagine.'

'Sounds just the ticket,' he said, eyes alight with humour.

Nancy rose to her feet, not wincing as her swollen toes hit the ends of her shoes once more. She wouldn't think about them. This was too good an opportunity to miss. It would most definitely take her mind off the trials of the morning, and if it meant her mother or sisters ended up looking after Georgie for a bit longer, well, serve them right, since they were so keen on babies and childcare. 'In that case, why don't you have a cup of tea or something, and wait here? Your own very special personal guide will be with you in no time at all.'

CHAPTER EIGHT

Violet stood at the parlour window, twitching the carefully starched net curtain. She'd always vowed she would never turn into one of those women who did this, nosy old gossips with nothing better to do, but today she couldn't help herself. Eddy was due home this afternoon and she couldn't stay still. If it had been a few degrees warmer she would have been standing out in the road waiting for him. The early April sunshine flooded the tired room with light, making the faded wallpaper almost golden, although Violet would never like it – the tangle of green stems that formed the pattern had always made her feel queasy. It added to her nerves. It had been so long. Would they find anything to say to each other? What if he'd changed?

Violet had worked in the shop that morning, opening up and dealing with the first rush of customers so that Rita could have a lie-in, knowing she would have been up half the night with Ellen. It had taken her mind off things, forcing her to concentrate on giving the right change, which she was never very good at, and picking up on the general mood of the dock workers. They were murmuring about a big offensive that was being planned – or that was the story they'd gathered from recent arrivals of overseas service personnel. Violet didn't know how much truth there was in it but it was impossible to ignore – every man had had his pennyworth to add to the rumour mill. It made her uneasy, but then again she was all jitters today.

Rita had taken over at just after midday, placing little Ellen just behind the counter in a wooden drawer lined with plenty of cosy blankets. True to form, the baby had been sleeping peacefully when Violet left, taking a careful peep under her little bonnet. It was just the hours of the night that she didn't like to slumber through.

Violet had run upstairs to her room, Eddy's room as was, and got changed from her worn corduroy skirt with its frayed hem into her best frock. Even that was old now; she'd got it just before war broke out. The buttons had been replaced and Dolly had kindly altered it as food rationing had made everyone lose weight. Violet hadn't had much to lose to start with, but at least the frock hung as flatteringly as possible on her lanky frame. She brushed her shoulder-length brown hair, as straight as if she'd ironed it, and took off her horn-rimmed glasses for a moment, but then put them on again as she couldn't see herself in the mirror without them.

The face staring back at her could never be described

as conventionally pretty, but she had a rosy complexion today, her cheeks flushed with anticipation. Normally she was sallow, but the thought of seeing her Eddy gave her an inner glow. It'll have to do, my girl, she told herself. After all, this was the face that Eddy had fallen in love with. That had come as a bolt out of the blue. She'd known as soon as she clapped eyes on him that he was the one for her, but the fact he'd felt the same was like a miracle. She hadn't been able to believe it. Yet here she was, several years later, married to him and waiting for him to come home.

Even Nancy had caught the excitement and lent her a rare bottle of nail polish, but Violet hadn't wanted to use it until she'd finished in the shop in case she chipped the varnish when shifting boxes of stock. Now she realised her hands were trembling with nerves and she wouldn't be able to paint it on properly. She would leave it. It didn't matter in the wider scheme of things.

Now she drummed her unvarnished nails on the window frame, its once-white gloss turned cream with age and years of smoke from the parlour fireplace. What if something had happened to him at the last minute? You heard of these things. A person would be waiting at home for a loved one's return and instead of the husband, or son, or brother, it would be the telegram boy at the door . . . No, she mustn't even think it. He hadn't said a specific time. Just that it would most likely be this afternoon.

This was no good. She couldn't stand still here. She walked swiftly across the room, over the threadbare rug and linoleum worn by three generations of Feenys, and flung herself out of the door and into the street. She didn't care who saw her. She caught a flash of movement in the house across the road, which must mean that Kitty was back. She had been due to return yesterday, Rita had said, but they'd heard her train got in late at night and nobody had seen her yet. Under different circumstances, Violet might have gone across to say hello to this woman she'd heard so much about but scarcely knew, but that could wait.

She wrapped her arms around herself to keep warm. It had been kind of Dolly to make her the bolero out of reknitted wool from her old cardie, but secretly she didn't like it – it itched and felt wrong across her shoulders. She stood in the best angle of sunlight she could find, and for a second or two her eyes were dazzled.

So she missed the moment that Eddy rounded the corner, a bulky figure in his chunky seaman's jumper, his kitbag slung over his shoulder. He saw her first and broke into a run, the weight of his heavy bag as nothing to him now he could see her, her hand shielding her face like a visor against the bright sunbeams. As he got close to her he flung the bag to the ground and swept her into his arms, laughing as he did so. 'Violet! I'm back!'

Violet laughed too and then she was half crying as well, full of relief and happiness, almost unable to believe he was here at last. She broke away to push open the front door and they fell inside, Eddy remembering at the last moment to drag his kitbag into the hallway, and then they were in the parlour, on the sofa, hugging each other as passionately as when they had been young newlyweds, eager to see what the other was like close up. Violet ran her hands along his back, sensing his muscles through the heavy wool of the jumper, as he pressed her to him and she knew she was where she belonged.

Finally Eddy pulled back and looked at her, drinking in the sight of his wife. 'I was waiting for this for all those days at sea,' he told her.

'Me too,' said Violet, her voice catching with emotion. 'It's been like forever, Eddy.'

'It has.' He dropped his head to the top of hers and breathed in, sensing the warmth of her. 'I've been counting the minutes. Now I'm back and it's for a whole week.' He faced her again, his eyes alight.

She beamed back at him, taking in his weathered face, the new wrinkles at his eyes from days out in the open on the fierce Atlantic crossing. 'It won't be long enough, Eddy; it will never be long enough.'

'We'd best make the most of every minute.' He stroked her cheek and grinned in return. 'Where's everyone else?'

'Pop's working on the salvage clearance, your mam's gone to the victory garden to get in some fresh food for your tea, Sarah's on her shift . . .'

'Then let's start as we mean to go on.' He stood up, took her hand and drew her to stand beside him. 'What do you say? Are we still in my old room?'

'Eddy!' Violet pretended to be shocked, but really she was delighted. 'In broad daylight! What would your mam say?'

97

Eddy grinned wickedly. 'What she doesn't know won't hurt her.' He began to lead her towards the stairs. 'And you know what? Even if she did know – she'd say go right ahead.'

'You look dead smart, our Kitty.' Danny regarded his sister with admiration as they stood in their kitchen. He couldn't help it – when he thought of her it was always in her old overalls from the days when she'd managed the local NAAFI canteen. Now she was in a vivid cherry red jacket and elegant dark blue tailored frock, with matching navy pumps. 'I thought you said there weren't any shops in your last place? Looks as if you've been using up your coupons all right.'

Kitty shook her head. 'Don't be daft. I couldn't have got this down in Sussex. I had to change trains in London so I met up with my old friend Laura, and when she learned I was going to be a godmother, she said I had to have something smart, so she gave me this.' She twirled around. 'She's not short of money and can always find a way around the clothing rations somehow. It's who you know, I suppose.'

'Lucky you know her then,' said Danny, straightening his collar and checking it in the tarnished little mirror over the sink. He was going to the christening in his naval uniform, which was the smartest outfit he possessed anyway. Somehow buying new clothes hadn't been a top priority for the past couple of years. 'How long have we got, do you think? It won't take us long to walk.'

Kitty thought for a moment that she'd forgotten

the way to the church and how far it was, because she hadn't been there since she'd joined up. Then she recalled how she'd always used to time the cooking of the Sunday roast around getting there, going to Mass and coming back. She did a quick sum. 'We've got about fifteen minutes, I'd say. We could have a cuppa.'

Danny shook his head. 'It's too warm. Anyway, we'll have tea coming out of our ears at the do after. That's unless Jack or Eddy have brought back some rum – that would improve things.'

Kitty pulled a face.

'Still not a fan of the odd tot then?' Danny teased. 'Go on, it'll put hairs on your chest.'

Kitty picked up a tea towel and flicked it at him. 'Away with you, Daniel Callaghan. I know you'd think it very funny if I got squiffy in front of everyone on my first weekend back home, but I don't think so. Besides, as the godmother I'm meant to be on hand to help out for any emergency. Come to think of it, so are you.'

Danny shrugged. 'Stands to reason they would ask you first. I'm meant to help out when she's older, with sage advice, and by giving her money at Christmas and birthdays.'

Kitty raised an eyebrow. She knew that – while Danny was fond enough of young children – he really preferred them once they were old enough to hold a conversation. She turned her thoughts to a more pressing worry.

'Danny, what are we going to do about our

Tommy?' she asked quietly, as their young brother was upstairs getting changed into his one clean shirt. They had insisted he did this at the last minute, or else it would be filthy by the time he got to church. Tommy had protested that he wasn't like that any more, he wasn't a little kid, but they'd taken no chances. To her, he was still her baby brother – although she'd had quite a shock when she'd seen him as he was now: taller, his boyish face changing into that of a young man, a new restless look in his eye. Perhaps he really had outgrown all that life on the farm could offer him.

'I don't know,' Danny confessed. 'What do you think?'

'Danny!' Kitty was exasperated. She'd been back home five minutes and already he expected her to take charge of things, just like when they were younger. 'It's not down to me. We should work out if we're going to be here for enough time between the two of us to look after him. I know he thinks he's grown-up now, but he's not. Also, just so's you know, I'm going to be working flat out at all hours, and I might not be able to do all the cooking and cleaning, so there's that to consider.'

'Hang on, Kitty, I never said I expected that,' Danny protested, even though one of the first things that had entered his mind when he got Kitty's news was that he wouldn't be so beholden to Dolly and Sarah for his food. 'How do you think I've been managing while you were away? I haven't exactly starved. I can look after myself, I'll have you know.'

Kitty tutted. 'Right. So Dolly hasn't been cooking you extras then? I bet she has. In fact I know she has. Don't try to fool me.'

Danny gritted his teeth. 'I can make a sandwich. Actually I can do several things. Scrambled eggs, if you can get them. Or eggs and bacon. Or . . .' He dried up.

'Or reheating Dolly's casseroles,' Kitty predicted. 'I'm right, aren't I? I know I am.'

Danny gave up. 'All right, all right, yes, Dolly and Sarah have been helping me get by, but I won't be expecting you to do everything now you're back, Kit. Honestly. I know what sort of job you're likely to be doing. You'll have your work cut out for you, no bones about it. I won't expect you to do everything like you used to.'

'Good,' said Kitty shortly, 'because I won't have time.' She folded her arms and then unfolded them, relenting. 'Look, I'll do all I can, of course I will, it's just that it won't be like when I lived here before, it can't be.' Her face creased in anxiety. 'That's why we have to decide about Tommy. I can't mother him if I'm working all hours, which I'm likely going to have to do. I'm worried how we'll cope, that's all.'

Danny nodded in acknowledgement, knowing she was right and that they would have to have a serious think about it, but before he could reply, the door from the hallway crashed open and Tommy stood there before them, in his best suit that was just too short for him, his dark hair swept back off his slightly spotty forehead. He was already up to Kitty's shoulder,

101

although he hadn't really begun to fill out yet. He was almost shaking with rage.

'You're talking about me behind my back.'

'No, no,' said Kitty, not wanting him to get upset right before they all set out for the christening. 'We're just trying to work out what's best for you, that's all.' She hastily reminded herself that they couldn't really go on about him as if he wasn't there; he'd never liked it as a child, and would tolerate it even less now he was that much older.

'No you're not. You're thinking about yourself,' Tommy exclaimed. 'You and your posh new job. Well, I don't care if you don't have time for me, I can look after myself.'

'Now look here, Tom . . .' Danny began, hands outstretched, coming towards his little brother who suddenly didn't seem so little after all.

'I don't want to live here only because you're here,' Tommy went on. 'I want to do my bit and help the war effort.' He paused, almost as if he wanted them to agree there and then to his joining up. When there was no such response his brow creased. 'You can't stop me. I can leave school at the end of the summer term and I'm bloody well going to.'

'Tommy!' Kitty had never heard her little brother swear before, and was taken aback both by that and the sudden turn of events.

'I hate you!' Tommy burst out. 'I'm not even going to speak to you again. I won't walk to the church with you; I'm going across the road. I'd rather walk with Auntie Dolly and Pop. So there.' He flung himself out into the hallway and there was a loud bang as the front door slammed shut.

For a moment there was silence as Danny and Kitty absorbed this new, older Tommy.

'Well,' Kitty said at last. 'We'd better let him calm down. Looks as if we have some serious thinking to do, Danny.'

Danny nodded, fiddling with his collar once more and brushing his jacket sleeves. 'Come on, we'd better get going. Can't have one half of the godparents holding up the ceremony, can we, even if our little brother's suddenly developed a temper.'

Kitty nodded and quickly glanced in the little mirror, patting back one of her unruly dark curls. Here we go, she thought. She'd wanted to be calm for the ceremony, because it was a solemn moment and she took her godmotherly duties seriously, but also because she knew Frank would be there with Sylvia. She would have to stand near him for the ceremony itself, wouldn't she? The last thing she needed was to have a seething mass of emotion going on. But Tommy's interruption had stirred it all up good and proper. She closed her eyes for a moment. She couldn't undo the past few minutes. She would just have to get on with things and make the best of it. Frank was nothing more than a family friend to her.

'Come on then,' she said to Danny, who stood waiting for her by the kitchen door. 'Let's go.'

CHAPTER NINE

Kitty breathed a sigh of relief as they all filed out of the church. She'd done it. She'd got through the ceremony without fluffing her words or making a fool of herself. She'd done her best to ignore the presence of Frank Feeny, who had stood on the other side of Danny throughout, almost close enough to touch. They hadn't had a moment to speak to each other, as she and Danny had arrived only just in time, thanks to the row with Tommy. Now Frank had gone ahead to walk back with Sylvia.

The sight of that young woman had somewhat thrown Kitty, even more than standing near to Frank – at least she'd been prepared for that. She hadn't been prepared for Sylvia, or at least not how she looked. Surely she wasn't the only person who had noticed it. Sylvia had dark curly hair, very similar to Kitty's own. They were about the same height. They were both Wrens – Sylvia was in uniform, and so Kitty could tell she didn't have the same seniority. Was all this a coincidence?

'Come on, Kitty, keep up!' Sarah teased her. 'Are you standing around admiring the scenery, or what?'

'Sorry, I was miles away,' said Kitty, realising that the girl she'd often dismissed as Rita's kid sister was now a very attractive young woman in her own right. She gazed around. She hadn't taken in until now just how much damage there had been to the houses around the church. She almost wouldn't have recognised some of the streets, they were so changed from how they'd been when she was growing up here.

'A bit different to how it used to be, isn't it,' said Sarah, guessing what Kitty was thinking. 'You'll find that a lot. We really caught it bad round here. Well, you'd know that better than anyone of course.'

'Yes, it's strange,' Kitty said ruefully, her mind transported back to the raid that had killed Elliott. 'I've seen the damage before, of course, on my visits back, but it's easy to forget it when you leave again – somehow I always imagine the streets and buildings back to how they were before the war.' She shook her head. 'You're right, we should catch up with the others.'

'Yes, we don't want to miss Ellen's party,' said Sarah. 'There's a lot to celebrate. Her christening, Jack and Eddy getting leave, you moving home. That's a lot of excuses rolled into one, so come on.'

'You must be Kitty,' said Sylvia, coming across to Dolly's kitchen window where Kitty was standing, a plate with a ham sandwich on it in her hand. 'I'm Sylvia Hemsley.'

Kitty put down her plate so that she could shake the Wren's hand. 'Pleased to meet you,' she said, hoping she sounded sincere.

'I've heard so much about you,' Sylvia went on in her strong Cumberland accent. 'You've just come home, haven't you? Frank said you might be working alongside us.'

'Did he?' Kitty wasn't sure whether to be annoyed or not. Usually she didn't like anyone discussing her work, out of habit, as you never knew who was listening in to your conversation. But what could be more natural than Frank talking about her return with his girlfriend? They would all know what she did – especially as Frank and Danny worked in the same place, although in different jobs. 'Well, I don't know if I'll be in the same building or not. Probably not, actually. I'll find out next week. But I expect we'll bump into one another.'

'It's a lovely party, isn't it,' Sylvia went on, seeming not to notice Kitty's hesitation. 'I was so pleased to be asked. There's so many people here and that's a lot of mouths to feed.'

'Oh, everyone pitched in with coupons and whatever they could spare,' said Kitty. That was always the case round here. It was the best way of making sure there was enough to go round. On top of that Tommy, Michael and Megan had brought fresh produce from the farm, so that Dolly had been able to use butter and real eggs, usually luxuries beyond reach. Kitty had of course been persuaded to make one of her famous cakes, which she'd baked the afternoon of her first full day back, even though there had only been enough rationed ingredients for one tier – the other tiers were false, merely cardboard imitations. Still, it took pride of place on the dining table, with its pressed white tablecloth only brought out for special occasions.

'I'm sure they did,' Sylvia said appreciatively. 'You won't find food like this in our mess, I can tell you that.'

'I know, I'm used to mess food, seeing as I've been transferred several times,' said Kitty, realising that it might sound like a put-down, as though she was stressing her own higher rank, but unable to stop the words from coming out of her mouth.

'Oh, of course, Frank said,' Sylvia replied, with no sign of having taken offence.

Kitty couldn't help but feel at a disadvantage. Clearly Sylvia knew far more about her than she did about the young Wren. She reminded herself that it was inevitable, and she shouldn't let it upset her. She would have to get used to this. To buy herself some time, she took a bite from her sandwich, savouring the home-made chutney in it. That must have been a product of the victory garden.

She looked up to see Frank had come across to join them. He hadn't changed much in the years she'd been away, though there was something in his demeanour that had changed. He had always been confident but now there was something else there too; a poise and maturity that only served to make him even more handsome than before. As her eyes met

107

his, she felt that familiar fluttering in her stomach – but was that a slight hesitation that she saw reflected in his? A small wavering in his easy manner? She forced herself to finish her sandwich, although her mouth felt unaccountably dry.

'Sylvia, you haven't met my friend Jack. Let me introduce you,' he said, passing his arm through his girlfriend's. 'Hello, Kitty, good to see you back home at last.' His eyes gave nothing away now – they held her gaze steadily. Kitty felt annoyed at herself for being so easily beguiled – Frank Feeny's blue eyes were of no concern to her now, she told herself.

Before she could reply, he had drawn Sylvia away and Kitty was left unsure as to what she should make of the brief encounter. It didn't look as if she was going to speak to him properly, and maybe that was just as well. It would give her time to absorb the reality of Sylvia, now she'd met her in the flesh, rather than just imagining her. Then she'd be able to move on, to become comfortable with the idea and not let it get in the way of her work. That was the most important thing. That was what she'd been brought back to do, not to dwell on her old friend and neighbour who just happened to have roused emotions in her that she'd never felt before. But that was a long time ago, she told herself firmly. She had to put that behind her if she wanted to succeed in this new position.

Rita came over, looking as happy as Kitty had ever seen her, her beautiful red hair shining and her blue-green eyes reflecting her deep contentment on this special day. Megan came trotting after her. 'Kitty, you were wonderful, you spoke so clearly,' Rita said, giving her friend a hug. 'Didn't she, Megan? You remember your Auntie Kitty?'

The little girl looked up at them both. She shrugged. 'Not really.'

'Megan!' Rita gasped, but Kitty smiled and shook her head.

'It's no wonder. We haven't seen much of each other for a long time, have we, Megan? Now I'm back home, I hope we'll get to know each other properly.'

'Yes please,' said Megan politely, then she dashed off as she caught sight of her brother holding some of the cake which had just been cut.

'Kitty, I am so sorry,' Rita said, mortified.

'Don't be silly,' Kitty reassured her. 'She's not seen me properly since, what, probably your wedding to Jack. She won't remember – that was over two years ago. She spoke the truth. You should be proud of her.'

'Oh, I am,' said Rita warmly. 'When I think of all she's been through, seeing her father treat me so badly, being taken off by him and treated like an idiot – it's a wonder she's turned out like she has. To think people used to reckon she was slow.'

'Well, no chance of anyone thinking that now. Just look at her.' Kitty and Rita turned to watch as the little girl caught up with her brother and loudly demanded that he get her a slice of cake because she couldn't reach the table. She wouldn't let him go until he agreed. 'She's one to watch, that girl,' Kitty told her friend, her pulse rate coming back to normal now that Frank and Sylvia were safely on the other side of the room.

'Oh Eddy, I'm glad you made it back for this,' breathed Violet, her eyes shining with pride at the sight of her husband in his best suit – to be truthful, his only suit. 'Aren't we lucky to have all these friends and family? I feel blessed, I really do, and it's all because I met you. I'm so grateful they took me in.'

Eddy gave her a squeeze. 'Of course they did; they love you.' His expression grew solemn. 'I tell you, Vi, it makes it easier for me to go, knowing you're well looked after here. Mam and Pop will see you right, no matter what.'

'Eddy, don't say things like that.' Violet's eyes clouded with worry. 'Not when we're having such a good time. Anyway, you're going to be all right now. You survived all those crossings with the U-boats coming after you. Things have calmed down now, you said so yourself. You can get over to America and Canada without having to dodge them any more.'

'Just the weather to worry about,' Eddy said with a wry grin.

'And even that's getting better now summer's on the way,' Violet answered stoutly. 'It'll be as good as a cruise the next time you make that crossing, you mark my words.'

'I'll drink to that,' Eddy smiled, raising his glass, into which he'd poured a generous tot of rum. 'Ah, that's better.'

'Here, let me have a sip.' Violet reached for the

glass and gingerly brought it to her mouth and tasted the dark amber liquid. 'Ugh, that's horrible, that is. How can you enjoy that stuff?'

Frank made his way over and laughed. 'Our Eddy's always had a taste for a drop of grog, haven't you, Ed? That's why he went to sea in the first place.' He'd left Sylvia cooing over little Ellen, who was resplendent in her embroidered christening robe, which had been worn by her mother and aunties before her. 'Didn't he tell you that, Violet?'

'No he did not.' Violet pretended to be cross but her heart wasn't in it. She slipped her arm around her husband's waist. 'I was just saying to him, how much safer he'll be now doing that Atlantic crossing. He'll be home with me for good in no time at all.'

'That day can't come soon enough,' Eddy said, his arm around her shoulders. 'You'll keep her safe for me meanwhile, won't you, Frank?'

'It'll be my pleasure,' said Frank, raising his own glass of rum and chinking it against his brother's. He kept his face cheerful, allowing no trace of what he really thought to show in his expression. He knew, as several others in the room most likely suspected, that there was going to be a big push soon into northern France. He couldn't say anything about it, and he couldn't tell from Eddy's face whether he also knew or not. Violet might presume her husband would be almost out of danger now, having come through the treacherous years when so many merchant seamen were lost in the Battle of the Atlantic. That would be true, if he stayed on that route. But it stood to reason that if the Allies were going into northern France, somehow they would need provisions, armaments, every kind of supplies, and the best way of providing those would be via the Merchant Navy. It wasn't up to Frank to burst Violet's bubble of happiness, and he had no way of knowing where his brother would be sent next, but in his heart of hearts he couldn't rejoice in the assumption that Eddy was out of danger.

There was nothing he could do about it either way, so he kept smiling, kept sipping the very welcome rum that both Eddy and Jack had managed to bring home, and carefully kept his thoughts away from Kitty's reappearance in his life. He'd been stunned by her appearance at the church, where she had looked more glamorous than he'd ever seen her. He was glad that Danny had stood between them – he didn't know how he'd have managed to actually be next to this new, elegant version of Kitty, her beautifully tailored red jacket emphasising her slim waist and trim curves. He had almost stumbled, something he hadn't done for a very long while.

Then he'd suffered a very strange mix of emotions at the sight of Sylvia and Kitty together, talking in the kitchen earlier. He wasn't a fool – of course he had known they bore some physical resemblance to each other, but seeing them facing one another brought out their similarities very clearly – and also their differences. Kitty now had an air of sophistication that was totally new. He supposed he shouldn't be surprised; she'd been away for years, sent to a variety of postings, becoming expert in her profession and learning social graces she could scarcely have come across in Empire Street. Then of course she'd had that doctor boyfriend, who must have brought her into contact with an entirely new set of people. He himself was now an officer, and he was well used to working and dealing with those who blithely assumed they belonged to the officer class by birth – and yet he had the feeling Kitty was now somehow far above him.

He gave a small shake of his head. He had to put all these feelings to one side. He could see how his family welcomed Sylvia into their midst, and he was grateful she was so friendly and open with them. He should count his blessings, be pleased with what he had rather than wonder about what he didn't. After all, the likelihood was that he might well bump into Kitty in a professional capacity now, and he couldn't allow her presence, or even the thought of her presence, to distract him from his vital work. Lives depended on it.

'Penny for 'em, Frank!' Jack came across, in his Fleet Air Arm uniform, and slapped him on the back, almost making him spill the last of his rum. 'How about a top-up?' He brandished a nearly full bottle. Frank looked up, and caught sight of Kitty leaning against the opposite wall. She was looking at him too and their eyes briefly met, Kitty turning away quickly with a tight smile. It was only wishful thinking that made him wonder if it was a blush he'd seen creep across her cheeks. . . *Damn it!* Frank cursed himself as he watched her turn away and speak to someone else. He'd have to shake off these stupid thoughts.

'Go on then.' Frank held out his glass and was pleased to see his hand was totally steady – unlike the beating of his heart.

'There, isn't she lovely?' It was Sarah's turn to hold little Ellen and she was every inch the proud godmother. 'She's been so good. Look, this is your godfather. Better make a point of behaving when he's around and you'll never be short of pocket money, though we won't tell your mammy.' She held the baby close to Danny's face, and he smiled but pulled away a fraction.

'Don't you go making her cry, now,' he warned. 'Just because she hasn't started wailing the place down so far, doesn't mean she isn't going to any minute. I'm not having Rita blaming me for that.'

'What nonsense you talk, Danny Callaghan,' Sarah scolded him, and Danny reflected that between her and Kitty, he couldn't do a thing right today.

'See, here's your Auntie Nancy come to say hello,' he said to the sleeping child, and made a hasty escape over to where Eddy and Frank were making inroads into the rum bottle.

Nancy smiled sweetly, even though she was still a bit put out at having been passed over as a godmother in favour of her younger sister. But there was no point in taking it out on the child – it was hardly her fault. 'She's cute as a button and no mistake,' she said. 'Look at her little fingernails. There, when you're grown up I'll teach you how to paint them. That's if you don't turn out like your mammy and godmother, working too hard in jobs that don't let you dress up.'

'Nancy!' Sarah objected, stung.

'Oh, no offence,' said Nancy lightly. 'Lovely food, Sarah – did you help out with it?'

'Of course,' said Sarah. 'You were too busy, I suppose.'

'Well, Georgie won't mind himself,' said Nancy, leaving her younger sister to infer that she had been busy with childcare last night, when in fact Georgie had been round at the Parkers' house again. Nancy had had her first proper date with Gary Trenton, and all she really wanted to do today was find a quiet corner and think about it. She shivered at the memory of him, his wonderful strong, lean hands holding hers across the table as they'd sat in a quiet pub miles from Bootle, where nobody would recognise her. He'd been such a gentleman, not trying anything on, but asking her all manner of questions about what she thought and what she was interested in.

She couldn't remember when anyone had thought to ask her things like that. She could feel her sense of self-worth growing. With him she wasn't the troublesome middle child whose siblings were all contributing to the war effort in far more demanding ways than helping out in a canteen; she wasn't the bad mother that old Mrs Kerrigan painted her as; she wasn't Gloria Arden's less pretty sidekick. Gary made her feel as if she was a fascinating and attractive young woman, and she loved it.

She gave a little sigh as she recalled the polite but firm way he had said goodnight, looking at her as if he longed to take her in his arms and kiss her, but knowing he mustn't go too far too soon. He cared for her feelings like that and she respected him for it. Next time maybe he would—

'Something wrong, Nancy?' asked Sarah.

Damn, thought Nancy, Sarah noticed everything and never cut her any slack. 'No, no,' she said, wafting her hand in front of her face, 'just a bit hot in here. Stuffy with so many people, you know.'

'Perhaps you should go out in the yard for some fresh air then,' said Sarah, clearly not believing her excuse.

'Perhaps I will an' all,' said Nancy, and she broke away from her sister and little niece. It was the perfect excuse. Now she could take a breath and have some blissful, uninterrupted moments to consider just what Gary might suggest the next time they met, and what she might agree to. There really wasn't a much better way of spending a sunny afternoon. She leant against the back wall and gave herself over to the delicious memories of last night, and even more delicious ideas about what might happen next. If only she was careful this time, and didn't let the likes of Sarah suspect what she was up to, she had the feeling that this relationship could go very well indeed. Gary wasn't like the young American men she usually met, or local lads like Stan Hathaway, who'd led her on only to let her down. No, he was mature, a man of the world, who was tough but gentle, and who appreciated her like nobody else did.

Back inside she could hear the piano start up, which must mean that they'd persuaded Eddy to give them a tune. He was the best of them; he got his musical abilities from Pop. There was the sound of Kitty singing – they'd all like that. Good, that meant everyone would be watching them and she wouldn't be missed out here. Because while she knew Eddy could tinkle the ivories with the best of them and Kitty had a lovely voice, it was so much more fun thinking about the strong, protective arms of Staff Sergeant Gary Trenton.

CHAPTER TEN

Violet was hoping she could shut the shop dead on time, if not even five minutes early, when the doorbell rang and Mrs Delaney came in, her eyes sharp and critical as ever. Vera Delaney had been one of Winnie Kennedy's close friends, and the two of them had spent many hours together, pulling apart the character of everyone they knew. This was back in the days when it had been Winnie's shop, and she'd spent her time indulging her beloved son Charlie and making his wife Rita's life merry hell. Thankfully both Winnie and Charlie were no more and Rita was now happily married to Jack. Vera Delaney still popped in regularly, though, much to Violet's regret. She forced herself to smile in welcome but she couldn't stand the woman.

'Good afternoon, Mrs Delaney. Well, almost evening. How can I help you?'

Vera sniffed. 'No Rita today, then?'

Violet kept her smile in place with an effort. It was a small shop – it wasn't as if Rita could be hiding anywhere. 'No, she's still taking it a bit easy now she's got the baby. She's over at Kitty's.'

Vera nodded, as if this confirmed what was wrong with the world at large. 'So she's back, is she. I'd heard as much.' She tugged at the sleeves of her jacket, and Violet could see the cuffs were frayed and heavily darned.

'Yes, Kitty's been posted back home,' Violet told her. 'Isn't that lucky?'

'Lucky? Is that what they call it?' Vera's expression would have curdled milk. 'Bad luck for anyone who has to work with her, I'd say. Terrible family, those Callaghans. Their father was a dreadful one for the drink, you know – well, you might not know, being as what you aren't from these parts, but he was a disgrace, wandering down the street half-cut at all hours, and those kids running about in rags.'

'I don't know about that, Mrs Delaney,' said Violet briskly, 'but she's doing very well now. She's been promoted several times.'

'Wonders will never cease,' snapped Vera. 'Time was when she wouldn't have said boo to a goose.'

Violet raised her eyebrows. That certainly didn't sound much like the Kitty she knew now. That was the trouble with some people; they got one view of a person and refused to change it, despite what was staring them in the face. That was Vera Delaney to a T.

'Anyway, Mrs Delaney, what was it you wanted?' Violet asked.

Vera glanced around the shelves, which were as

well stocked as Rita and Violet could manage, even if there wasn't the variety of goods available before the war broke out. Despite the cheerful display of Camp coffee bottles and the bright tins of Ovaltine, she looked dissatisfied. 'I've changed my mind,' she snapped. 'I'll make do with a tin of soup for my tea, and I'll write to my Alfie to let him know that Kitty's back. He always took an interest in her. He's good like that, has a heart of gold.'

Violet nodded dubiously, because that wasn't the Alfie Delaney she remembered at all. He had a reputation as a conscription dodger and a coward, but he hadn't been seen around for a while. Rumour had it that he'd offended a lot of people by selling contaminated meat which he'd obtained on the black market, and had had to make himself scarce when many of them fell seriously ill. 'Where's he now, then?' she asked, trying to make pleasant conversation as it didn't do to lose a regular customer, however unpleasant they were.

'He got a transfer to Clydebank,' Vera said, puffing up with importance. 'He's doing very well for himself, working his fingers to the bone for the war effort.'

Not what Danny used to say about him, Violet thought, but didn't speak it out loud. Danny and Alfie had worked together down at the Gladstone Dock and nobody had a good word for him.

'I see,' she said neutrally. 'Well, don't let me keep you, Mrs Delaney. There's still a nip in the air once the sun starts to go down.' She hoped the woman would get the hint. If she wasn't going to buy anything,

Violet wanted her out of the shop so she could shut up and go home.

Vera sniffed again but didn't linger, turning on her heel and leaving without saying anything further.

Violet breathed a sigh of relief as she drew the bolt on the door. There were times when she wished she was better at doing the books or other backroom tasks, as some of the difficult customers could try the patience of a saint, and tonight she didn't have any patience left. But it was her job to smile and get on with people, so she had to do it. She wanted to be back in her room, dwelling on the sweet memories of the time she'd shared there with Eddy.

He'd been back on duty for a fortnight or so now, but she could still picture him sharply in her mind, and what a wonderful week they'd had together when he was on leave. Truly, she was the luckiest woman in the world to have a man like him. She pulled down the blackout blind, just in case Rita or Ruby needed to come into the shop later on. She was dog-tired, even though she hadn't done anything exerting today. On some of her free evenings she'd begun to persuade Ruby to come to the pictures with her, but she hadn't had the energy even to suggest it since Eddy had gone back. Never mind. Dolly was making stew with some of the spring greens, and that would pep her up. As good as a tonic, Dolly's stews were. Wearily she took off her gingham apron and folded it away under the counter, picked up the handbag she'd made herself from remnants, and let herself out of the side entrance. She wondered what Eddy was doing at that very moment. Perhaps he was halfway to Canada, but he'd be safe now the U-boat threat had been averted.

'How about a cocktail?' Laura suggested, trying to be jaunty and not let her worry show. That was the last thing Peter needed. He was under enough strain as it was, preparing for the big offensive that nobody was meant to know about but which seemed to be common knowledge, at least in their circles. 'I'm simply dying for a martini. How very convenient that your uncle can get hold of the necessary ingredients. I swear I wouldn't last the week without one.'

Peter's handsome face broke into a smile, the frown lines relaxing for once. She nodded in delight, hoping that she'd distracted him from whatever was causing those lines to deepen by the day, almost by the hour. The creases at his eyes were deeper too – laughter lines, she called them, wanting to cheer him up. The truth was that the responsibility of being a captain in a navy at war had aged him, the good looks that had attracted her to begin with still there, but now tempered by two extra years of sleep deprivation, stressful shifts, and the knowledge that his every decision affected the lives of the men serving under him. On top of all that, there were the endless meetings.

It was one such meeting that had brought him back to London from his new base, close to Portsmouth on the south coast. At least it wasn't far to travel – although the train had been slow, he'd reported, and he'd only just made it in time. He didn't think it worth the risk of trying to return on the same evening, and so he and Laura were snatching a precious night together at his uncle the admiral's flat.

'You make it,' he said lightly. 'When it comes to cocktails, you're the queen. I wouldn't dare to compete.'

'There speaks a man who knows his own skills and recognises those of others,' said Laura, swinging around and letting her bias-cut flared skirt twirl around her shapely legs. 'No wonder you've risen far in the ranks. Giving credit where it's due will get you a long way.' She dug around in the admiral's fine antique cupboard for two suitable glasses, and held them up to the light of the sparkling chandelier. 'Excellent. These'll do.'

'Anyone would think you did this every day of the week,' said Peter, relaxing back on to the cream and gold cushions of the ample sofa. 'Rather than drinking lukewarm tea out of chipped cups in the Wrens' mess.'

'Or even more lukewarm tea out of enamel mugs while standing around waiting for my next passenger to bother to show up,' Laura reminded him, unscrewing the lid of a bottle. 'Let's not forget that, as it makes up so much of my working day. Ah, the glamour of it. Street corners of London I have known. Maybe I'll write a book about them once the fighting's over.'

'You're certainly the expert,' Peter agreed. 'In that and reversing into impossibly tight spaces.'

'It's why you love me, I know,' said Laura, holding the glass of viscous liquid at eye level and deciding it was perfect. 'I am under no illusions at all. My reversing skills were the top priority, I fully understand.'

She gave him a dazzling smile as she came across to the sofa, set both glasses down on the glass-topped coffee table and settled down beside him, snuggling close to him so that she could breathe in his distinctive scent – of his favourite cologne, a precious bottle of which he still kept at the admiral's flat, his freshly laundered crisp white shirt, and that extra musky note which was unique to him. For a brief moment she shut her eyes.

How many other chances would she have to do this before he had to return to action? She must make the most of it and treasure it, putting away the memory for safekeeping, just in case the worst were to happen. She would always have this moment, this evening, in this beautiful flat, with the most courageous and handsome man on earth. Please don't let this be the last time ever, she prayed fervently, screwing her eyes even more tightly shut. It had been bad enough getting the news when her brother had failed to return. She didn't think she could stand any more of it but, knowing there was no point in making a scene, she released him and sat back, reaching for her drink and passing him his. She noticed that he drew in a sharp breath but tried to hide it as he sat up. He would never, ever complain about the pain from the old chest wound.

'Happy days,' she said lightly.

'Happy days,' he echoed, raising the glass and sipping. His eyebrows shot up. 'Congratulations, Fawcett. Even by your standards, that is strong stuff. Good lord. I don't know why we have the finest brains in the country trying to come up with weapons to destroy Hitler and his crew. We could just send you in disguised as a waitress and have you serve them the likes of this. They wouldn't stand a chance.'

'Whereas you, my love, have had plenty of practice withstanding the punch of a knockout cocktail.' She sipped her own and smiled in satisfaction. 'Just how I like it. You must thank your uncle. He's too kind.'

'He is.' Peter nodded in acknowledgement. They were lucky, he knew, having the loan of the flat for an evening, and not having to make do with a half-empty pub with watered-down gin, or a restaurant that had little in the way of choice, or, even worse, trying to get past the dragons at Laura's strictly women-only billet. For this brief interlude they could persuade themselves that all was right with the world, and that they had a glittering future ahead of them. Had they met under normal circumstances that would have undoubtedly been the case; he knew they looked good together and both came from privileged backgrounds. Their prospects would have been gilded. Now everything was clouded with uncertainty. He didn't want to burden Laura with what he had just been told would happen. If they could keep this one evening special, he could think about it when he was in the thick of the action. He knew that would not be far ahead now.

'He's said I can come to see him here, when he's off duty,' she went on. 'What a poppet. I don't want to take up his time, though. He'll have other things on his mind.'

Peter shifted slightly. 'He'll welcome your company;

it'll be a diversion for him. All work and no play, and all that.'

'Well, you're one to talk.' She faced him with a quizzical expression. 'I know what you're like – you must get it from him. Promise me you'll get a good sleep whenever possible, when . . . you know.'

'I promise.' Peter knew there was little point in arguing with Laura. He might be the captain and used to giving orders, but she was something else again. 'Anyway, how was your day? How were the other lady drivers?'

Laura pulled a face. 'They're all right, they're good sorts really. They just think I'm fearfully standoffish. They always want to know every detail of what I'm doing, whereas I like to maintain a little privacy. I'm certainly not going to tell them that I came here with you. They'll go positively green. It's not fair on them; they don't get the odd night of the good life, so why torment them?' She paused for another sip.

'Bet they can't reverse like you can.'

'Of course not. Nobody can reverse like I can.' She said it jokingly but there was a core of truth to it. She was extremely good at her job, but that wasn't why he loved her to distraction. He thought she was the most beautiful, elegant, smart woman he'd ever seen, and knew she had deep reserves of courage too. She was also unbelievably stubborn and scarily deter-mined – but all those qualities put together made her the right woman for him. He only prayed they would have time together to enjoy life properly when all the fighting was done.

She rested her head on his chest – carefully, to avoid where the wound had been – and he wrapped his arms around her. She was wearing a silky blouse in buttery cream. 'This isn't parachute silk, is it?' he asked.

'Really! No, it is not.' Laura knew full well that plenty of women were making clothes from parachute silk, in the absence of anything better, and plenty of those were underwear. 'I got it when I last went back to see Mummy and Daddy. It's an old thing, nothing to make a fuss about.'

Peter could tell it must have been expensive once, but he didn't really care. She could have worn an old sack and he would have still wanted to hold her tight, stroke her precious body through the folds of the material.

'I wish you didn't have to go,' she said suddenly. 'Damn Hitler and the lot of them. Just stay here with me.'

'You know I can't do that. And you wouldn't want me to, not really.'

'I know. It's just so lovely here. Being here with you.'

'It is.' He nuzzled her shoulder, breathing in the scent of her warm skin. 'What do you say to putting these drinks aside for the time being and making it an evening to remember?' He stroked her more passionately. 'We could just go through there . . .' He nodded towards the spare bedroom, which lay through the beautifully carved living-room door. He could just see the soft rose quilt, plumped up and inviting.

Laura uncurled and faced him, then stood and took his hand. 'We could, couldn't we?' She tipped up her face towards him and he leant down and kissed her, gently at first and then more emphatically, as they moved together towards the open door.

'What do you fancy doing at the weekend, then, Sylvia?' Frank caught up with her as she came down the underground corridor in Derby House. 'You've got both days off, haven't you?'

Sylvia paused on her way back to her desk, her arms full of brown files. 'Clever you to have checked,' she said, grinning up at him. The late spring sunshine had brought out a smattering of freckles on her nose. 'Yes, but the thing is . . .' She paused, knowing he would be disappointed with her news. 'The thing is, I thought I'd try to go back to see my parents again.'

Frank swallowed. This wasn't what he'd been expecting to hear. 'Oh?' he said, hoping he didn't sound too put out. 'Well, if that's what you want . . .'

'It's not that,' Sylvia hurried to assure him. 'Not quite like that, any road. Of course I love going to see them, but you see, the thing is, Dad's not been well. Mum wrote to tell me, and of course I can't let him see that I know or he'd be horrified I've given up a weekend to go all that way, but I have to go all the same.'

Frank breathed out. 'Of course you do. Yes, I'm sure you're right. You don't have to say anything about why you're there; just turning up will do the trick. Otherwise you'll worry, won't you?' His eyes

128

crinkled into a warm smile. That was typical Sylvia – running to help where she could. His own disappointment was nothing compared to the anxiety she must be feeling about a sick parent, and not being close enough to just hop on a bus and go to see how they were. His heart went out to her.

Sylvia nodded. 'That's it. Oh, Frank, I knew you'd understand. I'd love to spend the weekend with you, of course I would, but I have to go to see how bad he is. And Mum will need my help. It's at times like this that I realise how cut off they are, all the way up there in the Lakes, and she might want me to sit with him while she goes out or send me on errands, or whatever needs to be done. Or I might get there and he'll be right as rain again – I just don't know.' Her lip trembled, and she bit it to stop it giving away how worried she was.

Frank could tell, though, and he briefly put a hand on her arm to comfort her. They were always very careful not to flaunt their relationship at work, as it was a tight team and in a confined space, and it didn't do to act unprofessionally. But he wanted to show her he knew how she must be feeling. 'You're doing the right thing,' he assured her. 'With any luck you'll get back there and he'll be striding around whistling for his sheepdog and heading out on to the hills. Then you and your mother can have a good laugh and she'll feed you up good and proper. You see if I'm not right.'

'Oh, I bet you are,' she said in relief. 'That's just how it'll be. But if I don't see how he is for myself . . .

well, Mum wouldn't have written unless it was serious, as she wouldn't want to worry me, so . . . I'm going to go.'

'Of course you are. I'd expect nothing less of you.' He withdrew his arm. 'And sorry, here am I holding you up when you've got all that work to do. You go, give them my best wishes, and we'll go out to the Phil another time.'

'I'd love that.' The Philharmonic Dining Rooms was where they'd had their first proper date, and it had remained one of their favourite pubs, despite it being slightly out of their way. The sumptuous art-deco interior always lifted their spirits, even if the route there was full of bomb-damaged buildings. 'I'll hold you to that, Frank Feeny.'

'I'll make sure you do,' he said mischievously as he watched her hurry back down the corridor.

CHAPTER ELEVEN

Nancy caught sight of herself in the mirror hanging on the wall of the quiet pub and thought that she looked all right, or as good as she was likely to manage these days. She was pleased. She'd wanted to appear as glamorous and attractive as she could for Gary, who was treating her to a romantic meal. Her hair shone, she'd used some of her precious reserves of proper make-up, and even her nails were freshly painted with deep red varnish. She felt she should pull out all the stops and show him British women were as good as anyone he might have known on the other side of the Atlantic. Not that he'd ever mentioned having anyone special on the other side of the pond.

She was only too aware that plenty of people resented the American servicemen, and complained they were 'overpaid, oversexed and over here', angry that they had more money to spend and better access to luxury goods than the boys from home. They were never short of female company for those very reasons, but Nancy wasn't with Gary because of that. Yes, it was nice to have someone who could treat her to drinks and entertainment that others couldn't, or who gave her little gifts that she couldn't have hoped to have otherwise. But the real reason she liked being with him was that he was such a gentleman. Some people said all the Yanks were brash and boastful, but she knew Gary wasn't like that at all.

He made his way back to her, carrying their drinks and smiling broadly. She noted how mature he looked compared to anyone else she'd ever been out with; it was another mark in his favour. She was tired of young men who – when it came down to it – were little more than boys, always thinking of themselves and not treating her right. Gary was a proper man and not afraid of the fact. He was confident in who he was – he didn't have to put on a show.

There were few other customers to notice his staff sergeant's uniform, and nobody seemed to object. They had chosen this place because it was away from the city centre and in the opposite direction to Bootle, so lessening the risk that anyone would recognise them. Nancy hadn't told Gary she was married, and hadn't mentioned her son Georgie after that first night, but she let it be known that her WVS colleagues might frown on her being taken out by a soldier who had used their services, particularly when he was an officer. Gary had accepted this and had praised her discretion and modesty. That had made Nancy smile. Not many people had used those two words to describe her behaviour before.

Now she raised her glass to him. 'Thank you, Staff

Sergeant Trenton.' She flashed her most brilliant smile and was careful not to spoil her lipstick as she took a sip of lemonade.

'My pleasure, Nancy.' He was tall, even when sitting at the old wooden table, which the landlady had polished to a bright sheen to compensate for all the cuts and scratches on its surface. His eyes danced with anticipation as he raised his pint of beer. 'Your very good health.'

'I hope so,' she said. 'And yours.'

'I hope so too.' He paused and seemed to be thinking. 'Well, I might be in need of a bit of luck soon. Not that I can say why, of course.'

Nancy raised a carefully plucked eyebrow. 'What do you mean, Gary? Is there something I should know?'

He shifted in his seat and looked around. Nobody was close enough to overhear them. He reached out and took her slim white hand in his large tanned one. 'The thing is . . .' He hesitated. 'Goddamn it, Nancy, sitting here with you is enough to put a fellow's mind in a bit of a spin. You got me saying things I shouldn't.'

Nancy bit her lip. 'Oh, Gary, you know I won't repeat a thing. You can trust me, you know you can. Not that I want you to get in trouble or anything like that.' She curled her fingers in his, suddenly aware of the warmth of his touch. She pushed to the back of her mind the uncomfortable fact that she'd slipped off her wedding ring earlier that evening, dropping it into her coat pocket wrapped in a hanky, after leaving Georgie with the Parkers once more.

'Nancy.' Gary's face grew very solemn. His eyes were still bright but they had lost their humour. 'You know what the rumours are. You're in downtown Liverpool and all those soldiers around you all day long. You're a sharp lady, you'll know that something's up.'

Nancy looked at him and nodded slowly in acknowledgement. She'd tried her best not to take any notice, recognising that there were always rumours and you couldn't live your life according to what they said or you would drive yourself crazy. However there was no denying it, they were all saying the same thing these days: that there was to be a major offensive into northern France. It was what she'd overheard Eddy and Jack say when they'd been home on leave. The one thing at home about being the ditzy sister was that nobody expected you to understand veiled hints and vague conversations, so they just carried on talking when she was in the same room. But she wasn't stupid. She could put two and two together as well as the next person.

'Sort of,' she admitted.

Gary held her hand even more tightly. 'Nancy, I gotta tell you. We're being moved out tomorrow.'

'Oh!' Nancy couldn't stop herself from gasping. 'Where? Or shouldn't you say?'

He made a rueful face. 'More like I can't. I don't know my whereabouts in England so the names don't mean much. But it's down south somewhere. There, I've told you far more than I ought to.'

Nancy stared down at the polished table top as the reality hit her: this might be her last evening with

Gary; this lovely, strong, caring man who made her feel cherished and protected in a way nobody else had ever done. How bitterly unfair, when she'd really only just met him and was still getting to know him. 'Oh, Gary,' she breathed. 'You'll take care of yourself, won't you?'

'Of course I will,' he replied, stroking her fingers. 'Now I know you'll be thinking of me, I'm gonna make extra sure I get back safe and sound. You will be thinking of me, won't you, Nancy?'

'Of course I will!' Suddenly she thought she was going to cry. She mustn't. Gary would be putting his life on the line. She just knew he was brave in the face of danger. She couldn't let him leave with the sight of her in tears. She would shed them in private once he'd gone.

'I'll be thinking of you,' he said, his voice completely serious. 'I'll see your pretty face before me and it'll give me a reason to keep fighting and get back in one piece. You'll be my comfort and my inspiration, Nancy.'

Nancy gulped. Nobody had ever said anything wonderful like that to her before. She struggled to keep the tears from her eyes and the tremble from her voice. 'Am I, Gary? Am I really?'

'Would I lie to you, Nancy? Over something as important as that? On my life, it's the truth.' He held her gaze. 'You're a very special lady, and I thank my lucky stars that I met you. The thought of you will give me hope in whatever's to come.'

Nancy could not take her eyes from his face, the

135

eyes full of solemn meaning, his strong but soft mouth, the little creases around his eyes and frown lines on his forehead that showed he was no inexperienced boy but a man who had seen real life. 'I'm glad I met you too,' she breathed. 'What a funny thing, wasn't it, fate bringing us together like that? Just imagine, if either of us hadn't gone out that evening, we'd never have met each other.'

He squeezed her hand again. 'I can't imagine it, Nancy. Can't imagine not knowing you. Even though it's only been a few weeks, they've been the most important weeks of my life.'

'And mine,' said Nancy, realising that she meant it. To think that she'd taken Sid's clumsy courtship for the real thing, and then she'd been stuck with having to marry him. Well, she'd paid the price for that all right. And Stan Hathaway, the smooth-talking local boy made good, who'd given her the push without a second thought, after having led her on good and proper. How wet behind the ears they seemed. They'd known nothing of the world or how it worked. They were full of hot air. Here before her was a man who was worth far more than the two of them put together. Not to mention all those callow young soldiers she'd gone for drinks with since then – and sometimes a little more besides. They didn't begin to compare to Gary Trenton.

'Gary,' she began, wondering if she was going to sound too forward. 'You mean everything to me, I know that now.'

'And you to me,' he replied. 'Don't upset yourself,

Nancy, I'd do anything not to upset you; that wasn't what I meant to happen at all.' He ran a gentle hand across her cheek. 'Give me one of those big smiles of yours. If this is our last evening together for a while, then show me that happy face so I can remember it.'

She looked up at him from beneath carefully mascaraed eyelashes. 'Would you really like something to remember me by, Gary?' The rest of the room seemed to be far away, and she felt as if it was just the two of them, cocooned from the world for one intense moment.

'Of course . . . ah, Nancy.' He suddenly caught on to what she meant. 'Nancy, really? Are you sure? I don't want to pressure you into doing something you don't want to, something that you might regret in the morning. I didn't tell you to try to make you do that. You know me better than that, don't you? I'd never force you to do anything you didn't want to, anything you weren't sure about.'

She held his gaze. 'Gary, you're wonderful and kind and a real gentleman. That's why I liked you to begin with. I know you'd never try to trick me into bed, and that's why I admire you.' She knew she was blushing in the low light of the pub room. 'But I'm sure. I've never been more sure of anything. That's if . . . if you'd like to, that is.' Suddenly she was afraid she'd been too bold, been too fast too soon. Yet if not now, then when? What if this really was their last evening together? The alternative, of not spending a night together ever, would be far, far worse.

Slowly he drained his pint and stood up, coming

around the table and taking both of her hands and lifting her to her feet. 'Nancy, that's an invitation I'd be mad to refuse. I've wanted to hold you properly ever since I saw you, but I never dreamed I could. Oh, Nancy, my lovely Nancy.' He leant close and gave her a tight hug, swiftly running his fingers through her soft red hair, the dull light glinting off it. Then he drew back before anyone noticed, mindful not to embarrass her. 'You'll make me the happiest, luckiest man in the world.'

'Danny, I swear, if I have to sit through many meetings like that he's going to drive me mad.' Kitty slammed through the front door and threw down her handbag on the floor by the foot of the stairs. Her brother stood in the doorway to the kitchen, watching her. His shift had finished before hers, and he was trying to work through a pile of crosswords he hadn't had time to do earlier in the week, but now it looked as if his peace was going to be disturbed.

'Steady on,' he said mildly. He wondered what this was all about. Kitty didn't lose her temper very easily, but she'd gone and lost it now all right.

'He's so particular about everything. Wants exact figures for this, that and the other. Puts everyone on the spot. Won't listen to reason.' Kitty shrugged off her uniform jacket, which was too warm for the June weather, even midway through the evening. She'd strode back from the bus stop at a great pace, trying to walk off her annoyance, and now she was hot and bothered on top of it all.

Danny raised his eyebrows. 'Are you talking about Frank, by any chance?'

'You see!' Kitty cried. 'You knew at once who I met. Clearly he's got a reputation for being difficult at work. You might have warned me.' She pushed past him and made for the kitchen sink to pour herself a glass of water, to cool down. She was more flustered than she'd been for a long while, and it was all thanks to being cooped up in that stuffy meeting room with Frank Feeny. She felt he'd singled her out for extra-strict attention, cutting her no slack at all. She'd just about batted back his requests, but hadn't been in the job long enough to be fully on top of everything, and she hated any such weakness being exposed. He really was the limit.

Danny followed her, pushing the newspapers to one side and exposing the old, well-scrubbed kitchen table. 'Not a bit of it,' he protested. 'Nobody thinks like that apart from you. Everyone else respects and admires him. It's just that he gets under your skin, then you come back here like a bear with a sore head.'

'I do not,' said Kitty hotly. She downed half the water in one go, then stood with her back resting against the wall. Its cool stone helped to calm her. 'Danny, really. No one else has to sit on those training committee meetings. If they did, then they'd soon see what he's like when it comes down to it. I don't know why I said I'd do it.'

Danny smothered a grin. 'You did it because you were asked to, as one of the best-qualified Wrens, and the whole point of you being back here is to help

139

with training, and you're the best woman for the job. So you'll just have to get on with it, Frank or no Frank.'

Kitty sighed. It was too hot to be cross, and it wasn't fair to take it out on Danny, who'd had his own tough day at work. Besides, they were all on edge. Last night there had been a broadcast by the king telling them all that the Allied troops now faced their toughest test, and everyone was keen to have news of what was happening. She glanced at her watch and saw it was nearly nine o'clock.

'Better switch on the wireless, Danny,' she said, steadier now. 'The news will be on in five minutes.' She shook her head, trying to get thoughts of Frank Feeny from her mind. It had been a shock to realise she was expected to sit on the same committee as him, closeted in a small room in the underground complex of Derby House. He'd sat there, immaculate in his uniform, seeming to know exactly what he was talking about, fully in command of his brief, and had made her feel like a total newcomer with no idea about anything. All her years of work and hard-earned expertise seemed to desert her. She'd have to be more careful in future – she hadn't been posted all the way back up here to fall at the first fence. She had to get a grip and maintain her professional attitude, not let it be waylaid by Frank's cool and commanding presence. She had to do better next time – the more junior Wrens depended on it and she couldn't let them down.

Danny turned to the old wooden Pye wireless set

and switched it on, but all that came out of it was a hiss of static. 'Damn, I must have knocked it earlier on and lost the station,' he said, turning the dial.

'Let me, I'm better at it than you,' Kitty offered, and then it was Danny's turn to grow annoyed.

'Don't be daft, our Kitty. How do you think I managed all those years when you were hardly ever here?'

Kitty groaned. 'Well, never mind, just hurry up, the headlines will be on in a couple of minutes now.'

There was a tap at the back door and Sarah let herself in, her expression revealing that she'd over-heard their heated discussion. 'Give over, the pair of you. We're all listening at home, so come across now and you'll catch the news. I was coming to ask to borrow a loaf tin, but it'll wait.'

'Thanks, Sar,' said Danny, abandoning the dial and switching off the set, the hisses and buzzing stopping as swiftly as they'd started. If he was honest, it was true that Kitty had the knack of finding the Home Service more quickly than he could, but he wasn't going to admit this now.

The three of them hurried across to the Feeny household, where Pop and Dolly were standing by their large wireless in the kitchen, while Violet peeled potatoes for tomorrow's stew at the sink, her faded apron splashed with muddy water. Dolly looked anxious. 'You're just in time,' she said. 'Sarah, did you get that tin—'

'Hush now,' said Pop gently, putting his hand out to Dolly.

At that moment a clear and calm voice filled the room. 'Here is the news, read by Joseph Macleod.'

They all stood totally still to take in Churchill's statement about what had happened that day in France, and what was still going on. The big offensive was under way at last, on the beaches of Normandy. Violet put down her peeler and leant against the sink, her hands clasped tightly, the last of the evening light falling through the kitchen window and on to her anxious face.

Kitty stared at the floor, wondering where her friend Laura's boyfriend was now – somewhere in the thick of it, most probably. She thought about Marjorie, setting off so steadfastly, unsure where she would be going or what she'd have to face. Maybe she was in Normandy too. They had no way of knowing. Despite her earlier mood, she found herself relieved that Frank Feeny wasn't caught up in the action but was safe in the underground bunker in Liverpool's city centre. No doubt he'd still be at work, just in case information came through that he was best placed to deal with, even though his shift should have ended by now.

Nobody spoke until the broadcast drew to a close, then they let out a collective sigh of breath.

'Sounds as if it's all going as well as it could do,' said Pop staunchly. 'Better than some might have hoped, in fact.'

Danny nodded. 'Well, like he said, they've reached inland as far as Caen already. And there hasn't been much loss of life.' Of course he knew that the reality behind the headlines might not be so rosy, but he wasn't going to say that here, not in front of this group of people, who meant more to him than just about anyone else in the world. He was acutely aware of those missing from the company: Eddy and Jack.

Dolly nodded solemnly, her face etched with worry, but saying nothing about her fears.

'Right, then.' Violet pulled down the blind on the back window as Sarah moved to light the gas lamp. 'I'll get back to the spuds.' She picked up her peeler once more.

Danny looked at Kitty. 'We'd best get back – we've got work in the morning. Thanks for fetching us, Sar.' He took a moment to observe her face, checking to see how she felt about the latest news.

Sarah smiled, taking it in her stride. 'You're welcome. Shall I pick up that tin tomorrow, Kitty?'

The women made arrangements for the following day, while Danny rerolled his shirt sleeves. He was heartened by the news and to see normal life resuming – but his thoughts were far away, over the sea in France, with the brave fighters now embarked on their biggest operation yet.

CHAPTER TWELVE

Violet held up the old knitted scarf to the daylight streaming through her bedroom window. She looked at it critically, then refolded it and put it back in the bag. It didn't fit the bill. She rummaged around in the collection Dolly kept of unused clothes or bits and pieces that could be remade until she came across a softer garment. Pulling it out of the pile she saw it was a shawl in pale green. That would be just the thing.

Baby Ellen was getting bigger by the day, and beginning to outgrow all the clothes that her doting extended family had made for her. Violet knew she herself was no great shakes at knitting, but she could help by unravelling the yarn of something that wasn't being worn, and then someone more expert could reshape it into a little garment. Dolly or Sarah, perhaps. Kitty wouldn't have time, and Nancy had never been seen to pick up two needles, much less do anything useful with them. Then again, she told herself sternly, Nancy had been noticeably subdued of late. Perhaps the news from across the channel was finally sinking in and making her more responsible. She shook her head. Pigs might fly.

Gathering up the shawl, she made her way downstairs. Her legs were weary and reluctant. She didn't know what was wrong with her – she'd never felt so tired before. Perhaps it was the strain of the war catching up with her, the constant sense of being on edge, and yet she couldn't fathom why it would hit her now. They'd been in far greater danger before, dodging the bombs as they landed on the city, and especially here near the docks. All the while she had known that Eddy was in deep peril out on the Atlantic with the U-boats lying in wait. Yet she'd kept on without complaint. Even though they'd lived with the knowledge that the country was at imminent risk of invasion, she'd found the energy to get out of bed, do a day's work, and live up to the expectation that she'd be the one to cheer people up.

Now, a couple of weeks after what everyone was calling D-day, news continued to be good and there was a cautious air of optimism around. She shared it, reasoning that Eddy was safer than he'd ever been, and that probably meant Jack was too – which made Rita more settled, and so Ellen was generally a happy baby. Maybe I just need a tonic, she thought, going into the parlour and setting the shawl on a side table. Then a glimpse of movement on the pavement outside caught her eye.

Rita was checking the shelves near the shop door, rearranging the jars of Marmite to make it look as if they had more than they really did, when she saw a figure draw up to the house opposite. For a moment she carried on counting the jars, making sure none of them had dust on their lids, and then it hit her. It was a telegram boy. He was propping his bicycle against the wall of her parents' house. With her heart in her mouth, she watched what he did next. Perhaps he was going to knock at the door of a different house. For a terrifying moment she thought it might be her door; that he was coming with news of Jack. Then he took something from his pocket before rapping hard on the fading paintwork. In her heart of hearts, Rita knew this could mean only one thing.

There was Violet opening the door, her expression welcoming and friendly to begin with, changing to stunned disbelief as the boy gave her the telegram. She held on to the doorframe and Rita could see her hands were shaking as she read the piece of paper. Rita waited no longer, but turned and ran to behind the counter where Ellen lay in her Moses basket. Scooping up the baby, she called through to the kitchen for Ruby to mind the shop. Then, baby on her shoulder, she dashed across the road to where Violet sat on the front step, telegram in her hand, face as still as a statue.

The boy on the bicycle rounded the corner at the bottom of the street and disappeared down the dock road.

Violet didn't glance up as Rita sank down beside her. 'Oh, Violet, I saw the telegram boy. What's happened? What does it say?' She reached across and took the telegram from her friend's hand, which was stone cold, even though it was a warm and sunny morning. Although Rita feared the worst, she still harboured a tiny fragment of hope that it was a mistake, or something trivial, or that if she didn't read the words then it wouldn't be true. But even as she thought these things, she knew she was clutching at straws. There was only one piece of news that merited the telegram boy in such a hurry and which would have had this effect on the recipient.

There it was, in black and white. There was no room for doubt. Eddy was dead.

Her hand flew to her mouth. No, it couldn't be true. Not Eddy. Not her beloved brother. He'd been here only a couple of months ago, laughing and joking and passing round the rum, playing the piano. How could someone so lively be dead? It wasn't possible. They had to have got the wrong Eddy Feeny. He must have swapped his uniform or . . .

Beside her, Violet suddenly began to shudder. Her mouth opened but no sound came out. Rita put one arm around her friend's shoulder as she held baby Ellen with the other. She was trembling herself, but knew she had to take charge. 'Come on, let's go inside. Is anybody else in?'

For a brief moment Violet looked at her as if she didn't know her, as if she was speaking a foreign language. Her eyes were wide behind their horn-rimmed glasses. Then she shook her head. 'Out. They're all out.'

Rita got up and pulled Violet to her feet, shoving

open the door and leading her into the coolness of the hallway, with its faded wallpaper rubbed shiny from where years of Feenys had brushed against it to hang up their coats on the hooks next to the cupboard under the stairs. 'We'll have some tea,' she said, pulling her friend into the kitchen. Violet made no protest but moved like an automaton. Rita set baby Ellen down on some cushions arranged in a corner of the sagging armchair, and went to the teapot. Violet stood blankly, her arms at her sides, staring seemingly at nothing. Rita turned her back to reach for the caddy and kettle, and then Violet bent suddenly forward. 'Sick,' she gasped, and bolted through to the back kitchen and then outside to the outdoor privy.

Rita ran the tap hard but could hear Violet heaving violently all the same. Then the noise stopped. Rita set down the kettle to boil and went out into the bright sunlit yard and drew her friend back inside. Her own thoughts were in complete turmoil, but her instincts were to calm Violet before she allowed herself even to begin thinking about what had happened.

Violet sank on to a chair at the table and mindlessly took the cup of tea Rita gave her. They stared in bewilderment at each other for a moment, and then Violet shook her head, as if by doing so she could make the news go away. 'Safe,' she said at last. 'He was meant to be safe. I thought he was going to Canada.' A sob broke from her. 'He should have been going to Canada. What was he doing in France? It's the wrong way; he shouldn't have been there, shouldn't have been there . . .' Then the tears finally came and she let her head fall into her hands, her shoulders shaking with the exertion, her whole body trembling as the enormity of what had happened struck home.

Rita went across and rubbed Violet's back, moving dumbly through her own pain and shock, wanting to let her friend know she was there all the same. Bitterly she remembered something Danny had said, not long after Eddy and Jack's leave had finished. Danny had dropped a heavy hint that just because the Merchant Navy vessels had mostly been deployed in the Atlantic up to now, it didn't mean that this was how things would stay. She'd brushed it aside as the sort of cryptic comment Danny was prone to these days, a result of him being too long underground and studying pages of gobbledegook. Yet Danny had known there was a risk. Probably Frank had too. Had Eddy? He'd said nothing when he was on leave. Neither had Jack. She pushed that last idea aside – she couldn't cope with that on top of this morning's news.

'There, there,' Rita said, comforting her sobbing friend, staring over Violet's shoulder in numb disbelief, fearful of facing her own grief until she was alone. Time seemed to stand still, but at last she heard the sound of someone – Pop or Dolly or Sarah – coming in through the front door. Quietly, and with a heavy heart, she made her way out to the hallway, shutting the kitchen door behind her, realising with increasing dread that she would have to break the news to the rest of the family. Violet had lost a husband, but they had lost a son – or a brother, just as she had.

*

Violet sat up at the sound of the door closing and saw she was alone except for little Ellen, wedged into her cushions. She sipped the lukewarm tea, clinging to the idea that it would be good for shock, but it made her feel sick all over again and she put it down. Ellen stirred and began to grizzle. Violet hauled herself out of her chair and went across to the armchair, bending over slowly, like a woman four times her age. Carefully she picked up the little girl and held her close, rocking her rhythmically, even as her own sobs subsided.

It seemed to do the trick. Ellen grew quiet again and then Violet could hear her small breaths turning into tiny snores as the little girl fell asleep on her shoulder.

Violet shut her eyes, smelling the top of the baby's warm head, her heart breaking as she faced the end of everything she had hoped for so keenly: the life that she and Eddy had planned ever since they had met – having their own house, a lovely garden, and children of their own. Now it would all come to nothing, and there would be no life with Eddy after the war. She would never see his beloved face or feel his strong arms around her ever again.

CHAPTER THIRTEEN

Alfie Delaney rubbed his hand over the top of his head and cursed that his hair was thinning and receding so quickly. It was a good job that everyone in the services had to keep their hair short to regulation length, and some went even further and had it cut as tightly to their scalp as possible, so his near-baldness didn't stand out too much. Not that he was in any of the services. He'd managed to avoid that, by claiming he was in an essential job on the docks. When he'd had to get out of Merseyside after the contaminated meat incident, he'd got himself taken on in Glasgow, but unfortunately they'd made him work so hard he'd almost regretted dodging the call-up.

The sun was beating down on him and he could feel his head getting burnt. He hadn't thought to bring a cap, which was careless, he realised now. In the city there was always shelter and shade. Out here in the countryside it was relentlessly hot and there was nowhere to hide from the sun's merciless rays. He hoped the trip would be worth it.

In the end he'd avoided being called up without the help of Danny Callaghan, but that didn't mean he'd forgotten Danny's refusal to go along with his scheme. All the man had had to do was to take Alfie's medical test for him and it would have been so easy, but no, Danny had to go all law-abiding and preachy and insist it was wrong. It would have been no skin off his nose, nobody would have guessed, and Alfie could have rested easy knowing his records would forever show he had a dicky heart and was unsuitable for everything but the lightest work. He certainly wouldn't have had to put up with the Clydebank conditions, which were nothing short of hard labour, he convinced himself. He would have had a nice indoor desk job – like Danny Callaghan had managed, so he'd heard. A lovely safe, warm, easy desk job. He'd harboured his resentment of Danny all the time he was away, until it had grown to the proportions of a grand betrayal.

Now the pressure was off and everyone was thinking about northern France and not getting poisoned by some bad meat, Alfie judged it safe enough to return to the Merseyside docks. His connections, principally local gang boss Harry Calendar, had ensured the process was smooth, and he was due to begin back on the Gladstone Dock next week. His mother had been delighted. He knew he could always rely on her. She'd written every week while he was away, regular as clockwork. That's how he'd known Kitty was back.

Alfie wiped the sweat from his forehead as he thought of Kitty Callaghan. She'd always taken his eye, back when they were all kids playing in the street.

She was pretty, and her hair curled in a way that had fascinated him when a boy. He would stare at it until someone noticed, but he had been too bashful when younger to do anything more than gaze from afar. Kitty had looked after her brothers ever since she was eleven, and everyone knew she was a wonderful cook. What else could a man ask for? Admittedly his mother had written to tell him she'd come back because of some sort of promotion, and people were saying she'd done well for herself, but after all it was only the Wrens. It wasn't like a proper man's job – how hard could it be? She'd still be the shy, gentle Kitty he remembered, he was sure of that.

However, it didn't hurt to take some precautions and do some background research. That was why he was dragging himself down this godforsaken country lane in the middle of nowhere, trying to find a farm. Some people might think this was a mad thing to do, but he wanted to cover all eventualities. His mother had mentioned that Tommy Callaghan had been evacuated out to Freshfield and was on the same farm as those horrible brats who had lived above the corner shop. Alfie reckoned it was time to renew their acquaintance. Tommy owed him. He'd saved his life a couple of years ago when the boy had been messing around in a warehouse that had caught fire. Alfie had basked in the glory of being a hero, even if his reasons for being down at the warehouses weren't quite as pure as he made out. He wanted to remind Tommy of how grateful he should be. Also, when Tommy was recovering in hospital, Alfie had gone to the trouble of obtaining some new football boots for the boy at Christmas. It wasn't a selfless gift; he'd made sure Danny knew it was so they were in his debt. Even if Danny wouldn't falsify the medical examination, he'd know that he still owed Alfie that favour. And owe him he did, big time.

Just when he thought he couldn't stand the heat much longer and would have to find a pub in which to slake his thirst, Alfie passed a milestone on which he could just about make out the carved letters for Freshfield. Of course, getting around anywhere now was a blasted nuisance, what with all the proper road signs having been taken away in case the Germans invaded. At least now he knew he was in the right place. There was the farm, just as his mother had described it. It had been a leap of faith coming here like this, as Vera had only got the description third-hand, from her late friend Winnie, whose son Charlie had come here now and again. It was unmistakable, though: the chicken coop around the back, the stable with the doors painted blue. Alfie paused to take in the scene and to plan his next move. He didn't want simply to barge in and demand to see Tommy. That would alert the farmer and cause suspicion.

The place was so quiet after Glasgow and Liverpool that it took some getting used to. Somewhere above a bird was calling, and a cow mooed long and low. Insects buzzed in the heat and a fly landed on his face but he swatted it away in irritation. He could almost feel sorry for those city kids, stuck out here with nothing to do. There was a goat running around in the enclosure near the farmhouse – it looked vicious. Give him a run-in with Harry Calendar's rivals any day.

His ears pricked up at the sound of a horse's hooves clip-clopping, and before long the animal appeared around the corner of the lane, pulling a cart. An old man sat on the driver's seat, reins in his hand. He nodded to Alfie as he approached.

Alfie decided to abandon any idea of a cover story and to make a direct enquiry. It was too hot to think straight, and he didn't want to get caught up in a web of lies if he didn't have to. 'Good morning,' he began, smiling and hoping he looked trustworthy.

The cart driver's expression didn't alter. 'Morning,' he said in a strong Lancashire accent.

Alfie kept the smile in place. 'I'm looking for a young friend of mine and I was told he'd been evacuated out here. Tommy Callaghan. Do you know him?'

The man shifted in his seat. 'Who wants to know?'

'Oh, my mother was a great friend of his auntie's,' said Alfie, stretching the truth, as Dolly wasn't actually Tommy's aunt and she couldn't stand Vera at the best of times. 'My mam's dead now and I wanted to get back in touch with them all, you know, for old times' sake. I was passing this way and thought I could make a start with young Tommy, if he's here.'

The man stared at him dubiously. Then he seemed to make up his mind. 'Aye, fair enough,' he said. 'But you've just missed him. He used to help out on the farm, so you got that bit right, but he's left now he's old enough to have finished school.'

Damn, thought Alfie, of course Tommy would be

155

older now – was he really fourteen? He supposed it was possible. 'That's a shame,' he said, trying to sound suitably disappointed and not as annoyed as he actually felt. 'I don't suppose you know where he's gone?'

The man shifted again, looking down directly into Alfie's face. The strain of trying to look open and pleasant was killing him, but he didn't let down his guard, grinning away for all he was worth, playing the part of fond friend of the family.

'Bootle,' the man said shortly. 'That's where they're all from, isn't it? He's gone back there.' With that he gee'd up the horse and moved off, the cart swaying along the lane past the farm and beyond it around another corner.

Alfie was left standing there, hotter than ever, and now cursing his luck. His eye twitched a little in frustration. He'd come all the way out here and Tommy sodding Callaghan had been just around the corner after all. Typical bloody Callaghans, sitting pretty while everyone else did all the work. But no, that wasn't fair. Kitty wasn't like that. He gritted his teeth. He mustn't give up; only fools were afraid to take what was theirs by right. He'd just have to go back home, find Tommy for a moment on his own in Empire Street and ingratiate himself that way. Yes, he told himself, it would be worth it in the long run. He had to keep his eyes on the prize: Kitty.

Dolly tried to summon up the enthusiasm to go to her make-do-and-mend group, but she just couldn't. To begin with the group had met in her parlour, but it had outgrown the modest room and now gathered at the church hall. Dolly was the leader, encouraging young wives to try different ways of sprucing up old clothes, using upholstery fabric for dressmaking, unpicking or patching or generally producing purses out of pigs' ears. They needed her with her years of experience, the result of raising five children and keeping them warmly clothed. She knew it, but she felt as if she didn't have it in her to leave the house, let alone make it as far as the hall.

The news about Eddy had floored her. It had been so unexpected. Like Violet, she'd been on tenterhooks for all those years that he was dodging the U-boats, but had relaxed and assumed he was safe now most of that was over. She had had no idea that he could have been part of D-day. Looking back, she realised that Frank had gently tried to warn her, without giving away what he knew, but she had brushed his vague words aside. Her Eddy – her baby boy. It seemed no time at all since he was a toddler, always trying to catch up with his big brother, putting up with little Nancy's tantrums, never making a fuss but always having his own way of doing things. She didn't know how she could go on without him.

Some people tried to be kind, pointing out that Frank was safe in his position, and that she still had her girls, so she should be thankful. It didn't help. For one thing, Frank had lost his leg on active duty, and you still couldn't say for sure that Liverpool city centre wouldn't be a target again. Rita's hospital had been attacked in the past – look at what had happened to

Elliott, killed by a bomb just after leaving his shift. Or when Sarah's colleague had died just outside their nursing station during a heavy raid on the docks. Even Nancy was at risk. Besides, the fact that you had other children didn't take away the pain of losing one. Eddy was irreplaceable. He wasn't a younger version of Frank; he wasn't just a brother to his sisters. She missed him as if she'd lost a limb. There was a permanent ache, a sense of something out of balance, a gaping wound.

She tried not to show it too much around the house because everyone was feeling devastated, everyone wrestling with their own sorrow. Dolly had managed to get to the church to see Father Harding, who had been a tower of strength, explaining that this was a test of her faith. He had helped her back when news had come of her parents dying, and also when Pop's parents had died, all of them over in Ireland, at respectable ages. That had been scant practice for how Eddy's death had hit both her and Pop. She was glad they had each other, even though Pop didn't, or couldn't, say much. But she knew he was feeling the pain and also sympathising with hers. They both had done their best to comfort their daughter-in-law, who was so dear to them.

Poor Violet would never know that support from her husband again. The young woman moved through rooms like a ghost, barely speaking, her face pale and her body shaking as if she was cold all the time, even though it was the height of summer. Much of the time she stayed in her bedroom. It was as if the old Violet, the one who never kept still but was always helping at the shop or the victory garden or the WVS, had totally disappeared. She hardly spoke. The only times she seemed at all lively were when Georgie or baby Ellen were in the house. Then she would stir herself and try to play with them like she used to, but it wasn't the same. Georgie had picked up that something was wrong, but Dolly couldn't find the words to explain to him. He was only four, and he had barely known Eddy, after all.

There was the sound of movement upstairs and then the creaking of the stair boards. Dolly looked up, pushing a lock of greying hair out of her eye, as Violet came into the kitchen, walking slowly and stiffly, her shabby dress hanging off her always-lanky frame. She said nothing as Dolly tried to catch her eye, but went straight through to the back kitchen and out of the back door, before Dolly heard the slam of the privy door. Then, although she tried not to listen, there followed the unmistakeable heaves of someone being sick. Poor Violet. But what had happened to her was enough to make anyone sick. Wasn't it? Dolly thought dully that for two pins she'd join her.

After a few minutes the back door opened again. Dolly could see Violet fetching a glass of water and sipping it standing at the sink. She set it down and held on to the draining board, as if she didn't have the strength to stand unaided. Dolly's heart went out to her.

'Come and sit down, love,' she called, hauling herself to her feet. 'What can I get you to help you feel better? How about a nice cuppa?'

Violet gulped but tried to smile. 'No thanks, Mam. It's too hot, really it is.'

Dolly pondered what else she might have to offer. 'We've got some peppermint cordial somewhere. Or our Frank brought over some ginger beer the other day.'

Violet shook her head then changed her mind. 'Maybe some ginger beer.' She managed to drag herself into the main kitchen, leaning on the cupboards for support, and collapsed into the saggy armchair.

Dolly went to the big slate larder shelf, where even in July she could keep foodstuffs cool. In behind the milk and precious ration of butter she found the ginger beer, and brought it through with a glass. 'There you are, my girl. That'll set you right.'

Violet sipped it gratefully and Dolly watched her with concern. The young woman was deep in grief, anyone could see that. But she was now wondering if she'd missed something, something that her mother's instinct would surely have picked up sooner if they hadn't heard the tragic news about Eddy. She shut her eyes briefly. How stupid she'd been, too mired in all their misery to recognise the signs. A healthy person like Violet, too tired to get out of bed, sick in the mornings, losing weight. Yes, losing Eddy would have thrown her out of kilter and caused physical symptoms, but those particular ones? Her eyes went to Violet's hunched figure, to see if there had been any change apart from the weight loss. Or maybe it was too soon.

Violet looked up from her glass and noticed her mother-in-law's expression.

'Violet,' said Dolly steadily, 'is there something you haven't told me? This isn't the first morning you've been sick. I know you're still in shock and it could just be that, but even so . . .'

Violet set down her glass and slumped lower in the chair. 'I don't know, Mam. I feel so poorly. I think it's finally hit me, what it all means, you know. That I'll be on my own and he's never coming home.'

Dolly's heart went out to her and she moved across the room to stand beside the old chair and pat Violet on the shoulder. 'I know, love. It's hard. It's so unfair, you two being so right together. He was a lovely lad and there's never been one like him.' She paused to sniff back her own tears. Now was not the time to break down. It wouldn't help Violet – and she had to find out the truth. 'What I wondered, though – and don't take on if I'm wrong – I just thought, there might be another reason you're sick?'

Violet looked up at her blankly.

'Violet, think,' said Dolly, trying to get through to her daughter-in-law. 'Eddy was back in April, wasn't he? Easter week, it was. Now it's July. Count back, love. Can you remember if you've had your monthlies since then?'

Violet almost dropped her glass. She gasped and her hand went to her belly. 'My . . . hang about, I don't . . . did I . . .' She shook her head. 'Oh, Mam, I don't know, but I don't think so. What with all the restrictions and everything, I stopped bothering to check.'

'And you've been giving extra food to Georgie off

your own plate for ages, don't think I haven't seen,' said Dolly, mock-sternly. 'You practically starve yourself, my girl. Well, that has to stop. Think, Violet. This is important. If I'm right, we've got to get you eating proper whether you feel up to it or not. There might be more than just you to consider.'

Violet slowly pushed herself to her feet. It was as if she was waking up from a dream. 'Maybe. Let me try to remember. Easter week . . . well, I know I had the monthlies in March because they were painful as can be and Sarah made me a special herb tea, but perhaps . . .' She looked at the smoke-yellowed ceiling as if the answer might be written there. Moments passed. Then she shook her head again. 'There's been nothing like that since. I'm sure now. To be honest I was tired out before we got the news that he'd died and I thought it was just one of those things. I'd forgotten that. Yes, I was like this before.' Her face changed and she turned to Dolly. 'Do you think it can be true, Mam? I might be carrying Eddy's baby? Really? Is that why I've been so poorly? If that's what it is, I don't care. I'll be sick all the time, I'll never complain. I can't believe it.' She started to cry, a mixture of sorrow and joy. 'Oh, Mam, we talked about having children all the time. I so wanted to have his children.'

'I know, love. I know.' Dolly went to hug her, carefully now.

'It wouldn't make up for losing him,' Violet went on, 'but this way I'd still have something of him; he'd be living on through his baby. It would be wonderful.'

'It would,' Dolly agreed, blotting out the fears that it would be hard for a young woman on her own to raise a child without its father. Well, she would just have to make sure Violet didn't have to cope alone, that all the rest of the family would help out – just as Violet had helped out up to now. 'And that means, my girl, that you really are going to have to start eating properly. Never mind being tired, you have to think about that child on its way. We'll have to get your rations sorted too. You'll get clothes points, you know.'

Violet huffed. 'That's the least of my worries, Mam. I can borrow Rita's things when I get big, I know she'll let me. I haven't felt like eating for weeks though.'

'Never mind that,' said Dolly firmly. 'That growing baby needs nourishment. It's our job to see that it gets it. So you finish that ginger beer and then let's see what we've got in the larder. You, my girl, are going to have a slap-up lunch, whether you like it or not. And I'll join you. At last we've got something to celebrate.' Her voice caught, despite her best efforts to be positive, because whatever happened, Eddy wouldn't be here to see it. A single tear escaped the corner of her eye. Then she resolutely dashed it away. He'd be looking down on her from the Heaven he most surely was in and he'd be expecting her to take care of Violet and the child when it came. She couldn't let him down.

CHAPTER FOURTEEN

Nancy stared gloomily out of the bus window as the ruined streets of the city centre passed before her eyes. The sunshine made the roads hot and dusty, and the buses were stuffy. It was hardly worth dressing up for her WVS shift. Everything got covered in a fine layer of the dust, making her feel grimy before she'd even begun.

She'd almost not come, she felt so low. The alternatives were worse, though. Staying in with her detested mother-in-law was to be avoided at all costs. The old bag had dared to take on the mantle of grieving for Eddy, adding it to her list of woes. Nancy bristled with fury at the idea. Eddy used to do a painfully accurate impersonation of the whingeing old woman. Now to hear Mrs Kerrigan go on, you'd have thought he was her favourite, a treasured member of the family.

The usual escape route of heading round to her mother's house was also more difficult now. The whole place reeked of sorrow – and no wonder. Nancy wasn't immune to feeling bereaved at her brother's death. She'd been truly fond of him, and knew he'd been a good brother to her, not tormenting her or teasing her in front of his friends. She'd miss him and his calm ways, the fact he would never let her wind him up, seeing through her temper tantrums and letting her quieten down in her own time. He'd been a breath of fresh air in the crowded atmosphere of Empire Street, and there hadn't been anyone else quite like him. She'd popped round earlier to drop off Georgie – Dolly had begged her to do this more often now, as it was one of the few things that brought Violet out of herself. She'd been in and out as fast as possible, unable to meet her mother's eye. When all was said and done, Dolly was her rock, and to see her so shaken hurt Nancy to the core. It was all too painful to think about.

What she couldn't tell anyone was that she was also worried sick that something had happened to Gary. She hadn't heard from him since D-day, and she was as certain as she could be that he'd been part of that operation. Realistically she told herself that he wouldn't exactly have been sitting around with time to spare, writing long letters home. She didn't want to begin to think of what he would have seen or what he would have been through. It shouldn't surprise her that she hadn't heard. The trouble was, if the worst happened, then she wouldn't know. They'd gone to such pains to keep their relationship a secret that none of the men serving under him would think to seek her out and tell her. Nobody at his base would know to do so. She was just the nice lady who served the tea or helped to organise dances, sometimes having a few turns on the dance floor, nothing further than that. When it came to information she would be last to find out – if she ever did.

She missed him. Their first and only night together had been everything she had hoped for and more. At last here was a man who treated her as she'd longed to be treated – and who knew what he was doing. He'd made Stan Hathaway look like an amateur. She'd never experienced such pleasure and he'd still been there in the morning, murmuring about what a privilege it was to make love to a woman like her. She'd never known anything like it. She was desperate to have that again, to make up for everything she'd been missing up to now. It had been worth the risk of leaving Georgie overnight with the Parkers; she'd invented a twenty-four-hour bug when she'd picked him up and thought she'd just about got away with it.

Nancy had known she had to be careful, as she didn't want to chance a pregnancy, what with Sid still being a prisoner of war, so it had reassured her to find that Gary had thought of this beforehand. That was another thing the Americans were known for – always having a supply of French letters, or rubbers as they called them. Well, she wasn't going to object. It was one less thing to worry about, and heaven knew there were plenty of other anxieties to fill her head.

So she had to resign herself to living in limbo, not

knowing if he was dead or alive and, if he was alive, when or if he'd be back. Meanwhile she had to carry on the pretence of everything being normal, and if people noticed she was a bit quiet they'd no doubt put it down to her brother being killed. Everyone was very understanding – so many others had lost a close family member, it wasn't as if she was the only one. Mrs Moyes had suggested that she take some time off, but that was the last thing Nancy wanted. Working at the canteen got her out of the house and took her mind off everything else. Now, as the bus approached her stop, she hoped that, despite the heat, they'd be rushed off their feet. That would be several blissful hours of thinking about something else. Wearily she stood, balancing expertly in her peep-toe sandals as she weaved between the seats to the exit.

'You can't make me!' Tommy shouted, his face reddening with emotion. 'If I'm old enough to leave school, I'm old enough to decide what I do!'

Danny grimaced and tried to keep his temper. He reminded himself that Tommy was far from being a grown-up, no matter what the boy thought, and it was his job to protect his little brother, even if he didn't want any protecting. 'It's no good, Tommy,' he said as calmly as he could. 'You are not joining the Merchant Navy. We didn't send you off to Freshfield for all those years just so's you could come back and get yourself killed.'

'It's not fair!' Tommy protested, throwing himself angrily into the back kitchen. 'You've all done what you wanted. You all started work when you were my age. Now it's my turn. The country needs fit young men like me – there's a war on.'

Danny counted to ten and tried again. 'I know. It's hard to avoid. But that doesn't mean you go and put yourself in the line of fire the minute you get out of short trousers. It was different for Jack and me. Now I wish I'd paid more attention at school. I've spent the last two years catching up. No, don't look like that, try to listen to what I'm saying and get the benefit of my experience rather than throwing a hissy fit.'

Tommy grabbed the handle of the back door. 'I'm going out. I don't care what you say, you're just trying to stop me doing my bit.'

'Tommy, no, it isn't like that at all.' Danny desperately tried to think what would stop his little brother storming off and signing his life away. 'Look, the thing is, the country does need everyone to do their bit—'

'That's what I meant!' shouted Tommy. 'Don't try to tell me what I just told you!'

'. . . but everyone has to do what they are best at,' Danny went on. 'When you were younger you helped on the farm, and that meant more of us got proper food, so that was the right thing for you to do then. So it's a matter of deciding what's the best thing for you now.'

'Joining the Merchant Navy!'

'If you won't listen to me, then listen to Jack,' Danny went on, picking up the letter that had started the latest row. 'He doesn't want you out there putting your life at risk.'

Tommy bunched his fists in frustration. 'Jack would say that. What does he know about it?'

'Well, seeing as he's been in the Fleet Air Arm protecting all the ships of the Merchant Navy for these past five years, he probably knows more than most,' Danny said, unable to keep the asperity from his voice. 'That's exactly why he's written to say you're not to join up. Think what happened to Eddy. You have to listen to Jack. You're not twenty-one yet and he's head of the household, no matter where he is at this moment.' Truth be told, the letter was so heavily censored that Danny had no idea where Jack had sent it from. What he did know was that some of the Fleet Air Arm squadrons had been involved in D-day, and he was not sure if Jack had been seconded to one of those. He was very experienced; he might well have been chosen. If that was the case, Danny didn't know how he could face writing the letter to say that Tommy had run away to sea. It didn't bear thinking about.

'I'll lie about my age,' threatened Tommy.

'You go ahead and try,' Danny countered. 'They might at a push accept you are fifteen, but that's it. And anyway, everyone round here knows your name. They'll all recognise you're Jack's brother and know all about you, so they won't take you on.'

'I'll run away and sign up somewhere else!'

Danny shook his head, although it wouldn't have been the first time Tommy had run away. The first place he'd been evacuated to had been a cold, cruel household, and he'd made his own way back home from there, although he'd been barely ten at the time.

He wasn't short of courage or resourcefulness, that was for sure. Danny decided to take a step back and let his brother talk it through, rather than push him to run off as he'd threatened.

'Come back inside and sit down, then we'll discuss it like adults,' he suggested. 'Can't say fairer than that. We'll sit down at the table and talk about it man to man, and then if you still feel like signing up after the end of that, we'll have to see.'

Tommy looked at him dubiously, but then accepted the flattery of being called a man and pushed past his brother to reach the table first. He pulled out a chair and turned it round so he could rest his elbows on the back. His expression was still mutinous.

Danny sat down opposite him and put Jack's letter back in its envelope, folding it carefully, playing for time. He had a strong sense that if he gave his little brother a few minutes he would calm down and not follow through on his rash threat.

'Right,' he said slowly. 'Before you commit yourself to anything, let's see what the options are.' He paused but Tommy just glared, not saying anything. 'There are lots of other things you could do that would be equally useful, you know – vital to the war effort.'

In reply, Tommy just kicked his foot against the table leg.

'For example,' Danny said, 'Sarah says they're always short of porters at the hospital.'

Tommy looked up sharply. 'Well, if Sarah says it then it must be true,' he snapped.

Danny felt a surge of anger rush through him. The

very idea that Tommy could be rude about their neighbour, whom he'd known and liked since he was a baby and who had always been especially kind to him, was shocking. His blood boiled at the insult to her. But he held on to his temper. 'Of course it is. Nearly everyone who's left is over forty, and some of them can't lift heavy loads any more. And you know very well that the hospitals have been bombed. It's not a cushy number.'

'Mmmmm,' Tommy mumbled, glancing away. He didn't want to work in a hospital. For a start lots of people would know Sarah or Rita, so his family would find out about every mistake he made. Also, though he would never have admitted it out loud, he was a bit squeamish. He'd helped out Seth and Joan on the farm, but he had often had to look away at the more sickening moments, like when Bessie the goat had complications giving birth to her kids, or a fox got into the hen house. He didn't think he'd last long in a hospital. There would be blood, and worse, and bad smells. He would never live it down if he fainted and someone told Sarah.

'Maybe,' he prevaricated.

Danny was warming to his theme now. 'We could ask Pop if he knows of anything through the ARP,' he went on. 'Not you being a warden or anything, but a messenger or something like that. You're good at remembering detail and you know your way around here like the back of your hand. What about that sort of job?'

Tommy brightened. He loved meeting lots of different

171

people and he could always find something to say – Kitty's main complaint, echoed by Seth and Joan, was that he could talk the hind legs off a donkey. But if he was with the ARP, then Pop would want to keep an eye on him. He was even stricter than Danny. That wouldn't be much fun.

'Don't know,' he said, swinging his leg and then stopping when he saw Danny glare. 'Suppose it would be better than nothing. While I'm waiting around, like.'

Danny recognised that this was progress indeed. 'All right, so maybe you think the ARP are a load of boring old codgers,' he said, knowing the way his brother's mind worked. 'But a messenger of some sort, then?'

Tommy shrugged, but his resistance was wavering.

'I know,' said Danny. 'What about delivering telegrams? You'd have to be quick for that, and completely trustworthy. You're giving people the worst news they could ever have; you can't be careless about it. You'd have to show you were level-headed and responsible. It wouldn't be a doddle getting in.'

Tommy now looked interested, although he was clearly trying not to show it.

'You'd need a bike,' Danny mused.

Tommy now sat up straight. 'Ah, come on, our Danny. You can get your hands on anything. You could get me a bike, no bother.'

Danny pulled a face. 'It might not be as easy as that. Things are different around here to when you went away. I don't have the contacts any more and, even if I did, I'd hesitate to use them.'

172

'Danny, you could do it,' said Tommy, eager now. 'Go on, say you'll try. Think what I could do if I had a bike. I could fetch things for you and Kitty while you're at work, for a start. You'll wonder what you ever did without me in no time.'

Danny had to stop himself from laughing at Tommy's abrupt about-turn. 'I suppose the General Post Office might provide the bikes. I never thought, we'd have to check.'

'Oh, that'll be easy,' said Tommy airily. 'Someone's bound to know. Pop might, he knows everything.'

'All right, we'll ask him,' said Danny.

'But can I have a bike for home anyway?' asked Tommy, taken with the idea now. 'Then you wouldn't have to worry about me getting home an' all. Kitty wouldn't have to sit up. We both know what she's like,' he said conspiratorially, suddenly all man of the world. 'Can't have that now, can we?'

Danny threw up his hands. 'All right then, Tommy, we'll see what Pop has to say and find someone to recommend you to the GPO,' he said. 'You win.' But actually, he thought to himself, it was me who won that conversation. Tommy hasn't gone running off to join the Merchant Navy and I won't have to tell Jack the news. And, who knows, Tommy might just end up in his ideal job, for now at any rate.

CHAPTER FIFTEEN

Laura set down her beautiful fountain pen and reread what she'd just written. She thought it just about made sense but her mind was whirring. Perhaps she'd got it all wrong and was making a fuss about nothing. Indeed, if she didn't have the physical evidence of the scrappy piece of paper now carefully flattened under her empty tea mug, she would have thought the whole thing was a figment of her imagination.

She couldn't even write what she really wanted to say as the censor would block it out. Never mind, all she really needed to do was make sure it sounded sufficiently urgent for Kitty to take notice and to agree to meet her.

She stared out of the window of her new attic billet in Kentish Town, across the rooftops of northwest London towards the centre of town. How she and Kitty and Marjorie would have loved to have lived here during their training – they could have walked into Piccadilly at a push and gone to all those bars and clubs that Elliott had known. Now such venues held little interest for her. It would just be one more place to dodge the buzz bombs, the new German weapon that had been causing havoc over the summer, no doubt launched in retaliation for D-day.

Peter had survived the landings and had made it back to his base near Portsmouth, and so she'd been able to hear first hand about the horrors and successes of the operation. He had come through unscathed, and full of admiration for the way it had been planned. 'That was down to you too, my darling,' she'd told him, on the one night they'd managed to snatch at his uncle's flat. 'Those boring old meetings paid off.' She was terribly proud of him, and mightily relieved he was back in one piece, but there was a strong likelihood he would be back at sea shortly. However, he had taken to persuading colleagues who were sent to London from their south coast base to seek her out if their paths looked likely to cross, passing her messages to cheer her up. It was an unconventional way of getting news, but it made her day to know that he was thinking about her.

It was one such encounter that had brought about her state of indecision. Yesterday she had just stood down from duty and had chosen to walk through Regent's Park to make the most of the sunny day, glad to have finished her shift driving a particularly unpleasant naval officer, who seemed to think that her company later in the evening would be part of the service. She had put him right politely but firmly, wishing she could have told him exactly what she thought of him. If he tried it again she'd report him, she thought angrily. She'd been wandering down one of the less frequented paths when a man in a drab grey jacket had approached her, his distinguishing features blocked out by the brightness of the sun behind him. 'Miss Fawcett?' he'd asked, in a voice she could only have described as nondescript.

She'd looked directly at him, neither denying nor confirming her name – she had no idea who this was and the light was such she would have struggled to recognise even a reasonable acquaintance.

'Message for you,' he'd said, pressing a small piece of paper into her hand, then he was gone.

Well, that was a new twist from Peter, she'd thought, and made her way back to the rather grim little attic room, which was too hot in the summer and would probably be freezing in the winter. She'd opened the flaking window as far as it would go, and stood by it before taking out the paper and unfolding it.

If it was from Peter, it wasn't his writing. It was a scrawl, almost as if it had been deliberately disguised. *Back soon. Safe and well. Don't worry.*

It had no name, date, or any way of telling where or who it was from.

She had stared at it, held it up to the light, sniffed it to see if it had any trace of lemon juice or substances said to be used in invisible ink, even while telling herself not to be so stupid. It was most likely a silly joke.

She'd put it to one side and left it overnight, half believing when she woke up that she'd dreamt the whole thing. But she hadn't. It was still there, curling in the dry air. In the morning light the ink looked a little faded, as if the message had been written some while ago. Could this letter possibly be from the one person that she desperately wanted it to be? Freddy – her brother – missing presumed dead.

This was all too much to decipher on her own. She didn't want to bother Peter – and he might not even be ashore right now. The only person she could think of who might have an idea was Kitty. There was no chance that she'd risk putting the details in a letter, but she could talk to her in person. She was owed some leave. She could go to see her parents, a long-overdue visit. And meet Kitty at Crewe, if they could co-ordinate it. She just had to stress how urgent it was, without unduly alarming her friend. She thought she'd got the tone about right, and with nothing that would annoy the censor. Nodding firmly, she slipped the letter into an envelope and made her way down the rickety uncarpeted stairs to post it.

She hated allowing herself to be taunted by false hope, but ever since Freddy had disappeared, she had thought about the ways in which he might make contact, if by a miracle he had survived. Of course it was a long shot. But she would be lying to herself if she didn't admit that it was what she wanted to be behind this strange little note.

'Well, well, if it isn't Tommy Callaghan.'

Tommy looked up from where he'd been kicking a stone along the dock road. He squinted into the sun. The voice sounded familiar but it took him a moment to put a name to the face. He realised that the man had changed since he'd last seen him – he'd almost gone bald. His scalp shone pink through the remainder of his closely cropped hair.

'Hello, Alfie,' he said.

'How's it going then?' said Alfie. 'I heard you were coming back. Home for good, are you?'

Tommy shrugged. 'Suppose so.'

'Bet you're glad to be back in the thick of things and not stuck out in the sticks any more,' Alfie went on.

Tommy looked dubious. 'How do you know where I was?'

Alfie gave a big, open smile. 'Oh, word gets round, you know how it is. I travel around a lot as well. It wouldn't have been my sort of place, I can tell you that for nothing.'

Tommy wasn't sure he liked the sound of that. 'It was all right,' he said shortly. If he was honest, he missed the farm and Joan and Seth, who'd been like family to him. He also missed Michael and Megan more than he'd thought he would. Acting the big brother to them had made him feel important and grown-up. Round here he was back to being the little brother once more. He wasn't going to say that to Alfie though.

'So, got any plans?' Alfie asked. 'Smart lad like you, you're bound to have something up your sleeve.'

Tommy perked up. 'Well, yes, I have.' He paused. 'I might as well tell you, Alfie, 'cos you've known me since I was little.'

'And I saved your life back in that warehouse fire, didn't I?' Alfie interjected, almost as if he'd just thought of it, rather than he'd been determined to get that little reminder in as soon as he'd clapped eyes on the boy.

'Oh, mmm, thanks, Alfie.' Tommy wasn't sure what he should say to that. He felt awkward at the subject being brought up.

'So, you were going to tell me about your plans,' prompted Alfie.

'Oh, right. Well. I just went to the GPO for an interview and I got the job.' Tommy beamed with happiness and pride. 'I'm starting delivering telegrams next week.'

Alfie raised his eyebrows and gave his big smile again. 'Is that so? Congratulations. That's a proper responsible job, that is.'

'It is,' said Tommy seriously. 'I might have to bring people the news that someone they love has died. It's not going to be easy. But I'm determined to do my bit.'

'Quite right, Tommy, quite right.' Alfie nodded solemnly. 'You'll do a good job, you will.'

'I'll have to.' Tommy brightened. 'And I'll have to ride a bike all over the place. Danny said he'd get me one to have at home an' all.'

'Did he now?' Alfie thought swiftly. 'That's kind of him. Aren't you lucky to have such a kind brother?'

'Suppose so,' said Tommy.

'You tell him that I can get hold of a bike for him if he wants,' Alfie said confidently, without knowing if that was the case or not. Still, he reasoned, it couldn't be that hard. If holier-than-thou Danny Callaghan could manage it, then surely he could too, and probably a much better model at a cheaper price. 'Yes, I'll do him a mate's rate, like, seeing as it's for you.'

'Blimey, thanks, Alfie.'

'It's no trouble to me,' Alfie said airily. 'That's what friends are for, right? And by the way, how's your sister? She's back home now, isn't she?'

Something about the way the man asked the question made Tommy uneasy, even though Alfie's expression hadn't changed. He couldn't put his finger on what it was, but he suddenly felt uncomfortable in his skin. 'She's all right,' he said shortly. 'I hardly see her, she's at work all the time.'

'Oh, that must be hard,' said Alfie, oozing sympathy, but his eyes didn't match his words as they stared at Tommy just a little too intently.

Tommy shrugged. 'She's happy enough,' he said. 'I must get on, Alfie. Got to tell Danny about my interview.' He couldn't wait to be gone now.

'Oh, right,' said Alfie, covering his disappointment that he wasn't going to hear any juicy details about Kitty. 'Yes, you'd best get back right away. Do say hello from me. And to Kitty, of course. Tell her I'm glad she's back home after all this time.' He gave what might have been meant as a broad smile, though it didn't really look like one.

'Okey doke, then, Alfie.' Tommy turned and headed off, relieved to have got away from the man, though he couldn't have said why. Then he brightened again as he rounded the corner into Empire Street. What was he worried about? He'd got the job. He'd have a red GPO bike for work and a smart uniform. He'd have to do PT drill first thing every morning with the other telegraph boys, and he'd be doing his bit. Life was getting better by the minute.

Sarah Feeny was about to go in through her front door when she caught sight of him. 'Well?' she demanded, coming across the street to greet him, her nurse's cloak slung over her arm as it was too hot to wear it. 'Did you get it?'

'Course I did!' Tommy was almost jumping up and down with pride.

'Course you did!' Sarah echoed. 'That's wonderful news, Tommy. When do you start?'

'Next week.' Then Tommy remembered his manners. 'Please say thank you to Pop for getting Mr Mawdsley to put in a word for me.'

'I will, but he was happy to do it,' Sarah said, recalling that Pop had called in a favour from the husband of one of her mother's close friends. Mr Mawdsley was a respectable civil servant, but he wasn't above drinking the occasional pint in the Sailor's Rest. His word would have carried some weight. Sometimes it was all about who you knew.

'Guess who I just saw,' Tommy said.

'No idea.' Sarah raised her eyebrows in encouragement.

'Alfie Delaney!' Tommy announced. 'I almost didn't know it was him. He's gone bald and his head is burnt so it's like a red snooker ball.'

Sarah drew in a sharp breath. 'Is it now? That's a turn-up for the books. No, not his head, the fact that he's back after all those years away.'

'Oh, has he been away?' asked Tommy. 'He didn't say. Sounded as if he was back here all right, though. He said he could get me a bike. Mate's rates an' all.'

'Did he?' Sarah shook her head. 'You know what, Tommy, if he's still got the same mates as before he left, I might be inclined to wonder where he'd get a bike from.'

Tommy's face fell.

'But don't mind me,' she said hurriedly, not wanting to spoil his triumph. 'You go on in and tell Danny about the new job. I expect he'll get you a bike, won't he?'

'Oh, yes, he said he would,' said Tommy, brightening again. 'Right, see you then, Sarah.'

'Bye, Tommy.' Sarah watched as he ran to his own front door and burst through. She was delighted and relieved to hear he'd passed his interview, as she knew how worried Danny had been about his young brother. He was a hothead – but so was Danny, even if he'd mellowed over the years, especially with the heavy responsibility of his work. Perhaps the same would be true for Tommy. She hoped so. Still, she couldn't shake the chill that had come over her at the mention of Alfie Delaney's name. She wondered if Danny knew he was back; he hadn't said anything. Then again, perhaps he wouldn't have told her even if he'd seen the odious man recently. Sarah was aware that Alfie had some kind of hold over Danny but she didn't know what it was. She only knew that his return could mean nothing good – and might well portend something very bad indeed.

'That seems to be all. Thank you, gentlemen – I do beg your pardon, ladies and gentlemen.' The senior officer rose, and everyone crowded around the table in the meeting room rose as he headed out of the door. The others filed out behind him, but Frank put out a hand to detain Kitty. The only other Wren, Moira Butcher, turned to catch her eye, but Kitty shook her head. 'I'll catch up with you in a moment,' she said, slightly annoyed as she was very busy, and yet conscious that the slightest touch of Frank's hand had burnt through her uniform jacket like fire. That annoyed her too – she still couldn't prevent it happening, couldn't break that circuit.

'I won't keep you long,' he said, his warm eyes gazing into hers.

'Thank you, I have a lot to do this morning as I'm sure you will appreciate,' she said in her most firm and professional manner.

'Of course.' Her heavy workload seemed to amuse him, and she felt like saying he could offer to share it if he found it so funny. 'I must get back to my desk soon as well. No, I just wanted to say that I might have found your Tommy a bike.'

'Oh, really?' That stopped her in her tracks. Danny had all but promised one to Tommy, but they were hard to come by, and he'd been asking around everyone he knew these past few days. So far the only

183

lead had come from Tommy himself, claiming that Alfie Delaney, no less, had offered to get him one. She and Danny were determined to avoid that at all costs. Nothing Alfie did was ever out of the goodness of his heart – that was if he even had one.

'Yes, you know Commander Stephens has a young family? Maybe not; he doesn't say much about them, as they're over in Cheshire most of the time now and he misses them.'

'He must do,' said Kitty, remembering that the superior officer was a kind man, although he didn't suffer fools gladly. But then Frank was no fool, and would only have seen the good side of him, she suspected.

'His younger son was given a bike for his birthday, but it's far too big for him,' Frank went on. 'They've found him a better one, one that's the right size, and he'll sell the first one at a bargain price as they don't have room to keep it until the lad's grown into it. How about that?'

Kitty felt a rush of happiness, knowing how much it would mean to Tommy. She felt she owed it to him to get this right, as he'd been so desperate to join the Merchant Navy and she didn't want him to feel that his new situation was second best in any way. 'Frank, that would be wonderful,' she said.

'I'll let him know you'd like it, shall I?' Frank offered, trying not to be distracted by the sudden gleam of delight in Kitty's eyes and the way her cheeks blushed rosy pink at the idea of giving a present to her little brother. He knew how responsible she felt for him.

'Oh, yes, please do that. I'm so grateful,' she said, all her previous annoyance gone.

'Right, I'll see him later today. Come, let me hold the door for you, you have so many files in that stack you're holding,' he said.

Kitty expertly balanced the manila files on her hip as she manoeuvred through the door, relieved Frank was holding it open, knowing it would have been tricky on her own. The idea of dropping them all and their contents spilling out was mortifying. She brushed past him, but the narrowness of the doorframe meant that for one brief moment his arm was around her shoulder. She tried not to notice, but wondered if he had spotted it too. She took a quick breath and moved along the corridor.

Frank let the door swing closed behind him, relieved that for a moment he was behind Kitty and she couldn't see his face. Just for a second there it was as if he'd had her in his arms. He told himself not to be silly. Why was he allowing himself to think like this? He had a date with Sylvia to look forward to this evening, and he had no business letting such thoughts enter his head. He took a longer stride to catch up with her.

The corridor was far from wide and he found himself holding back a little so he didn't come into contact with her again, not wanting to cause her embarrassment. But he couldn't come to a complete halt either; what if she thought his leg was bothering him? His pride wouldn't allow that. So he carefully kept a respectable distance, while being ever more aware of how neatly her uniform fitted her. From this slight distance he could appreciate her curves, although he was trying hard not to notice. She was no longer the slim girl over the road he'd grown up with, that was for sure. Wartime diet or not, she had filled out in all the right places.

'Frank?' She turned a little to face him as she walked and he almost stumbled. He hoped there was no trace of his thoughts on his face but couldn't be certain. 'I have a few days of leave coming, but perhaps Commander Stephens could arrange everything with Danny?'

'Yes, of course, that would be easy to do,' Frank assured her, regaining his balance.

Kitty nodded. 'That's so kind of you to think of Tommy, Frank. He'll appreciate it, he really will. We can't keep him cooped up at home, and at least this way I'll know he'll get back safely.'

'Don't mention it,' he said. 'It's no trouble—'

'We couldn't think how—' she began, then she blushed even more in embarrassment as they both apologised for speaking over each other.

She paused to make sure he had finished, and gave an awkward laugh. 'We were struggling to find a way to get a bike,' she began again, 'so thanks a lot, Frank . . .' She looked as if she was about to say something more, when Moira from the meeting came striding back along the corridor to look for her.

'Callaghan. There you are. Do you think you can spare a minute? One of the newer recruits has got herself in a right pickle.'

Kitty smiled at Frank and hurried after the other woman, leaving him with a strange mixture of emotions. He was pleased to help out, and Tommy was almost like a young brother to him, their two families had been so close for so long. But he couldn't deny that the main feeling rushing through him was pleasure at bringing that look of happiness to Kitty's face.

CHAPTER SIXTEEN

'This should do the trick. Do you like it?' Rita pulled a big checked shirt from her wardrobe. 'It used to be Jack's but he hardly ever wore it because he doesn't like anything too baggy. It was just the ticket for my last couple of months.'

Violet took it and noticed that it was a lovely soft flannel. 'Are you sure? Won't he want it when he comes home on leave?'

Rita laughed and shook her head. 'You must be joking. It won't fit under his pilot's jacket and he'll want to wear that all the time, if I know Jack. No, you take it and put it away somewhere for when you need it.'

'That won't be for a while,' replied Violet, touching her belly self-consciously. She reckoned she was five months gone but there was little to show in the way of a bump as yet. At least the constant sickness had stopped, and she wasn't quite as tired. Now it had become clear what had been causing her symptoms, she had far more energy, and she was determined to give her baby the best possible start, war or no war.

'You'll be surprised,' predicted Rita. 'Once you start to swell you keep on ballooning at a proper old pace. You'll be due in January, won't you? So this will keep you nice and cosy too.'

'It will,' said Violet. 'I'm ever so grateful, Rita. You've all been so good to me, more than I deserve.'

'Stuff and nonsense,' said Rita robustly. 'You've more than pulled your weight helping out everyone, so it's our turn now.' She knew that Violet didn't have any real family of her own. Her father had died many years ago, her mother had died in a raid quite early in the war, and she'd always hated her drunken step-father. The Feenys were her family now. Rita for one didn't know how she'd cope without her sister-in-law.

Rita's mind then turned to her other sister-in-law, even though she never called her that, since Ruby had never been acknowledged as Winnie's daughter while the vile old woman had been alive. Now, though, Ruby had stepped up to help out in the shop, not just to mind it for a moment or two when nobody else was around, or behind the scenes with the book-keeping. She was down there now, holding the fort, and with none of her former crises of confidence.

'I hope Ruby's all right,' she said, going to the door so she could hear if the young woman should call up the stairs for assistance.

'Oh, I think she will be,' said Violet with a grin, looking almost like her old self. 'As I was coming in, I could see she had a visitor.'

'A visitor? Ruby? Are you sure?'

Violet tapped the side of her nose. 'And it won't be

the first time. I'd meant to mention it before, but, you know . . . it went out of my mind, what with everything else that's happened.'

'And no wonder,' said Rita forcefully. 'Who is it?'

'Mr James.'

'What, the old fellow down at the allotments?'

'No, not him.' Violet tilted back her head and gave one of her horsy laughs, which, even though it was a sound that took some getting used to, gladdened Rita's heart, as she hadn't heard it since before the dreadful day when the telegram had come. 'His son. Reggie. Have you met him? You must have, he often brings the vegetables.'

'Oh, him. The one who limps a bit,' said Rita, remembering now. 'Are you sure he isn't just delivering more boxes of tomatoes?'

'If you ask me, Rita,' said Violet wickedly, 'Ruby's getting more than tomatoes from him.'

Rita gasped. 'No! Surely not! Not Ruby.'

Violet shrugged. 'All right, maybe I'm making more of it than there really is. But it's more than bringing the vegetables, just you mark my words.'

'So you don't think I should pop down and see if she's all right?'

'No,' said Violet firmly. 'Most definitely not. She'll call if she wants our help. And she's got to get used to being down there on her own as you're going back to nursing. How are you feeling about that?'

'Honestly? I'm looking forward to it,' said Rita. 'It will be hard to leave Ellen' – she glanced at the baby asleep in her basket, tucked beneath the windowsill

190

– 'but Mam will look after her and she's old enough to have her bottle. I'd rather do that than send her to one of those nurseries.'

'We'll all help with her,' said Violet. 'They'll need you back on the wards.'

'I'm sure it will all work out,' said Rita, hoping fervently that she was right. 'Let's go over and see what Nancy's brought round. I'm glad she offered to dig out some of Georgie's baby clothes. It's only right, the time you've spent looking after him over the past few years.'

Nancy was holding forth about the filthy state of the city centre as they reached Dolly's kitchen. She'd arrived back from her WVS shift to find her white sandals were more like grey and their little daisy decorations like withered weeds. 'And my poor collar!' She was wearing a neat broderie-anglaise blouse, the hem and collar of which were visibly the worse for wear. 'I'll have to spend ages scrubbing it. It'll ruin my nails.'

Rita shook her head. 'Never mind, Nance. Look on the bright side. You could dye it grey and be done with it.' She had little sympathy – her own nails were always kept trimmed short because lifting stock in the shop always wrecked them, let alone what she would encounter when back on duty as a nursing sister.

Nancy tossed her head. 'I might have known you wouldn't understand. Anyway, Violet, here's those clothes I told you about. I don't know what you'll want as you don't know if it's a boy or a girl, but help yourself.' She handed over a bulging canvas bag.

191

'So many, Nancy! Are you sure?' Violet lifted the top ones out. 'They're really good quality. Thank you.'

'It's the one good thing about Misery Guts,' said Nancy with asperity. 'She likes to see her little grandson looking right, or else he'll reflect badly on her. So she spent her coupons on him whenever she could. Then I got a few things in town when I was able to. Doesn't look like I'll be giving him a little brother or sister any time soon, so you might as well make use of them.'

'I should hope not!' said Dolly hotly, coming in from the back yard. 'Don't you be bringing disgrace upon this household.'

'Joke, Mam,' said Nancy. Then quickly, to distract her mother, 'See this little top – you knitted that. He wore that all the time when he was tiny.'

'So he did,' said Dolly, her face creasing fondly at the memory. 'Sure, he was a little angel, that he was.'

'And where is he today?' asked Rita, not taken in by Nancy's tactics for one moment.

Nancy's expression changed to one of worry. 'His chest is bad again. I didn't like to take him to the Parkers' in case he gave it to them, so I've left him in with Misery Guts. In fact I'd best be off.' She pulled a face. 'I know she can't do much to harm him now he's that bit older, but I still don't trust her an inch. She'll probably be telling him how unlucky he is to have such a bad mother.'

'Now don't take on so. I'm sure she isn't,' said Dolly, always suspicious that Nancy denigrated Sid's mother's method of babysitting so she could bring Georgie round to her more often.

'Well, I'm not going to risk it,' Nancy said, picking up her white handbag, which looked too small to hold anything useful. 'You sort through those things, Violet, and keep what you like. Actually, Rita, you might find something to suit Ellen in there as well. You might as well take anything that fits, I know they grow like mad at that stage.' She glanced fondly at her niece, asleep in the Moses basket that Rita had carried her over in. 'There should be some romper suits for a six month old in the pile somewhere.'

She gave a little wave and flounced out.

'What's got into her?' Rita wondered out loud, but she wasn't going to look a gift horse in the mouth. Nancy had never offered before, and Rita had resorted to hunting around for anything that Megan might have grown out of all those years ago. 'Oh, now, look at this. Didn't Georgie wear it for his first birthday? I might take that and put it to one side for when she's big enough.' She carefully set the brick-red chunky cardigan on the edge of the Moses basket. 'And this little siren suit. Let's hope we don't have to use it down the shelters again.'

'Amen to that,' said Dolly at once. 'It's very kind of Nancy, but don't you have to see to the shop? Have you got the time to go through the whole bag? It can always stay here, Rita, and you check the rest when you have the time.'

Rita dropped another small cardigan in soft cream on top of the other two baby garments. 'We're grand, Mam. Ruby's taking care of it all.'

'Is she now?' Dolly looked concerned.

'Yes, she's making a very thorough check of a big delivery of tomatoes,' Violet told her solemnly.

Nancy almost skipped down the street, despite the pain in her feet from wearing impractical sandals for a busy shift. She knew she should wear more sensible ones, and had told herself off time and time again, but she'd felt like dressing up this morning. The miracle had happened. Gary had managed to get a message to her. One of the GIs under him had been shipped home wounded, but had recovered enough to come back to the WVS canteen. He had been told to seek out 'the lady who looks like Rita Hayworth' and pass on the news that Staff Sergeant Trenton was alive and well, fighting fit but looking forward to coming back to Liverpool. That was all. He didn't know any details, such as when that might be, and he'd been wounded so early on in the proceedings that he couldn't really say where Gary was now. However Nancy didn't care.

Gary had survived the first onslaught, which everyone was saying would be the most dangerous part, and had thought so highly of her that he'd arranged this way of telling her how he was. She knew the young GI couldn't have been expected to say he sent his love or anything as sentimental as that. Still, he'd cared enough to take the trouble, and that had made her day. It was only yesterday that she'd heard. Since then she had been on cloud nine and had struggled to hide her joy from her inquisitive mother-in-law.

Then on top of it all she had all the brownie points from her family, sharing out the baby clothes like she had. It was no skin off her nose, and in fact it might even annoy her mother-in-law if she found out, except she wouldn't be able to say anything without sounding extremely mean. It just got better and better. Nancy was fond of baby Ellen, and knew that she'd look even more adorable in the clothes; Rita simply didn't have the time to go out and hunt down new ones. As for Violet, Nancy couldn't begrudge her the loan of anything, seeing as she'd been so good with Georgie and had gone through the hell of losing Eddy. Nancy sometimes was taken aback when Georgie spontaneously asked for Violet before anyone else, including her, if anything went wrong, but she found it hard to resent her sister-in-law. She was too sunny-tempered to fall out with. On a day like today, Nancy felt she might not ever fall out with anyone ever again. Even the prospect of hand-washing her delicate blouse and treating it with Reckitt's Blue didn't quench her joy. Despite everything, life was good.

Kitty looked around at the station as they drew in, recognising it as Crewe. She had changed here on several occasions and it was always crowded, its platforms thronged with servicemen and -women in all sorts of uniforms, many with big kitbags. There were often wounded personnel being escorted to hospitals around the country. No wonder the one on Linacre Lane in Bootle was so keen for Rita to return. The knock-on effect of D-day and the ongoing campaign in France meant a steady stream of injured Allies returning for treatment, and everywhere was feeling the strain.

It was also the station where she'd first met Laura, she thought, and laughed at the memory. Kitty had been nervous about leaving home for the first time, shut in a carriage with some young and impudent soldiers, when a very posh voice had asked her to shove up, then the young woman – Laura, as it transpired – had handed round cake. Now Kitty was meeting her here again, but she was unsure what the urgency was. Still, she knew Laura wasn't given to panicking or hare-brained schemes, so she must really need to see her about something. Kitty had been happy to give up one of her precious days of leave to learn what it was all about.

She checked her watch as she left the train. Laura should be arriving in a few minutes if her train was on time, but Kitty didn't hold out much hope of that. She wandered along to the end of the platform to get some fresh air, away from the milling crowd. A small group of young women in civvies stood anxiously waiting, and Kitty wondered if they were expecting the arrival of wounded loved ones. How hard that must be. Yet at least they wouldn't be left high and dry like poor Violet.

By a miracle only twenty minutes late the London train was announced, and Kitty positioned herself for a good view of everyone getting off. It was bound to be busy and she didn't want to miss her friend. As it turned out there was little chance of that, as Laura had chosen her most colourful dress in a bright geometric print in red, white and blue.

'Do you think I look terrifically patriotic?' she

greeted Kitty, swinging a neat leather weekend bag by its handle. 'I chose it specially. I like to think I bring a little cheer into the travelling public's life. What do you say?' She twirled theatrically and several more dowdily clad women turned and frowned.

'I bet you do that all right,' grinned Kitty. 'And there was I wondering if I'd be able to spot you. Come on, let's grab a cuppa, there's a counter over there.'

They made their way to a neighbouring platform where a queue of people was waiting for refreshments. The buffet was large and airy, with an intricately patterned tiled floor, and in peacetime had probably been a pleasant place in which to unwind between journeys, but today it was bursting at the seams.

'Do you mind if we don't?' asked Laura, peering dubiously into the big room. 'I'd like a smidgeon of privacy if at all possible. There's a hotel next to the station – maybe we could go there.'

'Of course,' said Kitty, happy to go along with Laura's suggestion.

She followed her friend as she swiftly wove her way through the exit and round to the hotel, which was indeed directly next to the station, and watched as Laura with her trademark combination of charm and determination secured them a quiet table in the bar area, next to a window. 'There, you see,' she said. 'Peace and quiet and a bit of a breeze. Just what we need.'

Kitty nodded. 'Let's get a lemonade,' she suggested. Keeping up with Laura was hot work. They ordered their drinks and she settled down to find out what all this was about.

'So . . .' she said.

Laura pushed a stray lock of blonde hair behind her ear, then opened her weekend bag and drew out a book. 'I'm not quite sure how to begin,' she admitted. 'I'm so glad you agreed to meet me, Kitty. You might think I'm going crazy, but at least you'll understand.'

'Whatever is it?' asked Kitty, slightly worried now. 'Are you in trouble of some kind?'

'No, nothing like that. Well, no more than usual. My fellow drivers hate me now they've found out about Peter, but it's just silly jealousy,' Laura sighed. 'Makes me realise how lucky you and I were to find each other and Marjorie. Kindred spirits, that's what we were. There's rather a lack of harmony in the current crew. Anyway, that's by the bye.' She opened the book and a scrappy piece of paper fell out. 'Take a look at that.'

Kitty leant forward and picked it up, reading the brief message and turning it over. '*Back soon. Safe and well. Don't worry.*' She looked up at Laura with a puzzled frown. 'Is that it? That's all there is? Who's it from?'

Laura told her of the strange man in the park and how she'd thought it was one of Peter's little jokes to begin with. 'It isn't, though,' she said. 'I actually asked him – his uncle's flat has a telephone and I managed to make a call to his base. Fearfully lucky to have got through, and of course I couldn't stay on the line for long, but I would have felt like a proper twit if I hadn't asked him. I just laughed and said it didn't matter, there's no point in worrying him.'

'No,' said Kitty, thinking hard. 'But if it wasn't him, then who has sent this?'

'Exactly,' said Laura. 'Who do I know who is away from home?

'Plenty of people we've trained or worked with, or people Peter knows,' Kitty pointed out.

'Yes, but who would go to the trouble?' Laura asked. She paused. 'Someone who thinks I might believe they're sick or dead. Someone who wants me to know they're all right.' She raised her hands in the air and let them fall again and then blew out a long breath. 'I'm trying not to get my hopes up . . .'

'Oh.' Kitty suddenly understood. She stared directly at her friend, trying to read her expression. 'You think it could be Freddy.'

Laura wouldn't meet her eye. 'I know it's unlikely – *highly* unlikely. But who else do I know who is far from home and cut off and would want to get a message to me like that?'

Kitty knew what she meant and yet didn't want to give her friend false hope. 'Laura, it's been ages. He disappeared before we even met, didn't he? It'll be coming on for—'

'Four years,' said Laura dully. 'Autumn 1940, it was. Look, I realise that's a long time for anyone to be missing and then to suddenly communicate.'

Kitty reached across and took her friend's hand. 'It is, Laura. It really is. I suppose anything could happen, but it's such a long shot.'

Laura shook her head, her usually carefree face now full of desperation. 'But it might be, mightn't it?

In theory it's possible, isn't it? You see why I think I'm going crazy. I've been tormenting myself from the moment I saw it. It could just, *just* be him, alive after all that time.'

Kitty felt unbearably sorry for her friend, and yet she still didn't feel convinced. 'Then why now? Why wait for years? It doesn't really make sense, does it?'

'I agree – but then I can't help wondering what if . . .?' Laura said. 'What if he's been captured and brainwashed or something, what if he's been held somewhere against his will all this time? And then I thought – with D-day and us gaining more and more territory in France – whether he might be there, whether circumstances have changed somehow, and he's finally been able to communicate . . . Oh, I don't know. You're not convinced, I can see it on your face.'

Kitty bit her lip. 'Maybe, but it's still such a long shot.'

Laura slumped in her chair, all the fight leaving her. 'It is, you're right. It's probably those beastly drivers ganging up and playing a cruel prank.'

'They don't know about Freddy, do they?' Kitty asked. She thought it highly unlikely that Laura would have made her situation generally known, given how painful her brother's disappearance was for her.

'No, I wouldn't tell anyone I wasn't close to,' Laura confirmed. 'It's too awful to explain over and over again. Really it's just you, Marjorie, Peter and now his uncle who know all the details. Naturally I was going to jump to the conclusion it was from Freddy, but I suppose it could be from someone I haven't thought of, or it's possible that it was delivered to me by mistake. I have no idea who the man was, and he could have handed it to the wrong person – it could have been meant for someone else entirely.'

'Yes, that's the problem,' Kitty said gently but firmly. 'There's just not enough evidence to go on at the moment. You don't want to be adding two and two and making five.'

'But how about the paper?' Laura tried one last shot. 'Don't you think it looks a bit French?'

'Well, it's a tatty piece of paper that looks as if it's been scrunched up and unscrunched scores of times,' Kitty said carefully. 'But . . . French paper? I'm not sure I've ever seen any.'

'Oh, you know. The lines are a bit closer together. All right, I'll stop, I can see you don't believe me.'

'I'd love to,' Kitty assured her. 'There's nothing I'd love more than for this note to be from your brother, except I can't honestly say I think it is. If it was, it would be nothing short of miraculous.' She took a long sip of her lemonade, which was blissfully cool on the hot summer day.

'That's why I needed to talk to you,' Laura said. 'I knew you'd listen to my muddled theory but be kind about it. Thank you, Kitty, and for giving up your day off when I'm sure you could have found plenty of other more fun things to do.' She sat up and took a drink from her own glass. 'So, tell me, what is it like being home? Are you finding new ways to have fun? I do hope so. It has to be livelier than where you were before, surely.'

Kitty smiled and ran her finger through the drops of condensation forming on the outside of her glass. 'Not fun like we used to have, if that's what you mean. I'm working too hard, but it's lovely being back and seeing my family. I wrote to you about Tommy, didn't I?' She described the trouble she and Danny had had with him before he agreed to become a telegraph boy. 'Then there's Rita's new baby, who's lovely, although I'm a bit biased as she's my goddaughter. And now Violet is having a baby too, which is the best thing that could happen after losing Eddy.'

'I was so sorry to hear about that,' said Laura sincerely. 'You're close to all that family, aren't you?'

Kitty nodded. 'Mind you, the older brother, Frank, is driving me mad. He works at Derby House and so I see him all the time. He's an officer now and he's so strict, a real stickler for detail, and he drives me round the bend. Even though I should be grateful to him as he's found a bike for Tommy, he just has this way of getting my goat every time I see him.' She finished the rest of her drink in one go, suddenly feeling far too hot.

Laura raised her eyebrows and gave a lopsided grin. 'Well, well. Seems as if he really has got under your skin. Surely he can't be that bad? Haven't you known him all your life – is it only now that you see a different side to him?'

'Maybe,' said Kitty. 'Or else, I've grown up and he can't treat me like a little kid any more.' She blotted out the few times in the past when she'd thought he saw her potentially as something else. 'He's too annoying for words.'

'Interesting,' said Laura mildly. 'I've never seen you get het up like this about a man before. Are you sure that's all there is to it?'

Kitty frowned. 'Absolutely. Don't go looking at me like that. You're deliberately getting the wrong end of the stick. Anyway, he's spoken for – he's got a Wren girlfriend and she works at Derby House too.'

'A regular family business, that place,' said Laura, more cheerful now. 'Isn't another of your brothers there too, some super-sleuth type?'

Kitty, as ever, looked around before answering. She hated talking about what Danny actually did, even when there was nobody else about. Walls had ears.

'That kind of thing,' she said warily.

'We should introduce him to Marjorie one day,' mused Laura. 'She might have outgrown her preference for Canadian pilots and be ready to settle down with a nice British boffin type.'

Kitty had to laugh. 'He's the least boffin-like boffin you could ever meet. Anyway, she wouldn't like him. His hair's too dark. She always likes them fair-haired.'

'So she does.' Laura nodded sagely. 'I wonder where she is now.'

'Don't suppose we'll find out for a very long time,' said Kitty. 'I wasn't expecting to get any letters from her and I haven't. I don't think that should worry us too much, though.'

'No, I suppose not. No news is good news when it comes to Marjorie. She'll be doing a good job, whatever it is,' Laura said fervently. 'Oh, blast, look at the time. My train is due in fifteen minutes – not that I think it'll be on time, but I'd better be getting back to the station. Can't have Pa hanging around waiting for me, wondering where I've got to.'

They reached the platform and Kitty impulsively leant forward and hugged her friend. 'I'm so glad we managed to meet up like this, Laura. You must let me know what happens. If I have any bright ideas, I'll let you know too.'

Laura hugged her back. 'Thank you so much for coming out of your way like this. I feel miles better. Don't suppose you have any access to a phone? You being a telephone operator and all that?'

'No, you'd better not start calling Derby House, you'll start an international incident,' Kitty warned her. 'I wish we could take social calls, but it's out of the question. Rita was talking about getting a telephone for the shop but, what with Ellen arriving, nothing has happened.'

Laura picked up her bag. 'Well, see to it that you tell me if that changes. Meanwhile, don't go killing your annoying friend of the family. I'm sure he's far too valuable for the war effort.'

'I'll try,' said Kitty wryly as her friend stepped towards the approaching train for the north. She waved as Laura turned at the door and did the same. Trust Laura to pick up on the underlying reason she was so annoyed with him. She'd just have to work harder at resisting the effect he always seemed to have on her.

CHAPTER SEVENTEEN

The sun was beginning to set as the train drew into Lime Street. Kitty knew she should have thought of this but she'd just missed the previous train when saying farewell to Laura and had had to wait for the next one. She'd taken her book to the buffet, and to her relief it had emptied out a little and she'd found a corner in which to pass the time.

At least it wasn't like groping around in the dark down in Sussex. There were plenty of people about as she slowly descended the steps and began to head towards the bus stop. Her mind was whirring with what Laura had had to say. Was this peculiar note Freddy's way of making contact after all this time, or was her friend deluding herself, because she'd wanted it so badly for so long?

She was wandering along at the edge of the pavement when a car pulled up just ahead of her, almost against the kerb. The driver got out and came around the back of the vehicle, and she saw with a start that it was Alfie Delaney. She'd heard he was back but hadn't seen him. Tommy had been right – his head was a bit like a snooker ball.

'Kitty Callaghan, as I live and breathe,' he said, his smile wide and seemingly friendly. 'What brings you out at this time of the evening? Off to meet your boyfriend, are you?'

When she was younger, Kitty might have blushed and admitted that she didn't have one. She had an idea that this was exactly what Alfie would have liked her to do. Instead she turned to look at the car and then back at him. 'Didn't know you had a car, Alfie,' she said.

'Oh, you know me, Kitty, I can get my hands on most things I want if I try,' he replied, still keeping it friendly, but Kitty could tell there was an edge to what he said, even if he was trying to hide it. 'Are you heading back to Bootle? Fancy a lift?' He moved swiftly to the passenger side door and opened it.

If it had been just about anyone else, Kitty would have jumped at the chance. The evening was cooling rapidly and she'd only brought a light cardigan as she hadn't expected to be out so late. She drew it round her, but its lack of warmth wasn't enough to persuade her to accept his offer. Even in the dull twilight, the car didn't look in great shape. Being stuck with Alfie Delaney in a broken-down vehicle miles from home was all she needed.

'Thank you, but I'm going to meet a friend,' she said firmly.

It was as if she hadn't spoken. 'Go on, Kitty, get in, and then we can catch up on what we've been up to these past few years,' Alfie urged. 'You can tell me all about this new job everyone's talking about. Mam says you're doing well. And how's your Tommy? You know I'm getting him a bike, don't you?'

Kitty tried hard not to be flustered by that comment. He was just trying to make her feel like she owed him a favour, she could see that. 'He's very well,' she said, 'but he's already got a bike, so don't go putting yourself out, Alfie. I'd hate you to go to extra trouble.'

'Very kind of you, Kitty,' Alfie said, edging nearer, 'but then you were always the generous sort. Never hurt anyone, would you, Kitty?' His hand came forward and took hold of her arm. 'Why don't you get in the car and we can have a nice ride home, eh? You'd like that. I can tell.' His grip grew tighter.

Kitty knew she mustn't panic, but inside she was squirming at his horrible touch. What a disgusting man he was. If anything he'd got worse in the years since she'd last seen him, and she'd never liked him much before. You couldn't trust him as far as you could throw him. There was no question of her getting in the car with him.

'Like I said, Alfie, I'm not on my way home, so I shan't be needing a lift,' she said in what she hoped was a steady voice.

'Is that really true, Kitty?' His shifty eyes stared into hers. 'You wouldn't lie to me, would you? You wouldn't be trying to get rid of me?'

She tried to twist away but his grip was too strong. 'Alfie, let go of my arm,' she hissed. 'I have to go.'

He didn't, but pulled her closer to him. 'I thought

we could go for a drive,' he said. 'Bet you don't get the chance of that very often. None of you lot down Empire Street have got a car, have you? Still relying on old man Feeny and his horse and cart, that's what I heard.'

'There's nothing wrong with Pop's horse and cart,' snapped Kitty, stung at the insult to the man who had protected her like one of his own ever since she was eleven. She glanced around to see how many people were nearby. Though the light had faded, surely Alfie wouldn't try anything serious. She couldn't really believe that he wouldn't let her go, that he might try to force her into the car. All the same, a little shiver of fear wormed its way through her.

Alfie must have sensed it, because he gave her a horrible excuse for a smile. 'Come on, Kitty, don't hang about. We're missing the best part of the evening.'

She pulled her arm away harder and heard the fabric of her sleeve rip as she got free.

'Now look what you've done, Kitty. You've gone and ruined your nice cardigan,' Alfie scolded. 'You'll get cold now. Go on, get in, my car's nice and warm.'

Kitty backed away, still facing him. 'Go home, Alfie. I'm not getting in that car with you.'

Alfie made as if to take a step towards her, his expression now far from friendly, when abruptly he halted. There were footsteps behind her – with a slightly irregular rhythm. She swung around and there was Frank.

Her eyes widened. 'F . . . Frank!' Her mind spun, then she gathered her wits in a hurry. 'I was just coming to meet you. You . . . you took me by surprise coming from the other direction.' She widened her eyes at him and hoped he caught her meaning.

He stared for a moment but then cottoned on. 'Sorry I'm late,' he said smoothly. 'I was waylaid, I'll explain later.' He looked at Alfie. 'Mr Delaney. I'd heard you were back.'

'Alfie's just going,' said Kitty. 'Aren't you?' She glared at him.

For a moment she thought he would protest and even try to take out his frustration on Frank, but common sense seemed to prevail as he realised he was outnumbered and Kitty really had no intention of getting in the car with him. He turned on his heel without another word, got into the car and slammed the door heavily, before accelerating noisily away.

Kitty felt her shoulders sagging in relief. Frank caught her by the elbow and noticed the ripped wool.

'Good lord, Kitty, what's wrong? What did he do to you?' He could feel fury boiling inside him.

'It's nothing, it's nothing.' She took a couple of deep breaths. 'He just saw me walking along and wanted to give me a lift. He wasn't very happy when I said no.'

'But your arm,' said Frank, touching the rip in concern.

Kitty felt her flesh react to his touch, even as she tried to minimise the danger she'd been in. 'It's just an old cardie, it rips at the slightest thing. He didn't hurt me. Really, it's all right.' Now she was embarrassed and didn't want to cause a fuss.

'Damn him, Kitty, he's got no right to behave like that,' Frank fumed. 'I'm glad I came along when I did.'

'So am I,' Kitty admitted. 'Are you going back to your digs?'

'Yes. I'd been to the cinema with Sylvia and just walked her to her bus stop. Shall I walk you to yours? You are heading back to Bootle, aren't you?'

For a split second Kitty's heart dropped at the mention of Sylvia's name, then she told herself not to be silly and to be thankful that Frank had been out with the pretty young Wren, or he wouldn't have been here to come to her rescue. She should simply tell him to go on his way, that she was all right. But here he was, looking at her with those warm, caring eyes, and suddenly the thought of his company, even if only as far as the bus stop, seemed very appealing.

'Yes, please,' she said.

Tommy was pleased with his first session of PT. He could tell everyone was looking at him to see how he would cope, whether he was fit enough to cycle around the city all day. But years of helping on the farm had toned his muscles and he breezed through the exercises without a problem, barely breaking a sweat. He noticed one or two of the old timers nodding in approval. He wasn't the only new recruit, and a couple of them seemed to be struggling, which drew several disapproving glances. He was glad he'd got through that part of the morning.

Now he was out on his first real job. 'You do know

where this address is, don't you?' his supervisor had said, unsure about the new boy in his team.

'Oh, yes,' said Tommy confidently. 'It's around the corner from Oriel Road station. I know it like the back of my hand.' He'd set off at top speed, handling the red bike as if he'd had it for years, negotiating the potholes in the road, feeling the sun on his face. What a stroke of luck he'd got this job. He was going to enjoy himself, he could tell.

It took him no time at all to find the address and he swung himself off the bike, propping it against a low wall. This must be the door: a tarnished brass number 5 hung at a crooked angle above the letterbox. He rapped smartly on the wooden panel.

He noticed a net curtain twitch in the neighbouring house but couldn't see more than an outline of a figure behind it. Now he could hear the sound of footsteps and the door opened. In front of him stood a young woman, pretty, with long chestnut hair neatly plaited, but in a threadbare apron and a print dress frayed at the edges. She must be about Sarah's age. When she saw who he was, her face fell.

Tommy's mood of happiness evaporated as the meaning of what he was about to do hit home. He knew he couldn't show his feelings, though. He checked the name he'd been given and asked her: 'Mrs Pelham? Mrs Vincent Pelham?'

'Y-yes.' The woman held her head up but her eyes were already beginning to fill with tears.

Tommy handed her the telegram and she immediately scanned what it said. A single sob escaped her.

'Oh, no. Not my Vince. Not Vince.'

Tommy squirmed awkwardly. He shuffled his feet, not sure what to say.

The woman slumped against the doorframe and shut her eyes. Then, as if remembering where she was, she felt in her patch pocket and drew out a small coin. She handed it to him. 'For your trouble,' she said very quietly.

'Oh, no, I can't . . .' From the state of her clothes, Tommy could tell she could scarcely afford to part with even the lowest-value coin, but she grabbed his hand insistently and pressed it into his palm.

'Yes. Please take it. Vince would want me to.' Her teary eyes met his and he knew this was something she needed to do for her husband. He couldn't say no.

'Thank you, missus. Now I have to go.' He picked up his bike as quickly as he could, as the neighbour's net curtain twitched again. He hoped the neighbour was friendly and would help the devastated young woman, whose world he had just brought crashing down.

Cycling along past Oriel Road, he replayed the conversations he'd had with Danny and Kitty about this job, and how it would require responsibility and tact. He'd said 'yes' and 'of course' to them, but hadn't really thought what it would mean. Now he had a better idea of what they were on about and his heart sank. He knew he would see that woman's face in his dreams for a very long time.

CHAPTER EIGHTEEN

Danny picked up his pen from the kitchen table and scribbled in the final answer to the crossword in that day's newspaper. He should have spotted it ages ago – it turned out to be an anagram and he could usually recognise one as soon as he read it. He must be distracted, he thought. His mind was still on the meeting he'd been called in to that afternoon.

He heard the door open and flicked the newspaper over to the front page. The headline said that Paris had been liberated. That must be good news all round. The allies had been making further inroads all across France, but to win back the capital was a huge success and he couldn't help but smile at the account of the Parisians cheering the troops as they marched through the streets. It was enough to give everyone hope.

Kitty came through to the kitchen. 'You beat me home, Danny. My bus broke down, and I ended up walking some of the way.'

'Bad luck,' he said automatically, wondering how he was going to broach the subject of his news. He

213

hoped Kitty would understand and not be upset. It wasn't as if he had much choice, when it came down to it. 'The kettle's just boiled if you want a cuppa.'

'I'm far too hot,' moaned Kitty, taking the top sheet of the paper and fanning herself with it. Then she caught the headline and stopped. 'That's such good news, isn't it? That's a real milestone. Imagine what those people must be feeling after all that time. Did you read this page?'

'Of course,' said Danny. 'I was as keen to find out what was going on as you are. It's what we've all been hoping would happen for ages. We've got Hitler on the run, now. I didn't just turn straight to the crossword.'

'Well, you usually do,' Kitty pointed out, sinking into a chair on the opposite side of the table to her brother. It was still early evening and the light was shining through the back window. It was far too warm to argue for long. 'How was your day? You look as if there's something on your mind.'

Danny squirmed. How was it that his sister could tell when he was worried? He thought he was pretty good at hiding his feelings when he had to, but it never worked with Sarah or Kitty. 'Make me a cuppa and I'll tell you,' he suggested.

'Danny, you are the limit.' But she rose again and did as he asked, as she could now see something was wrong. She ran the cold tap, putting her wrists under the cool stream of water, and instantly felt better. Reaching for the milk, she asked, 'Where's Tommy?'

'He went across to ask Pop about something.'

Danny was bending the truth a little – he'd sent his younger brother over the road with a question about spare parts for bikes. He knew that there was a strong likelihood Dolly would offer him something to eat and he'd be out of the house for a while. He didn't want to share his news while his young brother was in the room.

'So, then,' said Kitty, setting down the teapot in front of him, 'out with it.' She pushed a stray dark curl out of her eye and sank back on to the chair.

Danny poured his tea, putting off the moment as long as he could. He slowly stirred it, adding a drop more milk to cool it down. He had no idea how his sister was going to react.

'The thing is,' he began, staring at the old table top. 'I was called in to see Commander Stephens today. He asked me to go on a course.'

Kitty looked at him. 'But that's good, isn't it? It shows that they rate you highly.'

Danny shrugged. 'That's as maybe. The trouble is, it's not around here. It's down south somewhere. An old house that's been taken over. Bletchley something or other.'

'Oh,' said Kitty. 'Will it be for long?'

'Depends,' said Danny. 'I might not be any good, for a start.'

'Well, they wouldn't send you if they thought that,' Kitty pointed out at once. She wasn't taken in by that for a moment.

'Then it looks as if it'll be for several weeks, if not months,' Danny said. 'They wouldn't tell me exactly.

And now I'm wondering if this – ' he pointed to the headline on the front page of the newspaper – 'will mean we won't be needed for much longer.'

'Or it might mean you're needed all the more,' Kitty said. 'We don't know, do we? I don't suppose they asked you if you wanted to go, did they? They'll have told you it's what you'll be doing, like it or not.'

Danny raised his hands and let them fall back to the table. 'Pretty well. Kitty, you know what it's like as well as I do. They've decided that certain people with certain skills need to learn new ones, and I'm to be one of them.'

Kitty met his gaze. 'Aren't you flattered, just a bit?' she asked. 'I would be.'

Danny turned away. 'Well, I suppose so.' That was part of the problem. He knew he was good at what he did, and so it was pretty gratifying for that to be recognised, and to be singled out for special training. Nobody had helped him get to this position. He hadn't had years of private schooling followed by university, unlike many of the others. He simply had the sort of brain that flourished when asked to solve strange puzzles. It was a source of great pride to him, as he was physically unable to serve his country in any other way. 'But what about Tommy? He's only just come home and begun that job. Now I'll be leaving you in the lurch to look after him again.'

Kitty sighed. That was the first thing she had thought of too – how could she keep an eye on the boy when she worked all hours? Then she sat up straight. 'We'll think of something,' she said. 'You mustn't worry about us. Tommy's older now, and he's got his work to keep him busy. He won't have the time or energy to get into scrapes.' She hoped this was true. 'I can sort something out with Dolly or Rita if I'm on night shift. We've managed before, we can do it again.'

Danny's face relaxed with relief. 'Do you think you can, really? It would be a load off my mind if I knew that you two would be all right while I was away.'

'Of course we will be,' said Kitty, more sure now. 'Look at how many other people get by – we're lucky. Our house hasn't been damaged, we've got friends and neighbours nearby, and both Tommy and I are working with money coming in.'

Danny nodded. 'That's true, of course. But I know we've only just begun to settle down as a family again, and now something else happens to turn everything upside down.'

Kitty's expression was rueful. 'That's war, though, isn't it? You never know what you'll be called upon to do. Besides, it won't be for ever.'

Danny got up, draining his tea. 'Let's go over and tell Tommy, and then Dolly and Pop can hear it at the same time.'

As he and Kitty reached for their jackets, he admitted to himself that they could tell Sarah too. He didn't know what she'd think. He knew he'd miss her – their regular talks, the way she quietly helped out behind the scenes, how much he'd come to rely on her steady friendship as a constant in his day-to-day life. There was nothing to be done, though. He had to go.

Kitty ran her hands through her curls, shielding her face from Danny. She couldn't let his news rattle her. Her thoughts had flown to Alfie and the sly way he'd looked at her. Danny wouldn't be around to protect her from any more unwelcome threats from the horrible man. She'd just have to be careful. Anyway, that incident outside the station had been an accident; he hadn't planned it, and she shouldn't go worrying over something that most likely wasn't going to happen. She certainly shouldn't worry Danny about it. Their job now was to reassure Tommy. Kitty picked up her handbag and they headed out to break Danny's exciting news to the others.

'What time shall I meet you, Patty?' asked the Wren with the tight brown curls, calling across the yard to her friend.

'Better make it seven thirty,' Patty shouted back, locking the door on the black car she'd been driving American officers around in all day. 'Don't suppose we need to ask you, do we?' she said pointedly to Laura. 'I dare say you've got something far better arranged for this evening. Whatever we do, it won't be good enough for the likes of you.' Without waiting for a reply she strode across the yard to Patty, little puffs of dust rising into the air from her brisk footprints.

Laura sighed but made no move to follow the two young women, now glancing back over their shoulders and laughing in a deliberate way so that they knew she'd see and hear them. They were trying her patience, but she wouldn't let them realise how annoying she found them. That would be exactly what they wanted. They were being childish, and so she had to do the decent thing and act like an adult around them. She was barely older than they were, but she felt at least twice their age.

Shaking her head, she locked up her own car and began the tiresome walk back to her digs. The streets were very hot after the long summer's day, but even so she preferred this form of transport to the crowded buses or the Underground. Heat rose off the paving stones in wavy lines, making her dizzy. She paused by a doorway. It had been bomb-damaged, like so much else around the area. Nearby windows were boarded up and there were gaps in the terrace towards the end of the road. She could see the exposed walls of the neighbouring house, and the bright colours of the wallpaper that would once have decorated the bedroom and living-room walls. She wondered what had happened to the family who'd lived there. Had they made it to a shelter on time? It always struck her as sad, thinking of someone choosing that pattern, painting the skirting boards, making a home for their children. Now it was open to everyone's gaze.

Further along there was a doorway to the street set a little further back, and in the sunlight she couldn't be sure if there was a figure in it or not. Yes, there was somebody. Maybe some poor soul who'd been bombed out, surveying the remains of a family home. As she approached, she saw it was a man; he straightened up from where he had been leaning against the doorjamb.

'Laura!' The voice was husky, as if he had been breathing in the dust that was everywhere. 'I say, Laura! Over here!'

Laura stopped dead. A chill ran down her back despite the heat of the day.

'Laura!' The voice was louder.

She stared ahead. This couldn't be happening; she was imagining things. Time seemed to stand still as she gazed in disbelief; all the hustle and bustle of the surrounding city faded into silence as she focused on the figure in the doorway.

'Laura,' the voice said again. 'You aren't seeing things, it really is me, Freddy.'

She ran forward towards him, suppressing a sob as she acknowledged that it was truly Freddy, that dear, familiar figure she'd known all her life. She tried to take in the changes in her handsome brother since last she'd seen him – he was thinner and standing not quite straight, his face etched with worry. His tousled hair was uneven, and did not quite fully mask a deep red scar on his head. Yet she would have known him anywhere. It was Freddy. It really was her long-lost brother Freddy.

She gasped as the full recognition hit her. 'It's you. It *is* you. Oh, good lord. I can't believe it. It's you, you're here.' She put out a hand to touch his arm, as if to make certain he wasn't a figment of her imagination. 'Oh, Freddy, where have you been? What's happened to you? How did you get back? Are you all right? Your poor head. Do Ma and Pa know? How long have you been back?'

'Steady on, old girl.' Freddy's face broke into an amused smile, revealing deep laughter lines at the corners of his eyes. 'One thing at a time.'

She took in the sight of him, in his creased and faded blue shirt, trousers rolled up as if they weren't his and didn't quite fit, belt pulled tight because he was too thin for the waistband. This was not the dapper Freddy she remembered. What must he have been through to appear so changed? But she didn't care. He was back; her beloved, aggravating, dearest brother was alive after all. She had dreamed of this moment but scarcely dared to hope it could ever come true. Now here he was, standing on the pavement of a residential street in northwest London.

'Yes, sorry. Yes, of course. But all the same, how? When and what have you . . . no, I've a better idea,' she said, trying to organise her tumbling thoughts. 'There's a decent pub around the next corner. Let's go there. They've got a garden at the back and we can be cool there and you can tell me everything. Can you do that? Have you got time?'

He laughed. 'As long as you're paying. I've just about got what I'm standing up in at the moment. I'll treat you next time, once they've sorted me out. I'm on my way to being debriefed – the War Office know I'm back, but I had to see you first before I'm sent back to my unit. I expect they'll get all the information out of me first, before they give me a decent set of clothes and a bit of spare cash.'

He was smiling, but she could tell he was tired, that this was all a bit of an effort. She offered him her arm and together they rounded the corner and found the little pub, set back from the road, almost empty apart from a few older customers who had called in for a quick drink after their working day.

'You go and find somewhere quiet to sit in the shade and I'll get you a nice beer,' she offered, but he gave her a look she remembered from their childhood that meant he wasn't happy being told what to do.

'I'm not quite an invalid, you know,' he said mildly. 'Can't have a girl ordering the drinks, even if she is my stroppy little sister.'

Laura almost argued back out of deeply ingrained habit, but then could see that his pride would be hurt unless she gave way. So for once she didn't press the point, but let him speak to the barman and carry the glasses out to the garden, where they saw that the table in the corner was free. She waited until he was seated comfortably before taking the wooden bench opposite. There was a gentle breeze blowing the leaves of the neatly trimmed privet hedge. She waited for a moment to see if he would start, but then her patience ran out. 'Well? What's happened? Where were you, when did you get back and how did you know where I'd be . . .'

'All right, Laura, I'll start at the beginning and tell you as much as I can remember,' he said, giving way to the inevitable, 'but I warn you, there will be gaps. You'll have noticed I'm not quite the man I was, and there are some bits of the story I simply can't remember. So go easy on me.' He rubbed his hand across his face and blond hair, making more of it stick up.

'Of course, of course,' said Laura, eager to reassure him and to know more as soon as possible.

'Well . . . I was sent on a mission to fly over France,' he began haltingly. Then, as if the floodgates had opened, he described waking up in a field, his plane on fire beside him, faces staring down at him, speaking a language he could barely understand. The people had argued about whether to leave him, and some of them thought he was already dead. Then the one who appeared to be their leader came closer, realised he was still breathing, and ordered a piece of sacking to be fetched to use as a stretcher. He had been taken to a nearby barn. There he had stayed, he had no idea for how long. He'd drifted in and out of consciousness and had been so ill he hadn't even worried about where he was or if he was safe.

That had come later, when slowly he had begun to stay awake for long enough to understand he was a problem for the people looking after him. Several women had brought food and water, and he had woken one day and noticed he was in clean but threadbare clothes, not anything he recognised as his own. He still didn't understand much of what they were saying, but he was gradually catching more and more of it, piecing together fragments of their conversation with snippets that came back to him from lessons at school. But when he tried to think about his school, he couldn't remember where it was or when he'd been there. He could remember almost nothing, in fact. Try as he might, he couldn't even manage his own name. He became aware of the

223

seasons changing, working out that he must have been hidden in that remote barn for months on end – if not longer.

Laura's hand went to her mouth to stop herself from crying out. She knew she would have been terrified if such a thing had happened to her. It was unthinkable, her poor brother lying wounded and far from home, unable to do anything to help himself. 'What happened then?' she prompted gently.

'Slowly, really slowly, I began to improve,' he said. 'I started to talk back to them in French. I tried to help them out in small ways. I could see they were taking a big risk in hiding me. If I had been discovered by the enemy, or if someone had betrayed my whereabouts, they could have been killed. I owe them my life. Once I was up and about, able to move on my own, I started to do things for them around the farm, but I still didn't know who I was. One or two of them spoke a little English, and of course they knew I was British from my pilot's uniform. They'd had to burn that – well, they said that it was pretty burnt anyway after the plane crash. They'd try to get me to talk about my past, but it was like there was a big curtain drawn across everything before that day.

'I tried to ask where I was and they brought me a map. It was a very rough one, and of course all in French, but it made sense to me. Then I began to remember – not my name or where I was from, but that I'd been taught about maps.'

'That makes sense, you must have done heaps of navigation training,' Laura said, taking a drink from her glass. It wasn't quite a cocktail from the admiral's cabinet, but it would do. 'Go on.'

'It was very strange, the way all that detail returned but not the personal stuff,' Freddy said, shaking his head slowly. 'I told them what sort of things I'd learnt about and they began to ask me more and more. It became clear after a while that they wanted me to join them.'

'Join them? Doing what? Being a farmer?'

'No, silly,' Freddy said with a familiar mix of affection and exasperation. 'All right, I did do chores around the farm as so many of the young men who'd done the work before weren't around any more.'

'Just like home,' said Laura.

'But to be honest I wasn't very good,' he admitted. 'I still had trouble walking properly – I'd taken this huge bash to the head, as you can see, and I'd been burned a fair bit. All that time of lying still had affected my muscles too. I could barely lift a spade to begin with.' He sighed. 'No, what they really wanted me for was my map reading and knowledge of navigation. They were with the Resistance, you see.'

Laura nodded. It made sense now. 'So you stayed with them? Didn't you want to try to get home?'

Freddy shrugged apologetically. 'I might have, if I could have said where home was. But I honestly couldn't. So I thought the best thing to do was stay with them and be of use that way. I didn't know who to contact, and unless I stayed hidden I was a risk to them. So I kept below the radar, literally.'

Laura tried to understand what it must have been

like, but it was a struggle. Part of her wondered if Freddy hadn't really wanted to get back to his old life. Perhaps he hadn't wanted to let their parents or her know he was still alive and with the underground in France. Yet at the same time she told herself not to be so stupid. None of it had been his fault, and he'd ended up fighting the Nazis in a way that few others could have done.

'It would have been almost impossible to have got me back to Blighty,' he explained, sensing her concern. 'I had no papers, nothing. Everything that could have identified me went up in flames in the crash, they told me. So bit by bit I became involved in their organisation, making new maps, advising them, that sort of thing, and doing some translation too when my French got much better. I'm pretty fluent now,' he said with a grin. 'One of the perks.'

Laura frowned. 'What changed, then? Was it D-day?'

'Things had been going our way for a while, but out in the countryside it was often hard to tell,' he said. 'Getting exact news was very hit and miss. But yes, finally the Allies got near and I knew it was safe to try to get home. My memory was returning and I could recall my name, where I was from, and what I'd been doing before that final mission. I even remembered I had a sister and that she could be a frightful pain.'

Laura punched him on the arm. 'You deserved that,' she admonished him. 'So you sent me that note, then? How did you know where I'd be?'

Freddy lifted his pint of beer and took a long drink. He nodded. 'This is something I've been looking forward to for a long time, I don't mind telling you,' he said. 'Nothing beats a pint of proper beer. You should taste what they have in France. The wine is lovely but the beer, oh dear.'

Laura looked at him. 'I'm sure you're right. But go on, how did you know how to get that note to me? Why all the cloak-and-dagger business?'

Freddy glanced down as he set the pint back on the rickety table and his expression grew sheepish. 'Actually, there's a rum story behind it. One hell of a coincidence, you could say.'

Laura's face was quizzical. 'What was that? Freddy, out with it. I nearly went crazy when I got that note.'

Freddy's face fell. 'Oh, I'm terribly sorry. I thought you'd work it out. I didn't do it to make you cross, it's just that I had to be vague in order not to put anyone in the line of contact in jeopardy.'

'All right, I see that. And I hoped it was you, I just didn't know how it could have been. So what's the coincidence?'

A faraway look came into his eyes. 'It's the most peculiar thing. I met someone who knew you.'

'Knew me? In deepest France? How on earth . . .?'

'She was one of us, she was brought in for a special mission,' he explained. 'It had to be her, she was one of only a few who could have done it as she spoke both German and French so well she could pretend to be either. She was pretty good, actually. Very impressive.'

Laura gasped. 'That's . . . no, it can't be. Marjorie? You met Marjorie?'

Freddy nodded. 'I know. How unlikely is that?'

'Of all the Resistance cells in all the world,' drawled Laura, but stopped when she realised Freddy didn't have a clue what she meant. 'Sorry. That is incredible, I can't quite take it in. So you got to know her?'

That look came back into Freddy's eyes again. 'Yes, you could say that. Erm, quite well, actually.'

'Freddy!' Laura's eyes widened. 'No, you didn't – you and Marjorie? Really?' Yet, now she came to think of it, it had a certain rightness to it. Marjorie and her liking for blond airmen – many years ago she'd even danced with a Canadian who had a definite look of Freddy about him, which had shaken Laura to the core. This made sense in a totally impossible kind of way. 'So she could tell you where I worked . . .'

'Yes, and I confess we persuaded someone on the receiving end of some of our messages over here to seek you out and pass you a note,' he said. 'I realise it's a roundabout way of doing things, but we couldn't put the chain of information in danger. Your friend is a dab hand at signals, she could set up wireless transmissions and they'd be picked up over here. She really was terribly good at her job.'

Laura finally picked up on what he was saying. 'Wait a minute. Was? Isn't she any more? Freddy, is she all right?'

Her brother wouldn't meet her eyes. 'The truth is, I don't know,' he said quietly. 'The arrangements were all made to get me out at last. We got that message sent to you. I knew where to go to find you – I just had to wait near where you girls park your cars, and Bob's your uncle. That part of the plan worked like clockwork.' He seemed to be shaking a little. 'What happened was, I was moved in the last few days, so I could get away more safely. I was in territory held by the Allies right at the end. But Marjorie was needed behind enemy lines, you see. So she went off on a new mission. And . . . we didn't hear anything. We thought we would. That she'd get a message through of some kind. But nobody has heard.'

'Oh, Freddy.' Laura didn't know what to say. It was bad enough to discover that her friend had made it as far as France and was excelling at her job, only to find something had gone wrong; but how much worse would it be for Freddy? Her brother, who had been through four years of unimaginable hell, had found a kindred spirit, only to lose her.

'She might be all right,' Laura said staunchly, knowing this was echoing what she had thought about Freddy himself all those long years. 'She's fearfully clever, Freddy. You never know.'

'No,' he said, looking away, but not before she'd noticed the tear in his eye. 'That's the thing, isn't it? We don't know.'

CHAPTER NINETEEN

Tommy stuck his hands in his pockets and tried to whistle, but his mouth was dry. The wind had got up, bringing the familiar smell of the river into the streets around the docks. Autumn was here, and he wondered where he'd left his scarf. Kitty wouldn't be happy with him if he needed a new one.

He'd finished work and would normally have cycled back on the bike Frank had managed to get him, but its tyres needed pumping up and he hadn't been able find the pump this morning, so he had caught the bus instead. He hoped he hadn't lost the pump for good – that would be another thing Kitty would be cross about. It was the whole business of having to get up so early and in to work on time – he still wasn't used to it, and as the mornings began to get darker it was harder still. He'd managed not to be late so far, as he couldn't have borne the shame of it, but it was touch and go. It didn't leave any spare time to find anything he'd mislaid.

He hadn't really noticed the change of temperature and the note of chill in the air as he cycled about the city on his rounds. He was too busy, and needed to move as fast as possible between jobs, so he was plenty warm enough. He was gradually getting used to the notion that he was a harbinger of bad news, and as the Allies continued their successes in France, the stream of casualties kept rising. Now that he was strolling along he began to shiver.

A car drew up.

'All right, Tommy?'

Tommy looked up. It was Alfie Delaney. He wondered if he could get away without answering, but there weren't many people around and he couldn't exactly pretend he hadn't seen him. 'Hello, Alfie,' he said cautiously.

'How's the new job going?' Alfie asked, leaning across the front seat and talking through the wound-down passenger window. 'Got the hang of it yet?'

'I think so,' said Tommy, brightening. 'There's lots to do and I have to get it right every time, so I'm very busy.'

'I bet you are,' said Alfie approvingly. 'Tell you what, I'd love to hear more about it. Why don't you get in? We could go somewhere and you can tell me what you get up to. How about that?'

Tommy hesitated. He wasn't at all sure spending time with Alfie would be a good idea. On the other hand, Kitty wouldn't be back yet and he'd be kicking his heels around the house on his own, now that Danny had gone on his course down south. Alfie's car would be warmer than the street as well. 'All right,' he said and climbed in.

'I reckon that you're a proper man now you've got a full-time job,' Alfie said, slipping into gear. 'We should go to the pub, celebrate you not being a boy any longer.'

'What, the Sailor's Rest?' asked Tommy, his voice rising in alarm. He'd never been in a pub and knew Kitty would have a fit if she found out – and if they went to the pub at the end of Empire Street, it was a one hundred per cent certainty that she would.

'No, no, we can do better than that,' said Alfie, not mentioning the real reason he didn't want to go there – he'd been banned ages ago, after the poisonous meat episode.

'Bent Nose Jake's, then?' Tommy asked. That was the second-nearest pub, and he knew Danny used to go there, but he'd said it was a bit rough. When Danny said somewhere was a bit rough, it was definitely true. It took a lot to shock Danny. Tommy wasn't sure it was a place he particularly wanted to go to.

'Trust me, Tommy,' said Alfie easily. 'No, you don't want to go down there. I know a new place so we can have a nice private word. No chance of anyone from Empire Street seeing you – that's what's on your mind, isn't it?'

Tommy muttered but didn't want to admit it out loud. He'd sound like a boy, no matter what Alfie said. He gazed out of the window as the ruined streets of Bootle went by, so many of the houses damaged or destroyed by the raids of the blitz.

Alfie pulled off the dock road and on to a side street, coming to a halt by a brick building with a newly painted sign outside. Tommy squinted at it but the breeze had got up and the sign swung too much for him to pick out what was on it. Alfie didn't want to wait around. 'Come on, Tom. Get your skates on. Sooner we get inside, the sooner we can have something to warm us up good and proper.'

Tommy leapt out and Alfie urged him inside. It was a dimly lit room, with a wooden counter in the corner, and a couple of mirrors that hung behind it over some shelves which held a few bottles. Tommy thought that for his first pub, it was a bit miserable. Still, Alfie was buying.

'What's your poison?'

Tommy hesitated. He knew he should say lemonade, but he could get that from Kitty. 'I'll have a beer,' he said boldly.

'Pint of your finest,' said Alfie to the barman with a broad wink. The barman glared at him but made no comment about Tommy's age. 'Come to think of it, make it two.'

The barman grunted and slowly pulled two pints. Alfie picked up the glasses and carried them over to a table on the far side of the room, away from the big window at the front.

'There you go, Tom. Get stuck in to that.'

Tommy sipped at the drink and had to stop himself from pulling a face. He'd snatched swigs of beer before, whenever there had been parties at home – the last time had been for little Ellen's christening. He didn't mind the stuff Danny got in bottles. This wasn't as nice, it was bitter and smelt odd, but Alfie seemed to like it. He was smiling broadly, though Tommy couldn't make out what he was so happy about.

Alfie began by cross-examining Tommy about every aspect of the job – the bike, the PT beforehand, the bosses, the other telegraph boys, what it was like to be the bearer of bad news. He seemed sympathetic enough, and Tommy began to grow more at ease. The beer was slipping down nicely. 'Tom, what a thirst you have on you,' Alfie observed. 'Must be all that cycling around. I'll get you another.' He was back at the bar before Tommy could object. Never mind, it was warm in here, even if the floor was a bit sticky.

Alfie put the fresh pint in front of him and carried on with his questions. Tommy's answers grew longer and more rambling. Alfie didn't seem to mind. 'And how are things at home now?' he wondered. 'Settled back in, have you?'

'It's nice,' said Tommy. 'A bit quiet. Kitty's always at work.'

'And what about Danny?' asked Alfie innocently.

'Oh, he's on some course thing,' said Tommy. Didn't Alfie already know that? Half of Bootle seemed to. 'He's off staying in an old house somewhere down south. So it's even quieter.'

'Must be a bit on the slow side for a young fellow like you,' Alfie sympathised.

Tommy shrugged.

'It's just you and Kitty there, then. I'd be bored if I were you.' Alfie took a swig of his drink, which didn't seem to be going down very quickly.

'S'all right,' Tommy said, and burped loudly. He

wiped his mouth with the back of his hand. Good job Kitty wasn't here to see him.

'Her boyfriend doesn't come round often, then?' Alfie asked.

'Boyfriend?' Tommy looked at him, puzzled. 'No, you got that wrong. Kitty hasn't got a boyfriend.'

'Oh,' said Alfie, keeping any emotion from his voice. 'My mistake. Only a while back in town one night, I thought she was meeting what's-his-name, used to live near you.' He drummed his fingers on the table, as if trying to remember. 'Frank. Frank Feeny.'

Tommy laughed and spilt some of his beer. 'Oh, no, you got that very wrong. He's not her boyfriend.'

'No?' Alfie looked doubtful. 'They seemed very friendly.'

Tommy shook his head. 'They are friends; he's like another brother to all of us. That's all. I'd know if not. I think he's got a girlfriend anyway, from where he works.' He gave a small hiccough. Alfie didn't seem to be sitting as steadily on his stool as he had been. His outline was becoming a little blurry. The whole room felt blurry. It wasn't unpleasant, just odd.

'Careful now, Tommy,' said Alfie. 'Nearly came off your seat there, you did. Don't want you cracking your head on the floor now, do we?'

Tommy grunted. He was feeling odder still.

'Well, I'm sure you're right about Kitty,' said Alfie. He realised he'd overplayed his hand. He had planned to get Tommy on his side, maybe persuade him to report back on when Kitty's shifts were or which friends she was seeing, so he could get a better idea

235

of her movements, but the boy must be completely unused to drink as he was swaying where he sat. 'Come on, best get you back. I've places to go, I can't be sitting around drinking beer all evening, much as I'd like to.' He hauled Tommy to his feet and guided him across the near-empty bar and back to the car.

Tommy gave up after a few attempts to continue the conversation and dozed off, coming to with a start as Alfie pulled up at the kerb on the corner of the dock road, just down from the junction with Empire Street.

'I'll drop you here if you don't mind,' he said. 'Save me going out of my way. You all right to walk back from here?'

Tommy shrugged and squinted hard to make out where he was. It looked familiar. 'Yes, course,' he said, trying to open the car door and failing. Alfie leant across and did it for him.

'Right you are then.'

Tommy scrambled out of the car and stood unsteadily. 'Ummm . . . thanks, Alfie.' Kitty would be pleased with him, remembering his manners like that, he thought. The cold breeze reddened his cheeks and helped sober him up a little as he turned to wave goodbye.

'Make sure you tell Kitty I was asking after her,' called Alfie as he sped off.

Tommy wasn't sure he would say anything of the sort. He would have to explain where and how he'd been talking to Alfie, and he knew that would be a bad idea. He made his way along the main road and turned up into Empire Street, his feet unsteady. He wove along, narrowly avoiding falling over his shoelaces.

Sarah stood at the top of the road, watching the swaying figure's progress, growing more alarmed by the second as she realised who it was. At first she thought she must be mistaken. The person was obviously drunk and it couldn't be Tommy – he was far too young to get served in a pub. And yet the closer he got, the plainer his identity became. Sarah groaned under her breath. She couldn't let him cope on his own. Even though she was exhausted after a shift that had gone on three hours longer than it should have, she knew it was her duty to see to him. Kitty wouldn't be home yet and now there was no Danny to help his little brother.

Tommy looked up at her as he approached, his face confused. He squinted as if trying to make out who she was. 'Sarah,' he said at last.

'Well done, Tommy,' she said in exasperation. 'Who did you think it was? Of course it's me.'

'Nurse's coat,' Tommy said, pointing.

'Yes, I've just come from work.' Sarah stepped closer and then recoiled at the smell of alcohol. 'Tommy, where have you been? You've been drinking, haven't you?'

'I . . . I . . .' Tommy appeared to be trying to explain but not getting very far.

'Don't bother, I can see you have been,' Sarah said firmly. 'Right, we'd best get you indoors. Do you have your key?' Danny had told her they'd got one cut for his little brother for his first week at work, reasoning that if he was responsible enough to deliver telegrams, then he could be trusted with his own door key. Tommy had been proud and tied it to a cord around his neck. Now he brought it out.

'I can do it,' he said, but as he stumbled to the front door he missed the keyhole by a mile. He tried again but it was no good.

Sarah reached over. 'Here. Let me.' The sooner he was inside the better. She didn't want anyone else to see him in this state – the likes of Vera Delaney would have a field day, and Kitty and Danny would like as not get the blame. She didn't want that.

She took him by the shoulders and guided him into the kitchen, where she lit the gas lamp and bent to set fire to the kindling left in the grate. Tommy slumped into a chair and rested his head on the table. 'I'm not very well,' he moaned.

'No, you're drunk,' Sarah pointed out. 'Here, have a glass of water. Now, tell me, what's going on?'

Tommy looked up at her and clearly decided he wasn't going to get away with not explaining what had happened. So he recounted meeting Alfie and agreeing to get in the car, and ending up at the pub with him. 'I didn't mean anything by it,' he said mournfully. 'He was being nice, that's all.'

Sarah gazed up at the ceiling in frustration. 'Tommy, this is Alfie Delaney we're talking about. He's never nice – or if he is there'll be some other reason behind it. What did he want?'

Tommy's face contorted with the effort of remembering. 'Wanted to know about my job,' he said slowly. 'And asked if Kitty had a boyfriend. I said no, she didn't.'

Sarah gave an involuntary shiver. The man had had no business taking Tommy into a pub – he was far too young. Maybe, just maybe, he'd done it as a gesture of friendship, she told herself. Then she shook her head. That wasn't likely. What had he really wanted? It was unlikely to be anything good.

The boy had almost dozed off at the table. 'Tommy, when is Kitty due back?' She shook him by the shoulder.

'Dunno,' he said dully, slumping back down against the table. He looked pathetically young in the dim gaslight.

Sarah thought quickly. 'You should have something to eat, soak up all the beer,' she said. 'I'll go home and see what Mam has got and bring something over. All right? Probably best you don't come over and let everyone see you like this.'

Tommy mumbled something and Sarah took it for agreement. She didn't want to leave him alone, but knew that Dolly would have a fit if she knew the boy was in this state. That wouldn't help matters. If she could nip across and grab a bowl of something hot, she might manage to help him improve a little before Kitty returned. She couldn't leave him alone for long though. What if he was sick? She was pretty sure he wasn't used to alcohol. He'd never been allowed it at home, or not officially anyway, and there was no way on earth that

Joan and Seth would have given him any. She could not tell how much he'd had now, but she wanted to keep an eye on him, or at least until his sister finished her shift. Sarah knew from several cases at the hospital how dangerous a large intake of alcohol could be. She couldn't bear the thought of anything happening to Tommy.

She let herself out of the front door and made sure it was left so she could easily come back in. Moonlight was now flooding Empire Street, picking out all the details of the bomb damage – the missing tiles, splintered frames and the empty space where a house had once stood. She leant against the wall for a moment. If only Danny were here.

Briefly she closed her eyes. She missed him, and he hadn't even been gone for very long. She'd come to rely on their almost daily conversations, his humour, the knowledge that she could ask him anything – and that he would ask her too. There had been a bond between them for years. She had been the only one apart from him and the doctors who had known about his heart condition, and he'd sworn her to secrecy. She'd said nothing to anyone until the accident, when he'd been so badly affected and the cat was well and truly out of the bag.

She also knew, although Danny hadn't realised she knew, that Alfie had some underhand interest in him. That was one reason she was so alarmed that Alfie had sought out Tommy. She'd overheard the occasional comment over the years and put two and two together. That was why Alfie's return could not mean anything good.

She was also deeply uneasy about his ongoing interest in Kitty. However, she wasn't sure what she could do about it. In the usual run of things she would have immediately turned to Danny for advice, or as a sounding board to talk through her own thoughts. Sometimes he understood her better than she did herself. She realised she'd taken this for granted; it was as normal as breathing, until the day he'd packed his bags and gone on that blasted course.

Sarah had always known that she had strong feelings for Danny, but, being an unusually steady and responsible teenager, she'd told herself that things might change as she got older and she should do nothing hasty. After all, the Feenys and the Callaghans had grown up almost as one big family, so it was no wonder she felt so close to him. Then her sister Rita had married his brother Jack, to further cement the bonds between them.

But the feelings she now had for him were anything but sisterly. She had to admit it. While he was here every day she could go on as usual, enjoying his company, trusting him with her innermost thoughts, loving the way they seemed to agree on just about everything. Now he wasn't here she was lonely even in the midst of her friends, family and colleagues. None of them came close to him.

She couldn't tell him about Tommy now. What would he do if he read about this evening in a letter? He'd worry, but be unable to come up to sort things out, and that would be the worst of all worlds. It was better to say nothing. Kitty could make that decision, if it came to it. She could just imagine Danny's fury, fuelled by deep concern for his young brother. She knew how responsible he felt for him, how anxious he'd been that this course would take him away just when he was needed at home.

Did Danny feel the same about her as she did for him? She didn't know. She wouldn't force the issue when he came back. She dreaded losing his friendship, and suspected that he still thought of her as another sister. Besides, he was so clever. Nobody had recognised this when he was growing up, least of all his teachers, but now look at him, doing this really hard hush-hush job and being sent off to learn even more complicated work. He might think she was too stupid for him. She had been no great shakes at school either, but she loved what she did and nursing came easily to her. That was enough for her; but would it be enough for Danny?

Sarah looked up at the moon. Time to go and see what her mother had in the way of a meal so she could make sure Tommy recovered from his ordeal. Her feelings for Danny would have to wait – but they showed no signs of going away.

CHAPTER TWENTY

Nancy had arrived back later than she'd planned, having stayed longer at the Parkers' house than usual. Georgie was quiet, too cold to talk for once. Nancy had some thinking to do. Maggie Parker, as was, had always been kind and accommodating, but she'd pointed out they couldn't go on minding Georgie as often any more. Nancy had agreed because she'd had no choice. She didn't want them thinking she was taking advantage of their goodness, though in some ways she knew she was.

'He's spending almost as much time here as he is at his own house,' Maggie had said forthrightly. 'He's a lovely little soul, don't get me wrong, but it's getting to the stage where I can't go out when I need to because he's here again. We'll have to get him his own ration book soon.'

'I'm sorry, I hadn't realised,' Nancy had murmured, deeply embarrassed. She knew she'd have to think again about how she would manage things.

She considered her other options. Violet was growing

bigger and bigger, her own baby nearly due, and so her mother's house revolved around getting everything done before the child arrived. Any spare time was taken up with looking after Ellen, now crawling and getting in the way of everyone. On top of that Dolly sometimes saw to Tommy's evening meal as well, if Kitty was on lates. Nancy tapped her front teeth with one of her elegant nails. Tommy liked Georgie. Maybe he would like to mind him when he finished work? She could pay him a few pennies, make it worth his while. She'd think about it.

'Is that you?' called the hated voice of her mother-in-law.

'Here, Georgie, let me have your coat,' Nancy said, bending to help unbutton the toggles on the duffel coat that her son was fast outgrowing. 'Of course it is,' she shouted over her shoulder. 'Who else would it bloody be?' she muttered under her breath. It wasn't as if the woman had any close friends who might come round. Her general air of spite and misery had made sure of that.

The Parkers had fed Georgie, and so Nancy took him up to bed, tucking him in, pulling the curtains against the bright moonlight. She looked at his pinched face as it turned on his threadbare pillow. He looked like his father, which sometimes gave her a jolt. The child had never even met him. Nancy gave a little shiver. She tried not to think about Sid if she could help it. There was nothing she could do about his situation anyway. She ran her hand over her son's brow, and murmured to him to sleep tight. Then she slipped quietly from the room and down to the front parlour, which was hers alone.

Lighting the mean amount of kindling in the grate, she pulled a chair close to it and drew out her precious letter. There was just enough light to reread it by. She savoured its short message.

Gary would be home for Christmas. He'd finally found time to write to her properly and he said he'd been thinking of her all the while, as his unit fought its way across France, liberating the people and advancing the Allied cause. The knowledge that she was there back in England waiting for him had driven him onward, giving him a reason to survive. 'I hope you'll be giving me a warm welcome,' he'd said, and a little tremble of anticipation shot through her. It wasn't exactly a passionate letter on the face of it, but she could read between the lines. Gary was clever – he'd know that the censor would read it first and would have no wish to embarrass her by being any more graphic. But she could tell what he meant all right. Well, far be it from her to deny a fighting hero his comforts when he made it back.

Carefully she refolded the letter and tucked it inside a book on the shelves beside the mantelpiece. The *Encyclopaedia Britannica* – it wasn't very likely that her mother-in-law would look in there. She barely lifted the newspaper, even though her usually absent husband worked on the *Liverpool Post* on permanent night shift. Nancy nodded in satisfaction. It might be pie in the sky, but she had begun to dream that Gary would somehow get her out of this cold, loveless place, rescue her from Mrs Kerrigan's meanness and the soulless existence she'd got used to. Who knew what might happen once he came home?

Kitty hated it when she got back so late that she didn't have time to make a meal for Tommy. If she knew she would be working well past when he usually ate, she cooked the night before and left a pot of stew on the cold shelf in the larder, along with a note on the kitchen table to remind him to heat it up. The problem came when she was asked to stay on at the end of a normal day shift, which wasn't uncommon. She could hardly say no. It was never for a trivial reason and she knew it was her duty to agree.

Tommy wouldn't be going hungry; Dolly would see that he ate something hot, or if she was busy then someone else would step in. Kitty wasn't worried that her little brother would starve. It was more that cooking for them both and then eating together gave her a chance to talk to him, to find out how his work was going, to see if there had been any difficult deliveries in the day, and to check that there had been no repeat of the episode Sarah had told her about.

Kitty had felt a wave of panic when she'd heard. How dared Alfie take Tommy out and get him drunk? Anything might have happened to him. What if Sarah hadn't chanced to be there when he'd made it home? What if he hadn't made it home at all? Just walking along the street was dangerous, with all the potholes and debris, especially in the dark. Trying to do so when affected by drink would have been far worse.

Kitty had never been drunk herself, but she'd seen her father staggering around often enough to know what it did to your sense of balance and direction. She was filled with a confusing mixture of emotions: disgust at Alfie taking blatant advantage of someone too young to know better; frustration that Tommy hadn't simply said no; and almost overwhelming anxiety that she hadn't been able to keep him safe. Now that Danny was away it fell to her alone, and sometimes she felt that she wasn't up to the task. She was also alarmed when she took a moment to imagine what Alfie's deeper motives might be. She didn't want him anywhere near her house or family. He made her flesh creep. There was something not right about him – more than his reputation as a spivvy black marketeer warranted. If only Danny could come back soon.

Now here she was, late back once more, and wondering what awaited her as she opened the front door. She didn't really think that Tommy would be down the pub with Alfie again; she'd sat him down and had a long talk with him, about how she had to rely on him to act like an adult now, and he had to live up to her expectations. He had agreed, desperately sorry that he'd disgraced himself. They had hugged and made up and she hoped that he would abide by his promise. Yet, now that it had happened once, she dreaded him doing something similar again.

She broke into a smile as she saw that for tonight at least there was no cause for anxiety. Tommy had got the fire going and the kitchen was toasty warm, and he was sitting at the table with what Kitty recognised as one of Dolly's casseroles in front of him. She'd have to make sure to return the favour as soon as she could. Dolly was so generous but Kitty knew stretching the ration for this wouldn't have been easy.

'I haven't eaten it all!' was how he greeted her. 'Aunty Dolly made sure there was enough for you as well. You just need to warm it up.'

Kitty ruffled the top of his head, because she knew it would annoy him. 'Thanks, Tommy. It's just what I need. I'll go and hang up my coat.' She gave a heartfelt sigh of relief once he couldn't hear her. She really hadn't felt like cooking after such a long day. Now she could tuck in to one of Dolly's hearty meals, no doubt full of the root vegetables that she grew in the victory garden.

Tommy was scraping the last of the juices from his plate as she took her seat opposite him. Just as she had hoped, the food was delicious, as Dolly had always been a dab hand at making something out of nothing. 'Next time I have a day off I'll make Dolly and Pop a nice pie to make up for their kindness,' she said. 'Do you think they'd like that, Tommy?'

'They'd love it, I bet,' he said seriously. It hadn't taken him long to realise that he'd been very privileged these last few years, living out on the farm and eating all the produce there. He'd barely noticed that food was rationed. Now he had to come to terms with the grim reality of powdered eggs and very meagre amounts of butter, as well as all the other shortages and restrictions. He knew that Kitty and Dolly often swapped and shared what was available, but it didn't compare to what he'd taken for granted before.

Kitty polished off the last of the stew and reached across the table. 'Give me your plate – I'll wash up. Do you want to listen to the wireless for a bit? There might be a Glenn Miller concert – you like him.'

Tommy shook his head. 'I'll have an early night, I think,' he said. 'I had to cover a big area today and I'm dead beat.'

Kitty nodded at the maturity of this. Maybe he had learnt his lesson. 'All right then. I'll say good night now, and see you in the morning.'

'Night, Kitty.' Tommy gave her a grin and went clattering up the stairs two at a time.

Kitty went into the hall after him and locked the front door while she remembered. That had been Danny's job, and she always made herself do it in good time now, in case it slipped her mind when she was more tired later on. Then she set about doing the washing-up and left the clean casserole dish on the table so she could take it back to Dolly's the next day. She put on the kettle for a cup of tea and added one more log to the fire. Tommy might want an early bed, but she wanted to read for a while and to let the events of the day settle. Then she'd catch the late news on the wireless.

She took out the latest letter from Laura. Kitty shook her head in amazement. How she wished she could see her friend now that Freddy had made it safely home. Laura had dashed off a hurried note as soon as the miracle had happened, and then followed it with a series of longer letters, explaining more fully how he had returned to safety; Kitty had managed to work out the gist of the events, despite the censor's best efforts. He was now receiving treatment at a specialist hospital, as the blow to his head had caused long-lasting damage, and his burns had left their traces, but he was gaining strength day by day and his hair had even begun to grow more normally. Laura's relief was evident.

There had still been no word about Marjorie, though. Laura feared this was affecting Freddy's recovery, as he felt guilty that he'd survived when she maybe had not. Laura kept trying to tell him that didn't make sense, but she admitted to Kitty that logic didn't enter into it. All they could do was hope.

Kitty had to agree. Just about everyone she knew felt this in some shape or form: they were lucky to be alive when others close to them hadn't been so fortunate. The bomb that had killed Elliott could have landed on the hospital and killed Rita too. Any of the houses on Empire Street could have been destroyed in the raids, but only old Mrs Ashby's had suffered really badly. She knew she had to count her blessings. She and Tommy had a roof over their heads; so did the Feenys, and so did Rita and Ruby in the flat above the shop. Their sufferings were as nothing compared to those of the thousands who had lost their homes.

She picked up her book, which she'd left on the mantelpiece, but decided her eyes were too tired after all, and so she put it down again. Had she locked the back door? She checked it – of course she had.

She was about to turn on the wireless for the news when she heard a noise. Startled, she stood up straight and strained her ears, trying to tell where it had come from. Had she been mistaken? It was easy to imagine such things. There was nothing other than the usual sounds from the small back yard – the cat from the end of the road yowling or dislodging stones. There were always a few odd noises, she reassured herself. Old houses creaked and there was no getting away from that.

She had just convinced herself that she'd got it wrong when it came again, louder this time. It was from the front. Carefully she eased open the door from the kitchen and closed it again once she'd passed through, so that the low light of the fire did not illuminate the hallway.

Someone was outside – she could hear their heavy breathing. Then she gasped as whoever it was tried the door handle. They rattled it – that was what she had heard before. They were trying to get into the house. For a moment she wondered if it could be one of her neighbours, but knew that wasn't likely. Sarah or Rita would go round to the back door as often as not, and any of them wanting to come in at this time of night would have knocked and called her name.

There was very little light in the hall, but she could make out the shadows around the doorway. She had sewn a makeshift curtain out of an old chenille table-cloth to hang across the inside of the door, fastened to a rod at the top so that it would swing with the door as it opened or closed. That kept the worst of the draughts out. Now whoever it was must be poking their hand through the letterbox, as the curtain moved and jerked. Kitty could hear her heart hammering in her ears. All the same, she reasoned that she had locked up earlier in the evening and it was a good, stout lock – again thanks to Danny's forethought. Perhaps the person thought they'd find a key dangling on a string inside. Time was they might have left one there, accessible through the letterbox, or have left the door completely unlocked, but with the war making everything so uncertain, they didn't take risks like that any more.

After what seemed like hours but couldn't have been more than a few minutes, the person gave up trying to get in through the door. Then came several footsteps as the person moved away. Kitty held her breath. What if they tried to break the parlour window? She calmed herself by thinking they probably wouldn't; the noise would wake too many people. Did they know the way in around the back? She breathed out slowly. She knew she had locked and bolted that door too. Had Tommy left his bike in the yard – maybe this person knew about it and wanted to steal it? No, he'd propped it in the hallway, even though she'd repeatedly asked him to wheel it around the back into the yard to get it out of the way. Now she was glad he'd ignored her.

Cautiously she opened the parlour door and crept closer to the window. The curtain was closed but she could hear someone was there. There was a very slight scrabbling, then silence, which seemed to go on for ever.

Then came more footsteps from the bottom of the street, and a flash of light as if someone was carrying a torch. A voice called out, 'You there!' It was Pop, on his ARP rounds. Then there was a shout and more footsteps, this time running away from the front of her house. Carefully she drew back a corner of the curtain and saw the bulk of a figure running away. Pop began to give chase but stopped before the end of the road, she assumed because he knew he'd frightened the person away. His white hair made him clearly visible in the light of a waning moon.

She wanted to tell herself that it was just a random burglar, perhaps one who'd heard about the bike, or someone who'd chosen her house out of sheer chance. However, she didn't really believe it. She'd only had the briefest of moments to pick out the fleeing figure, but that had been enough. It was Alfie Delaney.

Pop came back up the road and tapped gently on her front door. She cautiously unlocked it and opened it a little. The cold air rushed in. 'You all right, Kitty? I saw your curtain move,' Pop said.

'Yes . . . yes, I'm fine,' said Kitty, trying to convince herself as much as anything. 'I heard what I thought was someone trying the handle of the door – and then when I looked out I thought I saw Alfie Delaney running away.'

Pop grunted. 'There was someone, but I didn't catch who it was. I'd be surprised if he dared show himself on Empire Street again after that affair with the poisoned meat. He'll have the good sense to stay well away,' he told her reassuringly. 'Good night, now.'

'You're probably right,' said Kitty, smiling at the kindly figure of her father before carefully shutting and locking the door once more. She wanted him to be right – but she had a sinking feeling he wasn't.

'Sylvia! Hang on, I'll just put this lot of paper down.' Frank dumped an armful of carefully clipped meeting agendas on to the nearest desk and then turned to smile at the pretty young Wren. 'It feels as if I haven't seen you for ages.'

Sylvia blushed a little. 'Hardly ages, Frank. We went to the pictures to see *Arsenic and Old Lace* a couple of weeks ago.'

'Well, two weeks seems like a long time,' he grinned. 'Fancy going again? I couldn't stop laughing.'

'It was funny, wasn't it. And that Cary Grant is so good-looking.' Sylvia smiled back but seemed more flustered than usual. Frank was surprised; he couldn't remember seeing her rushed or panicked by anything.

'So, how about it?' he asked again. 'We can go to anything you fancy. There's bound to be lots of good ones on now we're in the run-up to Christmas.'

Sylvia shrugged apologetically. 'I'm not sure, Frank. I'm a bit on edge at the moment.'

Frank fell into step beside her as they moved along the underground corridor. 'I can see. What's up?'

She came to a halt. 'Oh Frank, it's Dad again. He's been proper poorly. I can't think about going out in the evenings at the moment. If I get any time off I'll have to go home again, to help Mum out. I keep waiting for a telegram or a phone call; I'm dreading more bad news. It's terrible and I'm sorry, but it's on my mind all the time.'

Frank could hear the concern in her voice. 'I'm so sorry, Sylvia. Of course you must see what happens. What a thing to have to think about, and when it's almost Christmas, of all times.'

Sylvia nodded, and for a moment he thought she was going to lose her composure and start to cry, but she bit her lip and gathered herself together. 'It's not that I wouldn't like to go to the pictures, Frank. Of course I would. It's just I don't think I'd be very good company.'

'I understand, of course I do.' Frank's eyes were full of sympathy for her. He knew how hard she worked, and to have this worry on top of all that must be dreadful. 'If you want any cheering up, you come straight to me. You will, won't you?'

'Thank you, Frank.' Sylvia's face was full of gratitude.

'Oh, by the way. I meant to say before, but if you are free over Christmas then my mam says you're to come over and join the family for dinner,' Frank told her. Dolly had been most insistent – she wouldn't have Sylvia being lonely on her own in her billet while the extended Feeny clan sat down to the roast turkey. 'Mam will pull out all the stops; it'll be just like there was no war on. She's been saving bits and bobs for months.'

'That's very kind of her.' Sylvia looked embarrassed. 'I'd love to say yes, you know I would, and I think the world of your mum. Well, all your family. But under the circumstances, I don't know . . . I don't want to say yes and then to let her down. She'll already have a crowd to feed, won't she? Like Kitty and all her family too?' Sylvia hesitated and an odd look passed over her face which Frank couldn't read. 'And what if I have to hurry back to Mum and Dad? I don't want to put her to any trouble.'

Frank laughed. 'Believe me, it will be no trouble. She always cooks enough to feed an army. I'm the one who'll be in trouble if I don't invite you.' His eyes danced. 'Pop will get out the rum that my brother-in-law Jack brought back when he had leave a few weeks ago; all the neighbours will be over. Then Pop'll get out his accordion and we'll sing the place down.'

Sylvia sighed and leant back against the wall. 'Frank, that sounds lovely, but I don't know if I can come. Best if I say I won't.'

Frank shook his head. 'Let's see what happens nearer the time,' he suggested. 'You shouldn't decide now, not when you're all upset. You can come over if you feel like it, we don't need advance notice. You'll be very welcome, you know that.'

Sylvia looked close to tears again but then recovered. 'Aye, Frank. I do know that and I'm right grateful. You tell your mum that.'

Frank nodded soberly. 'All right. Can't say fairer than that. You let me know how things are going and what you feel up to doing. It's no fun feeling miserable when everyone around you is having a party. But in the meantime shall we make a date to go for a quick drink, even if you don't feel you can go to the flicks? A trip to the Phil?'

Sylvia smiled ruefully. 'Better not, or at least not right now.' She turned to go. 'Thanks, Frank.'

Frank made his way back to his pile of agendas. Poor Sylvia, she was obviously preparing for the news that her father had died. If times had been different she could have gone home and helped make his final days, or weeks, or whatever it turned out to be, more comfortable, sharing the burden with her mother. If he'd been a different sort of man he might have felt she was deliberately being cool with him but he re-assured himself he had no need for such suspicions. War made everything so much more difficult and complicated.

He knew Dolly wouldn't see it as a rejection of her hospitality. As long as she knew Frank had invited the girl, she would be happy either way. Frank knew half of Empire Street would be crushed into the parlour and kitchen. He was looking forward to it in some ways; Danny would be back, or that was the word in his unit. He'd be bound to want a tot or two of rum. And if Danny came, then so would Kitty, singing carols in that beautiful voice of hers. Frank thought there might be some advantage after all if Sylvia didn't come, and then admonished himself for even conceiving of such a thing. There was no denying it, though – few could sing a carol as movingly as Kitty Callaghan.

CHAPTER TWENTY-ONE

'Violet, are you sure you should lift that?' asked Ruby anxiously from behind the counter of the shop. 'Here, you come and check the change in the till and I'll do it. You must be careful.'

Violet straightened up slowly, rubbing her back. 'Maybe you're right. Thanks, Ruby. It's getting so that I can't bend over properly any more. It's all I can do to kick my shoes off.' She made her way heavily to the counter as Ruby slipped out into the aisle, and found she could hardly fit in her usual space. She moved the stool to give herself a bit more room and collapsed on to it. 'I'm sure Rita was never this big. She didn't have this trouble.'

'I suppose everyone's different,' said Ruby uncertainly, rubbing her hands and then plunging them into the patch pockets of her faded apron. Growing up with only mean Elsie Lowe for company, she hadn't known any expectant mothers. Rita was the only person she had to go by, and she'd carried Ellen in a neat bump, managing to work almost up to the birth. Violet was struggling in comparison.

'That's what they say,' Violet huffed. She'd seen her own mother carry four children, and she didn't remember her ever being as big as this, but then again Violet was much taller than her mother had been, so perhaps it followed that her bump would be bigger too. She didn't know. Dolly, Rita and Sarah kept reassuring her that she had no need to worry, and so she tried to take comfort from them. Between them they'd carried eight babies and tended to more births than they could count, so they should know what they were talking about. All the same, she could do without the nights of interrupted sleep and constant heartburn. It made her uncharacteristically tetchy.

Ruby crouched down to try to shift the big box on the floor. She was not used to doing much of the heavy work around the shop, as Rita and Violet had always done everything between them. Even during the recent stages of her pregnancy, Violet had managed, as Rita was back at the hospital most of the time, but now it was physically impossible for her to get her arms around a bulky box as her bump was always in the way. Ruby tried to lift the box before her in the way she'd seen Violet do it, but nothing happened. Her arms were shorter and weaker. She hadn't had a lifetime of building up her muscles, and the sheer weight of the box defeated her.

'Oh, Violet, what are we going to do?' She began rubbing her hands again. 'We can't leave it there, someone might trip over it.'

Violet sighed. She should have known Ruby wouldn't

be able to move the box. It wasn't the young woman's fault; she'd just never had the practice. The spirit was willing but the flesh just wasn't up to it.

'We could see if anyone's around in the street,' Violet suggested. 'Maybe Pop or Tommy.'

Ruby shook her head of blonde hair, so pale it was almost white. 'No, they left already. I saw them earlier this morning.' She looked on the verge of tears, distraught at failing to help.

'We could open the box and move the contents tin by tin,' Violet said. 'It might take a long time, but we'll get there in the end.'

Ruby looked dubious. There were a lot of tins in the box, but she couldn't come up with an alternative. 'All right.' She struggled to open it, and Violet could do nothing but watch.

Ruby had managed to rip back half of the lid when the door jangled. She looked flustered at being interrupted, but then her expression changed when she saw who it was. Reggie James stepped around the end of the shelves and saw what was going on.

'Hello, Mr James,' said Violet brightly. 'Chilly morning, isn't it? Don't tell me you've got vegetables to sell after last week's frost.'

'It's good for the parsnips,' he smiled. Then he turned to Ruby and her predicament. 'Now, what is the trouble?'

Ruby shrugged. 'It's this box, it's too heavy for me to lift,' she said, 'and Violet can't do it any more.'

'Allow me,' said Reggie. 'Where do you want it?'

'But your leg . . .' protested Ruby.

260

Mr James ignored her, bending and lifting the big box with ease. 'Do you want it back in the stock room?'

'Yes please,' said Violet, swinging open the internal door, realising that Ruby's fear was groundless. If the man could work an allotment he was probably safe to lift a box, she reasoned. She certainly wasn't going to turn down the offer.

Mr James manoeuvred the box out of the way as if it contained nothing but feathers. As he took it through, Violet could see his muscles working through the fabric of his coat, stretched tightly across his back. She'd never really noticed before but, even though one of his legs was damaged, there was obviously nothing wrong with the rest of him. He was fit and strong, and had come along at just the right moment.

Ruby was beaming with pleasure. 'Thank you, thank you,' she said as he came back into the shop, wiping his hands on a handkerchief. 'Would you like a cup of tea?'

'And we could break open a packet of biscuits to show our appreciation,' Violet said. 'Tell you what, Ruby, why don't you take Reggie through to the kitchen? I'll hold the fort here. I don't want any biscuits now I come to think of it, they'll just make my heartburn worse.'

'That's very kind of you,' said Reggie, but his eyes kept straying to Ruby. 'I only stopped by to take orders for Christmas vegetables. We'll have plenty if you are interested.'

'Why don't you sort that out with Ruby; she

261

knows more about ordering than I do,' Violet admitted honestly. Adding up figures had never been her strong point and now she was getting by on just a few hours' sleep a night, she was worse at them than ever. 'I trust her to make all the right decisions, you know.'

'I'm sure you're right,' said Reggie, his eyes alight as Ruby led him back through to the little kitchen.

Violet sighed as she gently shut the door on them. They deserved a bit of privacy. He really was a very pleasant man and he seemed genuinely fond of Ruby. She felt mean that she'd made fun of him a little before. If he brought Ruby happiness, who was she to mock him? Ruby came to life in his presence in a way she'd never seen before. Violet shut her eyes, cross with herself. The trouble was they'd all believed Winnie, who'd put it about that Ruby was simple and wrong in the head. Even when they'd seen for themselves that it wasn't true and Winnie had been saying it out of meanness and as a way of putting everyone off the scent to cover her own sin, the damage had been done. Yet Ruby was a young woman who deserved love as much as any other. Perhaps Reggie James was just the right man for her.

The door bell went again and in came Mrs Mawdsley, obviously in a hurry. 'Good morning, dear. I won't keep you, just let me buy a paper.'

Violet smiled and then grimaced as a twinge shot through her. She rallied and tried to sound cheerful as she handed it over. 'Here you are. Chilly out, isn't it?'

Mrs Mawdsley regarded her carefully. 'Yes, Christmas

262

isn't far off now. When are you due, my dear? Not long to go now, by the looks of you.'

From anyone else, Violet might have bristled at the intrusive comment, but she knew the woman's heart was in the right place. 'Early January,' she replied. 'Dolly says first ones can often be late, but that I'm doing well.'

'And she should know,' Mrs Mawdsley agreed. 'All the same, you must take care, my dear.' She shook her head. The poor young woman looked as if she was going to pop at any moment.

'Oh, I will,' Violet assured her, keeping her smile in place until her customer had left. Then she collapsed back on to the stool with a groan. January couldn't come soon enough for her, Christmas or no Christmas.

'Don't you think you're asking a bit much of Tommy?' Sarah demanded as Nancy breezed through the kitchen of their parents' house. 'He'll have done a full day's work, he'll be tired, though he'd never admit that to you. But you have to remember he's only fourteen.'

Nancy shrugged. 'Don't be such a killjoy, Sarah. He'll love it. He enjoys looking after Georgie. And Georgie loves it, don't you?'

The little boy nodded. 'Can I stay with Tommy?' he asked.

'It'll only be for a couple of hours, and then he can take you back to Granny Kerrigan and she'll give you your tea,' Nancy assured him.

George's face fell. 'Don't like Granny Kerrigan's tea.'

Nancy couldn't very well say that she knew exactly what he meant. 'Don't be silly, there's nothing wrong with her tea. If you're good she might give you a treat.' Even as she said it, Nancy knew there was fat chance of that, but she had to get away with this somehow.

George made a face as if he knew it too.

'So, Gloria's back in town on one of her whistle-stop tours, then?' Sarah tried to sound as if she wasn't impressed, even if she was secretly pleased that she had a connection to one of the nation's favourite entertainers.

'That's right,' Nancy gushed. 'She'll do one big concert before Christmas, then go up to Scotland, and then do one more in Liverpool on her way back to London. After that she's off on some ENSA trip and I don't know when I'll see her again. So it's tonight or never, really.'

Georgie looked up. 'Can I see Auntie Gloria?'

Nancy bent down to his level. 'Georgie, you'd be bored silly. Mummy and Auntie Gloria will just be sitting and chatting and there'll be nothing for you to do. You'll have much more fun with Tommy.' She felt a little guilty but not enough to make her change her plans.

George didn't look too unhappy about being told no. He was used to it, after all. He scuffed his shoe along the edge of the rag rug and wondered if Tommy might let him have a go on the back of his bike. He decided to keep this idea to himself.

'Well, it's certainly put you in a good mood,' Sarah

observed, picking up her warm scarf and looping it around her neck as she got ready to set off for the hospital. She was in a good mood herself; Kitty had told her that Danny would be coming back for Christmas. She was full of anticipation at seeing him again, and yet it was tinged with dread, wondering if he would be different, or if he'd have met someone else. She couldn't even say that they were a couple though, so it wasn't a question of 'else'. It was too complicated to think about. She had to concentrate on being ready for whatever her next shift might throw at her.

Nancy nodded cheerfully, and kept smiling broadly as her sister let herself out. The thought of seeing Gloria always pepped her up, that was true. But it wasn't the only reason for her happiness. Tonight she had two tickets to the show, and she'd be going there with Gary. She closed her eyes for a brief moment, remembering the electric connection between them when he'd got back a few days ago. She'd made an excuse to miss her WVS shift and had gone with him to a discreet hotel room. It had been everything she'd dreamt of and more. The separation had made things even better between them, and the long, passionate afternoon had filled her with delight and a keen desire for more. The illicit nature of their meeting just added to the excitement. She knew she shouldn't set too much stock by promises made under such circumstances, but the flame of hope had been relit, that she might escape her gloomy life as her in-laws' tenant, break free of the whole grey, depressing existence she led now. How or when she didn't know, but that hope buoyed her up, made her tremble with emotion every time she got a quiet moment to think about it. Very occasionally she felt a flash of guilt, such as the rare occasions when one of Sid's clumsy and brief letters tumbled through the letterbox, but usually she managed very successfully to overcome it.

Tonight she was going to introduce Gary to her best friend. They would share the evening, and then with luck they'd have time to run back to the hotel room and spend some proper time together before she had to sneak back home and avoid the baleful gaze of her mother-in-law. She shivered with the thrill of it all.

'Are you cold, Mummy?' Georgie asked, bringing her back down to earth with a bump.

'Not a bit,' said Nancy truthfully. She was still in her sensible coat, flat shoes and practical knitted twin-set. But later tonight she'd sneak into the theatre toilets and change into her beautiful silk frock and daring silk underwear, which wouldn't keep her warm at all. Never mind. Gary would.

'So I'm meeting him by the stage door at quarter to, because it's quieter and we're less likely to see anyone who knows us,' Nancy said later that evening as Gloria expertly applied her lipstick in the dressing room before the show.

'Surely if you're going to sit with him in the front row, then it won't matter how discreet you try to be beforehand,' Gloria pointed out. She dusted her nose with the powder puff, then turned her head to the left and the right to check there were no shiny patches on her face. It was important to look the part; her audience expected it of her and she couldn't let them down. Her beautiful bias-cut silver dress sparkled in the lights ranged around the somewhat tarnished mirror.

'No, but I can always say he came in with the people sitting on the other side of him and we just got chatting,' Nancy said quickly. She'd had the bus journey to get her alibi straight if it was needed. It wasn't perfect, but it would have to do. She was thrilled to bits to have the chance of sitting with Gary in the prime seats, watching her best friend perform.

'All right, I'll back you up,' Gloria said at once without having to be asked. 'I do like that frock, Nancy. Where did you find it? Do you want to leave your other things in here?' She pointed to the shabby canvas bag in which Nancy had stuffed the sensible clothes she'd been wearing earlier.

'Oh, could I? Thanks, Glor.' Nancy shoved the bag under a chair, once resplendent in gold paint but now very chipped. 'Gary got it for me, of course. It was my little present – well, it was more like his welcome home present if you get what I mean.' She rolled her eyes.

Gloria shook her head. 'You just be careful, Nancy Kerrigan. You've been caught out before, remember. We don't want anything like that to happen again.'

'Of course I'm being careful,' Nancy snapped, not wanting to think about the miscarriage that only she and Gloria knew about. 'This isn't some wet-behind-the-ears young lad trying it on. Gary's very mature. He's a real man.'

'Keep your hair on, I was only checking,' said Gloria, not rising to the bait. She couldn't afford to get het up before singing. Her breathing wouldn't be right. 'Well, off you go and meet lover boy, and I'll see you backstage afterwards.'

'Break a leg!' called Nancy brightly, as she hurried from the dingy little room towards the stage door.

'Don't you think she's good?' Nancy hissed in Gary's ear, as she hung on to his arm.

'She sure is,' said Gary, eyeing Gloria appreciatively from their excellent view in the front row. 'How did you say you know her?'

'We grew up on the same street,' said Nancy proudly. 'We were in the same class at school and have been best friends ever since we can remember.'

Gary nodded but couldn't say anything as Gloria started singing her encore, 'We'll Meet Again', and everyone joined in. She sang it as if it was the first time she'd ever done so, giving it all the energy and belief that she knew her audience wanted. People were openly crying by the end, but standing proudly, clapping and cheering as Gloria smiled and smiled, turning and waving to everyone.

Nancy almost burst with pride at her friend's performance. Having the chance to show her off to Gary was the most special thing she'd ever done. 'Let's go while they're all still applauding,' she muttered, leading him out of the row and swiftly down some back stairs.

'I see you know all the secret routes,' he laughed as he moved quickly after her. Nancy neatly zigzagged around some clothes rails and pushed through a door marked 'Artists Only'.

'Of course.' She turned to face him now they were alone in the cold little corridor, paint peeling from the walls and the lino on the floor cracked and stained. 'I used to come here with Gloria all the time.' She flung her arms around his neck.

'Mixing with the great and the good,' he teased.

'I wouldn't like to say how good we were,' she said cheekily, taking his arm once more and leading him to Gloria's dressing room.

'You sure she won't mind my being here?'

'No, she particularly told me to bring you,' Nancy assured him. 'She's very keen to meet you.'

'Well, likewise,' said Gary affably, looking around the place. It definitely didn't match the glamour of the front of house. It could have done with some heating and brighter light bulbs.

The door swung open and in came Gloria, still in performance mode. 'You must be Gary,' she said, coming forward to shake his hand. Her smile was radiant and for a moment he was at a loss for words.

'Gary, this is Gloria,' said Nancy unnecessarily.

'De . . . delighted to meet you,' he said, finding his voice at last. 'You were mighty good out there, Miss Arden.'

'Why thank you,' Gloria said prettily. 'I'm glad you

269

enjoyed it.' She batted her eyelashes a little, but was watching him carefully.

'Say, can I get you girls a drink?' Gary offered. 'I guess the bar will still be open.'

'Oh, it will, but no need to go so far,' Gloria said. 'The management are very generous with their back-stage supplies. We like a cocktail, don't we, Nancy?'

'I'll make them,' Nancy offered, knowing where everything was. She turned her back and went to the little cupboard that was almost in darkness in the corner of the room, fetching three mismatched glasses and the silver shaker. Carefully she mixed the drinks the way she had seen Gloria do it, adding a twist of lemon. She concentrated hard, not wanting to drop the glasses, which looked as if they were high-quality cut crystal, and tuned out the low buzz of idle conversation between Gary and her friend. This was the height of sophistication, she decided, as she took back two glasses and then returned for her own.

'Cheers, Gloria,' she said, thinking she'd never been happier.

Gary's eyes twinkled. 'To the two most beautiful ladies in Liverpool,' he said, and Nancy laughed affectionately at him.

'You're very kind,' Gloria said gracefully. 'Nancy's told me so much about you. You've just got back from France, haven't you?'

'He's been so brave,' Nancy couldn't resist saying. 'He led his boys on Omaha Beach, and he's been fighting ever since.'

'Me and many thousands of others,' Gary pointed

out. 'Yeah, it wasn't a pretty business but we did what we had to do. We didn't come all the way over here for a tea party; we knew what we were in for.'

'Well, we're very glad you did,' said Gloria, serious now. 'Without you GIs we'd be in a whole lot of trouble. As it is, it looks as if things are going our way at last.'

'To victory,' said Gary boldly, raising his glass. 'It's within our grasp at last, ladies.'

Nancy gazed at him with adoration. He was her hero and she would deny him nothing. She waited until he had finished his drink and then said, 'Gloria, you must be tired after your long evening.'

Gloria took the hint. 'Just a little, maybe. Don't let me keep you, Nancy. It's been lovely meeting you, Gary.' She smiled once more as the handsome soldier held Nancy's coat for her and then held the door open.

'It's been swell talking to you,' he said.

'And you,' said Gloria. As Gary moved to leave, she quickly took hold of Nancy and gave her a hug. 'Remember, be careful,' she whispered in her friend's ear.

Nancy tapped her playfully on the shoulder as she broke away. 'Of course. See you when you're next in town, Glor.'

Gloria stood at the door to her shabby dressing room and waved goodbye to the couple, so visibly excited to be back in each other's company. She hoped Nancy knew what she was doing. She didn't want to spoil her friend's enjoyment, but if she were in her

271

shoes she'd be a little more cautious. Something about Gary Trenton had put her on the alert, but she couldn't say what it was. Maybe he'd been just that little bit too flirty while Nancy's back was turned as she sorted out the drinks.

Or maybe it was because she was getting older and more cynical, Gloria told herself. She couldn't begrudge Nancy some fun. She could see her friend was falling hard for this man – and yet she herself didn't trust him one inch.

CHAPTER TWENTY-TWO

'Right, do we all know what we're doing?' Kitty asked. It was Christmas morning and the planning of the dinner was like a military operation. Dolly was cooking the turkey and some of the trimmings, but there would be so many people to feed that some of the preparations would have to be done in Kitty's kitchen and others in Rita's.

Tommy nodded gravely. 'I'm going to look after Michael and Megan as soon as they arrive. We're going to go to the victory garden and see if there's anything last minute to be brought back.'

'And you are not, on any account, to allow them to get dirty,' said Kitty forcefully, even though she knew this was a forlorn hope.

'Of course not,' said Tommy, stung by the very suggestion.

'And what are you going to do, Kitty?' asked Danny, leaning against the side of the mantelpiece, relaxed and relieved at having made it home on the last train on Christmas Eve. It had been a close-run thing, but he was heartily glad to be back in his own home. Kitty had told him of what had gone on in his absence, but they'd decided to say nothing about it today so as not to spoil the celebrations.

'I'm waiting for Michael and Megan too,' she grinned. 'Or rather, for Joan and Seth. Seth's managed to get hold of a van and so he's bringing more food and some real eggs and butter, so I'm going to make a cake. It won't give me time to make a proper fruit cake, but I can manage a sponge all right.'

'Now I know I was right to come home,' said Danny.

'Will it have real icing?' demanded Tommy, his eyes lighting up.

'No, we won't have the sugar,' said Kitty. 'But we'll have a filling of Dolly's home-made jam from all that fruit she saved from the victory garden, and I'll whip up the cream that Joan has promised to bring. You won't go hungry, believe me.'

Tommy beamed from ear to ear. 'Okey doke. What about you, Danny?'

'Me?' Danny held his hands wide. 'You aren't expecting me to make a cake as well, are you, Tommy?'

Just as he said this, the back door opened, and Sarah stepped through, balancing a wide box on her hip. 'I heard that, Danny Callaghan. Kitty, did you warn him?'

Kitty smiled conspiratorially. 'Didn't have time.'

Danny turned. 'What do you mean, Kitty? What have you got in store for me?'

Sarah put the box on the table with a thump. 'Sprouts, Danny.'

He gave her an amazed look and she grinned back, her eyes twinkling.

'What am I meant to do with them?' He looked into the box. 'There must be hundreds of them!'

Kitty laughed out loud. 'Now come on, Danny. You're always telling me how well you managed when you were on your own, and you didn't always rely on Sarah here. So we thought you could help out with the vegetables. Your job is to prepare the sprouts.'

For a moment he looked dismayed, but then he rallied, as he could see he had no way of saving face other than by accepting. Besides, if Sarah and Kitty were ganging up on him, it was pointless to try to resist.

'All right,' he said grudgingly. 'You'll have to show me what to do though.'

'Kitty will do that,' said Sarah. 'I've got to get back to Mam. I'm peeling the carrots. Don't forget to save the box, though – Mam keeps them for protecting her vegetable beds.' With that she swung out of the back door.

Stepping outside into the cool, fresh morning air, Sarah congratulated herself on not falling apart at the first sight of Danny for what felt like half a lifetime. He was still as handsome as she remembered, and as warm and funny, and she knew her heart was beating faster even as she'd good-humouredly mocked him. Whether his was doing the same, she just couldn't tell.

'We did it!' Rita gave her mother a hug. 'Mam, you managed it. Thank you.'

275

'It was a team effort, so it's thanks to everybody,' said Dolly happily, pushing a grey curl behind her ear. She knew Rita had really wanted her first Christmas with Ellen to be spent in their own home, and with Jack there, but he hadn't been able to get leave. He'd brought them plenty of rum on his last visit, and he'd persuaded a comrade from the Fleet Air Arm who had been lucky enough to come home for Christmas to come round with extra rum and presents for the children, but obviously it wasn't the same as having him there. Still, she could see Rita had had a good time, and to be honest Dolly had been glad of the use of Rita's kitchen, not to mention the extra pairs of hands. They would never have been able to make enough roast potatoes otherwise.

Dolly sighed contentedly. They'd squeezed as many people as possible round the kitchen table, extended with side tables and whatever else they could find of the right height. Somehow they had all fitted in. At some point they were going to have to work out who owned which plates and cutlery, as lots of items had been borrowed as well, but that could keep. She didn't intend to move from her chair until she absolutely had to.

'Sit down, Violet, and take the weight off your feet,' she called across to her daughter-in-law, who was rising in a cumbersome fashion. 'You've done enough. We wouldn't have had any parsnips if it hadn't been for you peeling and chopping them all.'

Violet gave her a smile, but it was mixed with a grimace. 'I'll just stretch my legs a bit. I'm more comfortable when I stand at the moment, for some reason.' She heaved herself fully to her feet and slowly went to stand against the sideboard.

Rita went across and stood with her. 'Are you all right?' she asked quietly.

'Oh, yes,' said Violet at once.

Rita looked at her dubiously. She could see that wasn't completely true, but recognised that Violet didn't want to make a fuss. She remembered what her own last few weeks of pregnancy had been like and sympathised. Little Ellen was lying in a corner, in an improvised cot made of a drawer from the back kitchen, lined with knitted blankets, fast asleep in the middle of all the noise and chatter. Soon Violet would have her own baby, and she knew how deeply her friend had longed for this. She just had to get through the next few weeks.

'Would you like a glass of water?' she said.

'Oh, no, don't worry about me. I'll get it. It might be a bit cooler out in the back kitchen,' Violet said hastily, obviously not wanting to draw attention to herself.

Rita gazed around the room, which Pop had decorated with branches of holly he'd found on his rounds. There were home-made paper chains, which Violet had laboured over with Georgie, who was just old enough to help out. He and Nancy were here, as old Mrs Kerrigan had apparently said she couldn't begin to think about celebrating Christmas when her poor Sid was still a POW. Nancy had complained that this was no reason to deny Georgie his fun and had joined her own mother's party instead. Rita had to admit that Nancy was glowing, unusually cheerful and agreeable, her cheeks rosy with the warmth of the room, her hair beautifully styled and shining. Long may it last, she thought. Although, knowing Nancy as she did, her angelic mood meant there was probably something going on behind the scenes.

There was a rise of chatter from the far end of the room, where Pop was shaking his head. 'Oh, go on,' Sarah was saying, and it looked as if others were agreeing with her.

'Yes, come on, give us a tune,' Danny chimed in, and Rita noticed her youngest sister flashing a glance at him. 'Our Kitty will sing the words, won't you, Kitty?'

Kitty protested. 'Danny, I'm going to help with the washing-up in a minute.' But she was shouted down.

'The washing-up can wait,' Dolly announced grandly, for once in her life not jumping to her feet to clear everything away.

'We'll do it!' shouted Michael. 'Then Auntie Kitty can sing!'

'That's very kind of you, Michael,' said Dolly at once, 'but you don't have to do that. Like I said, it can wait.' She didn't want Michael and Megan trying to tackle the mountain of dirty plates. They were too short to reach the sink and, while she didn't mind too much if her own plates got chipped, she didn't want any of the borrowed china to suffer. Besides, they were young and deserved their fun, this day of all days. 'There you are, Kitty, the children want you to sing too.'

For a moment it looked as if Kitty would protest again, but then Frank came through the door, from where he'd been setting out the rum in the parlour. 'Did I hear that right?' he asked with a smile. 'Kitty's going to sing for us?' He gave her a straight look and everyone turned to her. The thought flashed through Frank's mind that this was the most natural thing in the world, to spend an uncomplicated day with Kitty and their families.

Kitty gave in to the inevitable, standing and making her way out from behind the table, as Pop leant across to reach for his accordion. She glanced across at Frank, whose face was full of warm encouragement. She had been a bit surprised that there had been no sign of Sylvia today. She'd kept half expecting her to turn up at the door, but Sylvia hadn't appeared and Frank hadn't said anything about her not being there; he'd seemed perfectly cheerful at the big family gathering without her. Kitty had allowed a brief but guilty thought that they might not be an item any more, but then remembered she'd heard that the young Wren's father was ill. So it might not mean anything, and she wouldn't read anything into her absence. 'What will it be, Pop?'

Pop thought for a moment and then played the opening bars of 'Silent Night'.

The chatter came to a stop. The whole group of family and friends paused expectantly, and then Kitty began to sing: quietly but true, her gorgeous voice filling the room.

For a moment Violet, alone in the back kitchen but

watching through the connecting door, turned away. Eddy's favourite carol. Surely everyone would be thinking that – Pop would have chosen it deliberately. Her husband would never play it on the piano again. She wiped a tear from her eye with the cuff of her sleeve, wishing with all her heart he was here with them, waiting with her for their longed-for child to be born.

Frank watched Kitty as she sang; this was what Christmas was all about. He shut his eyes, blotting out all other thoughts, of the pressures of work, of the progress of the war, or of Sylvia. He let the tune float through his mind, all the familiar cadences, the age-old story, the harmony that someone – probably Pop – was humming. He wanted the moment to last for ever.

But then Pop broke into a livelier tune, 'Run Rabbit Run', and everyone joined in, breaking the magic spell. Kitty's voice was just one of many, and he knew he had to let her go, to turn away from whatever it was that seemed to connect them, no matter how he tried to persuade himself otherwise. There was no getting away from the fact he was damaged goods, and maybe she'd always think of him that way.

'Penny for 'em, Frank!' called Danny, and Frank smiled and laughed and said he was miles away.

'We know a cure for that – pass the lad another tot of rum,' said Pop, and Frank accepted a glass and pretended he was in the best of spirits.

After they'd gone through all the old favourites,

Dolly finally stood up and announced she was going to boil the kettle if anyone wanted some tea. She looked around the crowded room. 'Where's Violet? I hope she hasn't started on the washing-up on her own. She needs her rest, that one, but she hates doing nothing.'

Rita moved towards the back kitchen. 'I'll check.'

She knew Violet couldn't have come back through the kitchen proper without one of them noticing. Perhaps she'd gone to the privy and then stayed out in the yard as she'd said she wanted to cool down. Yet Rita was concerned, because the daylight had gone and it would be really cold out there now. Cautiously she pushed the back door open and called out. 'Violet? Are you there?' She could see her breath forming in drifting white puffs.

She gasped as she saw her sister-in-law, her friend, clutching on to the fence at the far side of the little yard. 'Violet! What is it? Are you all right?'

Violet turned her face towards the open door and the light shining from it. 'Oh, Rita. I don't want to make a fuss. I'm not sure but . . . it's early if I've counted right . . . perhaps it's a mistake, but I think the baby's coming. I feel very odd. It hurts.'

Rita rushed over. 'Then you've got to come inside right away. How often does it hurt? What's it like, is it all the time or on and off?'

Violet allowed herself to be led slowly across the yard, but as she reached the threshold to the back kitchen, she doubled over and gasped, bracing herself against the doorframe. It was several minutes before she could stand upright again.

'On and off,' she admitted, 'but the pain gets worse every time and it's happening more and more often. Is that what it's like? Or is there something wrong with me? Wrong with my baby?'

Rita gave her a hug. 'That's what it's like. Sounds as if that baby is on its way already. Come on, we'll get you upstairs before the next pain arrives, and then I'll get everything ready.'

'But the party,' Violet moaned. 'I don't want to spoil it.'

Rita shook her head. 'You won't. Everyone will be thrilled.' She had to pause as she felt the sudden urge to cry at the emotion of it all. 'It's like a miracle, Violet. The best present any of us could wish for. In the midst of all the death and destruction of the last year, a Christmas baby. So let's get you inside.'

CHAPTER TWENTY-THREE

The party had moved to the parlour and everyone joined in a singsong, followed by a game of charades made more raucous by the new bottle of rum being opened and passed round. Kitty kept a sharp eye on Tommy to see if he attempted to try some, but he didn't seem at all inclined. Maybe he had learnt his lesson the hard way. She breathed a secret sigh of relief.

There was a knock at the door and in came Maeve Kerrigan, Rita's closest colleague from the hospital, and by coincidence a cousin of Nancy's husband, Sid. Thankfully she didn't take after that side of the family, but had felt obliged to pop round to see her gloomy aunt as she was the closest relative in the city. She hadn't stayed long, realising she wasn't really wanted as Mrs Kerrigan had no intention of celebrating, and so she'd come round to see Rita. When she found out her friend was upstairs and very busy, she came in anyway.

'Let me take your coat, Maeve,' said Sarah, hurrying forward. 'You'll stay for a cup of tea and some cake, won't you? Even something stronger?'

'None of that strong stuff for me.' Maeve shuddered at the thought. 'I'll not be saying no to the cake, though. Kitty, is it one of yours?'

Sarah stepped through to the kitchen, aware of the noises from upstairs, but knowing Violet was in the best hands. She'd go up to help when necessary. For now she'd only be in the way.

Maeve rolled up the sleeves of her best blouse, which she'd cunningly brought up to date with new buttons and a dark green ribbon at the neck. 'Will I have a go on your piano?' she offered.

'Didn't know you played, Maeve,' said Danny.

'Well, there's a lot you don't know about me, Danny Callaghan,' said Maeve smartly. 'Sure I can play. Just watch me now. What'll we have?'

Soon everyone was joining in, and if Maeve's playing wasn't quite up to Eddy's standard, no one mentioned it. Sarah stood with her back against the wall, thankful that the happy noise would drown out whatever was coming from the bedroom above, giving Violet some kind of privacy. After a few songs she gathered up the plates and cups, piling them on to a tray, and took them into the kitchen. She tried not to think about the look Maeve had just shot at Danny as the clear sound of Kitty hitting a high note followed her through.

Slowly and methodically she stacked the plates and saucers beside the sink, brushing off any stray crumbs. Before washing them, she decided to make sure the kettle was full and to set a big pan of water to boil – not that she thought it would be needed yet, but it would be easier to heat through if she put it on now. Humming to herself, she turned back to the sink and noticed that Danny was standing in the doorway.

'Getting everything ready?' he grinned.

'Can't be too prepared for something like this,' she said, brushing back a wayward strand of her brown hair. 'First babies usually take a long time, but then again we don't know when Violet really started. Knowing her, she could have been hiding it so as not to interrupt Christmas dinner.'

Danny nodded. 'You've got it all under control,' he observed.

Sarah shrugged. 'As much as that's possible – you never know what will happen at a birth, especially a first one like this. But Rita's the best. She'll know exactly what to do, no matter how it goes.'

'Well, you're the best too,' said Danny seriously.

'Danny Callaghan, you've been at that rum,' Sarah scolded him mockingly. 'Will you listen to yourself. Aren't you missing Maeve playing the piano in there?'

'I'm not missing anything important.' Danny leant against the doorpost. 'I can say it, can't I? No harm in a compliment where it's due.' He raised his eyebrows.

Sarah could see he had indeed had a tot or two of rum, and yet there was a look about him that told her he wasn't entirely joking. There was something in his eyes that hadn't been there before – or, if it had, she'd always glossed over it. She felt something shift inside her. She couldn't quite believe it – after all that she'd been thinking about him, for all the long weeks of his absence. Could it be true that he'd felt the same? Dared she hope for it?

'It's been quiet round here without you, Danny,' she began, and moved one step towards him just as he stepped closer to her.

Then there was the sound of someone running downstairs and Rita's head appeared around the other side of the door. She all but pushed Danny aside.

'Sarah,' she gasped, 'I think you'd better come up. Right now.'

The party began to break up, with Nancy saying she should take Georgie home, Dolly keen to get Ellen settled and Maeve needing to return to her digs, the other side of the hospital. Danny suggested that everyone else should come to the Callaghan house so that whatever was happening upstairs could carry on uninterrupted. 'Good idea,' said Kitty. 'You and Tommy get everyone sorted out, and I'll just make a start on clearing up here.'

'No,' said Ruby, unexpectedly stepping forward for once. 'I'll do it. I can do it.' She blushed a little at drawing the attention of so many pairs of eyes. 'You take the rest of the cake, Kitty. I'll help here. I want to be here, for if Violet needs me.' She looked down at her feet in their highly polished but very old-fashioned shoes.

Dolly realised what an effort it had been for her to speak up like that, and gave her a hug. 'Bless you, Ruby. That's a very good idea. That way the party can go on but we can get everything tidied up here.

Between us it will take no time at all, as little Ellen's fast asleep in her Moses basket.'

'You make sure to tell us as soon as there's any news,' Pop said firmly.

'Don't you be worrying about that,' said Dolly confidently. 'Sure, it will be ages yet.'

She breathed a sigh of relief as the last person left to go the short distance to the Callaghan front door. She didn't want to spoil their fun but, although the dinner had gone beautifully, now there was something else to think about.

Danny brought out their collection of glasses, rather mismatched, while Kitty brought out cups and plates. His mind was still on what had taken place in the Feeny kitchen, though.

What would Sarah have said to him if they'd stayed there and Rita hadn't rushed in? Had she understood what he'd said to her? Was this the right time to be thinking of such things? He'd have to go back to Bletchley to finish the project he'd been asked to join, and not see her for weeks. Yet he couldn't deny how much he missed her, and somehow it had felt very important that she knew it. He thought he'd caught something in her look, but then she'd had to drop everything and rush upstairs to help – exactly as he'd have expected her to do. He'd just have to wait.

The fire was low in the grate and only Danny, Frank, Pop and Kitty remained. Ruby had dropped in to escort Michael and Megan back to the flat. Tommy had taken himself up to bed hours ago, but the others couldn't sleep – Pop from anxiety, Danny because he felt too churned up, Frank because he felt some vague obligation now that Eddy wasn't here to see this baby into the world, and Kitty from good manners at being the hostess and because, no matter how tired she was, she kept catching Frank's eye in the fading firelight. The conversation had dwindled to a murmur as they all sat waiting. Frank glanced up at Kitty and she felt her heart turn over, the evening that they'd just shared seeming to sum up all that was right with the world. Their families were together and, for some reason, Kitty wasn't sure why, the awkwardness between her and Frank had disappeared today. It was almost like the days before the war, in simpler times. . . before Frank lost his leg and things changed forever.

Frank seemed to mirror her thoughts when he asked her, 'Do you remember when we had that dance Kitty, at Nancy and Sid's wedding?'

Kitty smiled. As if she could ever forget it. 'Of course, it seems like a century ago, everything was different then.'

'Some things don't change.' He stood and moved over to the gramophone, removing a record from its sleeve. 'Can you remember the song that we danced to, it was Gloria singing wasn't it?'

'That's right, but what was the song. . .' Kitty was only pretending not to remember, she knew that it was, 'The Nearness of You'. She would never forget the last dance they'd had before Frank was called up.

'It was this one wasn't it.' The opening bars drifted

288

into the room and Kitty stood, almost without realising it and moved to stand next to Frank.

'You remember it! Yes, this is the one. It's a lovely song.' Kitty and Frank were so close now they could touch. Frank closed the gap between them by coiling his arm around her waist and gently swayed her in time to the music.

'I might have lost a leg, Kitty, but I can still dance a bit.' Frank looked down into her eyes, and Kitty could not only see his smile, his kindness and his strength in his handsome face, but something else too. Something that she could feel in herself. Something that couldn't be ignored. 'You never did write me those letters that you promised,' he said, mock teasingly.

Gone was the flutter from Kitty's stomach and her usual confusion around Frank. All she felt now was his arm around her waist, the nearness of him and how good it felt – just like the words of the song said. 'Didn't I? Perhaps it was because things had changed Frank, after. . .'

'After I lost my leg you mean?' Frank asked, sombre now.

Kitty nodded.

'You're right. I was a fool, so caught up in myself I shut everyone out. But I'm learning, Kitty, I've grown up. This war has changed me, and not just how well I can dance.'

Looking at Frank now, Kitty could see that was true. 'You're still a great dancer, Frank, the best.' And Kitty meant it. Being in Frank's arms felt like the most natural thing in the world. They had both changed, she was no longer the shy and timid girl she had once been. 'Sylvia's a lucky girl.'

Frank knitted his brow and made to answer, but before he could Dolly burst in. It was already after midnight. Dolly's hair was awry and her cardigan buttoned against the cold – though all the wrong way – yet her face was full of joy as she ran to Pop and took his arms. 'Pop. You'll never guess,' she gasped.

Frank dropped his arm from Kitty's waist and removed the needle from the record, bringing their moment to an abrupt halt. 'Whatever is it, Mam? Is she all right? Is the baby here? What is it?'

Dolly stood in the centre of the Callaghan kitchen, almost too overwhelmed with emotion to speak. Then she gathered herself. 'Pop, you have a new grandson.' She paused and swallowed. 'He's going to be called Edward. Teddy for short.' Words seemed to fail her then, as Pop gasped too and looked as if he was welling up at the thought of a new Edward in the house; no replacement for – but a fitting tribute to – their beloved son who had given his life for his country and who had longed so keenly for this very moment. He rubbed his face, joy at the new life mixed with heavy sorrow for the one who would never see this new child.

Dolly took a deep breath and released the bombshell. 'You've also got a new granddaughter.'

Pop stared and Frank and Danny looked at each other and then back to Dolly.

'Yes, it's twins,' she went on. 'That poor girl – that's

why her bump was so big. But Rita says she's fine, and both babies are fine. They're a good size for twins, she says. She and Sarah are staying with them for now and we can see them in the morning. How about that?'

Pop stepped closer to her and drew her into a hug. He was a big man who had seen most of what life could throw at him, but it was almost too much for him to take in.

'A miracle,' said Dolly, her voice faint but steady now. 'Our best ever Christmas present. We might not have our boy any longer, but he'll live on – in the twins.'

Nancy was as stunned as the rest of the family by the news when it reached her on Boxing Day, and Georgie immediately demanded to be taken to see his new cousins. He'd been fascinated with baby Ellen, and the thought of now having two babies to watch was irresistible. 'I'm going to look after them,' he said seriously. 'I'm big and they'll be too small to do anything, won't they? So it's my job.' He stood up straight as Nancy did up his toggles and pushed his fringe out of his eyes.

'That's right, they'll be glad of their big cousin to help them,' she assured him. But her mind was only half on what he was saying. Her plan had been to leave Georgie with Dolly this afternoon and to dash into the city centre to meet Gary, then return in time to take him home before bedtime. She might still manage to do it, but would there be objections to her leaving him there with so much else going on? She'd risk it anyway. She was desperate to see Gary again, desperate for his touch, for that warm glow he gave her that nobody else had ever done. It was worth taking a gamble. With luck her parents' house would be in such uproar that nobody would notice she wasn't there all afternoon.

Fate seemed to smile on her as, the instant she stepped through their door, Tommy took charge of Georgie, who was delighted to trail after his hero. Nancy dutifully took a look at the new arrivals and acknowledged they were very sweet, before slipping out again into the cold December air, hurrying towards the bus stop before any of her family could challenge her.

Of course there were hardly any buses running, and she had to wait for ages, stamping her feet to stop them from freezing, thrusting her hands as deep into her pockets as she could. Once on the bus she carefully reapplied her lipstick, to the disapproval of some of the older passengers around her, who gave her sharp looks. She ignored them. It was more important to look good for Gary.

He was waiting for her near the train station, in his heavy uniform coat, his face full of concern. 'Hey, you look gorgeous,' he said, sweeping her into a close embrace. 'Aren't you cold? What a day, that wind is enough to cut a man in two.'

'All the warmer for seeing you,' Nancy said, wriggling deliciously in his arms, not caring if anyone saw them. Who of their acquaintance would be around, anyway? All the people she knew would be with their families, sitting in their tedious parlours, eating yesterday's leftovers and trying to stay festive. It didn't bear thinking about. The WVS canteen was shut and so none of her colleagues would be about. Besides, she was so wrapped up in the delight of seeing Gary that at that moment she didn't give a fig.

'Come on, let's go and celebrate our own Christmas,' she said, taking his arm and drawing him along the pavement. 'You can tell me all about what you do in America. If you were back there now, how would you be spending Boxing Day?'

Gary smiled, his eyes alight. 'Well, I certainly wouldn't be doing this,' he said, leading her along and pausing before the door of a cosy but select-looking hotel doorway. 'Shall we go in?' He pretended to bow. 'I hear they do all sorts of Christmas specialties in here.'

Nancy looked up. 'Oooh, I've never been in. I've walked past loads of times, though.' She walked in eagerly, curious to know what the place was like inside, never having dared try it before. It was without a doubt what Gary would call a classy joint, with thick carpets deadening any noise and subtle lighting, making it feel warm and welcoming and yet with a definite touch of luxury.

Gary stepped across to the reception desk and spoke in a low voice to the smartly dressed woman on duty. She smiled and gave him a key.

'Come on,' he said, returning to Nancy. 'I've told her our luggage is coming along later. So we don't need no porter to follow us up to our room.'

'Oh, Gary.' Nancy shivered in anticipation. This was a big step up from their previous assignations in pubs far from the centre, even more special than the hotel after Gloria's concert. She felt as if he no longer cared if they were seen together either – that he was proud to have her on his arm, to be seen in public with her, like a proper couple. He must really care about her, to bring her somewhere like this. 'Come on, then, show me where this room is. I can't wait to see it.' She widened her eyes at him and it was all he could do not to break into a run while picking her up in his arms then and there. Eagerly they hurried upstairs.

Frank passed through security clearance at Derby House and made his way down the chilly corridor towards the two underground floors that held the Western Approaches Command. It was the day after Boxing Day but security checks were still rigorous. Plenty of people were on holiday or in holiday mood, but the business of communications for the war effort continued day and night nevertheless. He straightened his back. He didn't want to be caught looking sloppy just because he'd had a distinct lack of sleep over the past couple of days, thanks to the shock of the twins' arrival. He could have gone back to his billet, of course, but somehow he'd felt his place was with his parents and wider family, knowing they were all sensing the absence of Eddy, even as they welcomed the arrival of his children.

The Feeny house had been bursting at the seams,

what with two extra babies and a non-stop stream of visitors keen to give their good wishes and catch a glimpse of the twins. Frank had realised again just how popular his parents were and, by extension, their children and grandchildren. Dolly's WVS friends and Pop's ARP colleagues all stopped by, bringing little trinkets of goodwill. He'd suggested sleeping on the settee in the parlour, but Rita would have none of it. 'You'll stay with me,' she'd insisted. 'There's plenty of room. In fact I'd be grateful if you could, as Michael and Megan won't be going back to the farm for a few days and, now Violet's not able to see to them, I'd really appreciate it. They don't need much, but if I knew you'd be here overnight it would be a weight off my mind.' Frank could hardly say no after that.

Derby House was quiet, the corridor echoing as he made his way along it. At least it meant he wouldn't be stuck in meetings for half the day. The downside, he reluctantly admitted, was that this also meant he wouldn't have an excuse to seek Kitty out. The sight of her face in the firelight at Christmas had stayed in his memory, along with the sound of her singing. But he'd hardly spoken to her since, as the arrival of the babies had put paid to all the household routines. She'd been on shift yesterday and was unlikely to be back in today. Firmly he turned his thoughts elsewhere, to the pile of memos that had built up for him in the brief time he'd been away from the desk. He was sifting through them, putting them in order of priority, when he heard footsteps approach.

Glancing up, he saw it was Sylvia. Instantly he felt a wash of guilt, that she'd been dealing with such difficult circumstances at home and here he was thinking about Kitty. Sylvia's expression was strained, although she smiled at the sight of him. 'Hello, Frank.'

'Sylvia!' He moved swiftly around the desk, hesitating to put his arms round her as he wasn't sure who else was in that part of the office. 'Did you have a good Christmas? I didn't know you'd be back so soon.'

She tried to maintain her smile but it didn't work. Her mouth trembled and she looked away, reaching for her handkerchief. 'No, not really.' She took a moment to gather herself. 'Dad died. It's all right, I was there, and so was my brother. He didn't suffer. We were all prepared.' She let out a deep breath. 'Even so, it came as a surprise.'

'Of course.' Frank put his hand on her arm. 'I'm so sorry. He was a good man, and he was lucky to have you all around him. Why are you back here? Didn't you want to stay at home with your mother?'

Sylvia shook her head. 'My brother has leave at the moment and so I'd rather come back here, do something useful, and then take more days when it's time for the funeral and then after when my brother can't be there. Mum will need me more then. I've talked to my superior officer, she agrees.'

Frank nodded slowly. That was a practical way of looking at it. He admired Sylvia for thinking so clearly while, if he knew her at all, wanting with every fibre of her being to be there with her mother in the family home. 'You're very brave,' he said warmly. 'We all have to carry on as best we can, don't we.'

Sylvia shrugged. 'Oh, I don't know. It's not brave. It's just the best thing to do. But thank you, Frank.' She looked up at him sadly.

'Over Christmas as well. You poor thing.' He took her hand and held it between both of his. 'Is there anything I can do? Make you a cup of tea? Take you for a drink after work?'

Slowly she pulled her hand free. 'I . . . I don't think so. I don't really feel like going out.'

Frank inwardly cursed himself. 'No. Of course not. Silly of me to suggest it. I just want to help you if I can, you know.'

'I know.' Sylvia looked up at the ceiling, the dullish bulb overhead. 'Really, I don't think there's anything. I'm going to get through the next few days and then . . . well, I'll go back home.' She paused, turned away a little, then faced him again. 'As a matter of fact . . .'

Frank met her eyes. 'What is it, Sylvia? Is something else wrong?'

The silence that followed his question lasted for an uncomfortable few moments. Sylvia looked as if she was screwing up her courage to speak, and finally she came out with it.

'The thing is, you see . . . well, I did quite a bit of thinking when I was home . . . This kind of thing, it makes you see what's important.'

Frank's expression grew puzzled as he picked up on her different tone of voice.

'You've been lovely to me,' she went on, 'I couldn't ask for a better man, a kinder man, I felt I could tell you anything. But . . . but it's not enough.' She looked down miserably. 'We have a good time, we go to the cinema, and I've loved it, but . . . I think we should stop now.'

Frank's jaw dropped. Whatever he'd been expecting, it wasn't this. 'Are – are you sure?' he managed after a pause. 'You're not just saying this because of your father? You're upset, you're bound to be, but I'll wait, if that's what you'd like.'

Sylvia shook her head. 'No. That wouldn't be fair. It's not because of Dad – or rather, that shook me up, and made me see what was happening with you and me more clearly. I could see the way Mum was with Dad, even though they were old and grey and . . . and I just can't see us like that, Frank. I'm sorry.'

Frank turned away, his emotions churning. Then he glanced downwards. Was this because of his leg? Had she felt embarrassed by his disability all this time and kept it hidden? Quick as ever, she caught his movement and realised what it meant. 'Frank, please.' She waited until he met her eyes once more. 'It's not about your leg. Believe me, I don't mind about that at all. I think you're wonderful, the way you don't let it stop you doing what you want, and I've been proud to be walking out with you. It's not that. It's . . . oh, it's hard to put my finger on.' She screwed her eyes tight shut for a second, as if she was assembling the words in her head. 'It's like sometimes you're not quite there. As if there's someone else in between us.'

Frank's chin went up sharply. 'What do you mean? I've never two-timed you – I wouldn't do a thing like that.'

'I know. Perhaps that came out wrong.' She sighed. 'Not like that, maybe, but there's a barrier around you. And, Frank, I'm not blind. Back at your niece's christening, I could see how much Kitty and I look like each other, and I'm sure I'm not the only person to have clocked it. You might not see it, but it's there all the same. I just know I'll always be on the wrong side of that barrier. Sorry.' She reached out and touched his arm. 'Thanks for everything, Frank.' Then she turned and walked away.

Frank sank slowly into the chair behind the desk, his mind whirring. He was struggling to believe what had just happened. He'd wanted to reach out to Sylvia, to comfort her, and she'd pushed him away. She didn't want them to be a couple any longer. His pride was deeply hurt. It was hard to imagine that his injury wasn't somehow to blame; any woman would find it repulsive, surely, and yet Sylvia had been adamant that wasn't the case. To be fair to her, she'd never complained, always accepted him for who he was, even though she must have ached to go dancing like the rest of her gang of friends. His mind flew off at tangents. How would he explain this to his parents? Dolly in particular had been so fond of the girl. How would he spend his free time? Would all Sylvia's friends be laughing at him behind his back? Would he spend all his working hours trying to avoid her, avoid them?

Gradually he calmed down and realised he was

being stupid. His mother would understand. She'd be sorry he was hurt but would probably say something like it was better to find out now rather than if they'd ended up getting married – just look at his sisters and their misery: Rita with the abusive Charlie and Nancy with unreliable Sid, who'd been caught seeing another woman the night before their wedding. Sylvia was a lifetime away from either of those. She'd made a difficult decision because she thought it was best for both of them.

As if there was someone else, she said. A barrier she'd always be on the wrong side of. Caused by the obvious likeness to Kitty. Well, if he was honest, she was right. Why had he found himself attracted to her to begin with? Because she reminded him of Kitty – the hair, the height, the uniform. But she wasn't Kitty. Try as he might, he had to admit that Kitty had started to infiltrate his mind more and more, the effect she had on him as potent as ever, and yet she was forever out of reach because of his disability. Sylvia hadn't known what he was like before; Kitty had. She would always draw the comparison and find him lacking, of that he was absolutely convinced.

He got up, pushing himself as always to compensate for the imbalance of the false leg. His pride was deeply wounded but he wasn't devastated. He'd recover, although he would miss Sylvia's good humour and company. In time he might even admire her for forcing the issue and bringing their relationship to an end. Just not today.

CHAPTER TWENTY-FOUR

'I really wish I could see you sing again tonight,' said Nancy ruefully, sipping a cup of tea as Gloria brushed a slight crease out of the gown hanging in her dressing room. 'I can't manage it though. I've asked everyone if they can take Georgie, but they're all too busy.' She knew she'd been pushing it recently and now Dolly had told her firmly that this was taking advantage and it had to stop.

'Never mind, you came to the first concert and cheered me on,' said Gloria. 'It's always good to have a friendly face in the front row. Gives me confidence.' She flashed her big smile.

'You don't need that, Glor, you must be used to it all by now,' exclaimed Nancy, surprised. 'You've been doing it for years.'

'Still get those last-minute nerves though,' admitted Gloria, patting her tummy. 'I wouldn't perform as well without them, but I do appreciate it when you're there, clapping.'

'Well, me and Gary,' said Nancy.

Gloria sat down opposite her. 'Oh yes, Gary. How is he? Have you seen him over Christmas?'

Nancy's eyes brightened. 'Yes, we had a wonderful afternoon at this gorgeous little hotel right near the station. It wasn't as swish as the Adelphi's rooms but it wasn't far off. It was my extra present, he said.' Her expression grew dreamy as she remembered just how exciting the afternoon had been.

'You're taking a bit of a risk doing something like that,' Gloria pointed out as she reached for a nail file.

Nancy shrugged. 'Not really. The place was deserted, quiet as the grave it was. Anyway, it shows how much he cares for me.'

Gloria gave her a quizzical look. 'Suppose so. He seems too good to be true, your Gary.'

'Oh, he is.' Nancy's face lit up. 'He's the best thing that's ever happened to me, Gloria. Well, apart from Georgie,' she added quickly. 'He keeps telling me about his home and how lovely it is. I think he's preparing the way.'

'What for?' asked Gloria.

Nancy shrugged. 'Well, I think he's going to ask me to go back there with him.'

Gloria shook her head. 'What do you mean?'

'You know. Like one of those GI brides.'

Gloria gave her friend a sharp look. 'Hang on there, Nancy. Wait a minute. You can't marry him. You're married already – never mind that there's Georgie to consider as well.'

Nancy shook her hair, which she was wearing loose today, clipped back with a glittery grip that Gary had

302

given her. 'I'm sure he'll find a way somehow. That's how much he cares for me, Glor. Anyway we don't know if Sid is coming home or not, do we? All those years he's been away, anything could happen.'

Gloria raised her eyebrows. It was true she didn't have much time for Sid Kerrigan, the cheater and would-be Mr Big, but the man had served all these years as a POW, and after enduring Dunkirk too. He couldn't be erased from Nancy's life quite so conveniently. Also, her initial distrust on first meeting Gary was growing by the minute.

'Nancy,' she said steadily, 'don't take this the wrong way, but are you sure he's not married? Older man, good-looking, knows how to please women . . . doesn't that give you pause for thought?'

'God, Gloria, I thought you were my friend!' Nancy exclaimed hotly. 'What do you want to say a thing like that for? Of course he's not married, he'd have said. He's a good man, Gary is. That's exactly the kind of remark Mam would make. Fine sort of friend you are.'

'That's why I'm saying it,' Gloria told her. 'I'm not judging you, Nancy. You know me better than that. I'm just asking the obvious question. He might still be a good man – people keep secrets, that's all. You do.'

Nancy puffed angrily. 'You're only saying that because you're jealous. You don't have anyone like him.' Then her hand flew to her mouth as she realised what she'd said.

Gloria simply looked at her for a long moment.

Then she stood up. 'No, as you so rightly say, I don't have anyone like him. I did, though. Giles died saving me and I never forget it, not for one single day. He's gone and I can't change that. Doesn't mean I can't see what's going on right under my nose though.' She turned and put the nail file back in the little pearly pink case with a gold clasp that contained the rest of her neatly organised manicure set. 'I don't want to quarrel with you, Nancy. You're my best and oldest friend. Be careful, that's all. Don't let your dreams take you too far from what you've already got.'

Nancy stood as well, pushing the little dressing stool under the shabby counter, littered with make-up and brushes. 'No. I know. I'm sorry I said that, Glor. I didn't mean nothing by it.' She hung her head and her beautiful Titian hair swung down like a glossy curtain, obscuring her features. She couldn't bear to catch sight of herself in the speckled mirror. How could she have flung that at her best friend, who'd quietly mourned Giles ever since that dreadful night when the bomb had killed him as he'd shielded Gloria from the blast.

'I know. Come here.' Gloria opened her arms and Nancy fell into them, hugging her friend tightly. 'Wish me luck for later, then you're going to have to go. I've got to speak to the *Liverpool Post* and then get ready properly. Just be careful, won't you?'

'Break a leg,' said Nancy as brightly as she could. She hated it when Gloria left her behind. 'And I'll be careful, course I will.' She gave her one last hug and then left the little room, making her way to the stage door and out into the sharp winter air. She'd hurry back and rescue Georgie from his detested Granny Kerrigan, because she really needed her family to do her a favour at New Year's Eve, which she planned to spend with Gary. Her mind flew again to the wonderful hours they'd spent together in the discreet hotel. In fact they'd had such a marvellous time that for once they had forgotten to be quite as careful as usual. But she wasn't going to worry about that now. Gary would look after her, no matter what, of that she was completely convinced.

Rita stood at the sink in the kitchen behind the shop and rinsed out her cup. She had dearly wanted to spend New Year's Eve with all her children, but she'd been called in to do a night shift and she couldn't let the hospital down. At least Maeve would be on duty too, and so they could spend the time cheering up the patients, saying goodbye to 1944 and welcoming in 1945. She couldn't begin to guess what this year would bring.

Ruby came into the room behind her, a big ledger under her arm. Rita turned and smiled.

'Don't tell me you're going to see in the new year by doing the accounts, Ruby,' she said. 'Let them go for once.'

Ruby shook her heard, her pale blonde hair bobbing as she did so. 'No, they are all up to date now. Everything tallies.' She put the ledger down proudly. 'We made a profit this year, Rita. You don't have to worry like you used to.'

Rita let out a breath she hadn't even realised she'd been holding, but the very sight of the ledger always made her anxious, ever since that awful time when the shop had nearly gone bust. They'd have lost their main source of income and maybe the roof over their heads as well. Now, even though she knew she didn't have to panic – Jack's wages would always provide for them – the deep instinct was still there. 'Ruby, you are a marvel,' she said with real feeling. 'I can't begin to think how we managed without you.' Badly, she recalled. It was Ruby's unexpected gift for reading columns of figures that had set them on the right road. 'So, if you aren't balancing the books, how are you spending the evening? Are you going over to Mam's with the children?'

Ruby's face took on a bashful expression. 'She's very kind. She asked me.'

'Of course,' said Rita. 'You're part of the family and Michael and Megan would love you to be there.'

Ruby nodded. 'I know. They asked me. It's been so lovely spending Christmas with them, they've grown so big. All the same . . .' She looked away.

'You don't have to say, I'm only teasing,' Rita assured her, wondering what could be so important that Ruby would turn down the chance to spend the last evening with the children before Joan and Seth arrived tomorrow to take them back to the farm. She hoped Ruby wasn't intending to go out and return late, unlikely though it seemed. The children would have to sleep upstairs, as there would be no room with Dolly and Pop, especially as they had agreed yet again to have Georgie to stay.

Ruby bit her lip and looked at the ceiling. 'I'm having a visitor.'

'A visitor?' Rita asked with interest.

'Yes.' Ruby's voice grew a little more confident. 'Mr James asked me to spend this evening with him and I said no, I can't go out because I'm looking after Michael and Megan later. That's right, isn't it?'

'Well, yes, that's what I'd hoped,' said Rita.

'So I asked him to come round for the evening,' Ruby went on, 'and he said yes. He's going to teach me to play chess. He promised ages ago, but his father was sick and he couldn't come before now. Old Mr James is better now so Reggie can come after all.' Her face glowed with excitement.

'Chess?' Rita echoed in astonishment. If only Winnie could see the young woman now, she thought. Her late mother-in-law had treated Ruby with nothing but meanness. She'd been horrible to Rita too, but Rita had had the support of her family to fall back on. Ruby had had nobody, no reason to disbelieve the common opinion that she was soft in the head and good for nothing. Maybe Winnie could indeed see her, from wherever she had been consigned to in the after-life. Rita remonstrated with herself – Winnie must have had her good points once, she supposed; it was just by the time Rita had met her, they'd been well hidden. For years Rita had blamed herself for the failure of her own first marriage, but the cruelty Winnie had shown Ruby, never admitting that she was her daughter, palming her off to endure being raised by spiteful Elsie Lowe, then putting it about that Ruby was simple once she had come back into her life, never ceased to amaze Rita every time she thought about it. She could not understand how a mother could treat her own child like that – Michael, Megan and Ellen were worth more than life itself to her.

Even so, how would Ruby take to chess? The only person Rita knew who could play was Danny, and he'd taken it up only recently. You had to have a certain sort of mind, people said. Yet perhaps Ruby did. While she still struggled with plenty of everyday activities, she was strangely talented in many other ways, and so perhaps this would be another one of them.

'Yes, he said it's all about seeing patterns, and I can do that,' Ruby said, growing more assured by the minute. 'I'm really looking forward to it.'

Rita nodded in astonishment but in admiration too. 'Make sure you get out the special Christmas biscuits that Kitty made,' she said. Impulsively she leant forward and gave Ruby a hug. 'I hope you have a lovely evening. I'll take Michael and Megan over to Mam's and then go straight to the hospital. I'll see you in the morning.'

Ruby smiled, even though she had never really taken to being hugged. 'Happy New Year, Rita.'

Sarah drew her nurse's cloak around her as she headed along the dock road, battling against the wind. Just when she could have done with getting off shift early, there had been an emergency and she'd had to stay late. It was thankfully nothing to do with the war, but a young boy who'd come in with appendicitis. The surgeon had caught it in the nick of time. Then again, she thought, even this relatively common incident had been affected by the war after all, as the boy's father was away fighting in France, his mother had been killed in the Liverpool Blitz and the aunt who was caring for him had had to find somebody to look after her own two younger children before she could come to visit. So it had fallen to Sarah to sit with the young patient as he regained consciousness, and reassure him that he would soon be well again and that a familiar face would be with him any minute.

As she neared her front door, Tommy and Danny emerged from theirs.

'Happy New Year, Sarah!' Tommy called, his new scarf blowing behind him in the strong breeze. Dolly had knitted it for him for Christmas, as he'd confessed to losing his other one. 'I'm coming over to yours for the evening. Aunty Dolly said I could.'

'Of course you are,' said Sarah. 'How about you, Danny? Where are you off to?' She hadn't seen him to speak to properly since that incident in the kitchen on Christmas Day, what with working at the hospital and helping with the chaos the twins' arrival had brought. 'Are you going to see in the New Year with us?' She tried to keep the hope out of her voice. She didn't want to sound desperate, and it was a perfectly reasonable assumption that he'd come with Tommy, after all. She grinned at him; she'd make time to see him on his own, and find out if he was still in the same frame of mind as on that momentous night.

Danny looked at her, and she was sure that she wasn't imagining it when he took a second longer than usual to reply. 'No, I've got to go into town,' he said.

'Big party, is it?' she asked lightly, trying to mask her disappointment. Who would have asked him? Who would be there?

He laughed. 'No, not quite as exciting as that,' he said. 'I've got to go to work. Something's up and they need me overnight. Not quite what I'd planned, but nobody else can do this particular task and so they've asked me.'

'Oh, of course you have to go,' said Sarah, at once sad that he wouldn't be with them for the clock striking midnight, relieved that he wouldn't be spending it with an unknown group of friends, and proud that he'd answered the call of duty without a quibble.

'I'd rather spend it with you folks,' Danny said, but it was impossible to read his face in the near-darkness. Did his voice carry an extra layer of meaning, or was it wishful thinking on her part? She couldn't tell.

'Come on, our Danny, it's perishing out here.' Tommy was all but jumping up and down on the spot.

'All right, you go on in then,' said Danny. 'Er . . . how are the twins? I've scarcely had a chance to ask.'

'They're doing well. Violet's managing to feed them and we got a special delivery of goodies from Joan and Seth, so she's able to eat as much as she likes herself. She's going to call the little girl Barbara.'

'Oh, that's a new one,' said Danny. 'Is that after anyone in her family? You haven't got any Barbaras, have you?'

Sarah shivered in the cold air but tried not to let it show. 'No, we haven't, and Violet hasn't either. She said she wanted something different, sort of a new beginning. But the middle name is to be Rita. Isn't that lovely?'

Danny chuckled. 'Well, that's only right. She and Rita have been thick as thieves. Barbara Rita. Has a nice ring to it.'

Again, from the dim outline of his face, she thought he was gazing at her in a new way, but she couldn't be sure, and wouldn't put herself out on a limb by asking. She found herself tongue-tied. Part of her said this was ridiculous – here was the person she'd been able to tell anything, with whom she'd been totally relaxed for as long as she could remember. But suddenly the words just wouldn't flow. 'I'd . . . I'd best get in, they'll be wondering where I am,' she said. 'Will I see you tomorrow?'

He shook his head. 'Afraid not. I'm due back at Bletchley so I'll have to start out first thing. One of the others whose parents live over in the Wirral is giving me a lift.'

'Oh.' Sarah didn't know what to say. What was foremost in her mind felt too big, too important, to be rushed in a few seconds on a freezing cold street.

'So, anyway, Happy New Year,' said Danny, stepping towards her a little.

'Yes. Yes, and to you too.' She looked up at him and for a moment thought he was going to come even closer. But he reached out, touched her arm briefly and turned away.

Confused, disappointed, and yet sure that he'd meant something more than the simple words themselves, she took out her key and let herself in to the warm comfort of her noisy family home.

Kitty paused to look out of her office window at the darkening sky and what was visible of the city skyline. She'd been working in the Tactical Unit, allied to Derby House, and was the last to leave. New Year's Eve. She cast her mind back to the previous one, when she'd still been down at the south coast. She'd had the afternoon off and had managed to meet up with Marjorie, and they'd had a chilly but bracing walk along the coast before finding a café serving an amazingly luxurious real hot chocolate, rich and sweet. She savoured the memory of the taste, better by far than any champagne or cocktail. Though maybe if Laura had been there she wouldn't have agreed.

Kitty sighed as she straightened the small pile of paper; it would need to be attended to as soon as possible. She and Laura had exchanged Christmas cards, but neither of them had heard from Marjorie. They'd again reassured each other that no news was good news, but Kitty was beginning to lose faith in the phrase. She dreaded that the worst had happened.

And how dreadful it was for Laura, to have finally come out of the horrible limbo of not knowing Freddy's fate, only to be faced with an almost identical situation with one of her closest friends.

Nothing to be done about it, thought Kitty grimly, putting on her overcoat and picking up her bag. She didn't particularly feel like celebrating with Marjorie's fate hanging unresolved, but Tommy would expect her to join in the fun. After all, she told herself firmly, she should be glad of everything that had gone well in the past year. The course of the war, for one. The tide had well and truly turned and the Allies had continued to sweep through France. The end might finally be in sight. She wanted that more than anything, so that if Tommy did suddenly change his mind and sign up with the Merchant Navy, at least his life wouldn't be in danger, or no more than it would normally be in peacetime.

She could be proud of herself too, for taking on this position and doing it well. It wasn't big-headed to say so; she'd been praised by her superior officer only this last week, and she knew she commanded the respect of her colleagues. She and Danny had made a safe home for Tommy, and guided him into a relatively safe job; that was a very big thing to be thankful for. Rita had had her baby safely, Jack had had a few shore leaves in the last year, and he and Rita were happy at last, against all the odds. Violet had had twins and they were thriving, despite the tragedy of Eddy's death, which they had all felt so deeply. So there was much to be thankful for.

If only Danny didn't have to go back to his residential course. It wasn't for ever, but they evidently thought so highly of him that he'd been selected to continue working on a special project. She would never have admitted it to him but, after that night when Alfie Delaney had tried to get into her house, she kept expecting him to try again. He wouldn't dare if he knew Danny was there. Perhaps he didn't know Danny was going away again. She would have to hope that was the case.

If Frank had still been living across the road she'd have felt much safer, but he'd gone back to his billet and she hadn't seen him since Christmas, as their shifts hadn't coincided. She paused as she drew her scarf around her neck – a soft, warm one in elegant royal blue, a present from Laura. Heaven only knew how she'd come by such a gorgeous thing. For a second Kitty imagined Frank draping the scarf around her neck, tying it gently, tucking it into her collar. She shook her head to dismiss the image. There was no point. Frank had Sylvia, and anyway, when all was said and done, Kitty was nothing to him but a kid sister, no matter what her professional ranking. All the same, that look in his eyes as he'd sat by her fire at Christmas, as they waited for news of the birth – and then the stolen dance to the gramophone record . . . She took a deep breath, checked the blackout blinds were in place, and left the office. She knew what her midnight wish would be, no matter how fanciful it seemed. It was just that she couldn't see any way that it would come true in the next year.

CHAPTER TWENTY-FIVE

The pale winter sun shone through the old net curtains, but Alfie couldn't bring himself to stir. He turned over in his bed and buried his head under the pillow, trying to block out the light. He'd have happily left the blackout blind down all the time, but his mother insisted he had to know when was day and when was night. It made no difference to him.

He'd never known a case of flu like it. Usually he prided himself on being able to weather most minor ailments, and his fellow workers on the docks were quick to condemn anyone who bunked off claiming they were sick. It took a lot to fell most of them. Alfie had never had their dedication or commitment, but he didn't see it that way as he lay in his sickbed, powerless to alter the menace of the virus, weak as a baby.

He thought he was a martyr, bearing up as well as he could, but unable to lift a finger to help himself. Surely nobody had ever suffered so badly. One minute he was racked with fever, raging hot, the next he was shivering, and no amount of extra blankets could make him feel warm again. His mother piled his bed with everything she could find – old counterpanes, crocheted shawls and a moth-eaten candlewick bedspread – but they did no good. Then he'd be too hot again and throw them all off, calling for her to fling open the window and let in the cool air.

This had been going on for weeks. Alfie had been too ill to be bored to begin with, but now he was slowly growing tired of being stuck in this one room, the bedroom he'd had since he was a boy. He'd never been much of a reader, and his eyes hurt too much to squint at the newspaper. He couldn't stand all the radio programmes his mother loved so much – he could hear *ITMA* – *It's That Man Again* – floating up the stairs, and sometimes she would laugh out loud and join in with one of the catchphrases. He swore he would scream if she ever said 'Can I do you now, sir?' one more time, except he didn't have the energy.

He had to admit she had looked after him, bringing him hot soup when he was cold, and chilled lemonade when he was burning up. All the same, he resented her for it, having to rely on her so much, as if he was nothing but a little boy again. He'd always taken blatant advantage of the way she spoilt him, taking it for granted that she'd be happy to wait on him hand and foot, and he hadn't particularly noticed how she did it. Now every tiny detail jarred. The way she'd be so deliberately cheerful in the morning, pulling up the hated blind. The little song she'd hum as she brought him up his meals. The snippets of gossip she'd bring back, in which he had not the slightest bit of interest.

Even though his body was worn out, his mind was beginning to churn, rehashing old resentments and frustrations. He didn't in the least care about being off work. He would rather his fellow dockers didn't think badly of him for taking the time off, but he didn't miss the physical work itself – he was happy to leave them to get on with it. He missed the company, though, and the opportunities it brought him for little deals on the side, always with an eye out for a profit. That was what made life worth living – getting one over on somebody, winning a game the other person hadn't even realised they'd been playing.

The fact that he hadn't managed to get Danny to do what he wanted still plagued him. Danny had somehow won without even seeming to try. He was safe as houses, doing his soft desk job, not getting his hands dirty. Alfie had begun to imagine how he'd teach the man a lesson if he ever got him alone, where he couldn't cry out for help. The more he thought about it, the more it seemed like a reasonable thing to do. His feverish days and nights put strange images of vengeance into his mind. Before his illness, Alfie had done a deal with one of Clender's men and got himself a crate of whisky off the back of a lorry. He'd hidden it in his wardrobe so his mother wouldn't find it, and had been helping himself when his thirst got really bad. It was now nearly all gone, but it had further fuelled his hatred of Danny, and his obsession with the Callaghans.

Then there was Kitty. Even before the illness hit him, he'd decided to lie low. He could have sworn that with an extra few minutes he would have worked out a way of getting into her house that night, but that bloody interfering Pop Feeny had come along to spoil his fun. The real problem was, Pop might have recognised him. Alfie had scarpered as fast as he was able, but he knew Pop was no fool. He didn't know if the self-righteous old ARP warden would have said anything to Kitty. He knew they were close, that Pop was almost like a second father to her, so on the one hand he might have felt obliged to warn her, but on the other he might not have wanted to frighten her.

He was fairly sure Pop hadn't reported him to his boss down at the docks, or to the police. Alfie had prepared his excuse: that he had just been dropping round to see Tommy and check if the new bike he'd got through Frank was all right, or if the lad wanted Alfie to go ahead and get him a better one. He figured this would be plausible – Tommy could back him up that he'd made the offer in the first place. He hadn't needed to use it, though. This was the one advantage of being laid up for so long. The odds were that by the time he eventually made it back into the outside world, everyone would have forgotten the incident.

He hadn't though. He craved news of Kitty, but no matter how much salacious gossip his mother repeated when she got home from shopping, she never mentioned her. He was all too familiar with the progress of the Feeny twins, whose unexpected arrival

318

was the talk of the neighbourhood, and the never-ending sorrow of old Mrs Kerrigan, missing her POW son Sid and now mourning Eddy Feeny too, despite her never having had a good word for him as far as anyone could remember while he was alive. There was the report that Mr and Mrs Mawdsley had had a goose for Christmas dinner and invited lots of their neighbours to share it. Alfie had not appreciated that titbit – it had been stuck-up Mr Mawdsley who'd led the complaints about the poisoned meat that had got him banned from the Sailor's Rest and forced to go up to Clydebank.

Every now and again he would feign interest in his mother's gossip and drop in Kitty's name just in case it jogged her memory. It hadn't done any good. As far as he could tell, Kitty was still working at that combined forces place in the city centre along with her brother. Yet again, he resented that Danny Callaghan, who he knew for a fact was no better than he was when it came to sticking to the right side of the law, was now some highfalutin boffin, safe and warm at his desk, while he, Alfie Delaney, worked all hours God sent labouring away and breaking his back. There was no justice in the world and his mind churned with hatred.

Alfie cursed to himself as he heard the door go downstairs and his mother cackling away to the *ITMA* theme. He took a small swig of whisky. When he was up and about again, he'd find a way of getting through to Kitty. She was going to be his and his alone. He knew that deep down it was what she wanted; she just hadn't realised it yet. It was up to him to show her what she was missing.

'So they've got you working here all day every day now, have they?' Vera Delaney eyed Ruby with suspicion, her eyes narrowing into slits. She hoisted her wickerwork basket on her arm, like a weapon.

'Y-yes.' Ruby stepped back a little. She was much better these days with nearly all of the customers, but there were a handful who reduced her to the bag of nerves she'd been when she'd first arrived. Vera, being one of Winnie's old pals, had been fed the tale that the girl was simple and could never be expected to amount to anything, and she behaved as if nothing had changed.

'Well, that's nice for Rita and Violet, knowing they've got someone they can rely on while they're off having children,' Vera went on.

Ruby looked puzzled. She often had trouble working out exactly what this woman wanted. She could tell the words should have been a compliment, and yet they didn't sound like one, which confused her. 'Yes,' she said again.

Vera stood still, as if waiting for something more. Then she shook her head and tutted. 'I'll have some of those tins of soup for my Alfie,' she said, pointing to the shelf above the till. 'Chicken, if you've got it. That's his favourite. He needs building up.'

Ruby reached down all the tins of chicken soup she could see.

'Been took terribly bad with the flu, he has,' Vera

told her, as if this was the most important news in the world. 'He can hardly move, the poor lamb. It's breaking his heart to be off work so long.'

'Oh,' said Ruby. This wasn't what anybody else she knew had ever said about Alfie, but she realised it would be foolish to point this out to his mother.

'He works so hard, practically wearing himself out,' Vera continued, her voice high and whiny. 'It's no wonder he's been taken so poorly.'

Ruby nodded, wishing she would just take her tins and go.

'Of course some folks round here have it easy, swanning around,' Vera complained. Just at that moment there was a movement outside and the speeding figure of Tommy on his bike whizzed past the shop window. Vera puffed in annoyance. 'Those Callaghans, for a start.'

Ruby shook her head, knowing full well how hard they all worked and the hours they put in week in week out.

'That Kitty is no better than she should be,' Vera said viciously, 'and as for that Danny, my Alfie said he let him down. Then he goes and gets that cushy job in an office.'

Ruby wasn't sure what to say to that. What did she mean about Kitty? That didn't make sense. If she was no better than she should be, wasn't that a good thing, not bad? She decided to stick strictly to the facts. 'Danny's not here now, he's away on a course,' she said.

'Is he, now? Probably smarmed his way on to that

an' all.' Vera gave her an exasperated look. 'Winnie was right about you – you haven't an ounce of sense in you. Come on, give me those tins and I'll be off.'

'You have to pay,' Ruby pointed out.

'I know that, you stupid girl.' Vera threw her coins down angrily on the counter, just as Rita appeared from the stock room.

'Anything else I can help you with, Mrs Delaney?' she asked sweetly, shrugging out of her thick nurse's cloak, as she had come straight from her shift at the hospital.

Vera glared at her, took her shopping, and swept out without a word, slamming the shop door.

Ruby looked at Rita with concern. 'She's not a very nice lady,' she said, her voice trembling a little.

'No, she isn't,' said Rita. 'Don't you mind what she says. You get off and make yourself beautiful – you're seeing Reggie later, aren't you?'

At once Ruby's face transformed. 'He's taking me to the pictures. I'm so excited. It's *Bell-Bottom George*, because he knows I love George Formby. Then we'll get fish and chips.'

Rita beamed, delighted that this new friendship was growing stronger and stronger. Ruby had been through so much – she surely deserved a good man like Reggie James. He seemed genuinely fond of her and had been around several times since New Year to continue the chess lessons, and, if Rita wasn't much mistaken, to gently pay court to Ruby.

'Off you go, then.' Rita shooed her out of the shop. She glanced at her watch. Not long and she could shut the place up and take herself over to her mother's and pick up Ellen, giving her the excuse to check on her lovely new niece and nephew. She was deeply touched that Violet had called the little girl after her. It was the little things like that which made life worthwhile, she thought, struck by the contrast of Vera's spite and the loving generosity she'd find over at her parents' house. If you were brought up by the likes of Pop and Dolly, you learned how to take the rough with the smooth and to love and be loyal to your family and friends. If you were brought up by Vera, you ended up like Alfie. She said a silent prayer of gratitude that she had the parents she did.

CHAPTER TWENTY-SIX

Kitty did her best to keep her face neutral and her hands from shaking as she picked up her notepad from the training committee meeting which had just finished. She pretended to drop a pencil so that everyone else would leave before her. She couldn't cope with seeing Frank after the surprise announcement.

Commander Stephens had come straight out with it without any warning or preamble. 'Now that it looks as if we have Hitler on the run, it's vitally important that all staff dealing with communications of every kind are on top of their game, and that we all operate according to the same procedures, whether we're in Land's End or John O'Groats. I need two members of staff to attend the briefing in person in London. Lieutenant Feeny, you'll represent your men. We need someone from the Wrens – Miss Callaghan, I'm informed it had better be you. Kindly see to it that your colleagues are up to date with everything before you go, although I'm sure I don't need to tell you that.'

'Of course, sir,' Kitty had said automatically, even as her mind reeled in shock. She was going to be with Frank for this special meeting. She'd probably have to travel with him. She wasn't sure whether to be delighted or to dread it. Could it be that he'd asked for her especially? Maybe he'd engineered it somehow. Perhaps he knew just how she felt about him after all, particularly since Christmas . . .

As if in a daze, she shut the meeting room door behind her, to find that Moira Butcher was waiting for her.

'Well, looks as if you've got yourself a cushy number,' she said airily. 'You'll be able to live it up in the bright lights. You were down there before for a while, weren't you?'

'Yes, I was,' said Kitty, a little offended that this was how her colleague saw it. 'I don't suppose there'll be much time to live it up, though. These meetings go on and on, you know that as well as I do. They won't bring people from all over the place just to give them a chance to hit the West End.'

'I'd make sure I managed it if I were you,' said the Wren, and Kitty realised she was jealous.

'I might try to see someone I did my initial training with who's still posted down there,' Kitty admitted. It felt like a long time since she'd last seen Laura.

The other woman raised her eyebrows. 'See, I knew you wouldn't be on duty every minute,' she said. 'And, by the way, don't go thinking there's something special about you and that's why you were chosen. I happen to know that Lieutenant Feeny specifically

325

asked for your superior officer to go, but he was overruled and you're the second choice. So don't go giving yourself airs.'

Kitty was too shocked to answer and Moira walked away, head held high, without a glance back. Had the woman hated her all along? As if she'd give herself airs about anything. But now Kitty felt sick to her stomach, knowing she hadn't been top of Frank's list. He would probably resent being stuck with her when he'd wanted someone more experienced with a higher rank. She was just a poor substitute. He hadn't fixed this so they could be together – the very reverse. Somehow she'd have to get through the ordeal without revealing what she now knew. Well, she'd have to give it her all, to demonstrate she was no pushover. If Commander Stephens wanted a responsible Wren to represent the Western Approaches Command, then she would do her utmost to live up to what he'd asked of her – with or without Frank's approval.

'You never think I'm old enough to cope!' Tommy complained. 'I will be all right on my own. You don't have to worry about me.'

Kitty shook her head. It was one thing to leave Tommy for a few hours in the evening when he got back at his regular time and she was on lates. Even then Kitty knew very well that he often went across to Dolly and Pop's, or sometimes even to the shop. He very rarely spent many hours on his own. It would be another matter altogether to have him sleep alone in the house. He wasn't yet fifteen.

'Don't you trust me?' he went on. 'You just think I'll go to the pub again, don't you. Well, I won't. I won't let you down.' He was going red in the face just like he used to when he got cross as a little boy.

Kitty had wondered if he could stay with the Feenys but the place was, as usual, bursting at the seams. Maybe Rita could take him, but she'd recently decorated the smallest bedroom in the flat for Ellen and therefore Tommy would have to stay on the settee. Rita would be coming in at all hours and Ellen would wake up as likely as not. It wasn't a recipe for a growing lad to get a good night's sleep. Privately Kitty was unsure of how much use Ruby would be as a guardian, either.

The tension broke as there was a quick knock at the door before Sarah came in. 'Look what I found,' she said as she stepped inside. 'Tommy, this is yours, isn't it?' She held up a scarf.

'Oh, that's my old one! I've been looking for that for ages,' said Tommy, his expression changing from mutinous to relieved. 'Where was it?'

Sarah laughed and shook her head. 'Believe it or not, behind the sideboard. Heaven knows how it got there. Well, now you'll have two.' She held it out to him. 'Careful, I tried to brush off all the dust but you'll need to wash it, I should think.'

Tommy took it eagerly. Even if he now had a new warmer, softer scarf, he was delighted to get this old one back – you never knew when you'd need a spare. Besides, it had annoyed him that he'd lost it – just one more thing that Kitty would use in her argument that he wasn't sensible enough to take care of himself.

Sarah realised there had been something going on before her arrival. 'What's the matter?' she asked, sharp as ever.

'Oh, nothing,' said Kitty, at the exact same time as Tommy said, 'Kitty's going away and won't let me stay here on my own.'

Sarah glanced from one to the other and Kitty gave her the details, while Tommy chipped in with his objections at every possible moment. Eventually he was satisfied that Sarah had understood his point of view, not just Kitty's. He liked Sarah and couldn't bear her to think he was still the little boy they all considered more of a liability than a help.

Sarah nodded, and sat herself down at the kitchen table. 'I see,' she said slowly. 'Actually, you know, this might get me out of a tricky situation. As long as you don't think I'm being cheeky.'

'Whatever do you mean?' Kitty demanded.

Sarah met her eye and gave her a knowing look without Tommy noticing. 'Well,' she said, 'the thing is, the twins are gorgeous, of course they are, but they're having trouble settling. It seems as if one of them's always awake. It's all right for Mam and Pop, they're in the front bedroom, but my bedroom is right next to Violet and the babies and I can hear them crying all the time. I'm having trouble sleeping too, and it's starting to affect my work. I can't seem to make up the hours.'

Tommy looked concerned. 'That must be awful,' he

said in his best man-of-the-world voice. 'I know I don't work as well when I haven't slept properly.'

'Exactly, I'm glad you understand,' said Sarah seriously. 'So, and this is the cheeky bit, I was wondering, if I could have your room while you're away, Kitty?' She looked at the two of them. 'Even if it's only for a night or two, that would let me break the habit. At the moment I just lie there even when they're quiet, waiting for one of them to start again. If I was over here I could turn over and go back to sleep.'

Kitty raised her eyebrows. It was a clever idea. It would put her mind at rest, Tommy would think they were doing Sarah a favour and, in truth, Sarah probably could do with a couple of nights of unbroken sleep. But she couldn't appear to leap at the idea or Tommy would smell a rat. 'Well . . .' she began. 'It won't be for long – are you sure it wouldn't be more trouble than it's worth?'

'Don't be silly, Kitty,' said Tommy at once. 'We have to help Sarah. Look at all the things she's done for us. Now it's our turn.'

Sarah looked hesitant. 'If you're sure I won't be in your way . . .'

Tommy shook his head firmly. 'Not a bit. You have to come and stay here. I insist.'

Kitty nodded. 'Tommy, if you feel like that, then I won't object,' she said. 'Sarah, you'll be very welcome to my room. It's all settled.'

'It's not fair!' Georgie stamped his foot in an

uncharacteristic burst of temper. 'Auntie Sarah is going to stay with Tommy. I want to go too.'

'Good heavens, Georgie, we can't expect Tommy to look after you *and* Auntie Sarah, now can we?' Nancy crouched down so that she was on the same level as her son. She wasn't sure what all this was about. Ruefully she told herself that she'd got off lightly so far – Georgie had by and large been a compliant little boy, rarely complaining, happy to go to whichever babysitter Nancy could find for him. The only thing he really objected to was his Granny Kerrigan's food, and she could hardly blame him for that.

However, since Tommy had moved back home, Georgie had grown to idolise him more and more. Given half a chance he'd have followed him everywhere. He'd started to ask for clothes like Tommy's, and Nancy had caught him in front of the mirror trying to brush his hair so it looked the same. The older boy could do no wrong. Nancy tried in vain to persuade her son that Tommy had to have a bike for work and that Georgie didn't need one. 'Maybe when you're bigger,' she said with her fingers crossed behind her back. She didn't want Georgie riding off and falling down potholes.

'I'll help look after them,' Georgie said. 'I'm good at helping, Granny Feeny said so. And I'm old enough. I'm going to school soon.'

Nancy nodded, even though she sometimes found it hard to believe – her little boy almost old enough to go to school. In some ways she dreaded it – it was such a milestone for them both. Yet she knew he would love it as he was a sociable little chap, and it would give her more freedom in the daytime. For a moment she imagined more secret trysts with Gary in the early afternoon. Then she brought herself up short. Although of course Gary couldn't say anything definite, he'd given her to understand he would be back in action soon. He still hadn't asked her to come back to America with him, but she was certain he was building up to it. Perhaps Georgie wouldn't have long to spend at his infant school in Merseyside . . .

'Mam, you aren't listening,' he protested. 'Let me stay one night with Tommy and Auntie Sarah. Just one.'

Nancy thought again of lying in Gary's arms. Maybe they could snatch an entire night with each other, one last time before he went back into action. 'All right,' she said. 'We'll ask. You'll have to be good and do what they tell you, mind.'

'Of course,' said Georgie, offended by the idea that he would do anything else.

'Let me help you with your case, Kitty.' Frank reached for the rather battered overnight bag that Kitty had brought with her on to the train.

'Thank you, but I can manage,' Kitty said, rather more sharply than she'd intended, but she didn't want to feel beholden to him for anything, not even something as small as him lifting her case on to the rack. Now she knew he'd wanted someone else to accompany him on this trip, she vowed to keep her distance, or at least as much as possible, given they would be travelling together in the same small compartment of the carriage.

Frank showed no outward reaction to her refusal but inside he was seething. So she thought he wasn't capable even of putting a case on a rack. It wasn't as if he'd lost an arm, but she had to make her point. She still saw him as someone who was lacking in some way, and he was lesser in her eyes for it. Just when he'd thought they might be getting closer again – but no, he'd got that completely wrong. He'd misread her face in the firelight at New Year. It had been a trick of the light, not a softening towards him. Well, two could play at that game.

'Very well,' he said, settling himself opposite her, as for once they had the space to themselves. 'I take it that you have your copy of the agenda for tomorrow?'

'Naturally,' said Kitty brusquely, reaching for her handbag, which she'd left on the floor. 'It's right here. Shall we go through it now?'

'That's just what I had in mind,' said Frank. 'We should make sure we're properly prepared. I don't want any of the London bigwigs to think we're in any way inferior to them just because we are based in Liverpool.'

'I should say not,' said Kitty vehemently. 'Well, then. Here we are. We'd best be quick as we don't want to do this in front of any other passengers who may join us. Right, item one.'

Frank glanced up at her but she was staring at the piece of paper, the top of her pen resting against her mouth, resolutely not meeting his eyes. She was the picture of professional efficiency and he had no cause to complain. Yet every cell in his body wanted something else from her. He'd tried to make himself think it wasn't true, that he might have had a future with Sylvia. But now he knew Sylvia had been right: he *had* placed a barrier in the way of their relationship, and he realised he finally understood why. He was destined to long for Kitty, no matter what happened. It was her or nobody for him. Sighing, he forced himself to concentrate on the business in hand, the long list of dry points that they would labour through tomorrow, all without the comforting knowledge that she would be waiting for him after the meeting, to laugh about it together, to take the edge off the inevitable disagreements, and to add her spark of humour to the whole affair.

Kitty kept her gaze on the agenda, trying to put her heart into the work, knowing it was vital to her colleagues that she did the best she could. However, her thoughts kept slipping to Frank, so close she could brush his knees with her own if she sat forward, and yet so far away in every other respect. She must not on any account let him guess how humiliated she had felt when she realised she wasn't his first choice. She had to show him he was wrong, that she was at the top of her game. She was upset and angry he'd thought otherwise. She would prove to him that she was more than capable of taking part in this big meeting. She gripped her pen with determination and ticked off the points as they made their way through them. Whatever happened, she would not reveal her deep hurt.

CHAPTER TWENTY-SEVEN

'For God's sake, stop fussing.' Alfie pushed his mother aside as he reached for his coat. Even though it was now March, the weather was still cold and, as he'd barely set foot outside his own front door for what felt like a lifetime, he knew he'd be grateful for its warmth. However, his mother was standing by holding a scarf and thick gloves, anxiously pressing them on him.

'You'll catch your death,' she warned. 'You don't want to rush into things. What do you need to go outside for, anyway? I can bring you everything you need right here. Why don't you stop inside and build up your strength?'

'Because I've got to get away from you, and the one thing I really need is more whisky,' Alfie muttered under his breath. He felt like a schoolboy again, being forced to take the hand-knitted gloves he'd hated so much. He hadn't worn them back then – he'd always just shoved them in his pockets the moment he'd rounded the corner out of her sight – and he wasn't going to wear them now. He'd had enough; he'd reached his limit. If he didn't get away soon his head would burst, with all the furious thoughts that were swirling around it.

The shock of the outside air made him gasp, but he gulped it in, relishing the freshness of it, after so long being cooped up in the small terraced house, with its constant smell of cooked cabbage and damp walls. He turned his face up to the sky. It was grey and it would probably rain but he didn't care. He was free again. It was all he could do not to shout out loud.

He knew he should go down to the docks and see his boss, explain he was on the mend and would soon be back at work. He needed to start earning again, for a start. His feet decided otherwise, heading in the opposite direction, as if he had no choice in the matter. He moved along in a direct line as if driven by a secret mission. After a while he arrived at the nondescript pub to which he'd taken Tommy all those months ago. The sign still swung in the breeze, but now the new paint could be distinguished on it: a bright figure and the words, The King's Head. Alfie glared at it, squinting upwards. The king hadn't done much for him, he thought angrily. Still, it was a pub, and one he hadn't yet been banned from, so it would do as well as any other. He was gasping for the taste of proper beer.

If he'd hoped for any kind of welcome, any comments that he hadn't been seen in there for a while and he'd been missed, he was doomed to disappointment. The morose barman simply grunted at him and pulled the pint without comment, setting it down silently and holding out his hand for money. Alfie didn't care. He wasn't at home, his mother wasn't going to fill his head with information he didn't want, and he had a decent pint of bitter before him.

In fact, there was one piece of information he'd seized on the other day when his mother had come in from the shop, complaining about Tommy Callaghan being a danger and a menace, riding his bike too fast, and about how slow that daft Ruby was. She'd mentioned in passing that Danny wasn't around at the moment, having been sent off on some course or other. Alfie had stored that nugget away and brooded on it; it was typical of that smug devil that he'd landed yet another cushy number, but on the plus side it left the field clear for Alfie to pursue Kitty.

Now he was out and about he could set about following his plan. With Danny out of the way, there would be nobody to stop him if he tried to see Kitty again. All he had to do was tell her how things were – that she needed to listen to him because he knew what was best for her. It was simple. She belonged to him. She'd always known he had his eye on her, she must have realised how he felt. She might resist at first, especially now she had this job that everyone thought was so important, but she'd see reason eventually. Alfie didn't hold with women working. It simply wasn't right; it went against the natural order of things. She couldn't hope to do whatever it was she did as well as a man would do it. She was an excellent cook, everyone said so, and therefore her destiny was to be in his kitchen and, Alfie hoped fervently, in his bed. He licked the head of his pint from his upper lip, savouring the thought. He'd have Kitty just where he wanted her, and soon, before that stuck-up brother of hers came back. He'd strike while the iron was hot.

The meeting room had been too warm and stuffy, crammed with bodies, all elbow to elbow as they tried to write their notes. Kitty wished they could open a window, but the few panes of glass had been covered with tape to minimise damage if a bomb should go off nearby, and couldn't easily be opened. She tried to put out of her mind what Laura had told her.

They'd managed a very quick rendezvous the evening before, as the Liverpool train had got in just after Laura's shift had finished. They'd hurriedly run to the nearest café, Kitty glad of an excuse not to spend any more painful minutes with Frank, even as she felt a pang when he'd turned his back and headed across the station concourse in the opposite direction. They'd been assigned to separate billets anyway. Laura had been her usual energetic self, full of news of Freddy's recovery, but still no wiser about Marjorie's fate. Kitty had looked at her friend keenly, recognising the signs of stress around her eyes. She wondered what the cause was.

'Oh, honestly, it's nothing.' Laura had dismissed the idea, but then, recognising that Kitty knew her well enough to see through any defences, caved in. 'It's these damned bombs again. It was bad enough dodging the doodlebugs, but this latest lot don't give you a chance. You don't even hear them until after they've struck. It's pretty annoying.'

'I can see that.' Kitty shuddered. 'Have they caused much damage?'

Laura set down her mug of weak tea. 'Here and there. The worst was Selfridges, can you imagine? That was very inconvenient of them. A visit there was one of the few perks of working in central London.'

Kitty raised her eyebrows. 'That's a real shame. I know we felt the same when Lewis's got hit at home. Still, we've managed somehow.'

Laura nodded. 'Of course. That's what we do, isn't it? We manage somehow. Sorry to rush you, especially as I've only just seen you, but I have to go – I've extra duties this evening, some visiting bigwig or other. But I'll see you tomorrow for a proper chinwag, won't I? After your big meeting?'

'Of course,' Kitty had said, and hugged her friend.

Now she felt her mind drifting to the evening ahead, and the promise of swapping gossip with Laura. Peter was back on active service, and they would have the whole time to themselves, which felt like a long-overdue luxury. Then someone spoke her name and she realised she was being addressed directly.

Quickly she gathered her thoughts, covering her moment of hesitation by tidying the stack of papers before her. Then she rose from her seat and gave the brief report she'd prepared, speaking steadily and confidently. As she finished she looked around at the sea of faces. She couldn't help but notice Frank, watching her with what seemed to be pride; despite her earlier intentions, she was buoyed by his approval. That'll show him, she thought. Me, Kitty Callahan from Empire Street, standing up in front of all these important people, speaking in public. She almost pinched herself; for a moment it didn't seem real. Then, as the chairman nodded to her, she took her seat once more. The chairman turned to his left and muttered something in the ear of the officer sitting just behind him. Gold braid flashed as the officer half rose. 'Miss Callaghan, if I could trouble you for a quick word after the meeting.'

She nodded, but there was no time for any further explanation – they had already moved on to the next item. She forced her eyes to focus on the agenda, now covered in annotations and underlining.

It was another half an hour before the meeting dissolved for a tea break. She made her way to a bare side room, painted in institutional cream, following everyone else. Before she could join the queue for the hot drinks, the officer sidestepped her. 'Miss Callaghan, a moment of your time.'

'Of course,' said Kitty, pushing away her alarm at being singled out.

'Your report this morning was very informative,' he said, his eyes crinkling in a friendly manner. She guessed he must be about forty, and evidently very senior in the service. 'Our chairman thought you might care to share it with some of our communications officers who can't be here in person. They are based near Holborn – I don't know if you know where that is?'

Kitty nodded. 'I was based in north London for some time when I first joined the Wrens,' she told him. 'I know most of the city centre quite well.'

'Excellent,' the officer said. 'I believe one of my colleagues has suggested Lieutenant Feeny comes along as well, to give his view of the operations. We can arrange a lift for you, as Captain Harris has to attend a combined services meeting near there, but if you can find your own way back, that would be a tremendous advantage.'

'That is no trouble at all, sir,' said Kitty, careful that her face did not betray her true feelings. More time alone with Frank – but she'd coped with the long train journey down and so this would be bearable. She'd keep her mind on the evening to come, catching up with Laura.

'Then we'll have a car waiting for you outside the side entrance when this is finished,' the officer said. 'Don't let me detain you from your tea and biscuits, Miss Callaghan. You see we can run to biscuits here – it's not like being stuck out in the provinces, you know.'

'Yes, sir,' said Kitty, annoyed that he'd had to have a snide dig at where she came from. London officers – they were all the same.

'Now you be a good boy and don't cause any trouble for Auntie Sarah or Tommy,' Nancy instructed her son as they stood on the doorstep of the Callaghans' house. 'Remember to clean your teeth and go straight to bed when they tell you.'

'Yes, Mam,' said Georgie impatiently, hopping up and down on the spot. He couldn't wait to be inside. He'd visited this house many times but had never been allowed to sleep there, and he could hardly contain himself.

Tommy opened the door, a big grin on his face as he caught sight of the little boy beaming up at him. 'All right, young Georgie?' he said affectionately, ruffling the boy's hair. 'Come on in.'

'Don't you stand for any nonsense from him, Tommy,' Nancy said, half worried that it would be too much for the lad, but proud too that her little boy was having this small adventure. 'He's got everything he needs packed in that canvas bag.'

'I put in my picture book an' all,' Georgie said solemnly. 'So I won't get under your feet.'

'Course you won't get under my feet,' said Tommy warmly. 'We're going to have a grand time. So don't you worry,' he said to Nancy, who was hovering.

'I know you will. All right, give Mammy a kiss and then off you go,' she said, wondering why she suddenly felt a surge of trepidation. The little boy's cough seemed to be on the mend at last, and she'd left Georgie with lots of babysitters before, including Tommy himself. In any case, it wouldn't be long until Sarah got home from work. Her younger sister was one of the most sensible, capable people she knew, so there was, as Tommy said, no need to worry. She was just being silly. She bent and gave Georgie a brief hug and then waved goodbye as Tommy shut the door. As she walked away she could hear Georgie's shrieks of excitement.

Nancy drew the collar of her best coat up around her neck, shivering with her own excitement. Gary had booked them into the select hotel they'd been to once before. It was so much more risky now the days were longer and people would be around who might know them – but she didn't care. He'd be off on active service from tomorrow. He couldn't tell her where he was going; she wasn't sure if he knew himself. So it would be a night to savour. She was now all but certain he was going to ask her to come away with him after the war was over, which everyone said would be soon. She knew there were a few legal obstacles in the way, but she was sure they could find a way around them. Gary was so clever, so caring and protective. He'd make sure a little thing like a hasty marriage undertaken when she wasn't old enough to know any better didn't get in the way of their lasting happiness together. She just had to trust him.

Singing to herself, she hopped on to the bus, ignoring all the looks coming her way, knowing that her joy was radiating off her like heat from the sun.

Kitty had kept her eyes facing the front windscreen as they were driven across town and shown to the large office where she was to repeat her report from earlier in the morning. There was no need for small talk with Frank as Captain Harris, apparently unaware that she'd ever been to the capital before, kept up a running commentary. It mainly consisted of pointing out bomb sites, something she could have done without.

They were met by a polite but brisk senior Wren, who swiftly ushered them upstairs to an echoing corridor, leading to a meeting room with rows of chairs which had the air of having been hastily put together. Kitty suspected they'd had about as much notice of this as she and Frank had. Still, she delivered her report, and Frank added a few points from his side of things, which seemed to go down well. Within less than an hour they were back on the street again.

Frank looked at Kitty. 'That was rather a whirlwind, wasn't it?' he said, rubbing his forehead as he did so. 'I hope we were able to tell them what they needed.'

Kitty could feel her resolve to keep her distance slipping away. 'They wouldn't have asked us if they hadn't thought we could contribute something vital. It's not our fault we aren't as up to date on how some of our communications were designed – we're the ones who know how to work them, after all. I'm glad we had the chance to meet some of the people who do a similar job and check we're all working in the same way. Are you all right?' she added anxiously, as he continued to rub his temples.

Frank straightened up at once, always sensitive to any implication he was less than one hundred per cent. 'Of course.'

Kitty sighed, realising he'd assumed she meant his leg, when all she'd intended was to be considerate. 'Only you look as if you might have a headache,' she added.

Frank nodded slowly. 'All right, yes, I have. It's being cooped up in that stuffy place this morning, and I have to admit I didn't sleep well last night. Whatever my landlady's shortcomings, I must confess the bed in my usual billet is extremely comfortable. I've been spoilt. The one I was given yesterday had springs poking through it, so I finally slept like a letter Z. Funny, isn't it, when we spend most of our working lives shut inside an underground bunker, in a warren of small rooms – you'd think this would all be a breath of fresh air.'

'Well, maybe some air is just what you need,' Kitty suggested, determined now to be friendly but practical. 'Come on, we don't need to get a bus or Underground, we can walk back. I know the way. It'll do us good.' She deliberately didn't ask if he would be all right to walk, knowing it would cause offence and break the fragile truce between them.

Frank tipped his head and looked straight at her. 'Lead the way then, Kitty. You're more familiar with this place than I am.' For a moment she thought he was going to give her his arm, but then he put his hands in his pockets, so she was saved the embarrassment of reaching out only to have the offer taken away.

'Let's make our way via the back streets,' she suggested. 'It'll be quieter. High Holborn gets so busy, it will be noisy and do your head no good at all.'

'Okey doke, as Tommy would say.'

Kitty laughed. 'I hope he's all right and not driving your sister round the bend.'

'How's that?' he asked.

'Oh, you won't have heard. It was all a bit last

minute.' Kitty found the street she wanted and explained the arrangement she and Sarah had come to, in order not to wound Tommy's pride but still keep an eye on him.

Frank laughed when he understood how they'd achieved that delicate balance. 'It's hard to remember that Tommy's almost a young man now,' he said fondly.

'You haven't seen him on his bike, have you? Honestly, it's a wonder he hasn't fallen off yet, the speed he goes around corners,' she replied – but whatever she was going to say next was lost as a powerful blast hit them, without the slightest hint of any warning. It was only afterwards that the hideous noise of the V2 bomb's descent could be heard – but by then the walls of neighbouring buildings had crumbled, a vast hole had opened in the narrow street, and Kitty and Frank were submerged in a pile of bricks and rubble.

CHAPTER TWENTY-EIGHT

When Kitty came to, all she could see was darkness, with a few smudges of weak light way off to one side, but she couldn't turn her head to see where they were coming from. She was unable to move much at all, as she seemed to be wedged in tight by sharp, heavy objects on both sides. The smell was suffocating – damp stone, dry dust, and a troublingly earthy scent that she couldn't quite place but didn't want to think about too carefully. Cautiously she tried to move her fingers and toes. The toes were all right and so were the fingers on her right hand, but when she tried to move those on her left, pain shot through her all the way to her shoulder, making her gasp. She strained to remember where she was. Gradually it came back to her – the big meeting, the smaller impromptu one, walking along with Frank . . . Frank. Where was he?

She tried to call but nothing came out. Her throat was painful and dry. How long had she been trapped here? She coughed a little and had another go. 'Frank,'

347

she managed to half-whisper. Then, more strongly, 'Frank! Are you there? Are you all right?'

There was no reply. Slowly it came to her that there were faint low moans coming from different directions, and she had no way of telling if any of them came from Frank. She wondered how many people had been caught in the blast. They had been walking between tall buildings; they must have been full of Londoners going about their daily business. Now they were all caught in the ruins of what had been a normal street, full of normal workers and families.

She blinked and tried to cast her eyes towards the chink of light. Was it still daytime? Maybe that was the sun shining. Perhaps that meant rescue was at hand. She knew there would be teams assigned to each area, ready to spring into action on occasions such as this, just as there were in Bootle, where Pop played a part both in salvage operations and with the ARP. She would cling to that thought – that a London equivalent of Pop would come and find her. How she wished he were here now. He would save them all. In a flash of panic she wondered if she would ever see him or any of them ever again.

Stop it, she told herself. Panic won't help. She had to stay in control. She would continue moving her toes and the fingers of one hand, to make sure her circulation kept flowing, but nothing more in case she dislodged any more bricks, or whatever it was that pinned her in place so firmly. Now she was more alert she realised she was being held down by a heavy weight and it was very uncomfortable. 'Frank,' she called again, trying to keep the desperation out of her voice. 'Frank! Are you there?'

She shut her eyes tightly shut, forcing back a sob. Frank had to be still alive. She couldn't bear it if he wasn't. How stupid she had been, angry that he'd picked another Wren in preference to her for this trip, wasting time being cross when they'd had all day together yesterday on the train and today going round the city. They could have enjoyed each other's company, talked properly, not pretended to be formal and indifferent.

Life wouldn't be worth living if he wasn't there too, she realised. He was everything she looked for. He was funny and clever, he was the best-looking man she knew, and yet he meant so much more than all of that. He made her body sing just to look at him, and on the few occasions when they touched, her skin reacted as if he'd lit it with a dusting of magic. She was drawn to him by something so fundamental she couldn't put a name to it. If she was honest with herself, she would have to admit that she'd never felt like that with Elliott, even though she had been extremely fond of him and had begun to think of a future with him. She felt a connection with Frank on another level entirely. She'd known it for years, ever since they'd had that brief dance long ago. Up till then she'd still been like another one of his young sisters. He'd awoken something in her and then he'd had his accident and things had changed between them. Was she really never going to have the chance to put that right?

349

'Frank,' she said. 'Frank, I'm sorry. I was angry with you and I shouldn't have been. I just want you to be all right. Can you hear me?'

She strained her ears for any response, but all that came were the low moans, some close by, others further away. Somewhere there was a crumbling noise, as if the rubble was shifting. Would that be the rescuers arriving, or more buildings collapsing on top of them? No, she couldn't think of that. It was too frightening. She had to stay calm. But where was he?

'Frank!' she called again, realising her voice was muffled by the weight of stone above and all around her. He might be just yards away and unable to hear her. 'Frank!' she called as loudly as she could, and another sharp jolt of pain shot through her left arm.

There was more silence. Then, faintly, she thought she heard a different noise. She wasn't sure at first if she was imagining it. Then it came again. 'Kitty.'

CHAPTER TWENTY-NINE

It was dark by the time Alfie left the King's Head. He wasn't sure how late it was but it didn't matter. He'd make his way back home, pick up the car and then take it round to Empire Street and go to see Kitty. He didn't know why he hadn't thought of this before. All he had to do was present himself at her house and she'd be his. To his confused and seething brain, this tangled logic made complete sense.

The walk back to his house seemed far longer than the walk out, but that must be because of the dark. Everything felt as if it lasted longer at night-time, he assured himself. It was nothing to do with his by now somewhat unsteady steps. There was hardly anybody around. It occurred to him that he really had been in the pub for a long time.

Finally he reached his street. There, parked alongside the pavement, was his car. For a moment he wondered if he should go into the house and change into something smarter – Kitty might appreciate a gesture like that. Then he decided against it, as he was bound to bump into his mother and she'd only start interfering. Kitty knew him well enough to take him as he was. He didn't need to impress her with fancy clothes or nonsense like that.

Luckily his car keys were still in his coat pocket. He had the sudden worrying thought that the battery might be dead after so long without starting it up, but the car didn't let him down, sputtering to life after only a few attempts. Alfie sighed with pleasure as he put it into gear and released the handbrake. He'd missed being behind the wheel. He was glad he wasn't one of those people who was affected by drink. He'd be perfectly safe; he'd only had a few pints. He hadn't even had any whisky today – that proved how sensible he was. Anyway, there were no other vehicles about to get in the way.

After hitting the kerb only a few times, he drew up at the junction to Empire Street. His sense of self-preservation told him not to turn on to the street itself. Not many people owned cars here; his would be easily recognised. Better to park it on the main road and walk the last few yards on foot. It would be easier to get away without having to turn or reverse as well.

He eased himself out of the driver's seat and left the car unlocked. What he wanted to do wouldn't take long. He'd be back here with Kitty in no time. He walked unsteadily to her front door and paused. Should he knock? There was no sign of life inside. It was later than he'd planned, and she'd have most likely gone to bed. He tried the handle but the door didn't budge.

He thought of the times he'd visited Danny here, back in the days before he'd let him down so badly. They always sat in the kitchen, he remembered, and his family and friends often went in and out of the back door. He could make his way around and try that. He didn't want to cause unnecessary noise, as that might draw Pop out on to the street, the last person he wanted to see.

He stumbled his way around to the alley at the back and found the gate to the Callaghans' yard. It was bolted, but he soon worked out how to open it. He realised he was making a bit of a noise as he shoved the gate hard, but didn't think it would be enough to wake anyone. There wasn't much light but he could make out the shape of a bicycle against the inner wall – that would be Tommy's. He'd got the correct place all right.

He crept cautiously across the yard and reached the back door. It too was locked. Still, there was nobody to see what he was doing. His usual caution left well behind, he gave the door an almighty shove and the old lock gave way. He pushed it wide open and paused, alert for any noises inside the house, but there were none. He tried to remember what Danny had said over the years about who slept where. He was pretty sure Tommy had the smallest room, facing the back. So that narrowed down where Kitty would be. He knew the layout of the place and navigated his way around the kitchen furniture and into the hall. Silent as a thief, he slowly headed upstairs.

He could just about make out that the door to the

back bedroom was closed. He turned in the narrow corridor and traced his way along the wall till he came to the door that he was sure belonged to Kitty's room. He opened it carefully, and could immediately pick up the sound of somebody's deep, regular breathing inside. So he was right; she had gone to bed and was asleep.

He waited until his eyes were fully accustomed to the dim light. All he could really see were vague outlines, but that was enough to work out where the bed was. He could hardly believe it – he was finally in Kitty's bedroom and that shape under the blankets was her. Any moment now she would be his. Swiftly he moved across the room and shook her shoulder. 'Kitty, wake up, come with me,' he muttered, not quite able to keep his voice as soft and persuasive as he'd planned. He shook her more strongly. 'Wake up, I said. You're coming with me.' Now he was growing frustrated at her lack of obedience. 'Come on, stop fooling around, get your things, I'm here to take you away.'

The shape groaned and shifted under his grip. Alfie lost his patience and threw back the bedcovers, grabbing wildly underneath them. The shape screamed and half sat up.

'Shut up, Kitty. Come with me and look sharp about it. I can't wait all bloody night.'

He grabbed again, connecting with what might have been a nightdress, gripping the flesh beneath it, pulling her further out of the bed. She screamed again, resisting him, twisting away, and he lashed out, furious

354

now that she wasn't agreeing with him fast enough. Didn't she realise this was her way to a better life; that he could give her all the things she wanted, if only she'd do as he told her? He hit out again and felt something bony. Maybe her nose. His hand came away wet – he'd drawn blood. He put out his hand to check and felt her hair, long and straight.

Even in his befuddled state, he realised something wasn't right. Kitty had curly hair, in a short bob. It was one of the reasons he liked her so much, her pretty dark hair. Had she changed it somehow? Had he made a mistake? Had he actually hurt her, when he hadn't meant to do that at all? What sort of pickle had he got himself into now? Or was this an imposter? That might be even worse. Nothing was going to plan and it didn't make any sense. Blind rage took over.

'What have you done with Kitty, you bloody bitch?' he shouted, lashing out.

Whoever it was made a gulping noise as if it was in pain and couldn't scream any more. Angrily he shoved his victim back against the bed and aimed another punch at her to shut her up. Then he plunged back towards the corridor, ignoring the low moaning from behind him. A shaft of moonlight lit up the narrow hall as the door to the back bedroom swung open.

A small figure came out. 'Aunty Sarah?' It was a little boy. 'Aunty Sarah, I woke up. There were strange noises and I didn't like it. Can I have a drink?'

Alfie was nonplussed for a moment. Kitty didn't have a kid. What was this boy doing here? Then he decided it didn't matter. In his confused state, all he wanted was to punish her for not being here, for thwarting his intentions, which had all been for her own good. But she'd rejected him, by not being here. Whoever this kid was, he must be important to her and therefore she'd want him back. And he had to make the kid shut up, or else he might start kicking up a fuss and waking the neighbours. Whatever else happened, he didn't want to alert Pop.

'I'm not your bloody Aunty Sarah,' he snarled. 'But you're coming with me. I'll give you a drink all right.' He swept forwards, grabbed the child, slamming his palm over his mouth, and raced down the stairs, out of the back door and through the yard, not thinking any further than getting the boy bundled into the car and far away from here. He'd work out the rest as he went. The child managed to squirm away from his hand and screamed piercingly into his ear, but he shut it out, concentrating on running, putting as much distance between himself and the house as he could before whoever it was who'd pretended to be Kitty woke up the entire street.

'Kitty.'

It was barely there but she was certain it was her name. It had to be Frank. The rubble distorted the voice but it had to be him.

'Frank, is that you?' she shouted.

'Kitty!' It was him. She couldn't tell how close he was. 'Kitty, are you hurt?'

She almost sobbed again in relief and the sheer

delight that he was alive. 'I'm stuck under rubble,' she called, 'and one arm is painful, but otherwise not too bad.' She forced herself to sound cheerful. She didn't want him to worry about her. 'What about you?'

'Not too bad either.' He coughed. 'I'm caught under some stones but I can move one arm. Hold on.' There was a scrabbling noise and then the sound of something moving over to her left. Suddenly she could hear him much more clearly. 'Is that better? I've managed to shift a brick or something like that.'

'Frank, that's much better. I can hear you properly now.' She breathed out slowly. 'Are you really not hurt? Can you see anything?'

'Only a patch of light coming from behind somewhere. I can't twist around to see any more, though. Not because I'm injured, more because I'm pinned down and don't want to move any more stones in case I set off a rock fall.'

'I'm the same. I hope it's daylight but I don't know. How long have we been in here, do you think?'

'I've no idea,' Frank said. 'I must have passed out for a bit. I only came to when I heard you calling.'

'Me too,' said Kitty. 'It was like I woke up in a dark fog. I'm getting used to it now though. It's not so bad, is it? It could be worse.'

'That's the spirit,' Frank said at once. 'And we're bound to be rescued soon, you know.'

'I thought that too,' said Kitty immediately, trying to believe it. 'They'll be out there now, won't they, working out how best to clear the rubble and everything.'

'We'll be out of here in a jiffy.' He sounded so sure of it. Kitty prayed he was right. She didn't know how long the air would last in here or if there were more falls to come.

'Frank . . .' she said hesitantly. 'Frank, I meant to say.' She gulped. Somehow it was easier to talk here, in the dark, when he couldn't see her face. She was ashamed of how she'd felt over the past few days and couldn't bear for him to blame her. She knew that given the circumstances it should be the least thing on her mind, but her feelings seemed magnified down here somehow and it helped to think about something else other than the tons of rubble above and around them. 'I'm sorry. I was offhand with you yesterday and I was being silly. I was just upset that you'd wanted someone else to come on the trip with you; that you didn't think I was good enough.'

There was a moment's pause before Frank asked, 'What do you mean?'

Kitty swallowed hard. 'That, you know, you wanted my superior officer to represent the Derby House Wrens at the meeting, not me.'

Frank paused again. 'I don't know what you mean. I asked for you because you're the best when it comes to telephone communications and training. I know your boss has been doing it for longer, but she doesn't understand the day-to-day difficulties or how fast things have changed. I definitely asked for you.'

'Oh.' Kitty was caught off guard. 'But I thought—'

'How on earth did you come by such an idea?'

'Well, after that meeting with Commander Stephens,

Moira Butcher told me I was the second choice. She seemed to know what she was talking about, and so I believed her.'

'That's not true.' Frank sighed. 'It's probably because she's friends with Sylvia. She's being protective – not that she has any need to be. After all, it was Sylvia who called a halt to things, not the other way around.'

'What?' Now it was Kitty's turn to sound astonished. 'I didn't realise. I thought you were still courting her. When did that happen?'

'Between Christmas and New Year.' Frank cleared his throat, his voice seeming to fade a little. 'I didn't exactly make a song and dance about it. Not the sort of thing to spread around, really.'

'Frank, I'm sorry.' Kitty knew the two of them had been seeing each other quite regularly. 'You've been putting a brave face on it all that time. We didn't know.'

'No need to be sorry.' Frank paused again, then his voice changed, became stronger again. 'She probably did me a favour, to be honest. She said . . . she said there was always a barrier between us. As if there was somebody else there.'

Kitty wasn't sure how to take that. 'But you wouldn't have two-timed her.'

'Of course not. That wasn't what she meant. She had a point, though.'

'Did she?'

'Yes, she did . . . Kitty, you must know what I'm talking about.'

Kitty knew what she wanted him to be talking

about, but she wasn't at all sure that was what he meant. She'd jumped to too many wrong conclusions on this trip already. She paused for a moment, not daring to indulge any of her hopes, and then said, 'No, I. . . I'm not sure.'

There was no reply. Had she offended him somehow?

'Frank, are you still there? Are you all right?' There was a lengthening silence. She couldn't tell how long it went on for.

'Frank? Speak to me, Frank.' She tried to keep the growing anxiety from her voice.

After what seemed to be an eternity, he finally spoke. 'Kitty . . . sorry. Might have blacked out again for a moment there.'

'Are you all right? I was worried,' Kitty said.

'Don't be worried, I'm here Kitty and not going anywhere, tell you what. Can you give us a song? That'll keep me awake. Something to rouse our spirits.' He didn't sound right, but it was better than the dreadful silence.

'All right,' said Kitty. 'If you're sure it will help?'

'It will.'

Hesitantly at first, but then with more spirit, Kitty began 'Pack Up Your Troubles', not too loud, but with as much hope and energy as she could muster. Frank joined in quietly – she could just about hear him. She had to keep him awake if she could, to know he was safe. She absolutely could not lose him.

'What next?' she asked when she reached the end of the song.

'What was it we danced to at Christmas?'

She shut out the thought that she might never see Pop and all the others again. '"The Nearness of You", wasn't it?'

'Sing that one for me, Kitty.'

Kitty bit her lip at the memory and then, knowing it was to keep him alert, and possibly anyone else who was trapped down here with them, she sang the song, the one that meant something to both of them, wishing that she could be close to Frank now, holding his hand. Gloria would have been proud of the performance, she thought as she came to the final chorus. 'How was that, Frank?'

But he didn't answer.

Sarah slowly dragged herself downstairs to the kitchen sink and turned on the tap. She must have passed out briefly and she was disorientated. Her head was pounding and her nose felt swollen. Filled with dread, she carefully lit the gas lamp and glanced in the old mirror. She gasped in horror at the sight of her face covered in blood. She knew she had to clean herself up before Tommy or Georgie saw her. Drawing on all her training, she carefully dabbed at the mess, careful not to press too hard, swearing to replace the tea towel with a clean one when she had the chance. Kitty wouldn't mind, she knew. It was silly to worry about a little thing like that, but somehow it helped deal with the pain.

The full horror of what had happened to her was only now beginning to dawn. A man had come into her bedroom, had groped her under the blankets then beaten her. At first the memory was fuzzy but slowly her mind cleared. He had thought she was Kitty. He had smelled heavily of sour beer. She hadn't seen more than an outline of him but the voice had sounded familiar.

She was thankful in one way that beating her was all he had done. It could have been so much worse. From her work at the hospital and the Red Cross post, she'd come across horrendous stories: men forcing themselves on women under cover of the blackout, taking advantage of the most vulnerable. She shivered. All the same, her head was ringing with the agony from the punches and she was sure her body would be bruised in the morning. She hadn't exactly got off lightly.

When she'd done all she could, she rinsed out the ruined tea towel and wrung it tightly, before hiding it under the sink – she didn't want Georgie to see it in the morning. She hoped he and Tommy had slept through everything, and were safely in their beds. She thought she'd better find her first-aid kit, which she'd brought with her from habit. It would be in her bag, back up in the bedroom. She would check on the boys while she was up there. She stumbled a little as she mounted the stairs, at once weary and yet with no inclination to sleep, shaky with energy from the shock. She had no idea for how long she'd passed out, or been in the kitchen, or what the time was now.

Tommy came out of his room as she reached the top. She angled her torch so he wouldn't see her face.

'Sorry, did I wake you? I just needed something

from the kitchen.' She tried to make her voice as normal as she could.

Tommy shook his head. 'It doesn't matter,' he said. 'I had a bad nightmare. There was crashing and banging and screaming, I didn't know what was going on. I just woke up. But where's Georgie?'

Kitty awoke from a doze, confused and thirsty. She could feel pins and needles in her legs and the earthy smell was growing stronger. The air seemed more fetid. She knew she had to stay calm, but the temptation to give in to panic was strong. The tiny glimmer of light had vanished now.

'Frank?' she called hesitantly, afraid he still wouldn't answer. For a moment her heart nearly stopped as there was only silence, and then she heard him give a quiet cough. 'Sorry, Kitty, must have drifted off there for a moment.'

'Me too.' That was an understatement, and she knew he must have been drifting in and out of consciousness for much of their time underground.

'It won't be long now.' He sounded weaker this time, his voice hoarse. 'They're bound to be with us soon.'

'Yes, you're right,' she said, hanging on to his words for desperately needed comfort. She had to believe it was true. Anything else was unthinkable. She had to be brave. Many others had suffered worse than this. And yet there was that horrible suspicion at the back of her mind that the air couldn't last much longer.

'How's your arm?' Frank asked.

'Still letting me know it's there,' she said, forcing herself to make light of the pain.

'Well, that's a good thing, shows the nerves are working.'

'You sound like Rita or Sarah,' she said, smiling at the thought of his sisters, imagining them in their nurses' uniforms, and then wincing as a sharper bolt of pain shot along the length of her arm. She gritted her teeth. Better that it hurt than went completely numb.

'Bet they'd know what to do if they had you in their hospital,' he went on.

'Yes, and they'll have seen far worse than this. We're lucky, really,' she replied, trying to convince herself. Her ears caught a distant sound. 'What's that noise? Can you hear it, Frank?'

'Hang on.' Frank paused for a few seconds. 'Yes, it's . . . well, I could be wrong, but I reckon it might be stones moving around.'

'Moving around? You mean, more falling on us?'

'I don't know,' said Frank. 'It's possible, but of course it could be quite a way away from us. We shouldn't worry. We're going to be fine, Kitty.'

'Yes, of course.' Again the noise came; it really did seem like more stones falling. She tried to block out the image of being buried in here for ever by the weight of bricks and blocks, slowly running out of air. 'Frank, are you still there? It's getting closer, isn't it?'

'We don't know that. Sound does funny things underground. We mustn't jump to conclusions or panic.'

'No. No, of course not.' She closed her eyes again, willing herself to stay in control. Panic wouldn't help. She had to breathe slowly. She tried to hear Rita's sensible voice in her head, explaining how a steady breath helped you stay calm. It was hard to concentrate on that while the noise of stone on stone grew louder and closer. 'Frank, I'm sorry but I'm scared, I'm so scared.'

'I know. It is frightening. It's natural to be scared, but we're going to get out of this.'

'Frank . . . I—' She couldn't keep the depth of emotion from her voice. The effort of pretending was too much.

But Frank cut in on her garbled thoughts. 'Kitty, I'm sorry to interrupt, but I must tell you something. This isn't exactly how I'd planned to say this, but, well, lying here in the dark makes you realise what's important, doesn't it?' He must have caught her tone and understood it for what it was. 'And the fact is, you are. You're the most important person in the world to me, Kitty. I know I've had the accident with my leg and I'll never be the man I used to be, but I have to say this anyway. I can't go on kidding myself I think of you just as a friend. Sylvia could tell that wasn't so, even if I wouldn't admit it. You're the woman I love, Kitty. You always have been.'

Kitty gasped, in shock and yet in delight that his words echoed exactly what she'd been thinking. The terrifying darkness seemed to recede. 'Frank, I don't . . . I can't believe it. Really? I thought you looked down on me, like a kid sister or something. I never dared tell you how I felt. I don't care about your leg. It makes no difference to me. How could you even think it?'

'Because I was stupid and had my pride,' he said ruefully. 'I thought I couldn't condemn you to spend your life with a disabled man, especially when you'd known me before, in the days when I could dance and box and everything that normal men do. I never looked down on you, ever. Yes, you were like a sister to start with, but then things changed. I always wanted to take care of you, but it's something different now, you have to believe me.'

'Frank, you're the only one for me, I don't care about anything else,' Kitty breathed. 'If we get out of here—'

'No, *when* we get out of here,' said Frank staunchly. 'They'll come for us soon. They're bound to. Then we'll get your arm sorted, and after that we can make up for lost time. We can be together properly – as long as that's what you'd like, Kitty.'

'Of course, it's what I want more than anything.' She gave a small laugh. 'Really? Are you sure? Oh, Frank. We can't lose each other now. Do you think we would have ever said this if we hadn't been trapped like this? Would we have gone on misunderstanding one another and being unhappy? Perhaps we should be grateful that fate has done this.'

'Perhaps.'

'We're going to be all right, Frank. Fate couldn't be so cruel as to harm us any more now we finally know we're going to be together.'

'Exactly,' he said confidently, not allowing any

shadow of doubt to colour his voice. 'They'll be here in no time. All we have to do is wait. Pretend I can hold your hand. Imagine I'm doing that, and giving it a good squeeze. That's what I'll do when we get out of here. I'll give you a big hug; I'm never going to stop hugging you, protecting you.'

'I'll hold you to that. I won't care about my arm, as long as we get out of here.'

'We will, Kitty. We're going to be safe any moment now.' But she could hear his voice was fading once more. He must be as thirsty and hungry as she was. They hadn't eaten since the biscuits at the meeting. At least they'd had those. Her mind began to drift again and she could feel her eyelids drooping, the welcome muzziness of sleep – or was it just that she had no strength left? The lack of air was playing with her senses. Time was stretching away from her. Then Frank's voice came again.

'Kitty. Can you see it?'

She came out of her stupor, realising his voice was sharp now, stronger once more.

'See what? I can't . . . oh, perhaps, though. There's something on my left-hand side, a patch of . . . I don't know, it's not quite as dark.'

'I'm sure it's a beam of light. It is, Kitty. I'm going to call out. Over here!' he shouted, his voice croaky but full of force.

'Hello! Over here!' Kitty echoed as loudly as she could, tasting dust and dirt as she did so. Now she could make out the light more clearly. It moved around. It must be the beam of a torch.

'Hello there, miss,' came a man's voice. 'Shout out again so I can tell where you are.'

Kitty could have cried with relief but instead she called to him, 'We're over here. There's two of us – or at least that's all we know of. There could be more.'

'Steady on, then. We'll be with you in a jiffy.' The man sounded closer, and then there were muffled noises, perhaps as he turned and spoke to the other rescuers. 'That's it, that's it – almost there.' More stones fell nearby and then, with a grunt of effort, the man and his team rolled back a huge pillar. As the torchlight broke through their prison, Kitty could pick out the markings of the stone, and then the ARP uniforms of the men.

'Hello, miss,' said the first man. 'You're safe now. We'll get you out in no time at all.'

CHAPTER THIRTY

The first face Kitty saw as they lifted her out of the rubble was Frank's. He had been brought out just minutes before her – she'd heard the rescue party reach him and free him from the weight of the rubble. He had refused to go for treatment until he saw Kitty with his own eyes.

She was helped from the shattered remains of the building by an ARP warden, both of them covered in dust, but she was able to walk. Frank stepped towards her, took one look and then enveloped her in the hug he had promised her when they'd lain trapped under the weight of the collapsed block. 'Kitty,' he murmured, breathing in her hair, not caring about the dust. 'You're safe, you're safe. See, I said you would be.'

She rested her face against his chest, ignoring the smears of earth and blood and dust. 'You did. You were right. Oh, Frank, I thought we might die in there.'

He pulled back a little. 'But we didn't. And even if we had, yours would have been the last voice I'd have

369

heard. The most beautiful sound in the world. My darling Kitty.' He hugged her again, very carefully angling himself away from her left arm.

'Now then, sir, this young lady has to go for treatment at once.' The ARP warden spoke with sympathy but he wasn't about to brook any objection. 'And you need a transfusion, you've lost blood. Time enough for all of that when she's been given the all-clear by the doctor. You're still bleeding from your temple; you're to go and get that sorted out.'

Frank reluctantly let Kitty go, but before the ARP warden could direct them to the first-aiders, there was a minor commotion and somebody in a Wren uniform pushed through the crowd. 'There you are. Hoped I'd be in time. You're to come with me, admiral's orders.'

'Laura!' Kitty exclaimed. 'How did you know where we were?'

'Miss, these people are to go to the first-aid post,' the warden said sternly, but Laura was having none of it.

'Which will no doubt be completely overwhelmed with the number of injured from this site, so I'm here to take these two to somewhere less crowded,' she said blithely. 'Don't worry, they'll get the best possible medical treatment. The admiral's car is over there, waiting specially.' The warden stood back, too busy to argue the point, and Laura swiftly ushered them across the remains of the road to where a smart black limousine was parked. 'Get in and I'll explain,' she said.

Frank helped Kitty get into the back seat and then

followed her, resting his arm around her uninjured shoulder to make sure she sat upright and didn't jar her damaged arm. 'So you're Laura,' he said.

'And you must be Frank,' she said, pulling away from the kerb, meeting his eyes in the rear-view mirror. 'I've heard so much about you.' She smiled wickedly.

Kitty couldn't keep up the pretence of light-heartedness any longer. 'But how did you know we were there?'

'Oh, well.' Laura swerved neatly around a pothole. 'What's the point of being Peter's girlfriend if I don't make use of the connections? To hell with lying low. When you didn't turn up this evening, I thought something must be up, so I rang the admiral and he rang some other people and found you'd been at that extra meeting earlier, and that a V2 had hit there just after it finished. I put two and two together, he lent me the car, and Bob's your uncle.'

'I see,' said Frank, slightly overwhelmed by his first encounter with Laura.

'Anyway, I'm taking you to his doctor and then back to his flat. You'll need to rest up.'

'We're back on duty tomorrow,' Kitty said, her voice faint; the movement of the car was jolting her arm, even though Frank was shielding her. 'We're going back to Liverpool.'

'No you're not,' said Laura. 'Not till you're better. That goes for both of you. Don't worry, the admiral's cleared it. You're to have an extra night or two at the flat, which I should say you'll find very acceptable, it's a jolly nice place.' She grew serious again. 'Honestly, it's all right. You did the service a favour by attending the other meeting, and then you got caught up in all this – so this is the least they can do. Peter's uncle was adamant, and you don't say no to him when he's in that kind of mood.'

'Won't the doctor mind? It's the middle of the night,' Kitty protested.

'Don't you worry,' Laura predicted. 'He works shifts like all of us. Didn't you say Frank's sisters were nurses? Then you'll know all about it,' she went on. But silence greeted her remark and, looking in the mirror again, Laura realised her passengers had fallen asleep in each other's arms, worn out by the strain of the evening, but able to let go now they were finally, against the odds, safe.

Nancy felt numb. She couldn't even cry. She sat on the early morning bus as the dawn rose, the devastated city centre stark in the pale light. It looked as cold as the chip of ice now buried in her heart.

The evening had started so well. Gary had bought her the best food there was to be found, almost as if there wasn't a war on: delicious beef, followed by a fruit pudding with an unbelievable amount of sugar whipped into fancy swirls all around it. Then they'd ordered drinks in their room, before sinking into the soft bed with its gorgeous linen sheets, and she'd showed him how much she loved him and how a real hero was to be treated. Her body had hummed with delight, and when they'd finished she felt as if she was floating on air. What he'd said next, however, had brought her down with a bump.

'So, it's time to say goodbye.'

She'd thought he was referring to his return to active service, but it soon became clear he meant it for good.

'But why?' Nancy couldn't understand it. They were meant for each other, and he should be asking her to come back to America with him, not dumping her as if she'd been some toy he'd been playing with. 'Don't you want us to be together for ever?'

Gary had leant back against the pillows and stretched his arms above his head. 'Now what makes you think that? Sure, we've had a swell time while I've been here in Liverpool. But anyone can see the fighting's drawing to a close. I'll be back home in America with my wife—'

'Your wife?' Nancy had exclaimed, going white.

'Sure, my wife. What, did you think I didn't have one?'

'You've taken your time mentioning her,' Nancy said, stung into asperity.

'Never said I wasn't married though,' Gary replied evenly. 'I didn't promise you anything, did I? And anyway, you aren't exactly free yourself.'

'What do you mean?'

Gary had shaken his head and given a short bark of a laugh. 'Oh, come on. That first night we met, you said you had a little boy. So I reckon you're as married as I am.'

Nancy had felt sick. She'd spent so long pushing Sid to the back of her mind that she'd almost managed to convince herself that he didn't exist, and had reassured herself that Gary would make the inconvenient problem go away somehow. In a matter of moments, her ticket to future happiness had disappeared in a puff of smoke. She couldn't bring herself to believe it.

Now she sat on the almost empty bus as it slowly drove back to Bootle and knew that the dream was over. Damn Gary for his good looks and charming ways. He was no better than the rest of them. Gloria had been right – he *had* been too good to be true, but Nancy had been so dazzled by him she hadn't been able to see it. How she longed for her best friend at a time like this. Gloria was away with ENSA, though, and not due to return to England any time soon, much less come to Merseyside. Nancy was back on her own.

Wearily she dragged herself off the bus when it reached her stop, the cold wind chilling her through her best clothes, worn for glamour and not to keep out the weather. She sucked in her cheeks in order not to give in to the mounting need to sob out loud. She wouldn't. He wasn't worth it. She wouldn't give him the satisfaction. He certainly wouldn't be crying, setting off with his men, leading them back to the final and decisive fight that he was sure was just over the horizon. He'd be laughing, thinking about going back to his accommodating wife at home. A fat lot of use he'd turned out to be.

Nancy thought this was just about as low as she'd ever felt, that life couldn't throw anything more at her to make things worse. Then she rounded the corner into Empire Street and saw the gathering of people outside her parents' front door, and two policemen.

'Do you think you can sleep now?' Laura asked anxiously as Kitty propped herself against the dark oak headboard. Her arm had been strapped and put in a sling, and she'd been told not to lie down fully as her ribs were bruised. The spare room at the admiral's flat was the most luxurious she'd ever seen, with its plush furnishings and little touches of comfort, added to by Laura. A glass of water and some tablets were left on the bedside table in case she felt pain on waking.

'Yes, I'll be all right.' Kitty was beginning to feel guilty at all the attention she was getting, even though she told herself not to be stupid. 'What about you? Where will you go?'

'I've got the admiral's room – no, he's not going to be in there,' Laura said hurriedly. 'He rang his housekeeper and had her make up the bed for me.'

'So what about Frank?' Kitty fretted, unable to accept he might have drawn the short straw after all he'd just been through.

'He'll take the sofa. No, don't worry, it's a very big and comfortable sofa,' Laura assured her. 'He wants to come in to see you now you're settled. Is that all right?'

Kitty's face broke into a smile. 'Oh, yes.'

'So I was right about him all along, was I?' Laura asked, just a little smugly. 'I'll leave you two in peace, then. Night night. Or what's left of it. It's pretty well morning, but we won't worry about that just now.' She slipped from the room and Frank came in.

He sat carefully on the edge of the bed and took Kitty's right hand.

'How are you now?' he asked.

'Not too bad at all,' said Kitty staunchly. 'The doctor was marvellous, wasn't he? Staying up for us like that. He's patched me up good and proper. What about you, though? That was a nasty cut on the side of your head and you didn't say a thing about it. I was a bit worried when you kept fading away.'

'It's nothing.' Frank grinned. 'Believe me, I've had worse.' He tapped his leg. 'Now that was pretty bad, I don't mind admitting, after all this time. What a good job I had the false leg though. The ARP man took one look at it and noticed how crushed it was – if it had been my other good leg, I could have bled to death from the injury. So, in a strange way, it saved me.'

Kitty squeezed his hand. 'Then I'm glad too. I couldn't have borne it if you hadn't survived, Frank. You mean the world to me, I see that now.' She sighed but her eyes were bright, full of the knowledge that what was happening between them was exactly right. 'Thank you for all you said when we were trapped down there. I might have given up hope without you.'

'Nonsense.' He squeezed her hand back. 'You're made of steel, Kitty Callaghan. You might not look tough but I know you are. You weren't going to give up, not for a minute.' He gazed into her deep blue eyes. 'I just wish I could lie down here with you and take you in my arms like I've longed to do for so long.'

She grinned at him. 'Well, you can't. Doctor's orders. Or at least,' she added, 'only if you're very careful.'

'As long as I know you want to as well,' he breathed. She shuffled cautiously and he stretched out beside her.

Kitty looked at him seriously. 'Frank, you're the man I've wanted ever since I was old enough to know what these feelings meant. I can't wait to be with you properly. You are my only love, and the thought of being without you is more than I can bear.'

He moved towards her and kissed her gently, careful not to jolt her arm. 'There, that's just for starters,' he said. 'We need never be separated again, Kitty. When you're well again we can celebrate properly. Make up for lost time.' He folded her into his arms, stroking her back, breathing against her neck, closing his eyes, and taking in all the sensations that were pulsing through him.

Kitty sighed and stroked him back with her good arm, burrowing her forehead against his chest, where she fitted as if she was made to be there. Finally she gave a little sigh. 'Frank . . . I'm sorry, I can't keep my eyes open any longer.'

'Then sleep tight, my darling Kitty,' he said softly, carefully releasing her, but she was already asleep. He curled around her, vowing that this would be the beginning of many years of their lives together. Slowly he too fell asleep on top of the covers, one arm resting around Kitty's waist, protecting her from whatever the fates could send her way, for ever.

'So you are the little boy's mother, Mrs . . . Mrs . . .'

'Kerrigan,' Nancy said between gritted teeth to the policeman. She thought she really was going to be sick. Never in her wildest dreams did she think this would ever happen to her, that her little Georgie would go missing. She was trembling with shock as she sat on her mother's settee. Violet had gone to fetch her a cup of tea.

'And you were not at home last night?'

'I've told you already,' she gasped. 'I was with a friend in town and Georgie was staying with his cousin Tommy for a treat. Well, they're as good as cousins. He'd been going on about it for ages, but we only decided he could do it a couple of days ago.'

The policeman nodded. He'd been over and over the story to see if anyone's statement didn't match, but they had all said the same thing. Nobody outside the immediate families would have known the boy was there. It made no sense that someone could have planned to snatch him in advance. The family members themselves seemed very unlikely suspects; he'd been surrounded by anxious enquiries and offers of hot drinks and biscuits since he arrived, everyone clearly desperate to find the little boy. The grandfather had wanted to stay home from his salvage job, but the policeman had persuaded him to go, with a promise of getting a message to him if anything changed.

'And there's no likelihood he would have gone home and your mother-in-law has him?' he asked.

Nancy shook her head vehemently. 'No, there's no likelihood of that at all.'

The policeman nodded again. His colleague had gone to check that for himself, but he'd wanted to hear the mother's answer nonetheless.

'So do you have any idea of who would have wanted to take him?' he persisted.

Nancy looked up to the heavens. Years ago, before Sid had joined up, he'd run with a pretty rough crowd, and had even had the local gangland boss Harry Calendar's sister as his fancy piece. But that was all water under the bridge. None of his old mates had bothered calling by to see if there had been any news about him since he'd been taken prisoner after Dunkirk. They probably didn't even know of Georgie's existence.

'No, I can't think of anyone.' She accepted the tea from Violet and sipped it, but it made her feel sicker than ever.

'Well, it looks as if he was frightened by this burglar who attacked your sister. We'll enquire at every house to see if they know anything,' the policeman said reassuringly, but Nancy's mind was not put at rest by this. Everyone on Empire Street knew what was going on in everyone else's houses. There wasn't much of a chance Georgie could be anywhere nearby.

She bent forward, hunching her shoulders, her head in her hands. Georgie, her little boy. She knew she'd been selfish and taken advantage of her family's

379

willingness to look after him whenever she fancied going out, which was often. She hadn't been the best mother to him, in all honesty, but he was the centre of her world. Without him her life had no purpose. The hurt and humiliation of the last twelve hours had been stripped away, leaving one clear fact: Georgie mattered more than anything. She had to get him back.

The policeman was still talking to her, she realised, and she looked up at him with a tear-stained face. 'Try not to worry, Mrs Kerrigan,' he said as he moved to leave.

Nancy watched him go with no faith that he would find her child. He gave her the impression he thought Georgie had run away and was hiding somewhere close, but she knew he'd been looking forward to staying with Tommy for ages, and wouldn't have left voluntarily in a month of Sundays. Even if he had been scared he would have gone to Tommy for comfort, or to Dolly and Pop's house.

Violet came and sat beside her, passing her a hanky. 'Here, take this.'

Nancy nodded gratefully and wiped her face. 'Thank you.' She sat up straight again. 'What really happened, Violet? How can my boy have run off?'

Violet shook her head. 'I don't believe he did. He wouldn't leave us, even if he was scared by a burglar.'

'Where's Sarah now?' Nancy wondered, realising she hadn't seen her younger sister that morning in all the chaos.

'She's sleeping. She looks awful; she got beaten up quite badly. She can't remember much about it.' Violet bit her lip. 'I think Rita gave her something to help her sleep.'

'What about Tommy?'

'He's sleeping too, he's been up half the night,' Violet explained, but even as she spoke the door opened and Tommy came in, looking white-faced but determined.

'Tommy!' Nancy stood up and went over to him. 'What happened?'

'Are you all right?' Violet broke in. 'You're meant to be in bed.'

Tommy shook his head. 'I can't sleep. I keep thinking and thinking. What if it's my fault? I forgot to bolt the back door.'

'Don't be daft, you aren't to blame,' Violet said hurriedly. The boy had enough to worry about, without that extra burden of guilt. 'You locked it, the policeman checked and saw it had been broken.'

'So tell me what happened,' Nancy insisted.

Tommy drew a deep breath and tried as best he could to explain. He'd been asleep with Georgie in his room and had woken up when he heard a noise – he wasn't sure what it was. He'd had a nightmare, but now he reckoned that was the back door being forced open and all the activity beyond his bedroom door. Then there was another noise, which he now realised was Sarah stumbling on the stairs. He'd got up and found Georgie's little camp bed was empty – then gone out and seen Sarah on the stairs, blood on her nightdress. They'd checked the house together and found no Georgie but a broken lock on the back door.

'Sarah didn't see who broke in, but she sort of recognised the voice,' Tommy added. 'Whoever it was thought she was Kitty; he kept calling her Kitty.'

'But who would want to hurt Kitty?' Nancy wondered aloud. Kitty was one of those people who simply didn't have enemies. If it had been Danny, that would have been another matter – then again, nobody who knew Danny would be likely to risk breaking into his house like that. 'Can we wake Sarah up and ask her to try to remember some more?'

'I think we'll have to wait,' Violet cautioned her. 'She was in a pretty bad way and, like I said, Rita gave her a sedative or something.'

Tommy balled his fists in frustration. 'We've got to do something.'

'I can't sit here till she wakes up,' Nancy burst out. 'Every second counts. He could be freezing to death somewhere. He'll be frightened. We have to find him. Think, who could have done this?' She paced across the room, holding her arms tight across her stomach as if to keep in the pain. She still hadn't taken off her coat.

Violet sat on the edge of the settee and screwed up her face. 'I don't know . . . but there was something odd, back before Christmas. I don't rightly remember, I was so near my time and I wasn't quite thinking straight.' She took a breath, trying desperately to recall the stray comment over breakfast one day. 'Pop was coming home from his ARP round and he said he'd seen someone hanging around your front door, Tommy. He didn't do anything official about it because the fellow scarpered as soon as he saw him. He thought it was someone he knew.' She paused again, then her expression changed as the name came to her. 'Alfie Delaney. He said it looked like Alfie Delaney.'

Tommy gave a gasp of recognition. 'Alfie. It has to be him. You know when he conned me into getting drunk that time? I remember now. He kept wanting to talk about our Kitty. It struck me as odd at the time, but I got in so much trouble for going to the pub that I didn't say anything. He wouldn't shut up though. Wanted to know if she had a boyfriend, what she did, where she went, who with. His voice went all funny when he spoke about her.' He shivered in disgust at the memory.

'Right, I'm going to tell one of those policemen who must still be on our street,' said Violet, getting up, full of purpose. 'They can go round his mother's house and see if he was in last night. That's a start.'

'Tell him to check if his car's there,' Tommy said suddenly. 'He loves his car.'

Violet nodded. 'Right, I'm off. Mam is with the twins upstairs, but you'll keep an ear out for them, won't you?' She ran out before either of them could answer.

Nancy looked at Tommy. 'We don't need to stay here for the twins. Mam can cope fine without our help. We should go and see if we can find that Alfie.'

For a moment Tommy looked dubious, and terribly young. Then he nodded. 'Come on then.'

CHAPTER THIRTY-ONE

Mrs Kerrigan was beside herself when the policeman broke the news to her. 'That Nancy is a useless mother!' she screamed. 'I'll have her guts for garters, losing the boy like that.'

'Now, Mrs Kerrigan,' said the officer, watching the woman's wild eyes with alarm, 'there's no suggestion it was your daughter-in-law's fault. As I understand it, she wasn't even there. The boy was staying with her sister and young friend and a burglar broke in. That's all we know.'

Mrs Kerrigan was having none of it. 'And where was she, the little trollop? She thinks I don't know what goes on, but I do. She's a filthy stop-out, and now look where it's got her. My poor grandson,' she added with belated concern.

'So you've no idea where he might be?' the policeman persisted.

'Run away as far as he can from her, I shouldn't wonder.' The woman was working herself up into a proper state. 'I've a good mind to go round there and give her a piece of my mind.' She turned to the kitchen table and grabbed her handbag.

'Now, Mrs Kerrigan, wouldn't it be more sensible to stay here in case he takes it into his head to come home?' the officer suggested, but the woman was adamant.

'I'm going to see my daughter-in-law right away and you can't stop me,' she told him. 'There are things that have needed saying for a long time. I blame myself, staying quiet for as long as I have done. So now I'm not staying quiet any longer. Someone's got to put that young woman right, and it doesn't look as if anyone else is going to do it.' She reached for her coat hanging on a hook beside the back door. 'If you'll excuse me.' She held the door open.

'We'd better go down to his road to see if the car's there,' Tommy suggested, happier now that they were actually out and doing something. 'I reckon I could spot it easily, seeing as what I've been in it.'

Nancy agreed, as it seemed as good a place to start as anywhere. She was tormented by thoughts of what Alfie might do to her boy. What could he possibly know about small children? Would he have thought to give Georgie a blanket or something warm, or was he wandering around in his faded pyjamas? She shuddered at the idea but could not banish the fear from her mind.

Just before the turning to the Delaneys' road, they caught sight of a small, angry-looking figure marching towards them.

385

'Quick,' said Nancy, pulling Tommy back and into the mouth of one of the alleys that ran along the back yards of the terraces. 'It's Sid's mam. She hasn't moved that fast for years. She must have heard.'

'Won't she want to help?' Tommy asked.

'Not her,' spat Nancy. 'She'll be coming round to gloat. She'll add it to her collection of things to be sad about, that's what she's like.'

Tommy stared at the mouth of the alley as the woman passed by, looking neither to left nor right, face set rigid with purpose. 'She doesn't look very friendly,' he admitted.

Nancy pursed her lips. 'She doesn't know what a friend is. At best it's someone to moan to. Horrible old bag. To think they asked me if Georgie would have run off to go back to her. He can't bear her, and all she's interested in is making sure he looks good so it'll reflect well on her. But the poor little fellow, and he's only just got over that cough, and this will make him worse again. Sorry,' she added, taking one look at Tommy's dismayed expression. 'It's nothing to do with you, so forget what I said.'

'Okey doke,' he said apprehensively. 'Shall we go on now?'

They threaded their way down the alley and out at the end nearest Alfie's house. Tommy gazed along the road. 'It's not here.'

'Are you sure?' Nancy demanded.

'Of course I am. I'd recognise it anywhere,' Tommy assured her. 'Maybe he's gone down to the docks? He works there, doesn't he?'

'I don't really know my way around there,' Nancy said nervously, but Tommy was confident.

'I do though. Danny used to work there, so I went there all the time when I was young. I'll be able to search all the likely places he could hide a car, no bother.'

Nancy allowed him to guide her down to the docks, where she felt extremely conspicuous in her glamorous coat and heels, but beyond a few astonished looks, most of the dockers paid her very little attention. She'd been so upset she hadn't even thought to put on something more sensible before coming out again. Tommy ran swiftly around all the places he could think of, mostly where he used to hide when his brother wanted to fetch him home, but again he drew a blank. He knew just about every possible spot where a vehicle of that size could have been tucked away, but it was in none of them.

'It's no good,' he told Nancy disconsolately, hands shoved in his pockets as he came back to meet her. The wind was whipping off the river, and her hair, for once not immaculately styled, was flying wildly around her face. For a moment he thought she was going to cry but she fought it. Instead she nodded briefly and lifted her chin.

'Then we'll just have to try somewhere else,' she said.

Dolly came downstairs, having settled the twins down for a nap, to find no Violet and no Nancy. She knew she shouldn't, but she felt a quick rush of relief at having a moment of quiet to herself. It was a rare thing in her house and she needed to make the most of it, to use it to gather her strength for whatever was to come. Dolly naturally looked on the bright side of things, but she was having a great deal of difficulty finding a bright side to this. Sarah attacked, Georgie missing – what was going on? She was prepared for tragedy when it was caused by the war. Even though she would never forget her beloved Eddy, she knew he had died in a just cause and for something he wholeheartedly believed in. However, this new turn of events had taken the wind out of her sails.

That wouldn't do. She knew her family depended on her and she couldn't let them down. She had to trust that the police would find out what had happened to Georgie and that Sarah's own resilience would help her to cope with her injuries. She was still sleeping now and that was the best thing for her. Dolly herself must try to comfort Nancy and take care of Tommy when he woke, as well as trying to reassure the other members of the family.

She was under no illusions about Nancy, recognising her middle child would use every available ruse to get her own way and often shirk her responsibilities. Yet this morning had shown her, if Dolly had ever had any doubts, that Nancy genuinely loved her little boy and was heartbroken that he'd gone missing. Deep down her maternal instincts were there, despite what most people thought.

The back door banged and Violet came back in,

pushing a hand through her lank hair which had been caught in the stiff wind.

Dolly took in the sight of her daughter-in-law, face pinched with worry, and knew she was extremely anxious for Georgie. The little boy had won the heart of everyone who'd ever looked after him. He'd done nothing to deserve this.

Violet glanced around the room. 'Where are Nancy and Tommy? Are the twins all right?'

'The place is deserted,' Dolly said. 'Don't see that often, do we? Don't worry, the babies have settled down nicely and Tommy was asleep, last I heard.'

Violet raised her hand to her forehead. 'They've gone after him. I bet that's what's happened.'

Dolly was puzzled. 'After Georgie? How would they know where to go?'

Violet sank down on one of the wooden chairs. 'Because I told them about what Pop said ages ago. Do you remember? That he was sure he'd seen Alfie Delany hanging around Kitty's front door after dark, and he'd run off as if he was up to no good. Tommy seemed to think it made sense. I asked them to stay here but—'

'Well, they aren't here now,' Dolly said. 'That Alfie Delaney is a wrong 'un if ever I saw one. I hope they know what they're doing.' Her face creased with worry. 'I hope they aren't putting themselves in danger.'

Nancy had racked her brains for any ideas as to where a person like Alfie Delaney might take off to, if he hadn't gone to his mother or to his old place of work, but come up with nothing. 'I'm not going home until we find him,' she said firmly. 'We're doing no good there. If he makes his own way back, then Mam and Violet will see to him. We're better out here, even if we're just combing the streets.'

'Suppose so,' said Tommy, beginning to feel his lack of sleep. His feet were weary as he dragged them along the pavement, made heavier by the unshakeable guilt. He was the man of the place and yet he'd let them all down by failing to protect them, even though he'd bolted the back gate after propping up his bike.

His bike. When had Alfie talked to him about the bike? When he'd first hoped to get his job – and also at the pub. He'd seemed to know the man at the bar there, even though the recollection was hazy. But where was the pub? He hadn't been drunk when Alfie had taken him there, only on the way back. It struck him that it might be a good place to hole up for a while, especially if you were trying to hide a child too. He struggled to picture the sign above the door, but he hadn't been able to see it clearly at the time. All the same, if he could just remember the way there . . .

'Nancy,' he said, more lively now. 'I've had an idea. But it'll mean a bit of a walk. It could take a while.'

'I don't care,' said Nancy at once. 'You've had more to do with Alfie than I have. It's worth a try.'

'All right, well, we're going to find the pub he drove me to a few months back. Do you know of any that have been done up quite recently? I don't know its name, you see.'

Nancy shook her head. 'Not round here.' She thought fleetingly of the places she'd gone to with Gary, or way back with Stan, but they'd always taken care to avoid the area around her home. Then she consigned such thoughts to the past where they belonged. There was only one matter on her mind now. 'I trust you. You lead the way.'

Half an hour later, and with her feet aching, Nancy was beginning to lose track of exactly where they were. It wasn't an area she knew well, if at all. It seemed quiet, almost empty of people, with a lot of bomb damage in evidence. She could still smell the river though. She hoped Tommy knew what he was doing.

Tommy was growing in confidence with every step. This was the right road, he was sure of it, even though he'd been taken here at a completely different time of day. Looking about him at the area, he decided that if he'd wanted to lie low somewhere, this would be ideal. There was nobody around to ask awkward questions – not like where they lived, or down at the docks. You could probably disappear here for weeks and nobody would be any the wiser.

Rounding a corner, he saw the building he'd been looking for. The pub seemed shabbier in bright daylight, even though it had been recently painted. The name was now clear: The King's Head. 'That's it,' he said. 'That's where Alfie conned me into getting drunk. All because he was after Kitty and I didn't realise.'

'Then he took advantage of you,' said Nancy firmly. 'You mustn't blame yourself. He picked on you deliberately, so that makes him a coward. You're worth a hundred of him, Tommy.'

Tommy glowed with the praise, even though he still did blame himself for being so stupid as to be taken in like that. Still, it was good to know Nancy thought well of him. He hadn't had as much to do with her as the rest of her family, and up till now had assumed she didn't really know much about him either. He drew back his shoulders. Now he had to live up to the praise.

'We could keep to the shadow of that wall so they're less likely to see us coming,' he suggested, and she fell in line behind him as they proceeded more cautiously now. After a minute, Tommy came to a halt. 'See there? The pub has a back yard.' He pointed through a flimsy gate, to a yard with barrels stacked along one side. A few low storage buildings lined two other sides of the square. Parked close to one of their doors was a car. 'Nancy, that's it. That's Alfie's car, I'm certain of it.'

'Then we'd better be careful,' said Nancy, edging forward a little. 'Alfie could be anywhere.'

'He's probably in the pub,' Tommy predicted, taking a good look at the building. 'If he is, all the bar windows face to the front or round the other side. We could get into the yard if we kept well back.'

'But we don't know he's in there,' Nancy pointed out. The enormity of the risk they were about to take suddenly hit her. 'What if he's waiting in the yard somewhere?'

Tommy shrugged. 'We'll have to chance it,' he said. 'We'll just be as quiet as possible and keep to the shadows where there are any.' He paused for a few moments. 'I can't hear anything from the yard, can you?'

Nancy had a sense that they were stepping off a cliff into the unknown. 'No. Let's try it and see. Anything is better than sitting around waiting, not knowing anything.'

Silently they edged along the rest of the wall and through the gate. Staying in the shadow of one of the outbuildings, they approached the car. There was nobody in it and no sign of Alfie or the little boy.

'If we keep down below the level of the car roof, no one can see us from the upstairs windows,' Tommy pointed out. All his years of playing hide and seek with Michael and Megan on the farm were coming in useful, he realised. He just had to keep all his senses alert.

'Tommy.' Nancy stopped dead, her voice little more than a whisper. 'Look over there, by the door of that shed. Can you see something?'

Tommy squinted towards where she was pointing. There was something there – something blue. He couldn't quite tell what it was. They crept closer until the little object came into focus.

'Tommy.' Nancy thought her heart would break. 'It's Georgie's slipper.'

In London, Laura decided she had better let Frank and Kitty sleep in. She wrote a swift note saying she would be back later and crept out of the admiral's flat. She had to get back to her billet for a change of clothes, and then put in an appearance at her work, although they were aware of what had happened last night and had granted her the morning off. She was slightly muzzy with so few hours of sleep, but exhilarated from the thrill of seeing her friend rescued, when for a while she'd feared Kitty had perished in the bomb strike. She was also thrilled that Kitty had finally seen sense about Frank. It had been obvious to Laura that her friend felt strongly about him and, now that she'd seen them together, she was convinced they were meant for each other. Laura had been fond of Elliott, who had been a decent and loving man, and yet she could tell the connection between Kitty and Frank went deeper still. They definitely needed their privacy when they woke up in the admiral's flat.

She caught a bus that for once wasn't diverted, nearly all the way to her front door. She still couldn't think of this as any kind of home and, as she'd fore-seen, her attic room had been perishing cold over the winter, but now spring was here it had started to improve. Sadly relations with her tight-lipped landlady hadn't.

The woman was waiting for her as she stepped into the narrow hallway, with its mean selection of coat hooks and little else apart from a sorry-looking plant that Laura sometimes secretly watered. 'Miss Fawcett. A word, if you please.'

'Good morning. Lovely day for once, isn't it?' said

Laura brightly. She didn't intend the woman's gloom to rub off on her.

The landlady ignored her cheerfulness. 'A young man called for you. He was most offhand, rude even. I'll thank you not to bring down the reputation of this house with such guests. He looked most irregular. His hair was sticking up all over the place, not at all like a gentleman from any of the services.'

'Was it dark blond by any chance?' Laura asked.

'I assume you know him, then?' the woman fired back.

Laura fixed her with her most solemn gaze. 'If it is the person I'm thinking of, then I can assure you that he has served his country in ways that you or I can scarcely imagine. The fact that one of the only traces of this is visible in his slightly irregular haircut is nothing short of a miracle. If that is all, then I'll go to my room.'

The woman sniffed. 'Indeed. That's as maybe, but I'd be grateful if he wasn't seen around here again. Meanwhile, he left you this.' She took a small envelope from her pocket, then spun on her low heel and made her way back to her own quarters at the rear of the house.

Laura mounted the stairs wondering how soon she could transfer to a different billet. It was true that Freddy still didn't look much like the average airman in uniform, but he had improved tremendously under his doctor's care, the regime of proper food and special exercise, alongside careful debriefing, working wonders for his health in every way. That the narrow-minded landlady could insult him so readily was deeply enraging. Still, she probably knows no better, Laura muttered as she stepped into her cramped room and sat down on the window seat to read his note.

A moment later she was on her feet again, almost leaping for joy. The message was terse, evidently written in a hurry, most likely with the unsympathetic gaze of the landlady curtailing his time.

L. No time for details but Marjorie's made it. Message received via very brave French agent last thing yesterday. She'll be home as soon as can be arranged. More news to follow. Contact me when you've read this. F.

Laura shut her eyes and breathed a long, drawn-out sigh of relief. Her friend and Freddy's soul mate was alive, contrary to their deepest fears. On top of the lack of sleep, she felt as if she might crumple, and she put out one hand to steady herself.

She was severely tempted to rush back to the admiral's flat, wake up Kitty and tell her then and there. She stopped herself, knowing her friend needed her sleep and that a few more hours would make no difference. The second she finished her shift, however, she was going to be back there, sharing the news. Last night, for one bleak moment, Laura had thought she'd lost both of her dearest friends. Now they were both restored to her. To hell with her miserable landlady – life was wonderful again.

CHAPTER THIRTY-TWO

For a moment Nancy couldn't move. Then she ran, with Tommy hissing 'keep down!' as he followed behind. She halted by the shed door and bent to the ground. It was definitely Georgie's little slipper, blue to match his favourite pyjamas. She picked it up. He was here, she could feel it in her bones.

'Georgie!' she called softly. 'Georgie! Are you there? It's Mammy and Tommy, come to get you.'

She could hear nothing but her own short breaths and the hammering of her heartbeat. Putting her mouth close to the shed door, she tried again.

Tommy crouched so that his ear was right where the door met its splintered frame. 'Georgie!' he called, a little louder. 'Are you there? Can you hear me?'

For a moment there was silence, and then came a tiny scrabbling sound.

'Georgie? Is that you?' Tommy asked, turning so his mouth was next to the door's edge.

There was more scrabbling, closer now.

'Mammy!' came the little voice. 'Mammy! I'm cold!'

For a moment Nancy couldn't move. Fear, relief, anger and overwhelming love for her child flooded through her in waves, rooting her to the spot. Then she sprang into action, trying to open the door, tugging at the handle, but it didn't budge.

'Keep down!' Tommy hissed. 'Look, it's fastened with a lock. You're just making a noise for nothing.'

'We've got to get him out!' she exclaimed.

Tommy nodded, but he was thinking fast. 'I know. I know.' He addressed the door edge again. 'Georgie, we're going to get you out any minute now. You stay quiet and keep a little way away from the door. You'll see me and Mammy soon.' Then he turned to Nancy. 'Have you got a hair grip in your bag?' he asked.

'Tommy, this isn't the time for—' Nancy began, but he held out his hand and spoke over her.

'Then give it to me,' he insisted. 'I'm not fooling around, I know what I'm doing.'

Baffled and uncertain, she delved into her bag and hunted around in its contents for her precious store of Kirby grips. They'd been a present from Gary. Well, if Tommy could make use of them to free her son, it would be the best present he'd ever given her. She thrust them into Tommy's hand. 'What do you want them for?'

'Wait and see.'

Tommy steadied himself so that he was at the level of the lock and gently extended one of the grips. He forced himself to breathe slowly and evenly, as he'd been taught, to keep his hand steady. Carefully he manipulated the narrow prong of metal until he heard the clicks he'd been waiting for. Cautiously he tried the door. It moved.

'Let's go in and keep as quiet as we can,' he suggested, and the pair of them swiftly edged inside the damp, cold shed.

There was barely any light penetrating from the cobweb-covered small window, but it was enough to see Georgie, in his blue pyjamas, standing back from the door just as Tommy had told him to. His cheeks were smeared with grime and his hair stood up on end, but otherwise he looked unhurt. His face broke into a delighted smile and he ran into his mother's arms, hugging her tightly as she picked him up and spun him round. 'I knew you'd come,' he said. 'The bad man shut me in here and said you'd never find me, but I knew you would.'

Nancy came to a stop and set him down gently. 'It was Tommy who found you,' she said. 'He's very clever, he knew exactly where you'd be.'

Georgie beamed up at his idol and Tommy ruffled the little boy's hair. 'All right, scamp?' he said. 'Sorry it took us a while.'

Nancy looked around the mean little shed. There were some sacks in the corner, pushed into a heap, but not much else. 'Did you sleep over there?' she asked anxiously. 'Are you all right, the man didn't hurt you, did he? Did he give you anything to eat or drink?'

'No,' said Georgie, the corners of his mouth turning down. 'Mammy, I'm cold and hungry. Have you got any food?'

'Let's see,' said Nancy, but she knew it would be a fruitless search. Her bag contained some money and items of make-up, but she hadn't thought to put in anything else, anything useful.

Tommy dug around in his pocket and drew out a stick of liquorice wrapped in a paper bag. 'Here you go, scamp.'

Georgie reached out for it and began wolfing it at once. Nancy raised her eyebrows at Tommy but he didn't react. Instead he reached into his other pocket and produced a scarf. 'Here you are, Georgie. When you've finished eating you can have this. It's all right, it's a spare.' He paused and then took off his jacket and removed his pullover. 'As a matter of fact, I was feeling a bit warm walking round in this, so you can have this too. It'll be a bit big, mind.'

'You won't care, will you, Georgie?' Nancy asked, as she helped her son into what was for him a huge jumper, but the little boy was delighted. Since it was Tommy's pullover, it was the best in the world. He allowed his mother to tie the scarf around his neck and to put his missing slipper on him. 'There you are, that's better, isn't it?' She hugged him again, rubbing his arms to make him warm. 'Tommy, we'd better be going. I don't want to hang around in here.'

Tommy nodded. 'Alfie probably thinks it's all right as nobody will know to come here and that Georgie's safely hidden as he's locked in. But we can't stay here till it gets dark.' He looked down at the little boy. 'You'd better let me give you a piggyback, Georgie, then we'll be faster. I reckon if we head away from the river, we'll get to a main road and find a bus.'

'Or a police station,' Nancy murmured, but didn't want to frighten the little boy. Now he was warm and had devoured the liquorice stick, he had bounced back to his normal cheerful self, as if unaware that they were in danger. Given the chance to wear Tommy's clothes and ride on his back, it was almost a treat, she could tell from his face. She had to keep him thinking that way.

'Okey doke,' he said.

Violet gazed anxiously out into the street from behind the curtains in Dolly's parlour. Hours had gone by and they hadn't heard a thing, apart from a short and unpleasant visit from old Mrs Kerrigan. The woman had been full of venom aimed at Nancy, but Dolly had firmly shown her the door. Now Violet was trying not to think the worst, but her imagination was running away from her, casting up pictures of Georgie lying helpless somewhere, cold and frightened, and of Nancy and Tommy being attacked while trying to trace him. She knew these images were making it worse but she was powerless to stop them.

'Come away from there, love,' Dolly said from the doorway. 'You'll get yourself in a proper tizzy and then the twins will feel it and start crying. We don't need that, do we?' She tried to keep her voice light and positive, but even she was reaching the end of her reserves of cheerfulness. The twins were in fact safely asleep, but mentioning their need was the only distraction she could think of that would outweigh Violet's affection for Georgie. She dreaded to think what would happen if the worst had befallen him. He'd won the hearts of so many in his short life.

'When's Pop due back?' Violet asked dully.

'Any time now. The salvage boss won't make him stay late tonight, not when he's told them what's going on,' Dolly predicted.

'Then I might stay here till he comes up the street,' Violet said, turning back to the window.

Dolly came to stand behind her, putting her hand on her daughter-in-law's bony shoulder. 'I'll wait with you,' she said, not wanting the young woman to be alone, and feeling in need of company herself. Sarah was still asleep upstairs in her old room, time working its healing magic, and so it was just the two of them, standing and watching anxiously, staring into the middle distance as dusk fell over the few houses of Empire Street.

They were still there when the police car drew up, its shielded headlights bright in the gathering gloom. Dolly snapped to attention, jolting Violet out of her daydream, neither of them sure what this could mean. Dolly's heart was in her mouth, wondering if they'd come in person to bring bad news.

Then the rear door opened and Nancy stepped out, followed by Tommy from around the other side, and then the small figure of Georgie, wearing an enormous pullover with the sleeves rolled up, over and over into thick cuffs. Dolly gave a little gasp and Violet jumped, then ran to the front door and threw it open. She knelt down to Georgie's level and he ran forward to hug her.

'I'm wearing Tommy's jumper!' he told her.

'So I can see,' said Violet, trying her best to sound normal but not quite managing it. 'Do you want some milk?'

Dolly wiped a surreptitious tear from her eye as Violet led the little boy, apparently none the worse for wear, into the kitchen, then turned to Nancy. 'So, where have you been? Did you find Alfie? What's been going on?'

'It's a long story,' Nancy started to say.

The policeman, a different one to the couple who had been there that morning, intervened. 'I understand you are all acquainted with Mr Alfred Delaney,' he said slowly. 'I can therefore inform you that my colleagues are at this moment in the process of apprehending him. He won't be back to cause your family any more harm, I can reassure you of that, Mrs – Feeny, is it?'

Dolly nodded, as Tommy burst out, 'He was in the pub, Auntie Dolly. We could hear him as we got Georgie away. He was shouting and screaming about something.'

'Then we tried to find a bus but we went past an ARP warden's station and got help from there,' Nancy explained. 'Don't worry, Mam, we're fine, and Georgie doesn't seem to have been hurt. We're trying to say as little as possible in front of him, but really he thinks it's all a big adventure now.'

403

'You can tell me all the details later, then,' Dolly said. 'I'm still going to ask Rita to take a look at him. She should be back from the hospital soon. And that's Pop now, if I'm not much mistaken.' She hurried to greet him, keen to update him on all he had missed since leaving for work much earlier in the day.

Nancy looked at Tommy. She realised she'd always discounted him before as a young tearaway who was likely to cause trouble wherever he went. Now she saw he had grown up and was on his way to being a man – and one who could take responsibility and keep calm under pressure. He also seemed to know a few useful tricks.

'I meant to ask you before,' she said in a low voice so that Dolly and Pop wouldn't catch what she was saying. 'How did you know what to do with that hair grip? I mean, I was glad you did know, or we'd never have got Georgie away so soon or so quietly – but you didn't learn that at school, did you? Don't tell me they teach you that at the GPO in case nobody answers when you knock.'

Tommy blushed in the parlour's gaslight. 'Promise you won't say,' he replied. 'Uncle Seth taught me. Auntie Joan mustn't find out. He accidentally locked himself out one day when she was at market and we couldn't get in. He showed me what to do and let me have a go. We had to send Michael and Megan to play with the chickens so they wouldn't know.'

Nancy raised her eyebrows. 'And here was me thinking he just taught you how to fix a fence or collect eggs. Well, I'll thank him one day – don't worry, when nobody else can overhear.'

Tommy shuffled a little guiltily but was saved from further embarrassment by the arrival of Rita, still in her nurse's cloak. Dolly was all for hurrying her straight to check that Georgie was as unhurt as he appeared, but Rita paused, taking something from her bag.

'Hang on, we'd better see what this is. Ruby took delivery of this telegram, which is addressed to Sarah. Is she still asleep?'

'She was when I last looked,' Dolly said. 'I'd better have it instead.' She ripped it open, though Tommy looked anxious. He knew only too well what they so often meant – and yet who would be sending messages to Sarah?

'Oh, it's from Kitty,' Dolly said. 'She's been delayed in London – doesn't say why, but we aren't to worry. Well, as if we would. She's probably been asked to go to some more meetings or something like that. That's all right, Tommy, you can stop here with us. I don't want you in your own house until that lock is fixed.'

'I'll go and do that now,' said Pop, glad to be of use in this house of increasing chaos. 'Want to give me a hand, Tommy?'

Nancy looked across at the boy – almost young man – and smiled. 'Yes, you go and do that,' she agreed. 'You're good with locks.'

'Have you seen the kitchen here, Kitty?' Frank asked as he approached the sofa in the admiral's flat, bearing two cups of tea. Kitty was propped up there, much brighter for her hours of sleep. Her ribs and left arm still hurt, but she could wiggle her fingers and had faith in the doctor's judgement that rest was the best medicine. She grinned as she looked up at Frank.

'No, I haven't been here before, only heard about it from Laura,' she said, shuffling a little against the plush cushions to accept the fine porcelain cup. 'This is a bit different to Derby House, isn't it?' She sipped carefully.

Frank sat beside her and put his arm around her shoulders. 'I should say so. There's even a chock-full cocktail cabinet over there. Haven't seen one of those for a very long time.'

'I knew there'd be a reason Laura liked coming here,' Kitty laughed, and then winced as the movement caught at her ribs. 'I shan't be having anything from there though. I don't think it'd go well with the pain-killers.'

'You're probably right,' said Frank. 'Tell you what, when you're better I'll take you to the finest cocktail bar in Liverpool. How about the Adelphi? Bet they do all manner of them there. Would you like that?'

Kitty rested her head on his shoulder. 'Frank, I don't mind about posh cocktail bars. I'm not that keen on cocktails, to be honest. You can treat me to half a shandy down the Sailor's Rest if you like. As long as I'm with you, I don't care.' Her dark blue eyes shone as she turned to look up at his face, familiar and yet alight with a look that she now knew was love, love for her. The realisation nearly took her breath away.

She had waited so long for him, hardly daring to believe it would ever happen. Now here they were, together at last.

Slowly he bowed his head forward and kissed her gently, as much as her awkward position would allow. 'That's just for starters,' he said tenderly. 'We'll go wherever you like, Kitty. You'll make me the proudest man in England with you on my arm.'

She gazed up at him, still having to pinch herself that this was really happening. Yet it felt totally real and absolutely right. She was meant to be in Frank's arms – of that she had no doubt. She had the sensation that at last she had come home.

She had lost count of how long they had sat like that, wrapped in the half-embrace, taking in each other's eyes, when they heard a key turning in the lock of the front door. Reluctantly they pulled apart, and Kitty took a sip of the tea, which had gone cold.

Laura stepped into the room, smart in her uniform. 'Don't separate on my behalf,' she said at once. 'You don't know what a tonic it is to see you two together. Well, actually alive at all, after yesterday. That you've finally seen sense and worked out you're right for each other is the icing on the cake.' She turned blithely and hooked her jacket over a nearby chair. 'How are you after your sleep, Kitty? You don't look as pale as earlier, I must say, although that could be the therapeutic presence of Lieutenant Feeny here.'

'Much better, thanks,' said Kitty at once. 'I'll be on the mend in no time.'

'Good,' said Laura, 'because I have some news.' She retrieved the note from her pocket.

Kitty tried to sit up to see what her friend was doing, but with a gasp she sank back on the sofa. Maybe she wasn't as improved as she'd hoped.

'Steady on,' said Frank, immediately concerned.

'I'm all right,' Kitty said. 'What is it, Laura?' She had a strong inkling that Laura would have left them alone to enjoy their new-found love unless it was something very important. She tried to guess what this might be but could not.

Laura cleared her throat and for a moment couldn't quite say the words. Then she looked up at them with a broad smile. 'It's Marjorie,' she said. 'She's managed to get in touch with Freddy. Don't ask me how or where she's been, we simply don't know, but she's alive and she's coming home. Isn't that marvellous?'

'Oh, Laura.' Kitty shook her head and then was filled with almost incredulous joy. 'Is it really true? She's alive, after all this time? Does he really not say anything more?'

Laura pulled a face. 'He can be a man of few words, my brother, but this time I think he genuinely doesn't know. He would have said, or at least told me where I could phone him from here. I'm going to try to see him later on. But anyway, it's just such a relief to hear she has not been killed off in a Resistance cell somewhere. That's what I feared, I can tell you that now.'

Kitty nodded. 'I never wanted to say either, but that's what I was scared might have happened too.

We know she must have gone in undercover – it doesn't bear thinking about what might have happened to her. She was so brave before she went, though. So determined.'

'Yes, underneath that quiet exterior, she always was as stubborn as a mule,' said Laura cheerfully. 'No doubt that's stood her in good stead. Frank, I'm sorry, you don't know this person, but she's been like a sister to Kitty and me ever since we did our initial training, and she's been missing for ages. So you see, it's rather good news.'

Kitty sighed. 'It's almost too much to take in. Frank, you'd like her, she's terribly clever. She'd love you too – I mean she'd admire you, and would probably want to know exactly what you do at work. It would get her brain cells ticking and she likes nothing better.'

Frank nodded. 'I'm glad she's all right, then. It's not much fun waiting to hear if someone you love has made it or not, is it?'

There was moment of silence as Laura recalled the years she'd agonised over Freddy's fate, and then over Marjorie's. Kitty recalled the awful time near the beginning of the war when they'd thought Jack was lost at sea, and then the terrible blow of Eddy's death. That Marjorie had somehow survived her secret mission was nothing short of a miracle.

'Right, time to celebrate,' said Laura, heading with habitual accuracy to the cocktail cabinet. 'Frank, have you seen the admiral's treasure chest here? What will you have? Kitty, don't tell me, you still don't care for them.'

'I'll have whatever you're having,' said Frank bravely.

Kitty gave a wry grin. 'You two go right ahead. Laura, you know me too well. What I'd really, really like above anything is a cup of proper tea.'

CHAPTER THIRTY-THREE

'I don't know, I turn my back for five minutes and look what happens.' Danny pretended to be outraged, but really he was heartily relieved to be back home where he belonged. He'd been longing to return ever since he got the letters, from Tommy, Kitty and Sarah, giving what he immediately realised were heavily censored versions of the events he'd missed. His first reaction was to tell his superiors he could no longer continue with the project as his family needed him, and yet he knew he should not do that. He'd been chosen for this piece of work; it was vital for what they hoped and now expected would be the final phase of the war. Besides, as the letters had emphasised, they were all right, despite everything. Yet his primal urge was to get home and see that everyone was safe, and if he could have got his hands on that scum of the earth Alfie . . .

Now the project had finished at last and he was due to start back at his regular post in Derby House on Monday morning. He had the weekend to settle back in and had got up early, unable to sleep in, even though it was Saturday, and had gone to the shop for a paper. He'd bumped into Sarah as he'd left and invited her round to join him for his morning toast, though really he wanted to check she was as well recovered as she'd claimed she was.

The April sunshine was streaming through the kitchen window as they sat at the well-scrubbed table. Danny produced a small pat of butter and a jar of home-made jam, which Sarah immediately recognised as Dolly's, made from fruit from the victory garden. Dolly had been feeding Tommy more than ever, as he was now deemed a hero for saving Georgie, and had sent across a whole box of goodies for Danny's return. She wasn't going to turn down the offer, and hurriedly buttered her toast while it was still hot, so that the golden liquid soaked through it. She smiled broadly in appreciation, but inside she was apprehensive. To think that she'd sat at this table with Danny, day in, day out, and never thought anything of it. Today, though, she had butterflies in her stomach. It had been ages since she'd seen him and still longer since they'd been alone together. She cast her mind back to the last few times they'd spoken and knew she was blushing at the memory.

'Where are Kitty and Tommy?' she asked, thinking that the house was quiet.

Danny helped himself to a big dollop of jam. 'Tommy's still asleep and Kitty has a day off and left to go into town just before I went to the shop,' he said. 'Didn't say what she was doing. It was a relief

412

to see her last night, though – I didn't like the sound of her getting caught up in that V2 strike. I kept thinking she was badly hurt and putting a brave face on it – you know what she's like. Well, you'd know exactly.' He caught her eye with a meaningful glance. 'You're just as bad. Saying you'd had a bit of a fright, when in fact Alfie Delaney broke in and beat you up.' He put down his toast and his expression changed. 'Sarah, I'm so sorry. I feel responsible. I should have been here, protecting you. Instead you had to endure all that. I can't say how badly I wished I was here.'

Sarah didn't quite know how to take this. Was it loaded with the meaning she'd suspected at Christmas, or was he simply sad he'd been away and unable to fight off Alfie? 'Well, you know why she's gone into the city centre,' she said, trying to change the subject. 'Has she said anything to you? She'll be meeting Frank. Ever since they got trapped by that collapsed building, there's been no separating them. They're both floating on air, full of the joys of spring. The funny thing is, nobody's in the least bit surprised.'

'Sarah . . .' Danny shook his head. 'All right, no, I'm not surprised either. She did hint at something in her letters, and then when I reported back to Derby House last night straight off the train, Frank was there. He didn't exactly ask me if he could court my sister, but as good as. I said to him, if he thought I had any control over what Kitty did, he had another think coming.'

'Talk about falling for the boy next door,' said

413

Sarah, trying to keep her face neutral but knowing she'd let some of her true feelings show.

'Nothing wrong with that, is there?' Danny met her gaze full on.

Sarah didn't back down. 'No, nothing.' She paused. Even now, there was one question that had been plaguing her. 'Danny, I knew for ages that Alfie had some kind of dodgy business going on with you. What was it all about? Is that why he came round? I really want to understand.'

Danny sighed and bit on his toast to put off the moment of explanation. 'It goes back to when we were all getting called up,' he said finally. 'He knew I had a bad heart – well, everyone found out after the fire at the docks. So he kept putting pressure on me to take his medical test for him, knowing I'd fail, so that he'd be exempt for the whole duration of the war.'

'The coward,' Sarah spat. 'You could have got into a whole lot of trouble if you'd been caught.'

'I know. But I hadn't been totally on the straight and narrow when I worked on the docks myself, and he kept threatening to put the word out about me. He used pressure on all fronts – he got Tommy a pair of football boots one Christmas so we'd be beholden to him. He kept on asking even when I said no. Then I started at Derby House and he had to flee after he sold everyone that poisoned meat he got from the black market.' Danny sat back and screwed his eyes shut. He'd come to hate the man, no doubt about it. 'But that wasn't why he beat you up though. He'd

414

always had a hankering for Kitty. He'd hang around, hoping for a glance of her, make horrible comments to me about her.'

'Yes, I know he'd come to the house expecting her to be here, and then he lost his temper when he realised it was me instead,' said Sarah thoughtfully. 'I don't know what was in his mind. He was drunk – I could smell it on him. I didn't know who it was at the time, but it all fell into place after. I'm glad it was me, not Kitty. Who knows what he might have done.'

Danny impetuously reached forward and took her hand. 'Don't say that, Sar. I'd have done anything to have stopped him hurting you. You were doing us a favour keeping an eye on Tommy and yet that happened – it's not right.'

Sarah held on to his hand. 'I'd rather he beat me up than succeeded in getting into bed with Kitty. That's what he was after, wasn't it? It could have been so much worse if he hadn't realised who I was. But he did, and I'm still here to tell the tale and so is Kitty. And anyway, he can't harm us or anyone else any more.'

She fell silent. It had been a shock, she could hardly pretend otherwise, when she had finally felt able to leave her bed after the attack to come downstairs and hear the latest news. Apparently Alfie had attempted to flee from the police who'd come to arrest him by jumping into his car and driving off, even more drunk than he'd been when he'd broken in to the room where she'd been sleeping. Having left Empire Street, he had spent hours in the pub, leaving Georgie locked

415

up in the outhouse, staying on without realising the little boy had been rescued. The publican, when questioned, had claimed he'd had no idea that the little boy had been in there. He'd thought nothing of it – just the return of a regular customer, who'd often used the yard to park his car. It wasn't any of his business, as long as Alfie paid for his drinks. He'd been as surprised as anybody by the police arriving and accusing Alfie of his crimes.

Alfie had done a runner and sped off in his car, weaving erratically through the narrow streets. Inevitably his car had crashed, fortunately not involving any other vehicles, but he hadn't stood a chance. He'd died there behind the wheel of his beloved car, the bonnet buckled into the windscreen, and him not yet thirty years old.

Sarah shook her head. 'I know we shouldn't speak ill of the dead, but nobody's going to miss him, are they, with the exception of his mother.'

'It was no more than he deserved,' said Danny hotly. 'He was a bully, a coward, a drunk and a fool. I for one won't miss him. To think he could have had Georgie in that car with him when he crashed. It doesn't bear thinking about.'

'It seems cruel,' Sarah went on, 'to feel so little emotion. But with all the other deaths in the war, those who've paid the ultimate price for serving their country, I can't bring myself to mourn him.'

Danny stroked her fingers. 'You're always so kind, Sar, you see the good in everyone. Even when there's not much to see.'

'The things you say, Danny Callaghan,' she protested, but she didn't move her hand.

He gazed at her directly. 'I missed you, you know. When I was on that course, stuck in the middle of nowhere. It gave me time to think. All the men were going on about their girls and how they didn't know if they'd be waiting for them, or if they could trust the ones who'd joined up and were on active service themselves, meeting other men. Hardly any of them seemed to be happy; they didn't seem to have that trust between them. I thought then, how awful that must be, not to trust the woman you love. I trust you above anyone, Sar. I don't even have to question it. I'm sorry I never said anything before. It's just . . .' He looked away, embarrassed.

Sarah kept tight hold of his hand. 'Danny, are you saying what I think you're saying? You're being all cryptic, like one of your crosswords.' She kept her tone light but she was deadly serious.

'All right. Yes. Sar, you're the only woman for me, I've known it for ages but I never dared to say.'

'Danny.' Sarah gasped. It felt as if she'd waited so long for him to say this that, now he finally had, words failed her.

'Look, Sar, the thing is, you know about my heart and everything,' he went on. 'I felt I couldn't offer you anything – not when I could just go out like a light at any time. I mean, what sort of life together would that be? You'd be worrying about me all the time and I'd be worrying about you worrying about me. I couldn't ask that of you.'

'Danny, you trusted me to keep quiet about your condition before anyone else, so why would it worry me?' she asked, her eyes dark with concern that he might be pulling away from her even now. 'I'll take you as you are, Danny. As long as I'm good enough for you. I'm not clever like you, and I'm not cheeky and funny like some of the other nurses – like Maeve for instance.'

'Maeve? Maeve Kerrigan? What's she got to do with it?' Danny asked, confused.

'Oh, I was just being silly. When she came round at Christmas, I could see you liked her.' Sarah felt sheepish now, admitting to her fleeting fear.

'Of course I like her,' Danny said. 'Like you say, she's fun, and she's a good friend to Rita, and she's a pretty good nurse. But that's all there is to it. I don't love her, Sar. I love you.'

Sarah gasped again. He'd finally said the words she'd so wanted him to say. 'Danny. I'm so glad. I've loved you for as long as I can remember. Why wouldn't I? Your heart condition makes no difference to me – it's part of you and that's all there is to it.'

It was Danny's turn to look sheepish. 'I should have known you'd say that. I was too afraid to ask you. I should have trusted you in that, like I do in every other way.'

'Yes, Danny, you should,' Sarah said emphatically. 'We trust each other about everything, don't we?'

Danny nodded. It was true. He could say anything to this woman, knowing she wouldn't be shocked or horrified or let him down. 'There is something else,' he said quietly.

She looked at him intently.

'All those boffins down there, they came from all sorts of backgrounds, had all manner of connections. I happened to mention why I'd ended up in my line of work, you know, not being able to join up for the other services, and why. One of them had a brother who was a doctor based at a big hospital down that way. He got me sent there on a day off, for tests.' His hand began to shake a little as she held it. 'He said I'm not as bad as they first thought. My heart will never be normal, but there's new medicine being developed all the time. Basically, unless I'm really unlucky, it's actually not very likely I'll pop my clogs any time soon, after all.'

'Danny, that's wonderful.' Sarah could feel her eyes were brimming with tears. No matter what she said, the fear of suddenly losing Danny at a moment's notice had been there since she'd first found out about him, almost at the beginning of the war. She knew she'd love him, no matter what – but to have the unexpected gift of a proper future with him, not one curtailed by the threat of illness or untimely death, was more than she had ever hoped for.

'Well, I think so.' He grinned widely, the tension broken, and then they were standing and rushing into one another's arms, kissing as if they were making up for lost time and celebrating the time they now could look forward to together.

A noise from the hallway upstairs startled them and they pulled apart, just as Tommy came sleepily into the room. 'Hello, Sarah,' he said, taking her

419

familiar presence for granted. 'Oh, good, you've made toast. Don't you want all of yours?' he asked, noticing the pieces they'd left forgotten when the conversation became too important. 'I'll have it then.' He swept the remaining pieces on to one plate and began to munch them eagerly, completely oblivious to the scene he'd just interrupted.

Nancy held the letter and stared at it, unable to fully comprehend its contents. She sank into a chair and read it again. The message was still the same. As the Allies had advanced through France and the might of Germany had crumbled, prisoners of war had been rescued and freed. Some were already in Britain, in reception depots. Private Sidney Kerrigan was one of them, at present in a depot in Amersham near London, but soon to be on his way back home, once he was in better health.

Sid was coming back. It didn't seem real. Sometimes she struggled to remember what he looked like, it had been so long. She had photos of them on their wedding day, when he had stood there in his suit and made those promises to her, and yet her brothers had found him the evening before, out with Harry Calendar's sister, so those words were just so much hot air. He must have changed though. She knew she had – she looked different and she'd grown up as well. What would he be like now, having spent so many years in a prison camp? Would he even want to see her? Would he be at death's door, like the men in some of the pictures that had begun to appear in the papers? The

Red Cross had passed along his letters, but they had never given much away, just asking after his mother and Georgie. He'd never been one for letters, even before the war. She had written equally basic ones back to him. Heaven only knew what his mother had said to him in hers.

Nancy got up from her seat by the window in the parlour she rented from her detested mother-in-law, and began to pace around the room. Things were coming to a head, there was no doubt. Sid's arrival home would force the issue one way or the other.

She was pregnant again. Just like before, she'd tried to persuade herself it wasn't true, but there was no getting away from it. She and Gary had been careful, but apparently not careful enough. It might have been that time at New Year, or more likely just before he had dumped her. Whenever it was, he'd left her with more than a broken heart. She couldn't bank on having another miscarriage this time. She had to think, and think fast.

There was no Gloria to confess to this time either. Her best friend was entertaining the increasingly victorious troops and establishing herself ever more firmly as a household name. That was all very well, but right at this moment Nancy could have done with her back home. There was nobody else she could tell. Her mother and Rita were very strict on the subject of morals and she suspected that Kitty, Violet and Sarah would be the same. As for any of her WVS colleagues, they were out of the question. She'd just have to deal with this herself.

She couldn't rely on Mrs Kerrigan for any help, that was for sure. She found it hard to forgive the old woman for blaming her when Georgie was taken. It was beyond belief that the woman's first inclination was to badmouth Nancy, and only after she'd done that for some while to wonder if she could be of any help finding the little boy. That said it all – she didn't really love her grandson.

Nancy knew now without a shadow of a doubt that she herself loved Georgie with every fibre of her being, and that love had nothing to do with who his father was. So she reasoned she would probably also love this new baby, despite Gary being a feckless two-timing louse. It wasn't the baby's fault that its father had disappeared into the bright blue yonder. Nancy took a deep breath. If it came to it, she'd just have to be mother and father to this child. Before the war, that would have been a terrible prospect. In all honesty, it still was – but not perhaps quite as bad. She wouldn't be the only one. Plenty of children had lost a father, or a mother, or both parents, to the war in one way or another. She had raised Georgie with no help from Sid and precious little from his mother. Perhaps her own family would come round to the idea of the new baby eventually. If not, she'd have to manage somehow.

This was all assuming that Sid would get back and not want anything more to do with her. She had no way of telling how he would react – she'd have to pick her moment, if she told him at all. She'd have to be canny about it. But this time, she was determined. Yes, she'd had her fun and been caught out, but her baby would not suffer because of it. She was a good mother. She would just have to prove it.

CHAPTER THIRTY-FOUR

It was the day they'd all been waiting for. Germany had finally surrendered and it was official: the Allies had won the war. Kitty sang to herself as she surveyed her kitchen, the dull ache that still plagued her arm and ribs all but forgotten. She was going to celebrate, along with everyone else in Empire Street, and with however many friends and family came to join them. Her job now was to make a cake to suit the occasion, with no notice and no chance to pool rations as they were unprepared for the event. Still, this was what she was good at.

She'd spent the morning in the city centre, which was abuzz with the news. Wireless broadcasts had brought the joyful confirmation that the fighting in Europe was over, and Kitty wasn't the only person keen to buy flags to hang in celebration. She'd had to queue to get any, but everyone was so good-natured that she hadn't minded.

Now Tommy was outside with the ladder, insisting that he didn't need her help and he wouldn't fall. She knew she had to let him get on with it. He'd always be her little brother, but he was taller than her now, and to be fair she was in no state to stretch up and tie flags to the guttering at the front of the house. She was almost better, but that would be taking things too far. Tommy had proved himself by helping to rescue Georgie, and she had to accept he was well on his way to becoming a man – a sensible and responsible one too.

'Need any help?' asked Frank, coming in through the open back door. 'Don't you go lifting anything heavy, Kitty.' He set down a wooden box on the table. 'Can you make use of any of this?'

Kitty stared at the contents of the box in delighted astonishment. 'Where did you get this? Eggs and butter – that's exactly what I need, but they're as rare as hen's teeth.'

'Seth and Joan have just arrived, bringing Michael and Megan to join in the fun,' he said, stepping behind her and giving her a warm hug. 'They rightly guessed that we'd all be gathering for a party.'

Kitty relaxed and leant against him for a delicious moment. 'Let me guess, Dolly has sent them down to the victory garden to get them out of the way.'

Frank laughed and breathed in the beloved scent of her, all the more precious because for a minute or two back in March he had feared he'd never be able to savour this closeness; that Kitty would remain forever trapped under the rubble of the bomb site. He shut his eyes and enjoyed the moment, then he released her. 'Of course. Nancy's taken them.'

'Nancy?' Kitty couldn't keep the surprise from her voice, as she carefully unpacked the eggs and the big pat of creamy butter. 'Does she even know where it is?'

'Apparently so,' said Frank wryly. 'Georgie wanted to help his cousins and Nancy volunteered to help out. Everyone else is making sandwiches in Mam's kitchen – it's like a factory assembly line over there.'

'I can imagine,' said Kitty, reaching for her biggest mixing bowl, remembering all the times the women had joined forces to produce a family meal out of what felt like thin air. 'When I've got this into the oven, I'll pop across and see if there's anything more I can do.' She weighed her flour and expertly tipped it into a sieve without getting any on the table. Then she set about separating the eggs. 'What about Sid? He won't be able to control three lively children when they're out and about, will he?'

Sid's return had been the talk of the street, ever since the day the emaciated young man had stepped from an ambulance a few weeks earlier, a shadow of his former swaggering self. He was severely malnourished, and the word was that dysentery and other diseases had spread through the camps just before he'd been freed. He certainly needed building up again. He'd hardly been seen out, and nobody knew what he and Nancy had said to each other. After the incident when his mother had come round blaming Nancy for Georgie's disappearance, she had begun taking her ration books to another shop. It wasn't that Violet or Ruby had asked old Mrs Kerrigan to shop elsewhere, but she clearly felt uncomfortable. As for Nancy herself, she had given nothing away, but ever since that dreadful day she had been noticeably less demanding and thoughtless towards her family and friends.

'He's still at his mother's as far as I know,' Frank said, watching with fascination as Kitty cracked eggshell after eggshell, neatly pouring the whites into a small bowl while retaining the yolk unbroken in the half-shell, before finally tipping it into a teacup. He waited for her to finish the last one then said, 'Kitty, come here a minute, you've got flour on your nose.'

She stepped towards him and he brushed her face gently and then kissed her hungrily, more strongly than he'd ever dared to do for fear of hurting her. Now she kissed him back, passionate in her desire for him, and it was several minutes before they parted, gasping but laughing, full of pleasure that they could finally express how they'd felt for so long.

'Kitty,' said Frank, 'shall we make this a double celebration today?'

'What do you mean?' she asked, returning to the task in hand and weighing the butter.

'Put that down for a second, and give me your hand,' he said. 'Look, I can't get down on one knee, but you swore you didn't mind about my injured leg and so you'll have to forgive me. Still . . . Kitty Callaghan, I love you more than I can say and you are the most precious woman in the world. I can't imagine life without you. Will you marry me?'

'Frank.' Kitty's hands went to her face.

'Look, I'm sorry if I've rushed it. I know we've only been together for a couple of months. It's just that we've known each other so well for so much longer than that, I suddenly couldn't wait to ask you.'

Kitty gasped and then came into his arms again. 'Don't be sorry; don't even think it. I'm surprised, that's all. I didn't think you'd ask – or at least not so soon. Yes, Frank, yes, with all my heart. Of course I'll marry you. I can't imagine how anyone could be happier. Yes.'

For a moment they stood still, as the golden sunlight shone through the window, and outside they could hear somebody cheering, and the clattering of Tommy's ladder as he strung the flags from the house to the closest lamppost.

Then Kitty gently pushed him away. 'Duty calls, Lieutenant Feeny,' she said, her eyes bright with happiness. 'I've got a cake to make.'

Nancy watched Georgie trying to keep up with his bigger cousins. Michael and Megan knew exactly what they were doing at the victory garden, which is more than she could say for herself. She could count on the fingers of one hand the times she'd been there since her mother and Violet started it, although she'd been happy enough to eat the produce.

She took a deep breath as Megan began to pick rhubarb and Michel carefully explained to Georgie how to find out if the radishes were ready yet. Her son looked so solemn. He'd had a lot to get used to,

428

what with his father – a total stranger to him – turning up. He'd been polite but puzzled. Sid wasn't like his friends' fathers or the men he knew. He was very quiet, very thin, and very different to the few pictures he'd seen of him.

Nancy had been cautious at the first sight of Sid. She'd thought she was prepared, but when she'd finally come face to face with the shell of the cocksure man she'd married, she'd been almost speechless. Of course his mother had been all over him, and it had been some while before they'd managed any time on their own.

Sid had looked mostly at the floor, down at the parlour carpet Nancy so hated. 'Thank you for your letters,' he'd managed to say after a painful pause. 'It was good to have news of the nipper. He's a fine lad, you can see that.'

'He is,' said Nancy immediately. 'He's brave an' all. You can be proud of him, Sid.'

Sid had rubbed his forehead, as if that exchange had used up all his reserves of energy.

'Don't you overtire yourself,' she'd begun, but he'd waved his other hand at her.

'You're still a fine-looking woman, Nancy.' He kept his eyes down. 'I know I wasn't the best husband to you when we were wed. I see that now.'

Nancy shrugged. It was true, but then she was a fine one to talk. 'Doesn't matter, Sid. That was a long time ago. We weren't much more than children ourselves.'

Sid laughed wearily, and coughed. When the spasm

was over he cleared his throat. 'The thing is, Nancy, I don't know if I can be a husband to you now, if you know what I mean.' He'd glanced up and then away, embarrassed. 'I'm that tired all the time, I don't know if things will work like they used to. And lots of us got sick and weren't treated proper. I'm not the man I was, if you get my drift.'

Nancy didn't know what to say. 'Early days yet, Sid,' she replied awkwardly. 'We'll have to get used to each other all over again.'

'That's if you want to,' said Sid morosely. 'Just look at me, how I am now. I wouldn't blame you if you said no. Mam will look after me.'

'I'm sure she will,' said Nancy with asperity. Then she softened her tone. Sid's grim honesty deserved sympathy, she acknowledged. 'Look, you want to get to know Georgie properly, don't you? He'll want his parents to stay together,' she went on carefully, preparing the ground as best she could.

'He's a grand little lad,' Sid said, his voice brightening. 'You've done him proud, Nancy. I'm just sorry that I can't give you a little brother or sister for him, or not for a long while, I don't think.'

Nancy had clasped her hands and sent up a silent prayer for courage. Then she'd bitten the bullet. 'Well, Sid, about that . . .'

Sid had been shocked, but not as angry as she'd feared. At first he'd said he'd think about it, but over the next few days he'd come round to the idea of being the father of the new baby. Nancy had been heartily relieved, even if she foresaw her life being consumed with taking care of all three of them – Georgie, the baby and this semi-invalid Sid. Well, they'd work something out. They'd have to. At least Georgie could say he had his daddy home again. Even if Nancy was for now sleeping on the sofa in the parlour.

The one thing she hadn't raised, Nancy thought now, was where they would live. Come hell or high water, she would not spend one night more under her mother-in-law's roof than she absolutely had to. The woman's behaviour when Georgie had gone missing made it impossible. Nancy clenched her fists. She would not raise this new child in that poisonous atmosphere. Somehow she'd find a way for them to set up home elsewhere.

'You've done it again,' said Pop to Dolly, gazing in admiration at the row of tables, all covered with cloths or – when they'd run out of those – sheets, laden with sandwiches, pies and, in the centre of the row, the huge cake that Kitty had made. Everyone had contributed chairs and cutlery from their various houses and now sat around the tables, enjoying the food. Union Jack flags hung across the street, and the younger children all had matching red, white and blue hats, which Danny had brought back when he'd returned from work.

'It was a team effort,' said Dolly generously, although in truth she'd done most of the organising. She leant against Pop's familiar frame and sighed. 'Look at them, all together. They're safe at last, Pop.'

431

She turned her face to his chest so that nobody would see her silent tears. 'How I wish our Eddy was here to see it. There's not a day goes by when I don't think of him.'

'I know,' said Pop, putting his arm around his wife and remembering his brave son, lost for almost a year now. 'Sure we'll never forget him. He was the best son we could ever hope to have. Now it's up to us to make sure his own children are brought up right.'

'Yes, you're right.' Dolly swiftly dabbed her eyes with the edge of her apron. 'They'll want for nothing, those little twins. We'll see to that, won't we.'

'We will,' said Pop, glancing to where the big pram stood, one baby at either end of it, tucked in tight. Megan had fastened bunting to the handle. 'If they turn out anything like as well as our five, they'll have no trouble at all. You've been the best mother any of them could ever have hoped for. I'm so proud of you.'

'Pop!' Dolly could feel herself blushing. She knew Pop loved her, but he was a man of few words and didn't often say things like that. He was a treasure, to be sure. She knew she'd fallen lucky when she'd met him all those many years ago.

She looked around at her remaining children. There was Frank with his arm around Kitty – well, no surprise there. It only surprised her that they'd taken so long about it. There was Sarah, still in uniform, right up close to Danny – no surprise there either, though they'd said very little as yet. Of course Sarah was still her baby – but older now than Dolly herself had been when she'd married Pop. In all the upheaval of the war, Dolly had overlooked that. She'd become so accustomed to Sarah having to grow up fast and act far older than her years. Maybe now her youngest could let her hair down and reclaim some of that youth she'd lost.

Rita had worked late last night, but had done her turn making sandwiches and was now carrying baby Ellen around to see everybody. It was a shame that Jack was still on duty, but Rita had been thrilled to get a telegram from him, wishing he could be there with them for this longed-for day, but assuring her that he'd be home as soon as he could. Dolly smiled. She had no worries for Rita any more. She and Jack were so obviously meant for each other and baby Ellen was thriving. Ellen was waving her podgy arms at Maeve, who'd decided to join in the fun with her Empire Street friends. Dolly made a note to ask the lively nurse to play them some tunes later on.

She shook her head as she regarded her middle child, the most difficult of all of them. Nancy was standing with Violet and Ruby, deep in conversation. Dolly worried for her. Anyone could see that Sid would take a long time to recover, if he ever did. She thanked the lord that Georgie was such a sensible little chap, despite what he'd been through. Nancy had been markedly less flighty since that day – it was as if she'd grown up all at once. Dolly regarded the young woman's silhouette carefully – no, she was sure she wasn't imagining that little change around her middle. Well, she wouldn't push the matter but would wait for Nancy to speak. Dolly could do the sums as well

433

as anyone else, but if Nancy chose to announce this new addition to the family as Sid's homecoming present, then she wouldn't contradict her.

She sighed in gratitude. When all was said and done she felt blessed to be here, with the prospect of peace at last, among her beloved family. Of course they'd had their ups and downs, but when it came to it she couldn't have asked for a better husband, better children or better neighbours.

Ruby blushed to the roots of her white-blonde hair but smiled broadly. 'So what do you say, Violet?'

Violet had to take a moment to reply. It wasn't that she was surprised to learn that Reggie James had popped the question. He'd been paying court to Ruby for months now and evidently cared deeply for her. Violet and Rita had often discussed it when the young woman couldn't hear, deciding that it would be the best possible thing for Ruby if she were to marry Reggie. She'd been dealt such a tough hand in life – she surely deserved her chance at happiness.

What Violet hadn't counted on was Reggie's idea formally to set up in business, supplying fruit and vegetables to the shops around Bootle and, in time, beyond. He had the gardening know-how, and Ruby had proved she had a good business brain and head for figures. But, Ruby had pointed out, that wouldn't be enough. They'd have to have someone who was good with the customers, and ideally who knew about the growing side of things as well. Would Violet consider joining them?

Violet thought it through. She loved gardening and the satisfaction of producing nourishing food from seed. She also loved dealing with people. Working in the shop made her happy and allowed her to be only a stone's throw from the twins. Yet long-term it might not be as good for them all. The shop now belonged to Rita and Ruby between them – Winnie and Charlie must be turning in their graves. Rita had confided to her that when Jack came home, she wanted to move out of the accommodation above the shop, as it had too many memories of the years of abuse she'd suffered when married to Charlie. Besides, when Michael and Megan returned, they'd be bursting at the seams. It had been decided that they would finish their school year out at Freshfield, but then move back to be with their mother, baby sister and, eventually, Jack too.

Violet explained all this to Ruby. 'So you see, if I come and work with you, I'd only have a little time in the shop, as I can't ask Mam to mind the twins every day. Rita won't be there full time. So I can't see what would be best.'

Nancy cleared her throat. 'I could help.'

Violet's eyes widened. Nancy had never been known to do so much as move a box in the shop. 'Really?'

'Yes,' said Nancy, speaking quickly now the idea crystallised in her mind. 'I used to work in a shop, you know. All right, it was the big department store, George Henry Lee, but I dealt with customers and all that. It would be the ideal solution all round.' She looked at Violet squarely in the eye. 'If the flat is going to be free, I would be interested in that too. I'm not staying where I am, no chance, not after what the old bag said about me when Georgie went missing. Georgie would love it; he'd be right next to his favourite granny and you, Violet. Sid would have something to watch from the upstairs window as people come and go, and when he's feeling up to it he might want to help out as well. How about it?'

Violet and Ruby looked at each other and nodded. 'We'll have to ask Rita,' Ruby pointed out, 'but it might be good for Sid, mightn't it?'

Violet grinned. 'Nancy, if Rita agrees, you're on. I couldn't let the shop down, but I'd love to grow plants for a living. If we knew you were behind the counter, we wouldn't have to worry.'

Nancy beamed. She knew she'd just committed herself to a life of hard work. It might not be the glamorous existence she used to dream about with Gloria, or the fantasy of moving to America as a GI bride. However, it would give her little family security. That was the most important thing now.

Kitty watched the children devouring the last of the cake and smiled. As usual it had taken far longer to make than to be eaten, but that was how it should be. It was good to be out of uniform for once, in a full skirt, teamed with a pretty gingham blouse with puff sleeves and broderie-anglaise collar, topped with the rash purchase of a new cardigan. She'd decided that morning she deserved it as she'd scarcely touched her clothing coupons for ages – she was usually in uniform, after all. Laura had teased her about that often enough.

The thought of Laura reminded her of the letter she'd received a few days ago. It was from Marjorie. She was now recuperating at her parents' house, conveniently close to where Freddy was currently being treated. Evidently their romance, begun in the most testing of circumstances, had survived and was flourishing in the quieter surroundings of Sussex. While Marjorie still couldn't say exactly what she'd been doing, reading between the lines Kitty could tell that their guess had been right. The quiet, bookish former teacher had been working with a cell of the Resistance, going undercover at great danger to herself. Somehow she had come through it, unlike many other equally brave young women on similar missions. Kitty hoped to visit her soon. Perhaps she could co-ordinate it with Laura, if Marjorie was strong enough to take two visitors at once.

Then Frank brought her out of her reverie. 'Shall we tell them? Make it official?'

Kitty turned to face him, her expression full of love. 'Yes, why not, let's do it while everyone's here together. It's not as if you have to ask Jack's permission or anything. Unless you're afraid one of us will change our mind?'

Frank laughed and kissed her quickly. 'I don't think so. I've never felt more certain about anything in my life.'

'Neither have I.'

Frank reached down to the table and picked up a metal spoon, which he tapped against his half-full beer bottle until everyone looked towards them.

'We're here to celebrate the wonderful news that our country is at peace at last,' he began, 'but if I may have a moment of your time, I'd like to bring you some extra happy news . . . we're getting married!'

Kitty glanced across to where Danny stood with Sarah, and caught the glance that passed between them. So maybe there would be even more happy news very soon. For now, though, this was her moment – hers and Frank's. She looked around at all the faces turned to them and knew that she couldn't share it with a better group of people, the brave and resilient inhabitants of Empire Street and their closest friends. The war had destroyed houses, damaged workplaces, killed some of their nearest and dearest and turned all of their lives upside down – but it had not defeated them. On top of all that, it had brought her together with the man she loved most in the world.

'To Kitty and Frank!' called Pop, and everyone raised their glasses or bottles or cups and echoed, 'To Kitty and Frank.'

The End

Why not dive into more of Annie Groves' engrossing stories?

'**Heartwrenching** and **uplifting** in equal measure'

Take a Break